380

Dear Reader,

I have to tell you I am [...] the end of THE CHAME[...] time, Evie (my alter ego) has had one heck of a ride and deserves her happily-ever-after. But is it with Arch or Beckett? Like I'm going to tell you up front. *Heh.*

Speaking of...I was stunned and jazzed by the feedback from readers—50 percent cheering for Arch, 50 percent for Milo. Make my job difficult, why don't you! Gotta love a challenge.

So I did what I do. I listened to my characters. I followed their lead. I hope you're pleased with how things play out. I know I am!

Oh! And because I feel inclined, here's my stock Chameleon disclaimer.

I admit, *some* of Evie's adventures and tribulations are loosely based on my own experiences within the entertainment industry; however, she and all of the featured characters are purely fictional. In kind, although I extensively researched con artists and scams, Chameleon and A.I.A. are figments of my overactive imagination.

Enjoy the adventure,

Beth

Beth Ciotta

Evie Ever After

HQN™

Recycling programs
for this product may
not exist in your area.

ISBN-13: 978-0-373-77360-2
ISBN-10:   0-373-77360-9

EVIE EVER AFTER

Copyright © 2009 by Beth Ciotta

www.HQNBooks.com

Printed in U.S.A.

This book is dedicated to my agent, Amy Moore-Benson.
Your enthusiastic support and courageous spirit are a constant
inspiration. Here's to love, laughter and an exciting future!

ACKNOWLEDGMENTS

It's true. I spend countless hours holed up in my writing room
spinning adventures, but I am never alone in my endeavors.
I have an amazing support system, people I can contact for advice.
People who cheer me on when I'm down. Writers, readers,
my agent, my editor, key people at HQN Books—amazing friends
and associates.

Thank you—Steve Ciotta (my loving husband), Cynthia Valero
(my artistic soul mate), Mary Stella (my Semper-Gumby angel),
Heather Graham (my gentle-hearted champion),
Amy Moore-Benson (my dynamic agent), Keyren Gerlach
(my romantic, adventurous editor—you're the best!)
and the many readers, booksellers and librarians who have
shared their enthusiasm for The Chameleon Chronicles.

Thank you to the wondrous people at Harlequin Books
who've been there for me in a big way. Keyren Gerlach, Tracy Farrell,
Margo Lipschultz, Tara Parsons, Don Lucey, Jayne Hoogenberk,
Julie Chivers, Donna Hayes, Isabel Swift and Loriana Sacilotto.
Oh, God. I just *know* I've forgotten someone!

Then there are those I know only through reputation.
Read: their wondrous efforts.

Thank you to the talented artists, the marketing experts,
the dynamic sales team, the savvy publicists—the wondrous
departments that rock the house of HQN Books. You've treated
my work with enthusiasm and tender loving care,
and I am forever grateful.

Lastly, I'd like to extend a heartfelt thank-you to Emmy-winning
writer/director/producer/major league baseball announcer
Ken Levine. You're not only multitalented, you're generous
beyond words. As an avid fan of your work, I'm humbled that you
answered my questions pertaining to television. You're a joy and an
inspiration and I hope you enjoyed my mini-salute to M*A*S*H.
Cheers, my cyberfriend.

Evil Ever After

CHAPTER ONE

Private Jet Charter
Somewhere over Indiana

WHEN I WAS A KID I FANTASIZED about being a kick-butt crime fighter. You know, like Emma Peel of *The Avengers* or Agent 99 of *Get Smart*. Later, like most teenaged girls growing up in the seventies, I wanted to be one of *Charlie's Angels*. Specifically, Jill Munroe, but only because I wanted Farrah's hair.

Several decades and a career in the performance arts later, I'm still pining for the perfect hairstyle. The kick-butt crime-fighter fantasy, however, recently became reality. No one (except maybe my ex-husband) was more surprised than me. In this episode of my life gone wild, I'm winging through the friendly skies, escaping the scene of an anticrime.

My name is Evie Parish and I'm the newest member of Chameleon—a specialized branch of the AIA—which is something like the CIA only smaller and sneakier. Comprised of ex-grifters, former bunko cops, and now *me,* Chameleon creates illusions to expose despicable frauds. I used to sing, dance, and act on the stages of the Atlantic City casinos. Now the world is my stage and my idea of applause is the sound of a cell door slamming shut on the amoral keister of a scam artist. No, I don't have a background in law enforcement (or a criminal record), but my acting and sleight-of-hand skills (compliments of a stint as a magician's assistant) along with my scary-good memory make me perfect for this job.

Unfortunately, not everyone on the team agrees. Especially the man I'm sitting next to, the object of a fantasy fling come true, Arch "Ace" Duvall, a hunky bad boy with a Scottish accent and a soft spot for good-girl me. Call me crazy in love. Although Arch has yet to *say* the words, he did carve the sentiment in a tree: *Arch loves Evie.*

Yeah. I know. How sweet is *that?* And totally unexpected given his personal code. Let's just say he's never been in a committed relationship. Ever. Not that we've committed to anything other than *"trying to make this thing work."*

Where was I?

Ah, yes. My new reality. An adrenaline-charged cross between *Ocean's Eleven* and *The Thomas Crown Affair* sprinkled with the misadventures of a modern-day Doris Day. I kid you not.

A reformed con artist, Arch is one of two alpha dogs at Chameleon. The other being Special Agent Milo Beckett—known to the team as "Jazzman." Beckett—also sexy, but in a quiet, straight-arrow way—hired me without consulting Arch. He also kissed me—without consulting Arch—which resulted in fireworks, only not the good kind. I'm one of those people who can't jaywalk without getting busted, so naturally Arch walked in on the spontaneous liplock. I was mortified. Arch was pissed. And Beckett was no help whatsoever. But that's neither here nor there. Well, it's somewhere, just not a place I want to visit right now. I have enough worries, thank you very much.

I tried to put them out of my mind. Closed my eyes and willed the drone of the jet engine to lull me to sleep. It was nearly midnight. Hopped up on adrenaline all day and night, my body was exhausted, but my brain kept spinning scenarios worthy of a David Mamet film. Anxious, I fussed with my seat buckle and prayed for a smooth ride. My stomach was already churning. "Leaving a team member behind feels wrong," I blurted.

"*Dinnae* borrow trouble, Sunshine."

"It's just that—"

"Jazzman's more than qualified to manipulate a small-time chiseler like Frank Turner. *Dinnae* let his moniker snow you, yeah?"

Moniker. Grifter-speak for *nickname.* Turner's was "Mad Dog."

Yikes.

"Okay, but…" *I have a bad feeling.* Normally, Arch and Beckett *manipulated* bad sorts in tandem. I couldn't help feeling that if it weren't for me he would've stuck close to his partner. Maybe not as an active participant, but at least for backup. Though not intentionally, I'd driven a wedge between the two men. All because of that stupid kiss. Oh, and the time I confided in Beckett instead of Arch.

Oops.

I suppose most women would die to have two sexy men, two crime fighters, no less, vying for their attention. As fantasies go, it's a humdinger. In reality it's…unsettling. Even though they both denied it, I was certain, at heart, Arch and Beckett were friends. What if Beckett's plan curdled? What if he got hurt…or worse? How would Arch live with that? How would *I* live with that?

"*Dinnae* let that imagination of yours run wild," Arch said. He grasped my hand to still my nervous scratching.

My *tell.*

Crap.

"Let it go and trust Jazzman's judgment. He ordered us to fly *oot.* He had his reasons."

I just hoped they didn't have anything to do with me. "You're right," I said, faking an optimistic smile. "I'm just stunned that our part of the sting went so smoothly."

"I'm not." The green-eyed rebel flashed a cocky smile while stroking my cheek.

Zing. Zap.

My insides fluttered with something other than anxiety. Call me smitten. *Along with countless other women.*

I've heard the sighs. Witnessed the moony-eyed gawking. Heck, I've sighed and gawked myself. Arch is drop-dead gorgeous and deadly charming to boot. Talk about a dangerous combo. He's also six years younger than my forty-one. Not that that's an issue. Okay. That's a lie. I'm a *little* self-conscious in my older woman shoes. Arch—bless his warped soul—insists age isn't an issue. Then again, he excels at telling people what they want to hear.

"Jazzman's more than qualified to manipulate a small-time chiseler like Frank Turner."

Uh. Right.

My bad feeling escalated into imminent disaster. My pulse escalated, too. It didn't help that one of my two best friends, Jayne, had called me this morning in a tizzy over her psychic's warning after consulting a crystal ball. *"Mixing business with pleasure today is dangerous. Your friend must turn off the heat or someone will get burned."* Nic, my other best bud would snort, citing crystal balls as mystical bullshit. I prefer the term *hooey,* and normally I'd agree, but lately I confess I'm paranoid when it comes to this new life that seems too good to be true.

Don't scratch.

Arch asked the lone flight attendant for a bottle of champagne. *Lydia,* a twentysomething redhead with a knockout body and celebrity-perfect teeth, rushed to comply. Instead of watching her fawn over her sole passenger—me being invisible in her Scot-struck eyes—I excused myself to use the private jet's lavatory.

"You all right, lass?" Arch asked.

"Absolutely." *Liar.*

I moved down the narrow aisle before my heated cheeks gave me away. I didn't want to admit that I was feeling insecure in our new relationship. I didn't want to vocalize my lingering worries about Milo Beckett, prompting Arch to misinterpret my concern for his partner, my boss. I didn't want him to know I was freaking out about the recent web of lies we'd spun in order to avenge a U.S. Senator. I didn't want him to doubt my nerve. He already questioned my virtuous nature.

Where was I?

Ah, yes. Lies.

A product of my uptight Midwestern upbringing, I'm uncomfortable with purposeful deceit. A detriment in my new line of work. A liability Arch keeps pointing out. Although he believes I possess the motivation and talent, he's convinced I'm hindered by my goody-two-shoes morals.

I'm determined to prove otherwise.

Hence locking myself in the private jet's lavatory for a private meltdown.

It's not as if I could discuss my concerns with Arch: a) it would only support his theory that I'm not cut out for his line of work; b) born into a family of grifters, Arch's concept of right and wrong is blurred.

For the last several days I've been ignoring or suppressing serious issues that are destined to explode in my face. This moment I was obsessing on the *smoke and mirrors* mission that had involved blowing a lot of *smoke* up a lot of butts, some belonging to my own family and friends. Even though I'd played loose with the truth for the greater good, I couldn't shake the feeling that it would end badly.

"There are all kinds of lies," I could hear Arch say.

I gripped the rim of the stainless-steel sink, stared into the mirror and, instead of bemoaning my darkening roots (hey, I never professed to being a *natural* blonde), I concentrated on obliterating my guilt. "Everyone lies."

A global truth according to the research book I'm reading on scams and frauds. Turns out most of us lie daily albeit unconsciously. White lies. Etiquette lies. Lies of omission. Falsehoods intended to spare someone's feelings or to perpetuate goodwill. Like the friend who assures you your botched perm doesn't make you look like a deranged poodle. Or the parent who nurtures a child's belief in Santa Claus.

Then there are lies with selfish yet relative harmless intent. Politicians lie to win elections. Publicists lie to catapult an unknown artist to stardom. A form of manipulation we typically take for granted. Of course they're going to spin the truth, that's what they *do.*

But no one spins the truth like a con artist. Masters of persuasion and deception, con artists—aka confidence men, grifters, flimflammers, bunko artists, hustlers—excel in telling you what you want to hear. They target character traits ranging from arrogant to insecure, needy to greedy, ambitious to lazy, and pitch the irresistible deal. No social class is immune and the mark's intelligence is rarely a factor.

I should know. Last month I fell for a street hustle and *I'm* a smart cookie. Just gullible and naive, according to Arch. Then two weeks ago my mom, a mega-smart, supergrounded realist, fell prey to a Sweetheart Scam. Not that she knows, thanks to Chameleon. Point is, a good scam artist homes in on your needs and weaknesses and—*bam*—a sucker is born.

Where was I?

Ah, yes. Avenging and protecting U.S. Senator Clark. Once we'd determined how Frank "Mad Dog" Turner had cheated the senator's wife at cards, cheating the cheat had been cake. Mad Dog never knew what bit him and before he had a chance to wise up, the entire team, with the exception of Beckett—got the hell out of Dodge. Or in this case, Hammond, Indiana.

Tabasco, Gina, and Woody were en route to Atlantic City via Tabasco's single engine Cessna. While Arch and I, still masquerading as the Baron of Broxley and his fiancée, enjoyed the luxury of a private jet. Roomy accommodations, plush leather seats, expensive champagne, and an uber-sexy traveling companion. Who could ask for more?

Too bad I was battling a panic attack.

Someone knocked on the door. "Miss Parish, is everything all right?"

Lydia.

"I'm fine." *Liar.* My cheeks burned and my heart raced. Since I was alone, I scratched.

"In that case, would you please return to your seat? The pilot warned we're approaching heavy turbulence."

I slapped a palm to my clammy forehead. So now in addition to battling an anxiety attack, I had to endure motion sickness? I blinked at the door, felt a twinge in my jaw, and realized I was clenching my teeth. *Oh, no.* Though I hadn't had an episode in weeks, I still suffered from TMJ—a stress-related disorder. What if my jaw locked? It had happened before. Talk about embarrassing. Almost as mortifying as puking into an airsick bag.

Instead of exiting the lavatory, I sank down on the toilet. "Be out in a minute," I squeaked then dropped my head between my knees. *Breathe.*

Thirty seconds later, another knock. "Open the door, love."

Arch.

"Can't."

"*Cannae* or *willnae?*"

Both. My voice stuck in my throat as my imagination took flight.

What if Mad Dog goes rabid and attacks Beckett? Just because he's a two-bit cheat that doesn't mean he won't freak out and fight back when a Fed tries to run him out of town.

What if my family refuses to forgive me for convincing them I'm "engaged" to a wealthy baron, even though I deceived them for the greater good?

What if Arch fails to win my trust as he promised?

What if I fail him by putting my faith in the safer man—Beckett?

A millisecond later, the handle clicked and the metal door swung open. Another of Arch's talents: picking locks.

Hunched over, I glanced up. I wanted to blast him for invading my privacy, instead I wheezed.

"Bloody hell, Sunshine." He shut the door and stooped in front of me.

Hot-faced and short of breath, I stated the obvious. "Anxiety attack."

"I can see that."

He'd seen it before. During our first mission when he'd

dashed my assumption that he was a Bond-like super spy by confessing his true profession. *"I'm a con artist, Evie."* Yeah, boy, *that* was a shock. He left out the part about him working for the good guys. I learned that important tidbit later from Beckett.

He stroked a hand down my back. "Talk it *oot.*"

I shook my head, palmed my jaw.

"Did it lock?"

"Not yet," I said through clenched teeth.

He nudged aside my hand and massaged both sides of my face. "You're internalizing. Let it *oot* and the symptoms will subside."

Spoken like my dentist. Still, I refrained from speaking my mind. Instead, I yearned for my journal. Knowing I keep my feelings bottled, my dad had gifted me with my first diary when I was a kid. *"For when your heart and mind are jammed."*

Like now.

Only my journal was in my tote bag and Arch was relentless. "You're worried *aboot* Beckett."

"I'm worried about a lot of things." So much for the private meltdown.

Someone, Lydia, knocked again. "Excuse me, but…"

"Hold those thoughts." Arch kissed my forehead then rose and cracked the door to speak with the persistent flight attendant.

I massaged the ache in my chest with one hand, my jaw with the other. No problem on the thought holding. I'm an expert at internalizing. At least I used to be. Since my infamous "snap" at a not-so-long-ago audition, I'd been acting out and speaking out in ways I'd only dreamed of.

"What did you say to her?" I wheezed when Arch turned back to me.

"Something to make her go away."

He grinned and my breath stalled. Not because of the anxiety attack, but because he was so freaking gorgeous. When describing him to Nic and Jayne, I'd compared him to Gerard Butler, the Scottish actor who'd rocked our socks in a couple of action films and melted our bones as a romantic lead. We always compared people to celebrities. We're entertainers. Go with what you know.

Lately though, when I looked at Arch I only saw Archibald Robert Duvall. (Yes, that's his real name.) Aka "Ace" (his moniker), aka the Baron of Broxley. (His title. Bought, not inherited. Nevertheless legit.) Hunky body, dark, cropped hair, hypnotic gray-green eyes, and a knee-buckling smile. Did I mention the Celtic tattoo banded around his sculpted biceps? *Yowza.* And his warriorlike goatee? *Swoon.* Not for the first time I wondered what this charismatic rebel saw in Ivory-soap me. Not for the first time, I questioned our longevity.

And immediately dropped my head back between my knees.

Wuss!

Arch gently pulled me to my feet and into his arms. "Tell me your biggest worry."

The jet bounced and jerked as we hit the aforementioned turbulence. *Going down in flames?* "I understand that Chameleon is covert," I rasped, opening my mouth as little as possible, "but I don't want to keep my new life, my real job, from Nic and Jayne. I wouldn't be able to face them."

"The reason Chameleon is so effective is because we operate under the radar, you know? Can you trust them to keep our presence and purpose under wraps?"

"Absolutely."

"Then tell them."

"But what if one of them slips? What if I slip? What if—" The plane bounced and I gasped. Jaw aching, stomach spinning, I closed my eyes and imagined my happy place.

London. With Arch.

Scotland. With Arch.

Anywhere, my foggy brain whispered, with Arch.

"What you need," he said, sliding his hand up my thigh and under my dress, "is a distraction."

Zing. Zap.

My brain cells sparked and overheated. My body, including my jaw, melted as his mouth and hands, well, distracted. This was our thing. This getting it on in the weirdest places and wildest positions. Did I mention he was a fantasy come to life?

He kissed my neck and tugged at my panties. "Ever hear of the Mile High Club?"

"You wouldn't."

He continued to kiss and stroke. But of course he would.

And of course, I let him.

CHAPTER TWO

"YOU'RE HOME?"

Nic's husky voice usually cheered me. Usually. I sighed. "Such as it is." I glanced around my sparsely furnished apartment, despising every square inch. It lacked charm. Warmth.

Arch.

He'd turned down my invitation to spend the night. It wouldn't have bothered me so much, but by the time we landed and he drove me home it was long past midnight. I just assumed he'd sleep over. He begged off.

"I have some things to do, yeah?"

At three in the morning?

If I'd been more alert my imagination would've soared. Instead, I'd zombie-walked into my bedroom and passed out. Partly because of the hot sex and chilled champagne. Mostly because I was mentally and physically exhausted. I remember thinking I could sleep for days.

I slept for four hours.

"For how long?" Nic asked.

"Four hours."

"What?"

Ouch. Okay. Maybe it was a bad idea calling a night owl at the crack of dawn.

"You're only going to be home for four freaking hours?"

"What? No. I *slept* for four hours." Thanks to a recurring nightmare. A mish mosh of memories stemming from my first mission with Arch. A mission I'd bungled. As a result a man was dead. A bad man, but dead is dead. I worked my tight jaw and stirred sweetener into my nuked tea. "This conversation isn't going well. Maybe I should call back later."

"Screw that. I'm coming over."

"Now?"

"If Arch is there, boot him out. I want some private time."

"He isn't here."

"Is he still in the picture?

"Yes."

"Beckett?"

I flashed on the kissing incident, something Nic knew about because she'd flown to Indiana thinking I was having some sort of meltdown and ended up participating in the takedown of the man scamming my mom. Her dealings with Arch and Beckett had been tense. Even so, I suspected she was attracted to the latter, which was why I was doubly embarrassed that I'd told her about the spontaneous lip-lock. "Just friends," I said. "Coworkers."

"Uh-huh."

Okay. So admitting to her that I was a little confused about my feelings for Beckett had been a mistake. I just should have scribbled my worries in my journal.

Oh, wait. I did.

"Nic—"

"I'll be there in twenty."

"I'll call Jayne." What the heck? Arch had given me permission to tell them about Chameleon. No time like the present.

"Hold off on that, Evie."

"Why?"

"Jayne's been…weird."

"More weird than usual?"

"Tell you when I see you."

"But—"

She'd already signed off. Great. Leave me in suspense why don't you?

I didn't have time to shower and dress, so Nic was going to have to take me as is. Striped lounge pants, *Star Wars* T-shirt, fuzzy purple slippers. Trust me, she'd seen me in goofier getups. The mad scientist I'd once portrayed for an electronics sweepstakes came to mind. Oh, and the time I appeared as a mermaid, which would've been sexy except for the lobster on my head. Not a live one, of course, but still. Larry was his name. Larry the Lobster. These days he resides in a plastic chest of drawers along with a gazillion other props. Sherlock Holmes pipe and hat. Minnie Mouse ears and gloves. Clown nose, cigarette holder, flapper headband, pom-poms…

I plopped on my boring gray sofa and sipped my Earl Grey tea. I contemplated ditching those props to make room for, I don't know, something *useful?* I also thought about the various costumes, wigs, and accessories crowding my closet. A glitz and goof collection I no longer needed since I had retired (not entirely of my own choice) from entertainment.

Making a living on stage had never been easy, but I'd survived and even thrived at times for more than twenty years. But then the gigs were fewer and farther between and it only got worse. I learned I wasn't even being considered. *"They're looking for someone younger."*

Ouch.

Still, I persevered. Until that fateful day when I flashed my breasts. A moment of righteous defiance. So unlike good-girl me. But I was desperate. Standing on that casino stage, auditioning for a gig I was more than qualified for, being ignored simply based on my age, I saw my good-girl life flash before my eyes. I envisioned someone shoveling dirt over my career. My personal life was already six feet under. Losing my husband to a twentysomething hardbody was bad enough, but being robbed of my livelihood, my *passion,* simply because I'd had the nerve to turn forty?

That's when I snapped. That's when my inner bad girl came to my rescue and told those baby-faced executives what I really thought about their obsession with youth over talent. Okay. So maybe I torpedoed what was left of my entertainment career, but I unwittingly blew open the door to a new and exciting profession in fighting crime. The transition had been swift and adrenaline-charged, the stuff romantic action-packed movies are made of…only this was real life. *My* life.

And I was about to tell all to Nic, who only knew a little, but way more than Jayne.

As promised she showed within twenty minutes with— *bonus*—two mambo cups of Dunkin' Donuts java. Way better than Earl Grey. "How do you do it?" I asked as she passed me a cup and lounged on the sofa.

"Do what?"

"Primp, dress, make a pit stop for coffee, and drive here in under half an hour?"

"It's not like I live in another town."

"No, but… Never mind." I curled into the opposite corner of the sofa, trying to think of a time when I'd seen Nic look anything short of fabulous. I couldn't. She was one of those natural exotic beauties—kind of like Halle

Berry only with Penélope Cruz hair. A head-turner I'd love to hate but couldn't because underneath her lithe beauty and cynical personality, Nic was a marshmallow. Not that I'd ever said that to her face. Even though we were polar opposites we had an understanding. She was she and I was me and Jayne was, well, a whack-a-doodle.

"So what's going on with you?" Blunt. Typical Nic.

"I'll fill you in. But first, tell me what's up with Jayne." Evasive. Typical me.

"When's the last time you spoke to her?"

"Yesterday. Briefly. I feel bad now. I blew her off. But at the time I needed to be pumped up and she was a total buzz kill."

"She's been a neurotic spaz for weeks. That's why I didn't want to invite her over this morning. I wanted to give you a heads-up before you told her something that might send her into a tailspin. She still thinks you've been hired to sing at the Chameleon Club—period. She doesn't know about the undercover work with Arch and Beckett."

And Nic didn't know Arch and Beckett worked undercover for the government. Yet.

"Jayne's convinced your fate is at risk," Nic continued. "Karmic payback for something she screwed up in a past life."

"That sounds like Madame Helene talking." Jayne's crystal gazing, star-reading psychic. Nic and I had tagged along once and had both decided she was full of hooey. She was also a name-dropper, a favored psychic of B-headliner celebrities, and local hotshot execs—or so she claimed. Call me a nonbeliever. Pegging the psychic as a fake had only hurt Jayne's feelings and since then we'd kept our opinions of Madame Helene to ourselves. Well, at least I had.

Exasperated, Nic twisted her thick, long hair into a

makeshift bun. "That manipulative phony has Jayne wrapped around her cosmic-ringed fingers. I shudder to think what kind of money our friend has shelled out in an effort to predict the future. Her bimonthly visits are now up to once a week, not including phone calls."

My stomach turned. "I had no idea."

"That's because you haven't been around much lately." She winced. "Sorry. That was harsh."

I forced a smile. "Harsh, but true." I'd cruised the Caribbean then flown off to London, then, after only being home a couple of days, jetted to Indiana. Granted, I'd been working, but I'd also been having a pulse-tripping adventure and whirlwind affair. My life was on the upswing whereas Jayne's was spiraling out of control. Chagrined, I palmed my heated cheeks. "I've been so self-absorbed, I didn't realize…"

Nic waved off my apology. "Forget it. You've been on your own emotional roller coaster. It's just that the past few days… I think it's time to step in, Evie."

"What, like an intervention?"

"Someone has to be the voice of reason and it's not Madame Helene. We have to cure Jayne of this obsession. Sure, she's always had a new age spirit, and we've always supported that because, hey, to each his own. But now it's escalated into something scary. I'm worried about her. Financially *and* emotionally."

I felt sick. How could I have been so oblivious? "Maybe Arch and Beckett can help."

"By having them expose Madame Helene for the fraud she is?" Nic traced a finger around the cup's plastic lid. "I thought about that. Maybe."

Nic was a skeptic and she was hugely skeptical of the two new men in my life. She questioned their wisdom for drawing me into what she considered a dangerous profession. Also, I'm pretty sure she hadn't swallowed the story Beckett had fed her about him and Arch being freelance fraud investigators. Even though it was sort of true. Maybe she'd trust them more when she learned they worked for the government.

"Remember when Beckett told you he and Arch were fraud investigators?"

She settled back and nodded. Even though she looked relaxed, I could tell she was braced for a jolt.

"It's more complicated than that," I said.

"Go on."

"You can't tell anyone."

"Go on."

"It's big-time hush-hush."

Her green eyes sparked with annoyance. "What the hell, Evie? Do you want to spit and shake? Draw blood?"

"All right. All right." I took a deep breath then spewed. "Beckett wasn't lying when he said he's an ex-cop. He used to work in bunko. That's a unit that—"

"Investigates scams. I know."

"Right. Anyway, he saw too many grifters slipping through the system. According to Arch, con artists are hard to prosecute because technically there was no crime. They don't steal people's money. They persuade the mark to give it over—a willing participant as opposed to a victim."

Nic smirked. "Convenient reasoning, given his past."

I bristled in his defense. "Arch only targeted the rich and greedy. He never conned anyone who couldn't afford the loss."

"And that makes it right? You must really love this guy if you're trying to rationalize criminal behavior. You're the straightest arrow I know, Evie." She frowned. "At least you used to be."

I felt like I'd fallen from grace in her eyes and it didn't feel good. "Of course it doesn't make it right," I snapped. "But it does separate a scam artist from a scum artist. Scum artists prey on the vulnerable, the needy. They don't think twice about wiping out the savings of an elderly person or a lonely widow or…well, Arch would never do that. I mean he never *did* that. Past tense. Arch is reformed."

"So he says." Her frown deepened and I realized I'd only made matters worse.

The old me wanted to change the subject, to avoid confrontation. The new me, the me who was determined to fight for what I wanted, dug in my heels.

I wanted Arch.

I wanted this job.

Dammit, I wanted a new life.

I just hoped it didn't mean losing old friends. Or my integrity.

I chugged java and braced myself for Nic's aggressive opinions. If I could obliterate her concerns, easing Jayne's mind would be a cinch.

"I'm serious, Evie. How do you know Arch doesn't pull a con here and there on the side? How do you know he isn't scamming *you?*"

"I just know." Only I didn't. There were several aspects of Arch's life that he was unwilling to discuss. Take the mysterious "Kate" for instance. A woman from his past. A woman who's number was programmed into a special cell phone that he used for private stuff. Stuff he didn't want me to know about. Although he'd sworn his relationship with the woman wasn't romantic. All I'd gleaned was that they shared a mutual interest and it had something to do with grifting. I'd agreed not to press for details because it would mean sharing my own *private stuff*—thoughts, dreams, and rants I'd scribbled in my diary. In particular, I wasn't keen on him seeing the comparison chart I'd jotted listing his and Beckett's pros and cons. Let's just say Arch hadn't come out the wiser choice.

"No need to get defensive," said Nic.

"I'm not defensive."

She arched a brow and I ached to scratch.

"Okay. Maybe I'm a *little* sensitive where Arch is concerned. It's just that he's trying to do the right thing and that can't be easy given his upbringing."

"What do you mean?"

"His grandfather was an art forger. His mom was a grifter and so was his dad. Arch was the result of an on-off-on again long-term affair. His dad split for good before he was even born and, yes, he knew about the pregnancy."

"Prick."

"My thoughts exactly. Well, almost. I called the man *cold*."

"What does Arch call him?"

"Practical."

"You're kidding."

I hugged my knees to my chest. "That's what I mean. He had a skewed sense of right and wrong right out of the womb. He views his father's choice as practical because, according to Arch, emotional attachments compromise a grifter's judgment." The conversation played through my head word for word. It had been a rare moment. Arch was a closed book, yet one night on the cruise ship, when I'd been obsessing on my own troubles, he'd revealed a page of his life and I'd been stunned.

I was still stunned.

"Doesn't that worry you?" Nic asked.

"What do you mean?"

"Evie. Come on. Arch is condoning the behavior of a grifter who ditched his family for his career. How can you trust your heart to a man with iffy morals?"

Trust, as it happened, was the key sticking point between Arch and I. As he'd pointed out in another of those rare honest conversations, it went both ways. I wasn't the only one worried about getting my heart broken.

"For what it's worth," I said, "when I asked Arch what he would've done were he in his father's shoes, he responded, *'I'm not my father's son.'*"

"So you're telling me that although Arch has a twisted sense of right and wrong, he does have a sense of decency. A bad boy with a good heart."

I smiled. "Exactly. I know you'll find this hard to believe but he's actually quite vulnerable."

Nic snorted.

I wasn't offended because I knew it was a tough pill to swallow. The man was six feet of hard muscle. He smoked Marlboros, had a tattoo and cussed a blue streak. Not to mention he socialized and tangled with bad sorts. Vulnerable didn't fit the picture but that's because people only saw what he wanted them to see.

I flashed on a memory and cringed. "Oh, crap."

"What?"

"I just remembered, Arch told me about his family in confidence." He'd given me permission to talk about Chameleon, not his personal life.

"Why does it have to be secret?"

"Because he said the more people know about him, the

more vulnerable he becomes." I thunked my forehead. "I can't believe I betrayed him." *Again.*

"Calm down." Nic leaned over and squeezed my knee. A sweet gesture from a non-touchy-feely person. "I think your man is being paranoid, but we've all got our quirks. I won't repeat what you told me about his family. Not even to Jayne."

I massaged my pounding temples. "I hate keeping things from her, but I did promise Arch."

"I understand."

"I just wanted to give you some insight. I know you don't like him—"

"I like Arch, Evie. He's a likable guy. I just don't trust him."

That made two of us.

"Maybe I'll feel differently when I get to know him better."

Ditto.

"Moving on. So, do we break it to Jayne that you're working with a team of fraud investigators before or after we save her from Madame Helene's evil clutches?"

"Tough call. I'd like to get Arch's take, if that's okay. He understands the psychological aspects of the mark *and* the con artist. I don't want to make the wrong decision only to have Jayne turn on us instead of Madame Manipulator."

"Makes sense. Can you talk to him about it ASAP? I really want to get on this."

"I'll have an answer today."

"Good. Great."

There was a pregnant pause while we both regrouped. I didn't know what was on her mind, but I'd yet to share what I'd wanted to reveal in the first place. "Back to Arch and Beckett's profession."

Nic shifted and caught my gaze. "Ah, yes. Big-time hush-hush."

"Brace yourself."

"Spit it out."

"Chameleon isn't a freelance investigative agency," I blurted. "It's a covert branch of a government agency. You know, like the FBI."

"You're working for the freaking FBI?"

"No, the AIA."

"Never heard of it."

"Artful Intelligence Agency."

"Still never heard of it."

"Me, neither. But they exist. Don't ask me what they do, but Chameleon falls under their umbrella."

If I were Nic I'd be pacing the floor just now, venting and spewing rapid-fire questions. She just sat there, assessing. "You're telling me Slick is a G-man?"

Slick was her moniker for Beckett. One he didn't care for because she usually said it with sarcasm. I had no sympathy because he called me *Twinkie*. "Yes," I said. "Beckett's a federal agent."

"What about Arch?"

"Nope. Beckett's the only official member of the AIA. He answers to the director, a hardnose named Vincent Crowe, and everyone on the team answers to Beckett. Well, except Arch. They're partners. Sort of."

"Complicated relationship. I got that. Complicated further by you."

I smirked. "Thanks for reminding me."

"This is an awful lot to take in, Evie."

"I know."

"It's bigger than I first thought. More dangerous. And it plays right into Jayne's fears about a friend getting burned."

"I'm sorry I didn't tell you sooner. I'm sorry I haven't been here for you and Jayne."

She quirked a lopsided smile. "Yes, well, you're here now and we're going to help our friend."

I reached over and squeezed her hand. She squeezed back and my throat got thick as I thought about another friend in potential need.

"Any other bombs you wanna drop?" Nic asked.

"No."

"Anything you want to talk about?"

I swallowed and met her gaze. "I'm worried about Beckett."

CHAPTER THREE

Philadelphia International Airport

"I'M ON THE GROUND."

"How'd it go, mate?"

"Mission accomplished." Milo Beckett navigated the crowded terminal, fighting exhaustion and self-disgust. He'd manipulated and intimidated con artists before, but he'd never lost his composure. Then again, Turner wasn't a professional grifter. He was a former pro athlete with an arrogant streak and, as it turned out, an explosive temper. A dirtbag who cheated at sports, cheated the IRS and cheated at cards. Still, making him disappear for the sake of a politician's career left a bad taste in Milo's mouth. He'd spent several hours trying to put the ugly episode out of his head. Finally, he'd resorted to rationalizing. *I sold my soul to the devil for the greater good.*

Evie Parish, a virtuous soul who kept him connected to innocence and the pursuit of dreams, would view that rationalization as copping out or selling out. She'd certainly disapprove of the tactics he'd employed to accomplish the senator's goal. He hated that he cared. He wished he could stop thinking about that pleasurable but ill-timed kiss. He'd sent her away in order to focus on what he had to do. He'd sent away the entire team to shield them should his plan curdle. The separation had been an unexpected relief. The dynamics of the tight-knit group had been strained ever since Evie had tripped into their lives.

Now that they were in between cases everyone could go their separate ways. Maybe time apart would help ease the friction. Or maybe this was the end of Chameleon. He'd been contemplating leaving the AIA anyway. Screw his pension. His vision for the team had been compromised over the past year and he didn't see things improving under the leadership of the new director. Although maybe Crowe would get off Milo's ass now that he'd completed his *unofficial* directive.

Temples throbbing, he hustled toward baggage claim, anxious to get on with his life. The sooner he reported to HQ, the sooner he could decide his future.

"Still there, Jazzman?"

"Yeah." He'd called Arch out of courtesy. Next he'd call Samuel Vine, aka Pops, a trusted friend and the bartender and caretaker of the Chameleon Club. Word would trickle down to the other team members that he was safe and on home turf. "How's everyone doing?"

"Evie's fine."

"I meant the entire team."

"Sure you did."

Milo didn't argue. Truth was he did worry more about Evie because, unlike the rest, she wasn't trained in self-defense. Unlike the rest, she didn't have skin as tough as a rhino's. Not to mention he was infatuated with the good-hearted fireball.

"The Kid booked you a rental car," Arch said, skating past further talk of the woman who'd put a kink in their already complex friendship.

"He texted me the info." Woody, aka The Kid, was

Chameleon's computer geek. A wiz at all things technical. His role in the Mad Dog Turner sting had been vital as they'd relied on high-tech surveillance equipment to cheat a cheat.

"I assume Senator Clark was pleased when you handed him that briefcase packed with his wife's lost fortune, yeah?"

"'Impressive' was all he said. About the money anyway." Milo had driven to Senator Clark's estate directly after he'd handled Mad Dog. "Mostly he wanted assurance that I'd protected him from future scandal. I'm sorry to say I was able to give it to him." He reached in his jacket pocket for a packet of Tylenol.

"Want to talk *aboot* it?"

"What do you think?" He popped the pills dry, wincing when his hand bumped his split lip—compliments of Turner. Just then Milo noted two suits wearing dark shades. "Shit."

"What?"

"Trouble coming my way."

"Bad sort?"

"My sort. Gotta go."

"Call me if you need me, mate."

"Right."

Thirty minutes later, Milo stood in Vincent Crowe's office, clueless as to why he'd needed a personal escort to HQ. Agents McKeene and Burns had dodged the question. Didn't matter. This couldn't be good.

"Take a seat. Director Crowe will be in shortly," McKeene said on his way out.

"Thank you." He waited until the door shut then added, "Agent Ass-Kisser."

McKeene and Burns were new men, company men.

Brownnosers who made Milo's balls twitch. He didn't sit as directed. He hitched back his suit jacket and stared out the window, watching pedestrians navigate Independence Square on a sunny spring day.

For the most part, the new director of the AIA operated out of Philadelphia instead of Washington, D.C. A source of curiosity to Milo, although he'd never asked why. Crowe had been his boss for a month. Their relationship had been adversarial from the get-go. Because of a botched land investment sting in the Caribbean, and because Milo had been unwilling to explain why the team had operated outside of AIA jurisdiction, Crowe had put Chameleon on suspension. They were still on suspension. The mission they'd just completed had been unofficial. A *favor.*

Two weeks ago, Crowe had summoned Milo to this same office to inform him of Senator Clark's plight. His wife, an obscenely wealthy gambling addict, had lost a bundle to Frank "Mad Dog" Turner, pro athlete turned restaurateur, in a series of private high-stakes poker games. She swore she was cheated. Senator Clark enlisted Vincent Crowe to clean up his wife's mess. Crowe assigned Chameleon to infiltrate the game and win back the senator's money and then, to ensure there wasn't a scandal that could jeopardize the senator's political aspirations, to make the cheat disappear.

Milo had balked. Chameleon was his brainchild and he'd formed the elite group to champion Everyday Joes, not the rich and powerful. In his opinion Clark should have contacted Gamblers Anonymous instead of the AIA. But Arch and the team had talked him into taking the case, thinking if he refused he'd be damaging his career. Milo didn't give a flying fuck about his bureaucratic *career,* especially when it interfered with the work he really wanted to do. But he did care about the members of his team and if they wanted to stay tight with the AIA, he wasn't going to screw up that connection. Against his better judgment, he'd agreed to help the senator.

At least he'd had the opportunity to bail Evie's mom out of a swindle just prior to roping Turner. A win for the Everyday Joes. Unfortunately, it had also been a win for Arch. Even though something simmered between Milo and Evie it was Arch she loved. Leaving the better man, or at least the safer choice, shit out of luck.

The door opened and closed and Milo turned.

Crowe crossed to his desk. He didn't look happy.

At least they had one thing in common.

"We have a problem, Agent Beckett."

"Sensed that when you sent McKeene and Burns, sir." He didn't mistake the escort for a courtesy ride. The men had been cool and tight-lipped. Upon entering HQ, the receptionist and the five desk jockeys had greeted him warmly, which led him to believe few were privy to whatever was going down.

Crowe, a slouch-shouldered man with a puffed-up ego, settled behind an antique desk. The air crackled with arrogance and tension as he leaned back in his leather chair. "When I told you to silence the man who bilked Mrs. Clark, I didn't mean literally."

Milo eased into a chair as he felt the rug being pulled out from under him. "Are you telling me Mad Dog Turner is dead?"

"Are you telling me you didn't do it?"

"Hell, no. *Sir.*"

"Sources say otherwise."

"What sources?"

"My sources, Agent Beckett. Did you think I was going

to send your arrogant ass and hotdog team to handle something as sensitive as the senator's case without insurance?"

"You had agents spying on us?"

"I prefer to think of it as keeping tabs."

Milo's blood pressure rocketed. He eased a kink from his neck, breathed. "I won't bore you with the details. I assume you've already heard them. But I will tell you that when I left Turner, he was alive."

"And should anyone ask, I expect you to stick to that story. Don't worry Agent Beckett, we've cleaned up your mess. For the senator's sake and the sake of the AIA."

Fuck. "You don't have any proof—"

"Yes," Crowe said, "we do."

CHAPTER FOUR

As soon as Nic left I dialed Arch. Unfortunately, the call rolled over to voice mail. Instead of leaving a message I decided to try again later. If he rang back while I was in the shower, we'd end up playing phone tag.

I thought about calling Beckett. Not for advice on how to handle Jayne's dilemma, but to make sure he was all right. Except that seemed too intimate. Curse that kiss! If only I hadn't felt a little zing. If only he hadn't implied romantic interest. Before, I could've checked up on him as a concerned colleague. If I called now...would he read more into it? Would Arch read more into it?

I padded to the bathroom in search of Tylenol. Beckett would have one. The man carried an endless supply.

Stop thinking about Beckett.

I poured two pain relievers into my hand making sure they were what I thought they were before I swallowed them. I'd recently taken a pill by mistake and it had resulted in an embarrassing scene with the government agent.

I glared at my reflection in the medicine mirror. "Why do you have Milo Beckett on the brain?"

"Because you played with fire and you're afraid he'll get burned," I could hear Jayne say in an otherworldly voice.

I also had Madame Helene on the brain. But I couldn't do anything about her until I spoke with Arch.

I moved into my bedroom in search of something to wear. After I talked to Arch I'd shower and dress and then, hell or high water, I'd go shopping. Wall hangings, throw pillows…anything to make this wasteland more homey. I'd moved into this one bedroom apartment a year ago, after my ex, Michael, and I had separated, but I'd never really *lived* here. I'd been in too much of a funk to decorate. Then I'd just been oblivious. But after spending a week in Arch's grandfather's cluttered flat then time in my childhood home, not to mention a charming Victorian B and B, I just couldn't warm to this cold, stark apartment.

It was beyond depressing. It didn't help that I lived alone. I'd spent most of the past month sleeping with Arch. But that had been while on assignment or on holiday. *This,* I thought, soaking in the earsplitting quiet, *is my reality.*

"At least Dorothy had Toto."

I redialed Arch, wondering if I should get a cat.

"Yeah?" Arch's stock phone greeting.

I replied midthought. "Whoever said *'there's no place like home'* was full of hooey."

"Dorothy Gale," he said in his knee-melting accent. "*Wizard of Oz.* 1939."

I smirked. "I knew that. How could I not know that? It was a rhetorical statement."

"Ah."

"You're grinning, aren't you?"

"Aye."

"Because I'm cheeky or because I said *hooey?*"

"Take your pick, Sunshine."

I smiled. *I wish you were here.*

"What's wrong, lass?"

Going through sexy Scot withdrawal. "It's about Jayne. I'd feel better if I told you in person. I need your advice, Arch, and I need it soon."

"I can be there in…half an hour, yeah?"

"I'll be ready." My mind jumped tracks. "Have you heard from Beckett?" *Way to ruin a sexy exchange, Parish.* Only I was genuinely worried about my boss, a man I considered a friend…or something.

"He called a few minutes ago. Just landed in Philly."

Thank God. "And?"

"Mission accomplished."

The pent-up ache in my chest eased. "Great. That's… great." Beckett was home safe and Chameleon was once again in good graces with the AIA. I pumped a fist in the air. *Woo-hoo!*

"Evie."

"Yes?"

"I miss you."

Okay. That was sweet. That was…unexpected. My heart skipped and raced. "I miss you, too."

"Answer the door naked, yeah?"

Um. "Yeah. I mean, you bet. I mean…" *Holy Smoke.*

"See you in thirty."

I could imagine his ornery grin, the one that made the backs of my knees sweat. I could imagine what he was going to do to me when I opened the door—*hello*—naked. I peeled off my sleepwear and hopped in the shower. Thirty minute countdown to creative sex. Yeah, baby, yeah.

I'D JUST MOISTURIZED WHEN my cell rang. Naked and hot-to-trot, I adopted a Mae West drawl. "Thought about you when I was in the shower, Big Boy. Trust me. You don't want to be late."

"It's Nic."

"Oh! Sorry." Mortified. I slipped into the purple terry-cloth robe hanging on the back of the door.

"Whatever. Listen, Evie. We've got trouble. Zippo-the-Clown just called and Fannie's Flowers is in a snit. Fourth time this month Jayne didn't show on time. She has a scheduled telegram in less than an hour. I need you to get over there now and cover her butt. Otherwise she'll lose her job. I'm off to corral our wayward friend. Pretty sure I know where to find her."

"Okay. I'm there."

"Thanks."

"Sure."

She signed off and I scrambled to dress. If I remembered right and I usually do, Jayne had taken a job with Fannie's Flowers in order to make ends meet. Even though she was three years my junior, like me, she'd started losing casino bookings to younger, modelesque talent. It didn't help that the once-popular character actor gigs were almost obsolete. Rather than nabbing a nine to five to keep afloat she'd resorted to singing telegrams. Something that went against my creative grain, but as Nic said, to each his own. Except Jayne was my friend and I'd do anything for her. Singing "Happy Birthday" to an office worker while dressed as Marilyn Monroe or a clown or—*gak!*—a chicken wasn't going to kill me. Me, who'd once worked a high-roller Halloween party as PMS Pumpkin.

I think I set some sort of record blow-drying my hair and applying makeup. I was dressed and out the door in fifteen minutes. I shoved on sunglasses and race-walked to my car while dialing Arch.

"Yeah?"

"I won't be here when you get here. I mean, there's

been an emergency. Jayne. She's flipping out or something. I don't know. Anyway, I have to cover one of her gigs."

"Evie—"

"I know. I'm sorry." I whipped open the door to my beat-up Subaru and slid behind the wheel. "If I don't do this she might lose her job and I would feel awful. I already feel awful, but I can't get into that." I keyed the ignition only the car didn't start. "Oh, no."

"Evie—"

I tried again. *Dead.* Of course, I hadn't started my car in two weeks, plus it was old plus… "Dammit."

"Lass."

Someone tapped on my window scaring the bejeebers out of me. I gasped and smiled.

Arch.

First I noticed he'd shaved off that sexy goatee. I'd never seen him completely clean shaven. Before the goatee, he'd sported a perpetual five-o-clock shadow— also sexy. Not that a clean shave diminished his appeal. You know how some women look great in any hair color? Same difference. Any way you cut it, or um, shaved it, the man was gorgeous.

He looked like a *GQ* model in his hip, casual wear. Like me, he was wearing jeans, only his looked pricey. He'd left the tails of his paisley oxford hanging out and the collar opened. I imagined ripping off that shirt, skimming my fingers over his chiseled abs, licking his sexy Celtic tattoo… I squeezed my legs together to suppress an erotic tingle. *Get a grip, Evie. Think of Jayne.* Right. I chucked my phone in my purse and rolled down the window. "You're here," I said, sounding surprised and breathless and, well, sort of stupid.

Arch grinned and pocketed his phone.

"My car won't start."

"I'll drive you."

"Thanks." Honestly, I was happy for his company. I lived on Brigantine Island. Even though it was less than a ten minute drive to Atlantic City, it felt a world away. I felt semidisconnected here. If I didn't see the casinos, I didn't think about them. A blessing. I wish I could say those entertainment meccas conjured memories of the best times of my life. The incredible musicians I'd sung with. The wacky actress roles I'd nailed. Jeez, once I even sang backup for a famous boxer turned B headliner, and there was the time I'd been a featured swing dancer at a Big Bad Voodoo Daddy concert. But all I could focus on was the depressing fact that I was no longer "in demand." In my current mind-set the casinos represented rejection. They made me feel old. I ached to let go, to move on. I *had* moved on. The past month of constant travel had been a welcome distraction. But I guess it had also been a form of evasion. Now that I was back in the city, my former insecurities and disillusions threatened to crush me.

At least with Arch at the wheel, I could focus on him and not the cash cows that made me feel as if I'd been put out to pasture.

"Wow," I said as he opened the door of a black Jaguar. "Is this your car?"

"One of them." He handed me in then rounded the sleek-mobile and climbed behind the wheel. "What?" he asked as he revved the engine.

I gawked at the leather upholstery and a couple of console gadgets that looked like something out of a James Bond car. "It's just that, this looks really expensive."

He shrugged as if to say not so much, which probably

meant a small fortune. Again I wondered who he'd scammed in the past, how much he'd scored, and if he'd invested the money or stashed it in foreign bank accounts. He had to be rolling in dough because he lived and traveled in style. Not to mention, he'd bought a flipping Scottish Barony. I couldn't begin to imagine how much *that* had cost.

I felt bad for envying his wealth. Mostly because he hadn't earned it honestly. Then again, for all I knew, maybe he'd inherited a fortune from his family…although they hadn't earned an honest living, either.

Crimany.

Arch backed out of my apartment complex's parking lot and swung on to Brigantine Boulevard. "Where am I going?"

"Fannie's Flowers. It's on Baltic and—"

"I know where it is and if I *didnae…*" He tapped one of the fancy gadgets.

I buckled up and squinted at the screen. "Is that one of those GPS thingees?"

He shoved on his own dark sunglasses and smiled. My vocabulary was a constant source of amusement to the man. "It's a navigation system with a few perks."

He listed the perks and my eyes glazed over. I'd never been good with anything technical. I didn't even know how to text with my cell phone.

"What's going on with your mate Jayne?" he asked as he zipped over the bridge leading to the mainland.

His timing was great. Instead of looking at the upcoming casinos, I shifted and focused on him. In a long-winded ramble, I shared Nic's concerns about Jayne and Madame Helene, including some background history on the area's up-and-coming psychic. "Do you think we're overreacting?"

"Last year Chameleon took down a fortune-teller who fleeced marks out of hundreds of thousands of dollars by convincing them that the money—whether a result of investments or inheritance—was evil. She conned some of them into believing that the 'tainted' money was the cause of their personal or professional trials, you know?"

"Wow."

"Others were warned of impending doom should they not allow her to perform a ritual cleansing. The ritual, of course, involved the mark handing over the money." He glanced over. "Follow?"

"Unfortunately." I'd been reading up on various short and long cons. I thought I'd read it all. Boy, was I wrong.

"One woman alone handed over three-hundred grand. It all started with a ten-dollar tarot card reading. Using tricks of the trade, the fortune-teller gave a semi-accurate reading. The mark was hooked and started attending regular readings."

My arms prickled with goose bumps. "Sounds eerily familiar."

"The more the mark revealed *aboot* her life, the deeper the grifter's hooks. By earning her trust and manipulating her fears, over time the so-called fortune-teller was able to con the woman *oot* of a hefty inheritance. So, no," Arch said. "I *dinnae* think you're overreacting."

I shook my head. "Why does it seem like everyone in my life is being scammed in some way or another?"

"Because grifting is easier and more lucrative than ever, Sunshine."

A troubling statement on several levels.

"*Dinnae* worry *aboot* Madame Helene, love. I'll look into it. Just do what you have to do for your mate now and then we'll proceed, yeah?"

And just like that I felt better. Arch had an amazing knack of staying calm no matter the situation, a quality that impressed and irked me at the same time. Just now I appreciated his nonchalance. By the time he parked alongside Fannie's Flowers, I was even-keeled and ready to tackle Jayne's gig. Whatever it was. How bad could it be?

Arch slid his glasses on top of his head, revealing those hypnotic eyes. "Do you want me to come in with you?"

"No, that's okay. I just have to run in and pick up the costume and assignment." I scrunched my brow. "I think. I mean, I've never done one of these things."

"Singing telegram, yeah?"

"Yeah."

"With your background, lass, how hard could it be?"

"That's what I'm thinking. I just hope I don't have to wear anything too skimpy. I don't do sexy well."

"Sure you do."

Okay, that was sweet. That was…hot. "I'm hoping for a nerd or a Dame Edna or a dancing box of chocolates. You know, something goofy."

He leaned in, green eyes twinkling with mischief and…uh-oh. I knew that look. He winked. "I'm hoping for a belly dancer."

My inner thighs tingled and racy thoughts undulated through my brain. "Time's ticking," I squeaked while grappling for the door. "I'll be right back."

"I'll be right here," he said, stealing a kiss before I stole away. "Thinking *aboot* what I'm going to do to you later. Naked."

Zing. Zap.

I thought about the costumes in my closet and grinned. "How do you feel about French maids?"

CHAPTER FIVE

NIC HADN'T BEEN KIDDING when she said Fannie's Flowers was in a snit. Just my luck, or Jayne's luck, it was the boss herself.

A cashier showed me to a back room of the bustling store where Fannie labored over a gargantuan flower arrangement. Her work was lovely, her manner was not.

"Great," she snapped. "A substitute."

She paused and I fidgeted. She maneuvered random buds and I swallowed a lump of dread. She looked ticked and harried and I anticipated getting bounced from a job that wasn't even mine.

She glanced at her watch, me. "What'd you say your name is?"

"Evie."

"Listen, Evie, if you screw this up—"

"I won't."

"—Jayne's fired."

No pressure there.

"I'm thinking of letting her go anyway."

"Please don't." I tucked my hair behind my ears, wet my lips. I told the truth. Sort of. "She's been going through a rough time, but she's coming around and—"

"Yeah, yeah. Life's a bitch."

I wondered if Fannie was always this brisk or if she was

just having a bad day. I thought about my normally care-free, wacky friend and wondered if this job was worth saving. Except it *did* help pay the bills.

It also funded her Madame Helene habit.

One problem at a time, Evie.

Right.

Fannie jerked her head. "Follow me."

Instead of showing me to the door, she led me deeper into the storage room. Mostly it was filled with flowers and vases and baskets—florist stuff. But beyond a case of ribbons and cards, I spied two racks of costumes—entertainer stuff.

"Ever done anything like this before?" Fannie asked.

"Lots of times." Not a bald-face lie, just a spin on the truth. No, I'd never walked into a commercial office or a private home, singing birthday or anniversary greetings, dressed as a clown or some such stuff. But I'd appeared at plenty of parties or special events dressed as a clown or some such stuff. Sometimes I sang. Sometimes I danced. Sometimes I just roamed around in character making people laugh. I'm thinking that qualified me for this gig.

I was feeling jazzed and confident, but then Fannie produced my costume.

My mouth went dry. "You're kidding."

She narrowed her eyes. "Is there a problem?"

It was my worst nightmare, literally, come to life. "No problem."

I stared at the furry black costume, my mind reeling with the cosmic significance. For the past month I'd had sporadic dreams about gorillas. One involved wearing a gorilla suit, much like the one in Fannie's arms, hawking used cars with a sign that said, You'll Go APE For Our Prices. My ex-husband had been there with his arm wrapped around his new pregnant wife. He'd made an insensitive crack about my age. I took the dream literally, thinking it indicated the hairy demise of my career.

But Jayne had consulted one of her new age books, offering me a different account. *"If you dream about apes then beware of a mischief-maker in your business or social circle. Unless the gorilla is docile. Then the dream is a forecasting of a new and unusual friend."*

I knew this was probably one of a hundred interpretations, but it did pique my interest. Since Arch and Beckett had entered my life at that time, it was hard to dismiss as hooey. Call me intrigued. Or obsessed. I still didn't know if the ape dreams were warnings of trouble or forecasts of something good. I just knew I was still having them.

Fannie dumped the heavy suit in my arms then handed me my head, I mean the ape's head. I didn't even want to think about what it smelled like inside. Depended on who wore it last and if the shop had had it cleaned. I started itching and sweating and worrying about peripheral vision. But mostly I pondered the significance.

"You'll want to put that thing on after you get there," Fannie said, now searching through files. "Hard to drive wearing those big monkey feet."

"I have a ride," I said distractedly, flashing back on the time I'd arrived at an event via limo dressed as a bumblebee. Only this time Arch was my driver and I'm not sure I wanted him to see me as a gorilla. Dame Edna would have been sexier.

"Do you know the song 'Born in the U.S.A.'?" she asked while pulling out a folder.

I knew every Bruce Springsteen song ever written. Well, the biggest hits anyway. My ex-husband had been a Springsteen fan since the singer's Asbury Park days. As an entertainment agent, one of Michael's favorite stories was the time he almost signed The Boss as a client. That story had always made me a little sad, because I could hear the wistfulness in his voice. Like me, Michael had had bigger dreams than Atlantic City. I'm beginning to think it's the only thing we ever had in common.

"I know the song," I said, feeling more anxious by the moment.

"Lucky for Jayne." Fannie handed me two tickets and one long-stemmed rose. "You're going to sing that song with a twist on the title—'Born in the U.S. APE.'"

"Clever." *Not.*

"Then you present the guy with the rose and tickets. They're a gift from his wife."

Front row seats to an upcoming Springsteen concert. Lucky man. Generous wife. I shuddered to think what she'd paid. "What's the occasion?"

She looked at the file. "Second anniversary of their first date. Sappy. But sappy is good for business. They're having lunch at a gourmet restaurant." She handed me a piece of paper. "Here's the exact location, the guy's name, and his description."

My breath seized when I read the info. I'm pretty sure the blood drained from my face.

Fannie cleared her throat. "Is there a *problem?*"

I thought about Jayne. "No problem," I croaked.

I wondered what I'd done to deserve this? Or maybe it was some sort of cosmic test. If I could survive this, I could survive anything.

I pulled an elastic band from my hip pocket and tamed my hair into a ponytail. "If you don't mind, I think I'll slip into costume now."

"Whatever floats your boat," said Fannie. "Just make it quick. You're due in twenty minutes."

"Brilliant." Arch chuckled as I stuffed my bulky gorilla self—sans head—into the passenger seat of his car.

I slid him a disgusted look.

"You wanted goofy, love. I'd say this qualifies."

I didn't bother stating my issue with gorillas. I just passed on the pertinent information.

"Shite."

"You can say that again." I placed the ape head on the floor between my big furry feet then tried to fasten my seat belt and failed.

Arch reached over, made some adjustments and slid the buckle home. He stayed close, his face hovering near mine, his gorgeous gray-green eyes shining with concern. "You *dinnae* have to do this."

"Jayne will lose her job if I don't."

He gave me the once-over. "This monkey suit looks a bit big, Sunshine. Bet it'll fit me."

Tears pricked my eyes. "You'd do that for me?"

"*Cannae* think of much I *wouldnae* do for you, lass."

I kissed him. Hard. My heart pounded with affection as I cupped his gorgeous face with my furry paws and ravished his mouth. He matched my fervor, holding my head captive while conquering my tongue. Possessive. Seductive. The kind of kiss I would have dragged out forever if I weren't under the gun.

I broke off with a groan. "We have to go."

"My loss."

"Sweet talk like this is going to pay off big-time when I get you back to my place," I said with a little smile.

Grinning, he pulled back into the one-way traffic. "Never shagged a gorilla before."

I snorted. "Good to know."

He turned the corner and headed toward the boardwalk.

"*Didnae* know Stone and Sasha were back from their honeymoon."

"Neither did I." Over a week ago, Michael had called me from Paris, drunk and lamenting a fight he'd had with his blushing bride over me. Given the nature of this gig, I guess they made up. Whoop-te-do. "They're celebrating the second anniversary of their first date," I said, folding my furry arms over my gnarled stomach. "Michael and I weren't even separated then."

He reached over and smoothed the backs of his fingers over my cheek.

Sizzle.

That tender gesture was even hotter than that five-alarm kiss. I was definitely besotted. "To top things off," I said, squirming in my seat, "the casino they're dining in is the last casino I auditioned at. I'm not even sure I'm allowed on property after the stunt I pulled."

"All the more reason for me to take this on."

"Can you sing 'Born in the U.S. APE'?"

He slid me a look.

"Never mind. I can do this. I need to do this. For Jayne. For me. Call me crazy, but it feels like some kind of test." I plucked the gorilla head from the floor and fluffed the fur. "Just let me out at the main entrance. Park up there along the side. I'll be in and out in ten minutes. Fifteen tops."

He didn't look happy, but he didn't argue. A phone chimed—his.

I fiddled with the tickets and the flower while he took the call.

"Yeah?" He listened and frowned. "Bloody hell. No, I *didnae* know. Do some digging. See what you can find *oot.* I'll be there within the half hour."

"Who was that?" I asked as he pocketed the cell and pulled into the valet entrance.

"The Kid."

"Bad news?"

"Unexpected."

"You're not going to tell me, are you?"

He reached over and squeezed my hairy thigh. "Let's get through the gig for Jayne, yeah?"

"Then you'll tell me?"

"Aye."

"Okay." I forced a smile and lassoed my imagination. *One problem at a time.*

By the time Arch rounded the car and opened the door I had the head on, tickets and rose in paw—full gorilla regalia. Just like that I was *on.* Suddenly, it was just like any one of the hundreds of goofy gigs I'd done in the past. I was even on home turf. A casino I knew inside and out. All I had to do was stroll in and act as if I belonged. It helped that I was incognito. No one, not even the man I'd been married to for fifteen years, was going to recognize me in this monkey suit.

I gave Arch a cocky salute and waltzed toward the doors, enjoying the chuckles I heard as a doorman ushered me inside. I liked making people laugh. Bringing joy had always been a thrill and the top perk of being an entertainer.

I crossed the main concourse and headed for a bank of elevators, waving to customers as I passed by. Good thing I knew where I was going. My vision was compromised. The ape eyes were a creation of fabric and grill work. I could see, but not clearly, and only the things directly in front of me. Luckily, it didn't smell too bad in here. In fact, it smelled as if it had just been sprayed with some sort of cleaner. Pine scent. Not a personal favorite, but anything was better than stinky sweat.

I bolstered my nerve as I neared the gourmet Italian restaurant. It's not like I loved Michael anymore, but I had to admit, it was going to be rough seeing him with Sasha for the first time as man and wife. And worse, seeing her pregnant. Sadly, he hadn't been interested in having children with me. So, yeah, I was a little bitter about the kid thing. But they lived in this town and I lived in this town so it's not as if I could avoid them forever. In a weird way, getting my first look at them without them seeing *me* was a bonus. I could scowl or cry or roll my eyes and all they'd see is the stony pug-faced expression of a stuffed gorilla.

The hostess didn't stop me so obviously she was in on the joke. I saw Michael and Sasha right off—the handsome, sharp-suited agent and the much-too-young for him lingerie model. They were seated directly in front of me, at a table with an ocean view. Only they weren't alone. I recognized the casino's entertainment coordinator and the VP of marketing. Two of the execs who'd been present during my disastrous audition.

Pile it on, cosmos.

I wasn't anxious or intimidated. I was hopped up on indignation. I was going to be the best damned singing gorilla they'd ever seen. Put that in your banana and smoke it!

I marched up to the table and launched into song. The lyrics of the first verse actually matched my mind-set a few bitter months back. I sang them with a Southern accent and a gritty quality so Michael wouldn't recognize my voice. Although I suppose it was muffled anyway. I sang with gusto, gyrated my hips, and wiggled my big monkey butt. By the time I made it to the chorus, the surrounding customers were clapping in time.

"Born in the U.S. APE. I was born in the U.S. APE..."

After a double chorus, I ended with a bow and extended the long-stemmed rose and concert tickets to Michael. He looked half bewildered, half amused. Then he focused on those front row and center tickets and broke out in a face-splitting smile. The comments from the surrounding tables blurred into white noise. I only had eyes and ears for Michael and his new wife, whose belly was concealed by the table. I watched them kiss and hug, listened to their sappy endearments of love...and survived.

I felt nothing aside from the rush of a job well done. The surrounding patrons were *still* applauding and the fact that the casino execs looked impressed was a bonus. Ah, the sweet smell of rubbing their noses in my multi-talents—talents they'd rejected based on my age. *Yes!* I pumped my ape fist in the air and performed a victory dance before spinning off and making a hasty exit.

Only as I neared the elevator did I realize my mistake. That victory dance was my signature happy dance, one that used to amuse Michael before he grew bored with me.

Crap!

Was he looking my way when I did it? Or gazing moony-eyed at Sasha?

Sweat trickled down my face as I pressed the down button. *Come on. Come on.* The door opened but it was packed and no one got off. The laughing occupants waved and shouted corny monkey comments as the doors shut. I punched the button again, peeked around the corner and saw Michael coming.

Oh, damn. Oh...bloody hell.

I zipped around the other way, slip-sliding down the marble hall in my fuzzy feet. King Kong fleeing the slot-machine jungle. I heard my name, a shushed, muffled

"Evie" as I stepped onto the escalator. It was one of those really tall ones and I almost lost my balance. My heart leapt to my throat as I grabbed the railing and someone grabbed me.

"Fuck's sake, Sunshine. Are you *trying* to give me a heart attack?"

"Arch?"

"*Dinnae* turn around. Just hold on and…try to look inconspicuous."

I laughed.

"You were fucking brilliant by the way."

"You saw my performance?"

"From a distance."

"Michael didn't see you, did he?"

"No."

"Is he following us now?"

"No."

"Why did *you* follow me?"

"Backup."

Oh. "That was sweet."

"Standard procedure for team members, yeah?"

"Uh-huh." Wearing a big smile that he couldn't see, I bastardized a movie quote in a singsongy voice. "You were worried. Because you love me. You want to smooch me. You want to hug me."

"Sandra Bullock. *Miss Congeniality.* Sort of."

I craned my head around, but I still couldn't see him because of the ape's limited vision. "You're amazing."

"You're a pain in the arse."

"But an adorable pain."

"Aye," he said with a smile in his voice. "There is that."

"Oh!" I cried, experiencing a bout of déjà vu. "Let me know when we near the bottom. I don't want my fur to get eaten in the teeth of the last step. Once I was working with a group of Hollywood characters and the hem of Jean Harlow's gown got eaten and seized up the gears. She had to be cut out of the dress and—"

Suddenly I was whisked up and into Arch's arms. "Problem solved," he said as he carried me across the concourse and out the front door.

I giggled. "You probably look pretty silly right now."

"Not as silly as you, lass."

"True."

Ten seconds later I was seated in his car and yanking off that suffocating head. I swiped my arm across my drenched forehead. "I did it, Arch. I saw them together and I didn't feel anything. What a huge flipping relief!"

"Good to know."

Something in his tone. Something…fragile. I hadn't thought about it from his point of view. Had he worried I still harbored affection for my ex? Wow. More proof of the bad boy's vulnerability.

"You look flushed," he said as he pulled onto Pacific Avenue. "Are you okay?"

"Sure," I said, my mind zinging with a hundred thoughts. All of them having to do with Arch and the future. "Just hot. And itchy. I can't wait to get out of this suit. Speaking of… You're going the wrong way. Fannie's Flowers is south."

"The Chameleon Club's north."

I flashed on The Kid's phone call. My gut said this was about Beckett. I reached in the backseat, grabbed my tote bag and dug out my phone. "I'll call Fannie and let her know the gig went great and that I'll return the costume later today."

"Good idea."

"Oh, wait." I squinted at the screen of my phone. "I think I have a text message. I don't know how—"

Arch nabbed my cell, punched a couple of buttons and handed it back.

"Thanks." I read the abbreviated text. "It's from Nic. All it says is that Jayne's okay and that she'll call me later. Why didn't she call with more of an update?"

"I can think of a couple of reasons. Neither cause for panic."

"In other words, don't borrow trouble."

"Aye."

Speaking of trouble… "So what's the unexpected news?"

Fighting traffic, Arch cast me a quick look. "Mad Dog's dead."

CHAPTER SIX

THE CHAMELEON CLUB WAS LOCATED in Atlantic City's Inlet. Only not in the newly renovated section. And though it was situated on the boardwalk, it faced the bay instead of the ocean and was a goodly distance from the casinos and souvenir tourist traps. Let's just say I wouldn't walk around this area after dark. Even during the day, I held my purse close and watched for muggers and drunks. No wonder Nic and Jayne had flipped when I told them I'd been hired to sing full-time in this, well—calling a spade a spade—dive.

Arch veered into the pothole-ridden parking lot and I had visions of car thieves lurking in the abandoned building a block down. "Isn't there a nearby garage or a secret place like the *Bat Cave* where you can park this thing?"

"No."

"What if we come out and all of the tires are gone?"

"I'll buy new ones."

"What if the car is gone?"

"Jazzman's fine."

"I wasn't talking about Beckett."

"But you're thinking *aboot* him, yeah?"

I didn't bother to lie. Arch would know. "Aren't you?"

"Aye."

He didn't elaborate. I didn't press. He'd tried calling

Beckett twice since receiving the news of Mad Dog's death. Both calls had rolled to voice mail.

On the ride over my imagination had soared. Arch had no information other than Frank Turner had been found dead this morning in his home, the seeming victim of a burglary. So I'd filled in the blanks, creating two or three different scenarios. Surely Beckett hadn't killed the man and if he did, it must have been in self-defense only why then would he cover it up? Only maybe he didn't cover it up. Maybe the cops were mistaken. Or maybe it was a straight up burglary and the thieves—not Beckett—killed Mad Dog. Yeah. That was it. Only I kept going, relaying the plot of a classic caper flick, to which Arch responded, *"This is real life, not a movie, yeah?"*

Which was his way of telling me to stuff a sock in it.

I'd clammed up after that, until now that is. "Wait," I said as he helped me out of his spiffy car. "I have to get out of this costume." Even though Arch had cranked up the air, I was soaked to the skin and itchy. Unfortunately, I tend to break out in a rash when I'm nervous or anxious, although it's usually confined to my neck and chest. This was a full body itch so I guess that meant I was ultranervous about Beckett.

Arch tugged down the back zipper. I shimmied out of the gorilla suit, sighing when a breeze hit my sweaty skin.

He peered at me over the rim of his sunglasses. "Now *that's* sexy."

He was looking at my chest.

I glanced down, not getting a straight on view like him, but I could imagine. Initially, I'd been wearing layers, only I knew I'd be hot in the ape suit, so I'd peeled off the long-sleeved T-shirt, leaving my pale pink tank top. It was soaked and so was my sheer bra. I met his appreciative gaze. "So can you see my…you know."

"Nipples?" He quirked his first grin in several minutes then reached into his backseat and produced a denim jacket.

"Thanks." I didn't care that it was too big for me. Through twists of fate it seemed someone, somewhere was always getting a peek at my boobs. So far everyone on the team except... No, wait. *Everyone* on the team had seen my boobs. I didn't want to think about it.

Arch lit up a cigarette and I marveled for the zillionth time how I could possibly find the nasty habit sexy. I guess it's because it accentuated his bad-boy persona. It also stunk up the air and blackened his lungs. Lungs I cared about more and more, along with every other organ and limb of the man's hunky body.

"You should really think about giving those things up."

"Noted."

"And?"

"Thinking *aboot* it."

I rolled my eyes. Conversation with Arch wasn't always easy. But I wasn't daunted. After all, I'd been married to a man who spoke in circles for a living. As an agent, Michael had to appease both artist *and* buyer which often led to embellishing, twisting, and spinning his words. Sometimes the best approach was to leave off and come back to the subject later. In some ways, Michael had been a valuable training ground for Arch. Weird, but true.

We fell into mutual silence—Arch smoking, me scratching—as we made our way up the wooden steps and onto the boardwalk. Waves lapped at the shore. The sun beamed in a clear blue sky. A beautiful spring day, except for the cloud of doom I imagined hovering over the club.

Arch snuffed his Marlboro then steered me through the front door. As my eyes adjusted to the dim lighting, I flashed on the disappointment I'd experienced the first time I'd entered this run-down building. I'd expected a super spy facility, not a dingy bar that looked like it hadn't been modernized since the 1950s. It even had a beat-up cigarette machine and a jukebox. The pictures on the faded walls featured singers and musicians from days gone by. The only artists I recognized were Miles Davis and Billie Holiday. Then again, unlike Beckett, I wasn't a big fan of jazz. You can imagine my shock when I was told it's the only kind of music he allows in this joint. I sing pop, rock, country, disco and R and B. I do not sing jazz.

Although, I'd have to take a stab at it. When not in the field, Beckett expected me to perform here. A cover job of sorts. Just as this bar was a cover for Chameleon. Never mind that there wasn't a stage and that the mini sound system had been *appropriated* by Tabasco. At least it was better than flipping burgers in the kitchen. Maybe.

I hugged myself, scratching at my itchy skin through the sleeves of the jacket as Arch and I bypassed vacant tables and targeted the bar. Business wasn't exactly booming. Then again it was only one in the afternoon. I was pretty certain the two barflies buzzing over their draft beers were the same two geezers I'd seen in here during my last visit.

The bartender, an elderly dark-skinned gentleman with a fondness for vests and porkpie hats, was the team member who oversaw the club when Beckett was in the field. His name was Samuel Vine, but everyone called him Pops. He had a deep, soulful voice that seemed two sizes too big for his wiry body. Pops was also a man of few words. I didn't know his background, but I'm thinking he and Beckett went way back. Unlike Arch, he didn't hide his emotions. Clearly, he was rattled. Even so, he forced a smile and addressed me first.

"Welcome home, Twinkie."

Unfortunately, everyone on the team, except Arch, had picked up on my unwanted moniker. Fortunately, I'd grown used to it. "Thanks, Pops."

"Your ma and pa okay now?"

"Happily reunited. Thanks to…" I started to say Chameleon then remembered the barflies. "Friends."

"Good. That's good." His gaze flicked to the man beside me. "Ace," he said, gripping Arch's hand.

Arch squeezed the man's shoulder, smiled, and the old man relaxed a little. "Heard from Jazzman?" Arch asked.

Pops leaned in and lowered his voice. "All I know is he got hauled in by the AIA. Told me he'd be in touch later. That was—" he glanced at his Timex "—three hours ago."

I scratched my neck, my chest.

"Others are in The Cave," Pops said then moved back to his cronies.

Arch took my hand and pulled me aside. "Maybe you should wait here."

"Why?"

"From the way you're scratching, I'm not sure you can handle whatever's going on, Sunshine."

Of all the… "I can handle it!"

"Calm down," Arch said with a glance to the patrons. All two of them.

"I can handle it," I whispered through clenched teeth. "This isn't a nervous rash. I've never broken out on my arms before. I think it's a reaction to that monkey suit. The fur or whatever Fannie cleaned it with. I don't know."

"Right then. You should shower."

"I will. As soon as I get home."

"Now. Upstairs."

"Beckett's shower?"

"Aye."

"Forget it."

"He's not there."

"I don't care." No way, no how was I getting naked in Beckett's apartment. I'd been there. Done that. Almost. Thanks to ODing on a combo of over the counter medication. "I'm fine. Really. Let's go."

He didn't look or sound exasperated, but I'd wager I'd taxed his patience. "Fine," he said then steered me to a storage room.

My pulse accelerated as we navigated the jam-packed room and pushed through a concealed door. A set of creaky stairs led to the basement. A low-wattage bulb illuminated a washer and dryer and a freezer. Workout equipment. Tools. Crates of liquor and soda. All perfectly normal. Well, except for the appliances. The avocado finish screamed early 70s. Hello, *Brady Bunch*. The old-as-dirt dryer was probably a fire hazard. The ancient wiring couldn't be that safe, either. I immediately redirected my basement inferno thoughts.

I'd only been down here once before. But I knew Arch had to swing aside a wall clock to get to a security pad. Unlike Pops he didn't ask me to turn away when he punched in the code. Which intimated trust. Which gave me a warm fuzzy feeling. If only it would heal the itching sensation driving me batty.

Just as I knew it would, a wall slid open revealing *The Cave*. The super spy facility I'd imagined only it was hidden behind shelves of canned pretzels and assorted nuts.

I don't know why they called it The Cave. It didn't look like a cave. It looked like a state-of-the-art recording studio. Acoustic tiles. Plush carpeting. Leather furniture. A console of visual and audio gadgets.

A techno-geek's dream. Speaking of…

"I dug like you said, Ace, but I didn't get much," Woody said as we entered the room and the wall slid shut behind us.

The Kid, as everyone except me called him, was sitting alongside Tabasco at the console tapping away at one of three computers. The two men couldn't look more opposite.

Woody had a pasty complexion, scraggly hair, and a sparse beard. Skinny as a rail, early twenties—a dead ringer for *Scooby-Doo's* Shaggy. He'd had one girlfriend and he'd lost her. It didn't help that he was a social train wreck.

Tabasco probably had a girlfriend or two in every state. Any woman who'd ever drooled over Antonio Banderas would drool over Jimmy Tabasco. Same sexy, Latin lover vibe. Plus, he was sweet.

Tabasco's official role with Chameleon was dual: *Transportation Specialist* and *Location Scout*. But he was also pretty savvy with tech gear. Last night he'd worked alongside Woody in the high-tech surveillance van, spying on Mad Dog's poker game. Since the players weren't allowed to have guests, Arch (as the Baron of Broxley) had sent me back to our hotel, only I'd stopped the cab a block down and had backtracked, slipping inside the undercover van to view the sting over Woody's and Tabasco's shoulders. Being on the outside looking in wasn't where I wanted to be, but it was better than being in the dark. Due to strategically hidden cameras, Tabasco, Woody, and I had a prime view of every player and their cards via multiple monitors. Due to transmitting and receiving body wires, we had full audio contact. Between Arch and Gina, who were both in the game, Mad Dog never stood a chance even with his luminous contact lenses and marked cards.

"The only reason CNN picked up the story," said Tabasco, "is because Mad Dog was a former pro football player."

"Otherwise we wouldn't have learned the news so soon," Woody said. "A burglary that resulted in homicide. Local news stuff."

Just then Gina emerged from another room with a cup of coffee. Without a word she perched on the cushy leather sofa and thumbed through a stack of newspapers. She barely spared us a glance. I wasn't surprised. She hated that I was sleeping with Arch. I hated that she'd slept with Arch (something I'd learned from my meddling ex-husband). Arch, who'd refused to apologize to me for past affairs (which when I thought about it logically was, well, logical) was nevertheless sensitive to my discomfort. Hence, he'd been treating Gina with cool indifference. I was starting to feel bad about that. Especially, when I put myself in her shoes. I could fully sympathize with the plight of the woman scorned.

"Hacked into the local law's computer system," said Woody. "The initial report looks routine, though sketchy. Cops must be frustrated as all get out. No physical evidence. No clue as to the identity of the assailant."

"Yet," Tabasco said.

"Pull up that report for me, Kid." Arch moved to the console.

I scratched. I needed a distraction from the itching that was only getting worse. Eying the stack of newspapers, I sucked it up and sat down next to Gina. Not *right* next to her, but close enough to make her frown.

"What are you doing?" I asked.

"Looking for any mention of 'Mad Dog.' Doubt there'll be one since most of these papers went to press last night, but it's worth a look. Also keeping my eye trained for any blips about Senator Clark or Vincent Crowe. Anything at all."

"Can I help?"

I thought I heard her sigh, only Gina wasn't the sighing type. She reminded me of Nic—independent, cynical, worldly. She also resembled my friend in appearance, only her skin was paler and her eyes were brown. But she exuded the same sensuality. Had the same tall, slender but toned body. Except Nic was nice and Gina was mean. Okay. Maybe not mean. But definitely bitter. Again, I could relate.

She passed me the *Philadelphia Inquirer* without comment and I felt another twinge of guilt. Maybe if I tried harder we could strike some kind of truce. The tension I'd created between Arch and Beckett was bad enough.

Determined to fit in, I scanned the newspaper, every section, every page, every article. Meanwhile I listened to the men discuss the timeline and where they thought Beckett would have/should have been and what, if anything, could have gone wrong.

I didn't point out that I had made similar conjectures just minutes ago in Arch's car. I skimmed the paper and scratched, silently congratulating myself for thinking on their level.

Gina looked over her shoulder at Arch. "The Kid said you spoke with Jazzman this morning. How did he sound?"

"Tired."

"What did he say?"

"Mission complete."

"His part of the mission," Gina said, "was to make Turner disappear."

"Not literally!" I snapped. "He was just supposed to make him, you know, go away. Split the country. Change his identity and never mention the senator's wife's gambling problem or else—" I scratched my cheek "—something. He didn't *kill* Mad Dog," I grumbled while scratching my arms.

"Preaching to the choir, Sunshine. We're all on Beckett's side." Arch sounded calm. No surprise there.

Tabasco sounded calm, but his attitude needed work. "I have a sinking feeling we're going to be linked to Mad Dog's death."

"Agent Beckett did say he had a bad feeling about this case right off," Woody added.

"I want to know why the AIA pulled him in," Arch said, "and why he hasn't returned our calls."

"What's with the red blotches on your face, Twinkie?"

I glanced up and saw Gina staring at me with—here's a shocker—concern. I experienced a full body blush. "What do you mean?"

"You've been acting like a dog with fleas ever since you walked in," Woody said.

I realized then that I was scratching like a loon. My arms. My neck and chest. My face. Yet there was no relief from the incessant itching that felt as though it had wiggled beneath my skin. I felt irritable and anxious, and okay, a little scared. "Stupid gorilla suit!"

"What?" Gina laughed but she still looked concerned.

Arch moved around and crouched in front of me just as I yanked off his jacket in order to scratch my bare arms.

"*Shite.*"

"Shit," Gina echoed. "That's a serious allergy attack, Arch. Get her to a doctor."

My eyes widened. "What? No. I'm okay. Really. I want to help you guys help Beckett."

"Nothing we can do right now," said Tabasco. "Jesus, babe, you're covered in hives."

The Kid stood in front of me shaking his head. "You look awful."

"You always manage to say the worst thing possible," I snapped, because he did, but not on purpose. "I'm sorry, Woody. I…" I felt an anxiety attack coming on.

"Come on, lass." Arch pulled me off the sofa and into his arms.

I was going to die of embarrassment. I was going to die period. The itching was unbearable. But even as he carried me from the room I thought about Jayne. "What about Madame Helene?" I asked Arch. "You promised—"

"Tabasco."

"Yeah?"

"I need to you to check up on a local psychic," Arch said. "Madame Helene. I want to know her game."

"Will do."

"Kid. Gina. Call me if you learn anything more or hear from Jazzman, yeah?"

They said, "Sure," as Arch whisked me up the stairs.

I clung and fought not to hyperventilate. I couldn't think straight. I'd never been so physically miserable in my life. Except maybe when I had the chicken pox, but that was a faded childhood memory. Even the concussion I'd suffered in the Caribbean because of the Simon the Fish fiasco paled.

I scratched even though Arch told me not to, even though it didn't help.

Two minutes later, he placed me in his car.

I closed my eyes to stave off tears. "I'm going to die."

Arch kissed my forehead and buckled me in. "Not in my lifetime, lass."

CHAPTER SEVEN

MILO SAT IN THE RENTAL CAR, staring up at her condo. "You're a glutton for punishment, Beckett." They weren't on the best of terms. Hell, she didn't even like him. Still, he'd driven here instead of home. Somehow, he knew she'd make him feel better. Or at least she wouldn't object if he drank himself blind.

He'd been sitting here for fifteen minutes. "Screw it."

He rang her up.

"Hello?"

"It's Beckett."

Silence.

"I know this is crazy, but…I need to drink and I don't want to drink alone."

"Call a friend."

"My friends are my associates. Not up for that right now."

She paused and when she spoke again her tone was less abrasive, but not much. "What's wrong?"

"I'd rather talk about it over Scotch."

Silence.

His throbbing temples charged him a fool. His judgment had been off lately. Coming here was just another example. "Never mind."

"No, wait." She blew out a breath. "It's five o'clock somewhere, right? I'll meet you at The Irish Pub."

"Your place," he countered.

"Not comfortable with that."

"Neither am I, but I'd appreciate it."

"Well, damn, Slick." Another curse, then, "I live at—"

"I know." He knocked on the door.

A beat later it swung open and he was looking at Nicole Sparks. A lush-lipped beauty with a bad attitude. Nine days ago, she'd threatened to make his life hell if he ever hurt her friend Evie. She was an outspoken, pushy, skeptical pain in the ass. Seeing her again only convoluted his emotions.

What the fuck was he doing here?

His cock twitched in answer.

Easy, Mr. Happy. You don't want to go there. Okay. Maybe you do, but I don't.

The warm air sparked with mutual hostility as they sized up one another on the threshold of her third-story condo. He knew he looked bad. His lip was split and swollen. He hadn't slept in thirty-six hours. He needed a shave and his suit was rumpled.

She, on the other hand, looked chic in her slim-fitting pants and tailored blouse—black, like her long, glossy hair. Her unusual coloring—mocha skin, jade-green eyes—gave her an exotic look that solicited erotic images. He attributed his unwanted hard-on to her potent sexuality and his pathetic love life. It sure wasn't based on healthy desire. Nic was a threatening storm to Evie's hopeful rainbow. Not to mention she was Evie's best friend. The dynamics of his relationships with friends and associates was already screwed. Like he needed to add another twist. Nicole Sparks was trouble on several levels and Milo didn't want any part of her.

Yet here he was.

"Awfully sure of yourself, Slick."

"Just optimistic."

"You mean desperate." She quirked a brow. "What happened to your lip?"

"Walked into a fist."

"That fist belong to anyone I know?"

"No."

"Arch didn't lose his cool and pop you one for—"

"No." He took off his sunglasses and nailed her with weary eyes. "Are you going to let me in or not?"

She waved him inside and he tried not to stare at her ass when she led him through the foyer into a spacious living room. Tried and failed.

She turned and crossed her arms over her equally enticing breasts. "I don't have any Scotch."

His gaze caressed her curves then locked on her killer eyes. "I'll take whatever you've got."

"I'm not going to sleep with you, Beckett."

"Awfully sure of yourself."

"I know a come-on when I hear it and a hard-on when I see it." Before he could respond she slipped into the kitchen. "How do you feel about vodka?"

"Same as I feel about you. I can tolerate it."

He heard her laugh. A throaty sound that only heightened his predicament. He took off his jacket, adjusted himself then settled on the plush red couch. He rubbed a crick from his neck while noting the impeccably decorated room. So the pain in the ass had a flair for design. Classy taste. Designer taste. He wondered how she afforded it. As far as he knew, she made her living solely as an entertainer and according to Evie, times were tough.

She returned with a full bottle of Absolut Citron. Lemon-flavored vodka. Not a drink of choice, but just now he'd settle for Boone's Farm. She sank down beside him and set two glasses on the gleaming cocktail table.

"Given your mood, figured you'd want it straight."

"Good call."

"I know you made a pass at Evie and that she opted for Arch," she said straight out. "If this is some sort of rebound—"

"It's not."

"Because I've been through that more than once and—"

"This isn't about Evie." He poured, thinking, not for the first time, a wounded heart beat beneath Nicole's tough facade. He wondered if she'd ever let her guard down with him. Probably not. Which was probably for the best. "I didn't want to be around people I know—*well, that is*—and I didn't want to be alone."

Her eyes softened as she raised her glass in a toast. "What are we drinking to?" she asked.

"Me being fucked."

She stiffened.

"Not by you, sweetheart. By my own people."

"The AIA?"

"You know about the Agency?"

"Evie told me. Don't worry. I know it's…how did she put it? Big-time hush-hush."

He smiled a little. "She does have a way with words."

"Your secret's safe with me, Slick."

"I believe you, *Nicole*."

"Most people call me Nic."

"Most people call me Milo."

"When I was a kid we had a dog named Milo." She smiled when he grunted, then angled in and tucked her bare feet beneath that fine ass. "Just how big *is* this bureaucratic shaft?"

"I've been accused of murder."

The smile slipped. "That's big."

They slammed back two fingers of vodka in tandem.

"Knew I came to the right place," Milo said. Jury was out on who had drank who under the table the last, and only other time, they'd shared a bottle.

Nic refilled their glasses, chewing over his revelation. "Aren't you going to ask if I did it?"

"Did you?"

"Apparently so, though not by design." He still couldn't believe it, even after seeing the digital recording. He didn't want to believe it. Didn't want to feel the doubt and guilt clawing at his gut. He popped two Tylenol and slammed back a second shot.

"What does that mean?" she asked. "Apparently so."

"When I left the scene, he was still alive."

"So he died after."

"Soon after."

"Because of something you did."

Milo nodded. "Apparently so."

Nic watched him with a calm, cool gaze and sipped. "What does your partner say about this?"

"I haven't told Arch yet. The incident took place around 2:00 a.m. I just learned about the unfortunate outcome a few hours ago when a pair of agents met me at the airport and escorted me to HQ."

"Since you're free, obviously there wasn't enough evidence to hold you."

"I'm free, because the Agency tampered with the crime scene. Made it look like a burglary. Trust me. The victim's death will go unsolved."

Nic frowned. "Wait a minute. *Your* people discovered the body? How's that possible? Unless...were they there as backup?"

"They were there, unbeknownst to me, to make sure I didn't screw up. Which, it seems, I did."

"So they covered your ass. They compromised a crime scene, on purpose, which means they broke the law. Why would they do that? They're federal agents for chrissakes."

"Surely you, of all people, aren't that naive."

She angled her head. "Protecting one of their own?"

"So Crowe, my boss, says. He's also protecting a certain politician."

"You don't sound sold on your boss's motive."

"I'm not."

"Who's the politician?"

"Can't say." He looked away and poured more vodka.

"Privileged information, huh?"

"Sorry."

She shrugged, sipped. "How do those agents know for sure that you caused this person's death? Did they spy through the windows with super-spook binoculars? Slip a bug in your shoe?"

Milo's lip twitched. "For a second there, you sounded like Evie." He sipped vodka to drown out thoughts of the overimaginative half-pint. He focused back on his dilemma and Nic's question. "Spying was involved, yes. But more damning…"

"What?"

"Let's just say they have hard evidence."

"That sounds bad."

"It is."

They fell into mutual silence, drank more vodka. Milo could hear Nic's thoughts churning. "Just an observation," she said, "but given your background and training in law enforcement, seems you'd know whether or not what you did was intense enough to cause death. *Apparently so* says you're surprised. No offense, but this whole thing sounds like a grade B thriller. Maybe I've watched too many documentaries on conspiracy theories, but…any chance you're being framed, Slick?"

Damn, she was cynical. A quality he normally found off-putting in a woman. But there was nothing normal about this moment and he appreciated the benefit of the doubt. "The thought crossed my mind. Although I'm not sure how—"

"Forget the how. *Why* would the AIA frame you?"

"To keep me under their thumb. Maybe. I'm not a company man and Crowe is a control freak. On the other hand, could be wishful thinking on my part."

"What if it's not? What if there's some elaborate plan and you're the pawn?"

"Nicole—"

"Grow some balls, Slick. Buck the system. Investigate. Fight back."

He'd been bucking the system for years. Bucking the system is what had brought him to this point. "I need to sleep on this," he said honestly. "Only I can't. My mind won't shut down. It's not just this. It's…a lot of things."

"Want to talk about it?"

"No."

"Okay." She pulled a remote out of a mosaic box and turned on a thirty-two-inch plasma television. Nice. "Sports, news, sitcom or a movie?" she asked as she surfed channels.

"Anything but the news."

She messed with her TiVo and settled on The History Channel. He didn't know Nic well, but he knew she favored documentaries over sitcoms. "Ever watch this series?" she asked. *"Decoding the Past?"*

"Nope."

"This episode is of particular interest to me," she said. "Past U.S. Presidents who consulted psychics. Abe Lincoln, Woodrow Wilson, Franklin D. Roosevelt. Goes to show anyone can fall for that mystical bullshit, right?"

He cut her a glance, wondering at the hostility in her tone. Namely because it wasn't directed at him. "Right."

"Make yourself comfortable, Beckett. If you can't sleep, you can at least rest."

He didn't argue. The vodka was already taking effect. Smoothing the edges, slowing his thoughts. He'd been awake now—he glanced at his watch—thirty-seven hours.

"Think you should call someone and let them know you're okay?" Nic asked as she twisted her long hair into a loose braid.

He tried not to admire her stunning bone structure. Tried and failed. "Probably." Especially since he had numerous voice messages from Arch, Pops, and Woody. Arch was probably with Evie and that was a road he didn't want to travel just now. The less he thought about those two together, the better. He called Pops.

"Tell me you're not in jail, son."

Milo frowned. "Why would you think that?"

"We heard about Turner."

"How?"

"CNN."

"Killing the guy wasn't part of the plan, Pops."

"Course not."

"Tell the team…" He rubbed his eyes, blew out a breath. "Tell them I need some time alone. Tell them to meet me tomorrow morning. Ten o'clock. You know the place."

"You comin' home tonight?"

Milo glanced at Nic who'd drawn shut the curtains of the floor-to-ceiling windows. "Depends."

"Take care, Jazzman."

"Always." He thumbed the cell to vibrate then slipped it in his jacket pocket. If it went off, he wouldn't feel it. A few more shots of vodka, and he wouldn't feel anything.

"Thought it might help you relax if it was darker in here," Nic said as she settled back on the couch.

"Why are you being nice to me?"

"You've been accused of murder, Slick. I'm thinking you could use some consideration."

His mind focused on the last time they'd sat like this, watching TV, drinking. He'd woken up the next morning with her head in his lap. Nothing had happened sexually, but she'd given him the cold shoulder for the rest of the day and she'd cut her trip short. He wanted to ask why, but didn't. Instead, he commented on her eye roll when the program's narrator mentioned Roosevelt consulted a psychic about post-WWII world relations. "I take it you don't believe in the supernatural."

She topped off her drink. "Do you?"

"I'm in the business of exposing fraud, sweetheart. Do you know how many people a year are suckered by fortune-tellers, hotline psychics, and astrologers?"

"I know of at least one."

Again with the hostile tone. "Let's hear it."

"Are you sure?"

"Shoot."

She slammed back her drink and lowered the TV volume. "It's about my free-spirited friend Jayne and a whack-job psychic."

CHAPTER EIGHT

CONTRARY TO MY PREDICTION, I did not die.

Thanks to prescription-grade antihistamines and a topical cream, I would indeed live to see another day. Although, I sort of dreaded it. My current track record promised some sort of calamity. A screwball moment that would end in mortification. Hadn't I endured my share of embarrassing moments this past month?

Apparently not, because they just kept coming.

Gina had been dead-on in her diagnosis. A severe allergic reaction. A hypersensitivity response to an outside influence, according to the emergency room doctor. Said influence being a combination of heat, cleaning chemicals, and emotional stress.

If I would've showered when Arch urged me to, I could've avoided the hives. He'd had the decency not to say I told you so. Just as he'd been kind enough not to rib me about the time my jaw locked open or the time I got stuck in a tree. Although he'd been pissed about the latter since he'd thought I'd unnecessarily risked my neck to spy on my mom. Don't ask.

Just now I was trying to think of a way to get rid of him without hurting his feelings.

I didn't want him to see me like this. The gorilla suit had been sexier.

"*Dinnae* make me pick this lock, Sunshine."

Cocooned in my purple robe, I braced my weight against my bathroom door. "I told you I'm fine, just…ugly."

"What?"

"Did you ever see *That Touch of Mink?*"

"Doris Day and Cary Grant?"

"Bingo."

"Not one of their better films, yeah?"

"What are you talking about?" I glared through the door. "It's a classic!"

"He was funnier in *Bringing Up Baby* and *My Favorite Wife,* to name two, and had more chemistry with Hepburn or Dunne, take your pick."

"I thought Day and Grant were adorable together."

"Mismatched."

"Are you talking about their age difference? That would be pretty hypocritical, considering, you know…us."

"Age is moot when there's chemistry, yeah?"

I perked up. "You think we have chemistry? Like Bogie and Bacall? Gable and Lombard?" *Lucy and Ricky?*

"You know we do."

The connection. I'd mentioned before how we didn't make sense, but we connected. *We just need to find our rhythm.*

"Hard to dance with a door between us, you know?"

I sighed. "I know." I rested my forehead against the painted wood and imagined him doing the same. We'd had numerous conversations on the threshold of one or another bathroom, only the door had always been open and Arch had usually been wearing a towel, his upper body gloriously exposed. I imagined his broad shoulders and chiseled abdomen. His strong arms and that sexy tattoo. I let out a pathetic sigh.

"What's wrong, lass?"

Aside from being worried about Beckett and Jayne? Selfishly, I was lamenting my own crappy luck. "We were supposed to get naked tonight," I said with a hitch in my voice.

"Aye. And?"

"Now we can't."

"Why not?"

"For one, I'm too distracted."

"You mean worried," he said. "No need, yeah? Pops called a few minutes ago. Beckett phoned and he's fine. Said he'd fill us in tomorrow at a team meeting."

"He's not under arrest?"

"No."

Which implied he was innocent in the death of Mad Dog. I pumped a fist in the air. *Yes.*

"What else?" Arch asked.

"I'm worried about Jayne. I wish we had something on Madame Helene."

"Tabasco's working on it. He'll have something by tomorrow."

More good news.

"What else?" His patience was amazing.

"Well," I said touching a hand to my face. "Remember that scene in *That Touch of Mink* when Cathy broke out in hives because she was nervous about sleeping with Mr. Shayne?"

"You're getting cold feet *aboot* us? Shagging in your apartment is too intimate? What?"

He didn't sound mad, but I knew him well enough to know I'd tripped a live wire. Uh-oh. "It's not that. It's…"

The lock clicked and I hopped back just as the door swung open.

He took one look at me and smiled.

"Are you happy now?" I didn't know whether to cry or punch him.

"It's not so bad."

"It's awful." The topical lotion I'd slathered on my hives had dried in pink pasty splotches all over my arms, chest, neck and—*ack!*—face. I wasn't exactly confident about my looks as is. I'm sure there are some perks to being over forty, but random gray hairs, crow's-feet, and less taut skin aren't included. At least I have perky boobs. That's something. And I'm limber. A definite bonus.

Until recently I'd refused to let Arch *shag* me missionary-style. Too intimate. All I wanted was a fling. Sex, just sex. Falling in love with a man I didn't trust, a man who didn't do relationships wouldn't be smart. I knew it wouldn't take much for me to lose my heart to the sexiest, most dangerous, most caring man I'd ever known, so I'd avoided the ultimate intimacy.

Talk about a losing battle. I'd crumbled three weeks into our hot and heavy fling.

Though Arch appreciated my agility (call me Gumby), he surprisingly enjoyed the missionary-style most. He said he liked to look at my face and into my eyes when he, well, sent me over the moon to the Big O.

I didn't want him looking at my face tonight.

"You know what your problem is?" he asked as he nabbed my robe's sash and tugged me into the bedroom.

"Aside from the obvious?"

"You focus too much on the physical. The external, yeah?"

"Yeah? Well, my roots are in entertainment. Call me shallow." Or realistic. Granted, it had probably been this way for decades. Youth and sexuality taking precedence over talent. Not *all* the time, of course, but more often than it should. Not that I'm bitter. Okay. Maybe a little.

He angled his head. "So you're only hot for me because of what you see?"

"What? No. I mean I like what I see." *A lot.* "But that's just, I don't know, cake."

"Icing."

"Right. The frosting on the top."

"Cherry on the top."

"Whatever. I can name a hundred reasons why I'm attracted to you that have nothing to do with your movie-star looks."

His mouth quirked. "Name one."

"You make me feel sexy."

"You are sexy."

I snorted. "Nic is sexy. *Gina* is sexy."

"There are all kinds of sexy, yeah?"

Kind of like there are all kinds of lies? "Also, you always say the right thing. I don't know why I find that appealing since I know it's a honed skill. Con artists always say the right thing. It's part of your toolbox. Squeezed up against confidence, sincerity, and calm. Qualities that allow you to manipulate—" I squealed as he yanked off my sash and wrapped it around my head, covering my eyes. "What are you doing?"

"Helping you to focus less on the external."

Not only had he blindfolded me, but without the sash my robe gaped open. I felt violated and exposed and, *hello,* aroused. "But I look—"

He kissed away my protest. I wondered if he had anti-itch cream on *his* face now, but only fleetingly. Hard to think coherent thoughts with a sizzling Scot's tongue in my mouth. Not that I could see the man. But I could taste and smell and… *Zing. Zap!*

Desire snaked through my body as he palmed my bare butt and ground his erection into my belly. Erotic thoughts boogied through my head as he maneuvered me…somewhere. Or maybe that was the world shifting beneath my feet. Could this man kiss!

Delirious with desire, I think I actually whimpered when he eased away. I figured his little experiment was over and I was feeling a little ridiculous between the blindfold, my gaping robe, and my smiley face socks. Not to mention the splotchy pink cream. I reached up to untie the sash.

"Leave it."

I'm not sure which was sexier—the fact that he'd *ordered* me to do so or the anticipation of his next move. I scrunched my brow. "Are you still wearing all of your clothes?"

"Aye."

Hmm.

Before I could ask another question, he tore the robe off my body.

Um. Okay. *That* was exciting. I couldn't see his mesmerizing eyes or that tribal tattoo or his ripped torso, but yeah, baby, yeah, I could *feel*.

Before I knew what hit me, I hit the mattress. I could feel my soft comforter beneath my bare back and Arch's hard body—fully clothed—on top of me. "What—"

"*Dinnae* talk."

Another order.

Zing.

I was officially, totally turned on. *Clothes off,* I said to myself while fumbling with the buttons of his shirt.

"*Dinnae* touch." He grasped my wrists and pushed my hands over my head.

Zap.

I felt my knuckles brush the brass railings of my head-board.

"Grab hold," he said close to my ear, "and *dinnae* let go."

My heart pounded. Should I be nervous? We'd had a lot of creative sex, but never anything kinky. This was kinky. For me anyway. At least he hadn't used handcuffs. Although if I disobeyed and let go, he could always lash my wrists to the headboard with my socks. Which reminded me, I still had them on. Arch has a thing for my collection of cartoonish socks. He thinks they're sexy.

Definitely kinky.

My thoughts scrambled when he bit and sucked my nipples—no allergy medicine there. I gripped the brass rails and endured sweet ecstasy as he lavished attention on both breasts before kissing his way south. My heart raced as he kissed and nipped at my thighs, his warm hands urging my legs apart. I listened for the sound of his jeans unzipping and instead felt the pressure and warmth of his mouth down *there,* working magic. I bit back an enraptured, *oh-my-God*—no talking allowed—and settled on a lot of moaning.

Twice I almost climaxed. Twice he pulled away. Delirious with need, I wanted to anchor his head between my legs until I peaked, but…*no touching allowed!*

I could've ripped off the blindfold and taken back some control, but the experience was so erotic, so amazingly exciting, I didn't want it to end.

I held tight to the headboard and endured Arch's teasing. I squirmed and moaned, and when he finally took pity and tongued me to climax, I uttered gibberish which in my mind did not count as talking. Not that I could form a cohesive sentence right now anyway.

I lay in blindfolded darkness, breathing hard, heart racing, waiting for him to tell me to let go of the rails, only he didn't.

"My turn," he said, and my imagination galloped. Numerous erotic images pounded my brain only to be blown away when he mounted me missionary-style.

Given the kinky circumstances, I expected a fast and hard shag. But Arch wasn't cooperating with my predictions. He took it slow. Achingly slow. My body trembled with delicious sensations as he tormented me with his thick, hard shaft, withdrawing completely before filling me once more.

Just when I thought I couldn't take anymore, he pulled off the blindfold and nailed me with a gaze that sent me over the moon. I relinquished my hold on the rails and latched on to his shoulders. I cried out his name. I came and I came and, "Oh, my God!" came.

Arch shuddered with his own release and dropped his forehead to mine.

My body and mind sparked and sputtered. "That was…"

"Aye."

After a moment he rolled aside and pulled me into his arms. His heart pounded as hard as mine and he gazed at me as though I were the most beautiful woman on earth. I thought about how awful I looked and how wonderful he'd made me feel. He was right. I did focus too much on outer appearance. I thought about all the whining I'd done over the past few weeks. How I constantly compared myself to women in their twenties or Bond-type women and came up lacking. Yet I'd given a bad boy, a *younger* bad boy, a hard-on even with my less than perfect body slathered in chalky pink medicine.

I felt a shift deep inside. A snap.

I palmed Arch's cheek, smiling when I noticed a pink smudge on his chin. "Thank you."

"My pleasure."

"Not the sex. Although that was…"

"Fan-fucking-tastic?"

I grinned. "Actually I was thanking you for the life lesson."

"Just reciprocating, Sunshine."

I blinked. "*I've* taught *you* a life lesson?"

"A couple, yeah?"

"Really?"

He kissed me. "Really."

I wondered what, but I didn't ask. That could wait. My need to exert my newly found confidence, couldn't.

Looking down, I palmed John Thomas. "All tuckered out, big guy?"

"If he could talk," Arch said, clearly amused, "he'd ask what you have in mind."

I rolled out of bed, naked as a jaybird and more comfortable in my skin than I'd ever been. So, I looked like a flamingo threw up on me. So, I had a few smile lines and could stand to lose a couple inches in my hips. So, what? I strode to my closet and whipped out two costumes for his pleasure. "French maid or harem girl?"

Arch's eyes twinkled and I knew he was a goner. "Bollocks."

Yup. Toast.

CHAPTER NINE

MILO GLANCED AT HIS DIGITAL alarm clock. Three-fucking-twenty in the morning. Seven minutes later than the last time he checked. He lay in bed, his own bed, alone. Nothing new there. Aside from a few random *dates,* he'd slept alone most every night since his divorce. That had been more than a year ago.

As for sex, he hadn't been laid in months. Not for lack of opportunity, mind you. At first, he attributed his low sex drive to depression over his broken marriage, then later, to his frustration with the AIA. After a few scattered one-night stands, he realized he wanted something more than a disconnected lay. He wanted mind-blowing sex with a woman who got under his skin, a woman who challenged him, a woman who brightened his dark world.

That would be Evie in spades.

The hell of it was, he sensed something between them aside from mutual respect and likeability. He'd been toying with the idea of fighting for her, thinking himself the better man. Unlike the cagey Scot, he wouldn't keep his past under wraps, because he had nothing to hide. There'd be no secrets, no fear of commitment. He wouldn't break her heart.

Arch would. Given his partner's personality and make-up, it was inevitable. All Milo had to do was hang tough and pick up the pieces except…he no longer considered himself the better man.

Wood creaked—the sound of his front door opening and closing.

Swiftly, silently, Milo grabbed his Sig from the nightstand and moved across his bedroom. Someone had gotten past the club's security system and broken into his second floor apartment. A skilled thief? One of Crowe's lackeys?

He knew every creak in the scarred and warped hardwood floor, knew exactly where to aim his weapon when he flicked on a living room light and… Adrenaline surged and ebbed. *"Fuck!"*

"Bugger."

"Mind explaining why you broke into my place?"

"Mind pointing that thing somewhere else? Fuck's sake, Jazzman."

Now Milo was just plain pissed. He placed the loaded handgun on a bookshelf. "You're lucky I didn't shoot first and ask questions later."

"Not your style." Arch settled on the worn couch, gestured to the gun. "Bit jumpy, yeah?"

"You broke into my home."

"Wanted to have a word."

"You could have called."

"I did. You ignored my calls. All five of them, yeah?"

"Did we get married? Because you're acting like I'm accountable to you."

"Sit down before you fall down. You look like *shite*."

Milo mentally assessed his appearance. Boxers and a wrinkled T-shirt. Two day's growth of whiskers. Split lip compliments of Turner. Bloodshot eyes, compliments of a hangover.

Arch on the other hand looked sharp and rested—even in the middle of the night. Milo gave up and slumped into his beat-up recliner. Everything in this run-down apartment was beat-up, worn-out, or at least well-used. Given his current attitude toward life, love, and the AIA, he fit right in. "You could have knocked."

"Would you have let me in?"

"Probably not."

The Scot smiled and shrugged as if to say "There you have it."

His arrogance chafed. Then again, his arrogance always chafed. When they'd been adversaries, Arch had always kept one step ahead of Milo. Even as partners, the infuriating bastard continually took the lead even though Milo was technically the one in charge. The only reason he put up with the aggravation was because he wanted to milk Arch Duvall for his grifter expertise. And, although they'd never acknowledged it, they had developed a friendship of sorts, warped though it was. Except now, that unspoken friendship was strained.

Because of Evie.

Because of Milo's discontent with the Agency.

Weary, he rubbed his hands down his face. "Didn't Pops call you about tomorrow's meeting?"

"He did," Arch said. "I wanted to talk to you alone. Beforehand."

"Eight, better yet, 9:00 a.m. would have been beforehand."

"I asked Pops to call me when you showed."

He'd fallen asleep on Nic's couch, slept a good six hours. Part of the reason he'd had trouble falling asleep after he'd driven home and fell into his own bed. "I got home less than an hour ago. How the hell…" He flashed on the old man who'd been more like a father than his own blood. "Tell me Pops is sleeping in the basement." The club was rigged with CCTV cameras. Exterior and interior movements could be monitored at the control panel in The Cave.

"He *didnae* want to leave until you were home safe. I told him to bunk on your sofa, but he *didnae* want to intrude. *Didnae* want you to think he was spying on you so he opted for the sofa in The Cave."

"And kept watch via the monitors."

Arch leaned forward and braced his forearms on his knees. "A lot of people care *aboot* you, Beckett. Cutting us off today was thoughtless."

Maybe. He waited for the man to ask where he'd been all day and night. Milo conjured an evasive reply. Mainly because his visit to Nic's suggested romantic interest. In truth, she felt like a kindred soul—disillusioned with life and love—but that just sounded pathetic. Better to dance around his whereabouts.

"What's going on?" Arch asked.

To the heart of the matter. All the better. "I fucked up."

"How so?"

Somehow saying it out loud made it true. He'd been fighting acceptance, because his gut screamed he didn't do it. Even though he'd seen it with his own eyes, *apparently so* was the best he could muster.

He started at the beginning. Maybe talking it out would shed some light. "As planned, after you and the team split the sting, I parked outside the restaurant and waited for Mad Dog to make his exit. It didn't take long."

"Losing ten grand will take the wind out of your sails, yeah?"

"He was pissed more than depressed. Heard him ranting

to himself as he walked to his car. *Fucked by a fucking foreigner* pretty much sums it up."

Arch smiled.

"He drove straight home. I waited outside. When I was certain he'd turned in, I let myself into the house via the back door. Woody was right about the lame security system."

"So you crept into his bedroom and caught him with his knickers down."

"Caught him unaware, that's for certain."

"I know Turner's small-time," Arch said, "but he could've had a handgun near his bed for home protection."

"Didn't give him a chance to react. Hard to think straight when you're staring down the barrel of a SIG SAUER P299."

Arch frowned. "You held him at gunpoint?"

"I did."

"Shite."

He knew what Arch was thinking. Con artists never employ violence. They manipulate people with words. Only Milo wasn't a grifter and Arch hadn't been with him to play good cop, bad cop. He'd gone in alone not knowing how Turner was going to react to the intrusion and intimidation. The Sig had doubled as protection and a threat. In order for Milo's plan to succeed, Turner had to believe he was ruthless.

"Guns are a bloody menace," Arch said in a distracted voice.

Milo wondered if he was thinking about the Simon the Fish shooting. The Caribbean sting had curdled and the thug had pulled a gun. In the midst of the scuffle, Evie had been knocked out and Simon had taken a fatal bullet. Arch accepted blame though he claimed the gun had gone off accidentally. Since the Scot had a personal vendetta against Simon the Fish, Milo doubted his word. Something about Arch's story didn't ring true.

Then again, Milo was stuck in his own murky tale.

"Naturally, Turner was confused," he went on, the scene playing in his mind like a bad movie. "He wanted to know why the baron had sent his personal assistant to harass him. It's not like that bastard Scot had lost his shirt in the poker game. He'd won. Big-time. What the hell more did he want?" Milo massaged his temple, cursing an ever-present throbbing. "That's when I told him who I really was. Told him he'd fucked with the wrong people and that his best option was to disappear. He could do it under his own steam or I'd gladly help him along. I mentioned everything we had on him. Tax evasion. Collusion with a casino employee. Card cheating. Gave him a play-by-play as to what he could expect in prison. Warned him if he said a word about any one of the high rollers he'd suckered in the past…"

Milo broke eye contact and lazed his head against the recliner. "I'll save you the details, but by the time I finished, the man was shaking and pale. Claimed he was going to be sick."

"Bloody hell. You actually fell for that?"

"Wasn't at my best." He'd felt somewhat ill himself. Strong-arming a man to protect a politician's career. Wouldn't have been as bad if he at least respected said politician.

"The moment you let down your guard," Arch surmised, "Mad Dog got the best of you."

"He was frothing at the mouth. Not only had we fleeced him out of ten grand, we were robbing him of his life. The bastard had a good seventy pounds of muscle on me. All I know is, my gun got knocked away and suddenly I was dodging the punches of a pissed-off former linebacker. My cop instincts kicked in and I got him in a choke hold."

"Bugger." Arch dragged a hand over his face. "The report said cause of death unknown. Tell me the autopsy is going to reveal death by strangulation."

"Except he was alive when I left there, goddammit. Used appropriately, the bar arm takedown renders the aggressor unconscious for a few seconds tops. As soon as he went limp, I released the hold and grabbed my Sig. He came around and I issued a parting threat. Yes, he was flat on his back, but he was alive."

"So what happened?"

"He didn't get up. From what I saw on the DVD, he convulsed a minute later and fucking died." Milo rushed through the rest of his tale. He told Arch about the agents who'd tailed him. The ones who'd tampered with the crime scene. The ones who'd discovered the hidden camera and the DVR.

"Are you saying Crowe has a recording of the shakedown?"

"The agents found a collection of homemade porn," said Milo. "Mad Dog had rigged the room with a hidden camera. Seems he had a wild sex life and he caught it all on DVD. There must have been a remote under his pillow or, I don't know, but he tripped Record at some point. Probably thought he could use the evidence against me, reverse blackmail, only he didn't figure on dying."

"*Cannae* believe Mad Dog's dead," Arch said, looking a little dazed. "Evie was right. We shouldn't have left you behind."

"I didn't give you a choice."

"Are you going to be able to get past this?"

"You mean can I live with the fact that I killed someone?" Milo quirked a brow. "You killed Simon the Fish and you're living with it. If memory serves, you said you haven't given the shooting a second thought."

"That's because it was an accident."

"I could say the same."

Arch sighed. "You had a bad feeling *aboot* this case from the beginning. I'm sorry I pressed you to take it."

"I'm sorry I listened to you. Sorry I bent to Crowe's will."

Arch drummed his fingers on the arm of the couch. "Crowe's had a bug up his arse *aboot* you from day one, yeah?"

"He's not fond of our team's independent streak, no. Unlike the previous director who preferred to know as little as possible—results are all that matter—Crowe wants to run the show. Our show. Trust me. He sensed I wasn't keen on playing ball."

"Yet he saved your arse. Why not let you go down? Replace you with McKeene or some other bootlicker?"

Milo grunted. "Would you work with McKeene or some other bootlicker?"

"No. Neither would anyone else on the team."

"Exactly. Chameleon is a unique and valuable branch of the AIA. Though we prefer to focus on blue-collar scams, we have the ability to bust frauds on a much higher level. Scams aimed at the rich and powerful. Crowe seems particularly fond of helping people in high places."

"Like U.S. Senator Clark."

"Mmm."

"By protecting you," said Arch, "Crowe's protecting Clark. If it came *oot* that you were acting on the senator's wishes when Mad Dog Turner died…" He whistled low. "Talk *aboot* fuel for a scandal. His wife's gambling problem pales in comparison."

Milo caught his partner's gaze. "So Crowe has dirt on me *and* the senator."

"Which makes you both his puppets. Any chance you were set up?"

"I'd like to think so, but I don't know how."

"Let's find *oot*." Arch rose from the couch. "Repeat this story at the scheduled meeting. Let's get everyone's take and move forth accordingly, you know?"

Milo stood and buzzed a hand over his cropped hair. "If I am being set up, Arch, going head-to-head with the director of the AIA could be dangerous."

"I'm up to the challenge. You?"

"Sure. Although I can't say I'm looking forward to admitting to the team that I possibly killed a man. That's why I sent you away in the first place. To distance you from the dirty work."

"*Dinnae* worry, mate," Arch said as he opened the front door. "Evie *willnae* think less of you. Pretty certain she thinks you walk on water."

"I was talking about the entire team."

"Sure you were."

Milo didn't argue because, damn, Arch was right.

CHAPTER TEN

WAKING UP WITHOUT ARCH in my bed was more disappointing today than yesterday because, well, he'd been here, and we'd had great sex, a life lesson, and more great sex. I'd just assumed he'd sleep over. But around eleven he'd gotten a call on his second phone, the one for private stuff, and *poof,* he was gone. I'd burned to ask if the call had been from Kate, but I didn't. I thought maybe he'd volunteer the information, but he didn't.

By the time he left, I was seething. Curse his secretive hide! I couldn't call Nic or Jayne. Well, I could, but that would be rude given the lateness of the hour. It's not as if it were an emergency. Just me needing to vent. So I did what came naturally and poured my heart into my diary. After scribbling my frustrations about Arch, I'd fallen asleep and dreamed of Beckett.

I woke up feeling guilty.

I love Arch. So why the sensual dream about Milo Beckett? Aside from the fact that he zinged me a little with that kiss. Aside from the fact that he's handsome and attracted to me and, okay, I'm a teensy bit attracted to him. I wouldn't be concerned except it wasn't the first time I'd *snogged* with Beckett in dreamland.

I pushed my bed-mussed hair out of my eyes and nabbed my diary from my nightstand. I treasured this journal because it had been a gift from Arch. The cover featured tropical skies and a bright ball of fire. *Sunshine.* On the inside he'd scrawled: *For private stuff—Arch.* A kind and thoughtful gesture, and though I'd written a lot of wonderful passages about Arch, I'd also scribbled a lot of rants. Not to mention the occasional musing about Beckett. Stuff for my eyes only.

Just like Arch's secret cell is for his ears only.
Right.
I flipped through the journal until I found the page where I'd listed Arch's and Beckett's pros and cons.

ARCH
Unpredictable
Smart
Dangerous
Sexy
Shady past
Kind
Skewed morals

BECKETT
Stable
Smart
Safe
Sexy
Commendable past
Kind
Solid morals

Obviously, Beckett was the safer choice. Plus he was older than me so that wiped out my younger man/older woman insecurities. *Plus* we had a similar track record with relationships. Like me, he'd survived a failed marriage. Like me, his spouse had dumped him for someone else. Arch had never been in a committed relationship. Not one. His personal code: *Never attach yourself to someone you can't walk away from in a split second.* A survival technique for a professional grifter. Except he was no longer grifting for a living and given his vow to win my trust, I guess he'd sort of attached himself to me. Plus he'd carved his feelings into a tree, surrounding his declaration of love in a heart. I swooned every time I thought about it.

I grabbed my purple pen and added a line to Arch's list. *Romantic.*

Then I thought about the past few days and added three more. *Thoughtful. Protective. Secretive.*

At least three out of the four were positive. I felt a little better now that Arch had more pros than cons. As for the dream, I didn't need to consult Jayne and her dream interpretation book to know that Beckett represented security. A caring relationship with a man I already trusted. Which was nice. And safe. I got that. Remnants of the old me. The new me, however, the me who'd recently discovered my inner bad girl, wanted unpredictable and exciting and that was Arch Duvall. I just needed to get over my fear that he was too good to be true. Then the dreams about Beckett would cease.

Yeah, that was it.

My doorbell rang and my heart raced.

Arch!

He'd said he'd be back to pick me up for a scheduled meeting at the Chameleon Club. Only he was early. *Yes!* Maybe I could coax him into the shower. As eye-openers went, a wet and naked romp with a bad boy trumped a cup of bean juice any day.

I stuck my head out my bedroom door and yelled, "Just a minute!" then zipped into my bathroom and gargled— goodbye morning breath! My hair was tousled but it looked sort of sexy so I left it alone. Nor did I waste time washing off the anti-itch medicine. Arch was waiting and this was the new confident me.

Wearing lounge pants and a tight pink T-shirt, I race-walked into the living room and flung open the door.

Call me shocked and disappointed. "Michael."

"I need to talk to you."

"You could have called."

"I needed to see you."

"Oh." I stood inside the threshold feeling all kinds of uncomfortable. This was the first time we'd been alone together since I'd talked him into letting me do the cruise ship gig. Which, ultimately, led to me doing Arch. Plus now he was married to Sasha and they were expecting their first child. All that and more in less than a two month period.

"Let me guess," he said, gesturing to my face and arms, "an allergic reaction to the gorilla suit."

Busted.

"Uh…" *Smooth, Evie, smooth.*

"Can I come in, hon?"

Hon. His standard nickname for anyone of the female gender. I actually preferred Twinkie. At least it was unique to *me.* "Sure," I said, because it would be rude to slam the door in his face—albeit a cheater's face. Besides, it would be good to clear the air. I led him into the living room. "Would you like a cup of coffee?"

"I won't be staying that long."

Thank God.

Since he was dressed in a suit and tie, I assumed he had

a pending business meeting, otherwise he would've been in jeans and a casual oxford shirt. Stone Entertainment Inc. consisted of Michael and his secretary. Though the agency was successful, the office was small and cluttered. Dress code: casual.

I noticed him looking around the place as he hitched back his pin-striped jacket and sat on the end of my bargain sofa. "This place doesn't look like you, Evie."

I sat on the chair across from him. "I haven't had time to decorate."

"You've been here a year."

I crossed my arms over my braless chest. "I've been busy." No way was I going to admit that I'd been in too much of a postdivorce funk to make this house a home. "What gave me away?" I asked, referring to the gorilla suit. "My voice? The victory dance?"

His mouth curved and I was reminded of how handsome he was when he smiled. Except I didn't feel the old pitter-patter. Zip. Zilch. Nada. What a relief.

"That ridiculous dance is unique to you, hon. It certainly made me wonder enough to chase you down, only I lost you at the elevators."

If I gave a rat's patootee what he thought, I'd be hurt by that *ridiculous* crack. Instead, I smiled. "It was a fluke, my being there I mean."

"I know. I asked Sasha where she hired the gorilla from and I made a call. I know you were subbing for Jayne. Can't imagine you were thrilled when you saw who the singing telegram was for, but I'm not surprised you followed through. You've always had stellar work ethics."

"Yeah, well, some habits die hard." A less than gracious reply to a compliment, but I felt unsettled by his curious regard. "So why are you here?"

"I want to offer you a job."

"As a gorilla?"

He laughed. "Not quite."

"Not the job in your office." My mind latched on to a previous conversation. "I thought I made it clear I'm not interested in training to be an entertainment agent." Shoot me now.

"Definitely not that. Listen, Evie. I know this year has been a struggle. Financially. Emotionally. I just landed a strolling entertainer program at Caesars. I'd like you to be the on-site coordinator. Per the casino's wishes, I've hired a dozen young girls from a modeling agency."

"Naturally."

"They need to portray select Hollywood celebrities, circulate throughout the casino as greeters, emcee the occasional sweepstakes, work as party motivators at high-roller events."

"All the stuff I used to do."

"And do well."

Okay. That was nice. That was…gratifying.

"These women have potential, but their background is strictly in modeling. They need someone to show them the ropes. You're the perfect mentor."

No argument there. Except, I didn't want the job. I could name a dozen reasons why, but I'd save that for my diary. "I appreciate the offer, Michael, but I already have a job. I've been hired as the house singer at the Chameleon Club."

He frowned. "That place is a dive."

"It has its perks. Besides," I plowed on, desperate for him to hit the road, "I couldn't take you up on that gig anyway. You're no longer my agent."

"I'm not?"

"I fired you. Only I didn't tell you. Sort of like you didn't tell me that Sasha was pregnant and that you were planning to elope."

Michael readjusted his funky glasses and sighed. "I didn't tell you because I didn't know *how* to tell you."

"Because you thought I'd fall apart? News flash, *hon,* I'm over you. Completely. I wish you and Sasha nothing but happiness."

"That's…good. That's…thank you." He met my gaze. "What about Duvall? Are you over him?"

"As the song goes, we've only just begun."

"Jesus, Evie, he's—"

"I know what he is. I know what he did before and what he does now." I pushed to my feet and marched to the front door. It was that or smack him. *Violence is wrong,* my mom lectured from afar. "You both make your living manipulating people and talking in circles. You casting stones at Arch is like the hustler calling the hustler crooked. Or something like that. You know what I mean."

"Unfortunately." He scratched his forehead. "Didn't know you had such a low opinion of me."

I cringed at his hurt tone. "I'm sorry. It's just…I don't feel like I ever really knew you. And that's okay because we've both moved on. So stop trying to control my life. Where I work and who I sleep with is none of your concern."

I opened the door wide. *Take the hint, Michael. Leave.*

He rose from the sofa, slid off his glasses and slipped them into the inner pocket of his suit jacket. Two seconds later we stood toe-to-toe. "You've changed, Evie."

"Yes, I have. And it's a good thing."

"It's certainly interesting."

I started to say goodbye but he grabbed me and kissed

me. *Kissed* me! Tongue and everything only I didn't open my mouth. I pushed him back and smacked him— Mom's lecture be damned. "What's *wrong* with you?"

"I just…I want…" He reached for me again only someone wrenched him around and planted a fist in his face.

Arch.

Michael's knees wobbled, but before he could crumple, Arch shoved him outside. "Touch her again, Stone, and I'll kick your arse from here to Edinburgh." He slammed shut the door and ran his hands over me as if I'd been the victim of a hit-and-run. "Are you all right, lass?"

I nodded.

"Are you sure? You look stunned."

"I am. I mean…" Words failed me. Arch was against violence. He almost always had a firm grip on his emotions. When he did lose it, it was more of a verbal rage or a cold blow off. Even when Beckett had invited him to take a shot after our ill-timed kiss, Arch had thrown up his hands. So, yeah. I was stunned. "You hit him."

"Aye." He scraped a hand over his hair as if just now realizing his actions. He quirked a befuddled grin. "Guess I love you even more than I thought, yeah?"

I froze. I burned. I rocketed to the moon and beyond. "You just said—"

"I know."

"That was—"

"Surprising?"

"Wonderful. Romantic." *Hot.* Carving his sentiments into a tree was one thing, but putting his feelings into words? Every girl's, or at least this girl's, dream come true. "Say it again."

He caressed my cheek, dropped his forehead to mine. "I love you, Evie."

Ah, yes. I was definitely in another galaxy. Floating. Soaring. A dull buzzing between my ears.

"As the song goes," he said with a smile in his voice, "just breathe."

I laughed even as an emotional sob welled in my throat. "Now you're quoting country singers?"

"If the boot fits. Just so you know," he added, sincerity shimmering in his eyes, "that's the first time I've ever said that to a woman and meant it, yeah?"

From any other man that would have been cause for worry. Someone who'd made false declarations of love? Maybe multiple times? But from Arch, knowing Arch… "I believe you," I said, which I knew meant more to him than the expected, *I love you, too*. Besides, he knew that already.

He threaded his fingers through my hair. "You're the one, Sunshine. The only one."

Call me toast. "Bollocks." Royally seduced, I threw myself at Arch, literally, tackling him with a kiss that melted the paint off of the walls. To hell with breathing.

CHAPTER ELEVEN

I RODE A EUPHORIC WAVE all the way to the Chameleon Club. I couldn't help it. For the first time ever, I was certain Arch and I would work out our trust issues. I was certain we'd make this fantasy fling a longtime reality. There's someone for everyone, and he was the one for me. Love conquers all! Love is a many-splendored thing! Love makes the world go round! A dozen clichés pinged through my brain, along with *love will save the day!*

I couldn't wait to introduce him to Jayne, although her opinion of him might suffer when he pegged Madame Helene a fraud. That's why I intended to invite Tabasco to dinner, too. Since he was the one investigating the psychic, he could break the news. Better she despise Tabasco than Arch, although I'm sure her anger would be short-lived. First, Jayne didn't despise anyone except maybe Michael. Second, once she accepted the truth about Madame Helene, she'd view Tabasco more as hero than enemy.

I'd called Jayne and Nic and spoken briefly with them on the ride over. Neither was talkative, but even that couldn't dampen my spirits. I felt ridiculously bright about the future and that included restoring Jayne's positive and carefree attitude. Dinner tonight at my place would be followed by an intervention. I had no illusions that it would be pretty, but every faith that it would turn out beautifully.

Jayne needed someone to gently open her eyes to the real world the way Arch had opened mine.

Speaking of Arch… He tugged me aside before we walked into the club. "Hold up, Sunshine."

"What's wrong?"

He smoothed my windblown hair out of my face, traced a finger along my smile. "Might want to key your good humor down a notch, yeah?"

"Why?"

"Beckett's in trouble."

Yeah, boy *that* cooled my jets. "What do you mean?"

"The AIA has him *manipulating* Turner on video. Things got ugly and he had to subdue the bastard with a choke hold."

I imagined the worse. "So, Beckett *did* kill him?"

"Looks that way, but looks can be deceiving, yeah?"

I palmed my pounding head. "I don't understand."

"Jazzman will explain."

"You told me he was fine."

"Told you what he told Pops. I *didnae* know *aboot* this until late last night."

"So that's the call that took you away from me last night?" I asked with a hopeful heart.

"No. That was—" he glanced away "—something else."

Kate, I wanted to say but didn't. My stomach turned for myriad reasons. *Love hurts.* "Why didn't you tell me this before now?"

"Stone distracted me. Then *you* distracted me." He kissed me on the forehead. "For what it's worth, Sunshine, there's a chance Beckett is being framed."

That made me feel a little better, but not much. Guilt plagued my formally gleeful heart. *We shouldn't have left him behind.*

THE VIBE IN THE CAVE was somber. Everyone was there. Tabasco, Woody, Gina, even Pops. We sat on the edges of our seats, drinking coffee and listening intently as Beckett told his tale.

Even though he sounded calm and professional, I could tell he was struggling with dark emotions. Guilt? Anger? Unlike Arch he didn't school his feelings to perfection. Although his attire was casual—faded jeans and a loose gray T-shirt—his manner was stiff. He looked freshly showered and shaved, but there were shadows beneath his intelligent brown eyes and his lower lip was puffy. Given Mad Dog's height and bulk, I'm surprised Beckett wasn't in worse shape. Not that he was puny or anything. He was at least six feet and had the toned build of a runner— probably because he jogged daily. I'd seen his upper body a couple of times—don't ask—and I had no doubt he had the strength and flexibility to defend himself, but like I said, Mad Dog is, *was,* a big guy.

I imagined Beckett getting the man in a choke hold. Okay. Vision ingrained. Given his former cop status and current agent status, surely he'd been trained in all kinds of self-defense. But as hard as I tried, I couldn't conjure the image of him squeezing the life out of another human being.

He'd been there when I'd woken up in the Caribbean hospital. He'd given me a job at the club. Taken me on as a real team member even though I didn't have a back- ground in grifting or law enforcement. He'd volunteered to help my mom out of a jam and comforted me when I'd had a mini-meltdown. He was kind and committed to sav- ing unsuspecting innocents from unscrupulous hustlers. He was one of the good guys. If he *did* kill Mad Dog it was an accident. Just like when Arch had accidentally killed Simon the Fish—something I still felt guilty about. And now this. As far as I knew there had never been a death associated with any Chameleon sting. That is until I entered the picture.

I felt a little ill. It didn't help that Beckett hadn't looked at me once. Even when I'd first walked in, he'd said hello without making eye contact. Had I done something wrong? Or was it that *he'd* done something wrong and was ashamed.

"No one here believes that you entered Mad Dog's house with murder in mind, Jazzman," said Gina.

"But?"

"Fatalities due to choke holds are not unheard of. You remember the class action suit filed against the City of Los Angeles for fatalities allegedly caused by the bar-arm choke. Soon after the L.A.P.D. forbade use of the air choke and restricted use of the carotid hold."

I started to blast her for being the voice of doom but Arch cut me off. "Your point?"

She kept her eyes fixed on Beckett. "I'm not saying you weren't trained properly. I'm not saying you didn't know what you were doing. I'm just pointing out that there's room for error. It's happened before."

"How can you be such a pessimist?" I blurted. "He said Mad Dog was alive when he left."

"But the DVD shows that he didn't get up," Gina said. "Jazzman said a minute later Mad Dog convulsed, which suggests fatal cardiac arrhythmia."

"What are you, a doctor?" I couldn't help myself. I was beside myself. This was awful. "We should be digging Beckett out of this mess, not digging a bigger hole."

Beckett shifted. "Relax, Twinkie."

It was the first time he looked my way and I swallowed

hard because it hit me: Milo Beckett—the good guy—was indeed capable of killing someone. If he wasn't he never would've pursued a career in law enforcement. Apparently, he carried a gun and he'd pulled it on Mad Dog Turner and threatened him. Then the choke-hold thing. I wasn't sure how I felt about this facet of his personality. Unsettled, I looked away.

"Gina's stating facts," he continued. "As a former cop she's trained in self-defense and knows the possible ramifications of a choke hold. In hindsight, a carotid takedown would have been a safer choice, but Mad Dog had the strength of a coked-up giant and I reacted on instinct."

I didn't know one choke hold or takedown from another. I'd have to look it up just like I'd researched various grifter lingo. The team constantly tossed around words like *mark, roper, inside man, come-on, long con, short con, shill,* and so forth. Just when I'd found my comfort zone, they threw me a curve. I caught Arch looking at me and could fairly read his mind. *"You're not cut out to operate in my world, Sunshine. You're too soft. Too sensitive."*

I sucked it up and buttoned my lip.

Tabasco leaned forward. "Question. If the agents discovered the DVR while they were in the process of covering up the crime, why weren't *they* caught on video?"

"I'm wondering the same thing," said Pops.

Beckett rubbed his hands over his face. "Like I said, these agents, whoever they were, had been ordered to tail me. They followed me to Turner's house, not sure how they knew what went down, but they went in after I left to check Turner's status. Before entering, they cut the power for stealth purposes."

Arch spread his hands. "Hence disabling the DVR, yeah?"

Pops grunted. "Convenient."

Woody, always formal in Beckett's presence, raised his hand. "Was there a timecode, sir?"

We all looked at the team's techno wiz who, up until now, had been silent.

"When you watched the DVD," he continued. "Was there a running clock in the bottom corner?"

"There was," Beckett said.

"Notice any discrepancies?"

"No. Why?"

The Kid's eyes lit up. "Each frame of video is identified using a number called a timecode. When you edit video on a computer, the timecode serves as a specific identifier when making edits."

"Are you suggesting the Agency doctored the DVD?" Arch asked.

"It was a thought," Woody said. "Except if they edited something in or out there'd be a discrepancy in the timecode."

Beckett worked his jaw. "There wasn't."

"Darn."

Gina elbowed Woody. "Good thinking though, Kid."

"Wait." He scooted to the edge of the sofa. "Here's a possibility. They could've cropped the picture to exclude the timecode, stretched the frames to fill the screen, then inserted a new timecode."

"A stretched picture," said Arch. "*Wouldnae* that be obvious?"

"Not necessarily," Woody replied. "You'd be amazed at what you can do with a Mac, Final Cut Pro, and After Effects."

"We might be able to prove tampering if we can get hold of that DVD," said Gina.

"Not gonna happen," said Beckett. "It's either locked away at HQ or in Crowe's personal possession."

"What about the DVR?" asked Tabasco. "The recording would be on the hard drive."

"Unless they deleted it," said Woody.

"One way to find *oot,*" said Arch. "Is the DVR still at Mad Dog's?"

Beckett shook his head. "They stole it along with a few other things."

"To make it look like a burglary," Pops said.

Beckett nodded. "That DVR's probably locked in the evidence room. Getting hold of it or the DVD would be…a challenge."

Everyone, except for me, smiled.

Beckett angled his head. "If we get caught—"

"We *willnae.*"

Seriously? Arch thought they could get away with breaking into and ripping off a government agency? I had horrific visions of the team peeling potatoes in ugly prison garb. If I weren't all scratched out, I'd break out in a nervous rash. Instead, I scrambled to counteract their boneheaded arrogance. Lightning quick I replayed everything Beckett had said. Thank God for my stellar memory. "Crowe doesn't like you or your methods," I said to Beckett. "By letting you take the fall he would have been rid of you. But he saved you, and in doing so you owe him your allegiance. You and the senator are both at his mercy. That's power."

Tabasco cut me a glance. "She has a point."

I couldn't believe I was stating anything any one of them hadn't thought of, but just in case, I kept rolling. "Given the circumstances, whatever he wants you and the team to do, you'll be hard-pressed to say no. Same goes for Senator Clark."

"He did tell me to go about business as usual at the club until he sent a new case our way," Beckett said.

"No doubt a case of his choosing," said Gina.

Pops looked my way. "You're saying we should concentrate less on that recording and more on the man who ordered the cover-up. The man who dumped the senator's mess in Jazzman's lap to begin with." He nodded. "I agree."

I smiled. Wow. For a man who usually spoke in three-word sentences, that was a mouthful. Then again, I wasn't surprised. If Pops was going to speak up and out for anyone, it was Beckett. I still didn't know their history, but I knew the bond was strong. "Any government official who instructs his people to cover up a crime is deceitful." A Pollyanna view, but if the shoe fits… "Instead of risking your necks breaking into AIA headquarters, I think you, we, should investigate Vincent Crowe. If we get something bigger on him than what he has on Beckett…"

"Give me forty-eight hours," said Woody. "I'll give you Crowe's butt on a plate."

"Your enthusiasm and confidence," Beckett said with a crooked smile, "is appreciated, Kid. As is your observation, Twinkie."

My lungs blossomed. Not because Milo Beckett, the man, had complimented me, I told myself, but because my boss had acknowledged my wherewithal.

"Forty-eight hours," Woody said and moved to the computer console.

Gina unfolded her lithe body from the sofa. "I have my own methods for obtaining information and I know just where to start." She waggled her fingers at Beckett. "Later, boss."

Beckett looked a little off balance but he didn't balk,

which said to me that he trusted the instincts and judgment of everyone on his team. Or maybe just now he was a little leery of his own judgment.

My brain spun on how *I* could help. I hadn't the slightest idea. I started to ask Arch, but he delayed me with an apologetic smile and drifted off to take a call.

Pops rose and followed Gina out. "I have a bar to tend."

"Have some avenues to explore myself," said Tabasco, "but I need to speak to Twinkie about another issue first."

He tugged me aside and Beckett joined Woody at the console. It was hard to concentrate on Tabasco's brief rundown of Madame Helene when I was straining to hear tidbits of Arch's conversation. Then I noticed Beckett watching me watch Arch and realized Tabasco was also aware of my divided attention. I suddenly felt like the suspicious, absurdly jealous girlfriend. Arch could be talking to someone about Vincent Crowe for all I knew. Just because he was using his *private stuff* cell, that didn't mean he was talking to Kate.

I'd just invited Tabasco to dinner and an intervention when Arch approached looking oddly frazzled. *This is bad,* I thought and he said, "*Aboot* tonight."

So much for riding a euphoric wave of love.

CHAPTER TWELVE

"WHAT DO YOU MEAN he's not coming to dinner?" Jayne asked after releasing me from a bear hug. For a petite woman she was surprisingly strong. A living doll with a pert nose, big brown eyes, and thick long lashes, she was the epitome of cute. What made her sexy was her carefree spirit and the vibrant red hair that bounced around her shoulders. Women spent a fortune trying to recreate the corkscrew curls Jayne came by naturally.

I was relieved and delighted by her good cheer considering Nic had portrayed her as an obsessed mess.

Heart full, I accepted the bottle of wine she'd brought and led her into my living room where Nic was already opening a bottle of merlot. "Arch was called out of town on business," I said, my apologetic smile mirroring the one he'd given me when he'd said, *"It's important."* Because I'm a damn good actress, I delivered the explanation casually as in no big whoop, even though it was a honking big whoop to me. I didn't know where he was going or when he'd be back. I certainly didn't know what that important business entailed. Not wanting to appear the suspicious, jealous girlfriend, I didn't ask. I sort of hoped he'd offer details of his own free will. Ha!

I wasn't sure if I was more miffed that he'd bailed on me or on Beckett. Although at the time, Arch had tempered my disappointment by reminding me I had Tabasco as an ally and Beckett had four other Chameleons working to crack that nut, Crowe. *"When I'm truly needed,"* he'd said, *"I'll be here, yeah?"* He'd kissed me goodbye and in that moment I'd believed that somehow, someway he'd be in two places at once if things turned dire for me or Beckett.

Hours later, the potency of his charisma had worn off. Curiosity chewed at my gut along with fears and doubts. Where was he? Who was he with and what was he doing? Deep down, it wasn't that I felt deserted as much as disappointed. He'd promised to earn my trust, yet he didn't trust me with his secrets.

Jayne plopped down next to me on the sofa with a teasing grin. "If Nic hadn't met your sexy Scot herself, I'd declare him a figment of your fertile imagination."

"Arch is real," Nic said as she poured us each a glass of merlot. "Just untrustworthy."

Jayne frowned. "That's not good."

"It's not like it sounds," I said. Amazing. Even though I was mad at him, I still felt compelled to defend him.

"It's exactly like it sounds," said Nic.

"He can't help it," I said to Jayne. "It's in his blood." I spent the next few minutes giving her a brief overview of Arch's background. No specifics about his family, just that he'd been raised under unusual circumstances. I admitted that he used to make his living as a grifter but emphasized his view on the differences between scam artists and scum artists.

"He's a bad boy with a good heart," Nic teased, topping off our wine.

"Who now works for the good guys," I said which led me into talk of the AIA, Chameleon, and succinct intro-

ductions to the players. I came clean about the past seven
weeks, about how I'd played a part in thwarting three
bamboozlers, although I skimped on details, especially the
parts involving the deaths of Simon the Fish and Mad Dog
Turner. I knew it was a lot to take in. I knew it sounded
absurd. The stuff fantasies and movies were made of. The
stuff we made up when we needed a theme and characters
for an interactive murder mystery. I expected Jayne to
laugh and say, *"Yeah, right."* Or to freak out and spew a
string of doom and gloom predictions. At the very least I
anticipated a bazillion questions.

I didn't expect the smile and a simple "Wow."

Nic and I looked at each other then back at Jayne.
"Don't you find it odd that I was hired to work with a
covert team of fraud investigators?"

She shrugged. "From what you told me they spend a
lot of time dressing up in costume, pretending to be people
they're not, and creating illusions. You're an entertainer.
A versatile, talented performer with an incredible gift for
improvisation and memorization. They're lucky to have
you."

Flattered and humbled, I smiled. Her praise meant the
world because Jayne herself was an extraordinary talent.
*Who'd resorted to singing telegrams to pay the bills and
feed her psychic habit.* "Thanks, Jayne, but…" *I thought
you'd be more concerned about the dangerous aspects of
the job.* I glanced at Nic. She was thinking the same thing.
Where was Jayne's astrological and crystal-ball-based
warnings? She'd given me an earful over the past few
weeks and now when I gave her a springboard for *I told
you so, I knew it* and *beware of,* I got "Wow." Then again,
Jayne's mind worked in mysterious ways.

Since Nic and I had agreed to follow Tabasco's advice

and not to broach the subject of Madame Helene until after he arrived, I indulged another concern. "I'm just… I'm surprised. Aren't you angry with me for not telling you about the Agency and Chameleon weeks ago?"

"Why would I be angry? You weren't at liberty to tell me. One of the things I love about you, Evie, is that you'll take a secret to the grave. I'll admit I'm envious that Nic learned about this before me, but that's the bonus she gets for being financially independent."

Jayne made the observation with a shrug and a smile. She didn't sound resentful or sarcastic, but all the same I saw Nic fidget. Her financial independence was a touchy subject. She came from a wealthy family. She'd inherited a good amount of money that she'd wisely invested. She struggled to work in the field she loved, but unlike Jayne and I, wasn't struggling to pay the bills. The inheritance embarrassed Nic for some reason, so it wasn't something we talked about.

Jayne realized her slip. Red-faced, she looked at Nic. "Did that sound petty? I didn't mean—"

"One thing I love about *you,* Jayne—" Nic said with a sincere smile. "You're never petty. You have a steady job now. I don't. It was easier for me to fly away for a few days at the drop of a hat. That's all you meant, right?"

Jayne's curls bounced with a firm nod. "Right." She slid her doe-brown gaze to me. "Speaking of my steady job, I'm lucky I still have it. Fannie's miffed because I've been preoccupied lately. The only reason she didn't fire me yesterday was because you bailed me out and the client was thrilled with your performance."

Although she was smiling, her color was high. Whatever Nic had said to her yesterday, she knew she'd screwed up by flaking out on her scheduled gig and that her friends were aware of her unprofessional behavior. She gulped wine as if to dissolve the lump in her throat, "Thank you for subbing for me."

"No big deal."

"Very big deal."

"That's what friends are for."

Nic screwed up her face. "If either one of you break out in song, I'll puke."

We laughed, but Jayne was still contrite. "Seriously, Evie—"

"You're welcome." I reached over and squeezed her ring-laden fingers. "You thanked me twice on the phone as well, remember?"

"Twenty times wouldn't seem adequate given you had to sing for that cheating creep. Although I guess it was meant to be, given your recurring dreams about apes."

Nic snorted. "Coincidence."

Jayne was still looking at me. "Did you dream about gorillas last night?"

"No."

"I'm betting those dreams are history, Evie. They were premonitions leading up to a defining moment. The moment you faced Michael and Sasha for the first time. Talk about a hairy situation. Now that it's over…"

I furrowed my brow. "You said those dreams signified a new friend or mischief-maker in my life."

"That was a text interpretation. Generic. Not that it didn't apply. Obviously it did. Arch fits either bill. However, these dreams carried additional significance. Hidden meanings specifically attached to your inner hopes and fears."

"My head's spinning."

"That's because you're trying to make sense out of psychic-babble," Nic said.

Jayne frowned. "You're such a cynic."

"No, I'm not. I'm a realist."

"That's just sad." Jayne sipped more wine and sniffed the air. "I don't smell dinner."

"That's because it's not here yet." Since my car was in the shop, I hadn't been able to hit the grocery store. Originally Arch had offered to serve as chauffeur, but then he'd gotten that phone call and flown off to wherever. Instead, Tabasco drove me home from the club. When I'd mentioned the shopping dilemma and the fact that I wasn't much of a cook—*don't expect much*—he'd insisted on handling dinner. In addition to being a location scout, transportation specialist, and a guitarist, he was also a wiz in the kitchen—caring, too, always looking out for his friends. Plus he was handsome. All in all, an interesting catch for some woman, not that he seemed dying to settle down.

"So what are we having," Jayne asked. "Chinese or subs?"

"Italian," I said. "Home cooked. Not by me." I segued into the next phase of the evening. "Tabasco's bringing over his secret recipe lasagna."

"I brought Caesar salad," said Nic. "It's in the fridge."

"Jimmy Tabasco?" Jayne asked. "The guy who owns and flies a plane?"

"Mmm. I invited him to dinner. I hope you don't mind. I wanted to introduce you to a faction of my new life. It was supposed to be Tabasco and Arch. Now it's Tabasco and Beckett."

Nic choked on her wine.

"Are you all right?" Jayne asked.

"Wrong pipe," she rasped, setting aside her glass and shooting me a deadly look.

That cinched it. I'd been right to withhold that twist in our plans. If she'd had advance notice that Beckett was coming, she would have begged off. I felt a little bad about blindsiding her, but I'd been stuck between a rock and a hard place. Overhearing, the conversation between Arch, Tabasco, and I about Madame Helene and the intervention, Beckett had volunteered to step into Arch's shoes. Arch hadn't argued, Tabasco had pointed out the benefits, and what was I supposed to do? Say thanks, but no thanks? What kind of message would that send?

You're not welcome because you possibly strangled someone to death and that freaks me out.

You're not welcome because I'm a little attracted to you and you're a lot attracted to me and that makes me nervous.

You're not welcome because you and Nic don't get along and you're the reason, though I don't know why, she had a one-night stand with tractor-boy in Indiana then split for home ahead of schedule.

Even though all of those things crossed my mind, I wouldn't dream of hurting Beckett's feelings. Especially when he seemed a little depressed. The man already battled insomnia and relentless headaches. How did it feel to take another human being's life?

My own temples throbbed and my stomach clenched. I couldn't imagine. I didn't want to imagine.

Someone rang the doorbell and saved me the misery.

"Showtime," I mumbled as I hurried to greet my dinner guests.

Only it wasn't Beckett and Tabasco.

"Evie Parish?"

I blinked at a shaggy-haired throwback to the sixties dressed in a blue velvet suit and a ruffled poet's shirt. "Austin Powers?"

"Yeah, baby, yeah!" He waggled the brows behind his thick black-rimmed glasses then thrust a vase of flowers and a bottle of champagne at me and pressed Play on a mini boom box. "It's time to swing, baby!"

Stunned, I stepped aside as he "ponied" over my threshold, singing to a karaoke version of a Kinks song.

"Girl, you really got me goin'. You got me so I don't know what I'm doin'."

Nic's wide-eyed expression mirrored my own. Jayne, on the other hand, "ponied" alongside the hipster secret agent and joined in the chorus. *"You really got me! You really got me!"*

For a split second, I worried that this was a bizarre payback and come-on from Michael. But then I got it.

Austin Powers, *International Man of Mystery.*

Besides, Michael would have sent standard roses, not exotic orchids.

Nope. This was an over-the-top apology from Arch.

Juggling mixed emotions, I set his exquisite gifts in the center of my secondhand cocktail table.

The bespectacled actor ended his routine with a spin and a flourish, our cue to applaud only he wasn't finished. He nabbed my hand, twirled me into his arms and quoted a line from the movie. I knew the line so naturally, I rattled off the follow-up, just as I would with Arch.

The cheesy impersonator passed me a card and smiled. "Groovy, baby. He said you were the queen of movie trivia."

And Arch was the king. Our love of movies had been an instant bond. Since we had little else in common, I clung to our shared interest like a security blanket. Obviously he was working that to his advantage. *A con artist pinpoints a mark's vulnerabilities and weaknesses and plays to them.*

It occurred to me that researching his chosen profession was turning me into a suspicious cynic. A concern Arch had voiced more than once. *"I worry that subjecting you to deceit and manipulation on a regular basis will desensitize you. It's the way of things, yeah?"*

Hmm.

"Great job, Zeke," said Jayne.

"Thanks, Red." Two seconds later the singing telegram man was gone.

Nic shook her head in wonder. "At least he didn't strip."

"Guess *Zeke* works for Fannie's Flowers," I said to Jayne as we reclaimed our seats and drinks.

"To supplement his income, yes, but I didn't know anything about this. What's the card say?"

I opened the envelope, smiling when I noted the scenic setting featuring a big tree. I skimmed the short message then read it aloud. "'Apologies for missing dinner, Sunshine. My best to Nic and Jayne. Drinks on me. Cheers, Arch.'"

Jayne nabbed the card. *"Aww,* look," she cooed, showing it to Nic. "There's a heart with their initials inside. A & E."

"Sweet," Nic said, though she didn't look impressed. She glanced at the bottle of Moët & Chandon. "Expensive taste in champagne."

"Expensive taste in everything." His car, his clothes, a barony for gosh sake. For the bazillionth time I wondered where the money came from.

"Must have paid a fortune for those flowers," said Jayne. "They're beautiful."

And magical, I thought. A dozen long-stemmed exotic orchids bursting with color—fuchsia, orange and yellow. They breathed life into this sterile living room.

Nic arched a brow. "Singing telegram, orchids, champagne. An extravagant apology just for missing dinner, don't you think?"

Exactly why I couldn't fully enjoy the gesture. It smacked of a guilty conscience. Did he really feel that bad about skipping out on the intervention? Or was this about wherever he was, doing whatever with whomever? Not that I was jealous or worried. Okay. That's a lie. I was both, plus envious. What if this important business wasn't for selfish gain or pleasure, but for the greater good? I wanted to be his sidekick personally *and* professionally.

"Well, I think his manner of making amends shows imagination," said Jayne. "You really lucked out with this guy, Evie. Thoughtful. Funny. Generous." She smiled. "I like Arch."

Nic folded her arms. "You haven't even met him."

"When I do, I'm sure my intuition will be affirmed." Our big-hearted friend jumped up and whisked off with the champagne. "I'm putting this in the fridge. I think we should save it until Arch can enjoy it with us."

I was still trying to wrap my mind around the grand apology when the doorbell rang for the second time. "Let's try this again."

This time I opened my door to Special Agent Milo Beckett and former grifter, Jimmy Tabasco, who, like Austin Powers, looked like they'd stepped out of a movie. Clooney and Banderas with personalized twists.

Tabasco's dark hair was pulled into a low ponytail, showing off his angular features and sinfully dark eyes. He'd dressed down in jeans and a loose-fitting pullover.

Beckett had opted for khakis, a striped oxford shirt and a trendy suit jacket. He wore his salt-and-pepper hair short, the sideburns longish. Sexy. I hated that I noticed. Self-conscious, I avoided his gaze and motioned them inside. Jeez, they even smelled great, and so did the food, a tantalizing mixture of manly cologne, recently baked sweets, and spicy pasta. *Yum*.

Nic and Jayne stood side by side. Beauty and the beauty. In my eyes anyway.

I made brief introductions, feeling ridiculously nervous. It wasn't solely because of the intervention. It was the meeting of my two worlds. The entertainers and the crime fighters.

Arch should be here.

Nic and Beckett had already met, and I watched them closely to see if I could gain a clue as to their animosity. But they exchanged civilized greetings, and I released a pent-up breath. Whatever had happened, maybe it was in the past.

Jayne, on the other hand, was enthusiastic in her welcome and Tabasco exuded charm.

As an ensemble cast, we made a colorful and stylish impression. Nic radiated class in her tailored black pants and indigo satin blouse. The three-inch stilettos gave her a sexy edge. I'd kill myself in those heels.

Jayne looked like a Bohemian wild-child in her flowered batik dress. Even her flat sandals were adorned with cheerful daisies. I felt sort of boring next to my friends, even though earlier Nic had dubbed my Gap ensemble adorable.

"*Charlie's Angels,*" Tabasco said, after assessing the three of us.

"*Starsky and Hutch,*" Jayne said, gesturing to the two men.

Nic rolled her eyes. "They don't look anything like *Starsky and Hutch*. Original or remake."

"Thank, God," said Beckett, but there was a twinkle in his eye.

Jayne looked from him to Tabasco. "Is there some sort of rule that you have to be movie-star gorgeous to be in Chameleon? I mean Evie said you guys were handsome, but—"

"Wine?" I asked a little too shrilly, but Nic backed me up. "Merlot?"

"Sure," they answered.

"Kitchen?" Tabasco asked.

I realized suddenly that he'd been standing in my living room holding a hot baking dish for a good five minutes. "I'm sorry. I should have—"

"I'll show him," Jayne chirped and steered him away. "Nice pot holders."

"Nice shoes."

Nic groaned. "Tonight has disaster written all over it."

"Jayne's right," I said. "You are a cynic."

"Part of my charm." She held out a glass of merlot to Beckett and gestured to the box he was holding. "Trade you."

"Picked up some pastries at Aversa's."

"There better be a cannoli in there."

"You're kidding, right?"

"Good man."

She made the trade and left me alone with Beckett.

It should have been Arch.

"Movie-star gorgeous, huh?"

"Don't get a swelled head, Beckett. We compare everyone to celebrities. Blame it on our profession."

"So who did you compare me to?"

"I'd rather not say."

"But he's gorgeous."

"According to *People* magazine."

"Huh."

Shoot me now.

"Meg Ryan," he said.

"What?"

"You remind me of a petite Meg Ryan."

My cheeks burned. "I've heard that before."

"Is that bad?"

"No. It's flattering. I just wish I had her hair."

"Why?"

"She has great hair."

"So do you."

Okay, that was nice. That was…unsettling. So was the fact that he was standing too close. *Thank him for the compliment, you ninny. And, for God's sake, don't think about that kiss. Don't tempt fate. Don't—*

He brushed my bangs out of my eyes.

Zap.

I jerked back and…went ass over backward over an ottoman.

To my credit, I didn't shriek. It happened too fast and left me stunned.

Beckett didn't help my stilted breathing when he hauled me off the floor and into his strong arms. "Are you all right?"

"Peachy," I squeaked, damning his unsettling touch. Damning Arch for putting me in this position. But mostly I was mad at myself. Being physically *aware* of two men at once was too much for my good-girl sensibilities especially since I was positively, absolutely in love with one. "I have to…" I motioned to the kitchen. "I should help." I whirled and rammed into Nic.

Eyes on Beckett, she whispered in my ear. "Thought I smelled something cooking."

CHAPTER THIRTEEN

THE IRONY, MILO THOUGHT, was priceless. This dinner had been planned to save Jayne Robinson and so far Jayne Robinson was saving this dinner.

From everything Nic had told him, he'd expected an anxious woman fixated on a bangle-wearing psychic. Thirty minutes into dinner, and so far, the redheaded free spirit had yet to mention Madame Helene. She'd kept the conversation light and focused on Chameleon. She understood she had to keep their existence under wraps and promised to do so at least three times between the time they were introduced and when Tabasco dished out the main course.

Like Evie, she was hungry for information regarding con artists and fraud investigators, except instead of burying her nose in a dozen research books, she asked the source, or sources in this case, directly. Unlike Nic, she wasn't skeptical or critical, accepting everything he and Tabasco said at face value, which suggested—like Evie—she was too trusting.

Milo didn't mind answering Jayne's questions because it allowed him the chance to describe various short and long cons. The pigeon drop, inheritance swindles, and vanity scams. He and Tabasco had agreed beforehand they'd casually segue into the time they'd busted a so-called medium who could converse with the dead, which would no doubt spur talk of gypsy psychics. Jayne wasn't merely taking the bait, she was leading the way.

"I don't get it," she said. "Don't drugs have to be approved by the FDA? How can someone advertise and sell diet pills if the product is ineffectual or dangerous?"

"Your average person's reasoning," Milo said. "Precisely why so many marks fall for the come-on."

"*Mark* is another word for victim," Evie explained. "The *come-on* is the con artist's pitch."

"Simply put," Tabasco said, "there are too many weight-loss products circulating, whether through television, the Internet, or mass mailing, for the FDA to regulate."

"Even the Federal Trade Commission is overwhelmed," Milo said.

Nic feigned shock. "You're telling me the breast-enhancement pills I saw advertised in the back of a magazine are bogus?"

As if she'd given that ad a second thought. She didn't need enhancing. Nor was she gullible. Milo met her gaze. "Let's just say you won't see me responding to the e-mail I received promoting supplies of penile enlargement pills for a mere $49.99 a month."

Nic smirked. "That your way of telling us you don't need any help down there, Slick?"

"Haven't heard any complaints, *Nicole*."

He'd thought they'd struck a truce last night over shots of vodka.

He'd thought wrong.

Annoyed, Milo glanced at his other companions. Evie looked uncomfortable, Tabasco amused, and Jayne deep in thought.

"But some vanity products have merit," the redhead said. "Take that infomercial I saw on that device that uses a special light to whiten your teeth. The Before and After pictures were amazing."

"And no doubt doctored," Tabasco said, forking up the last of his lasagna.

Milo wondered how many panhandler and telemarketing scams Jayne had been suckered into over the years. Wondered how much the psychic had soaked her for and how many other *clients* were handing over hard-earned cash to see their past and future. Damn, he itched to expose that fortune-teller. Not because Jayne was Evie and Nic's friend, but because it was the right thing to do. Crowe would view this case as a waste of Chameleon's time and talent, but saving people like Jayne from tricksters like Madame Helene filled him with drive and purpose. It made him feel like an honorable warrior, not like a thug who'd avenged a troubled senator.

Not wanting eyes to glaze over from lengthy accounts, he advanced the conversation, keeping his references vague while getting across the gist of the cons. Tabasco described past cases with more color and detail. They both stifled grins every time Evie translated grifter-speak into layman's terms because the woman's dedication to her new craft was commendable and her enthusiasm, cute.

But where Evie and Jayne were intrigued with the stories, Nic grew increasingly restless. He assumed it was because she wanted them to get to the heart of the matter. Milo cast her a look. *We're getting there.*

Instead of relaxing, she stiffened. "You would think someone would try to educate the public to these despicable frauds."

"If you go on the Internet," said Evie, "there are all sorts of sites that try to do just that. Even the IRS has a consumer alert about tax scams. AARP warns seniors about identity theft and dishonest telemarketers. The trouble is people don't typically seek out this kind of information until they've already been wronged."

Jayne looked at her in awe. "How do you know all this?"

Evie shrugged. "Figured I should learn all I can about my new job."

Jayne smiled. "You always were conscientious about your work."

"What I want to know," Nic bulldozed on, "is why local law enforcement isn't doing more to vanquish these leeches."

A former cop, Milo took the question personally. "Bunko squads are committed to squashing fraud. Unfortunately, because a mark's pride is at stake, con artists are rarely reported. When they are, they're hard to prosecute. We're talking crimes of persuasion. The mark wasn't robbed. The mark willingly gave over funds."

"Also," Evie said, rising to his defense, "bunko cops are overworked and underpaid and," she added, using her breadstick to emphasize her point, "overwhelmed. If you knew how many scam artists were out there, you'd second-guess every purchase and business opportunity, no matter how big or small, for the rest of your life."

"Then I'd rather not know," said Jayne. "Suspecting the motives of everyone you meet is—"

"Smart," said Nic.

"I was going to say cynical."

"I know."

Jayne shook her silver heart pendent, filling the air with calming chimes. "I don't want to be a cynic."

Evie frowned. "Neither do I, but I don't want to be a victim, either."

"The compromise," Milo said, "is to be cautious."

Nic snorted. "This from someone who didn't watch his own ass."

"What do you mean?" Jayne asked.

Evie looked from Nic to Milo and back.

The ballbuster flushed and pretended interest in her half-eaten pasta. "Never mind."

What the hell? He'd told Nic about the Mad Dog debacle in confidence. Her sudden belligerence, he decided, had to do with her catching Evie in his arms. The circumstances had been innocent, but she didn't seem convinced. She'd once warned him she'd kick his ass should he hurt her friend. Guess she was revving up to kick-ass mode.

It didn't help that Evie kept avoiding his gaze. Their friendship had been off-kilter since the infamous kiss. Tonight his touch had completely unnerved her. He wished he could blame it on mutual attraction. Unfortunately, he feared her intensified discomfort had more to do with this morning's revelation. He'd killed a man, possibly, and that offended her gentle disposition. He wasn't surprised, just disappointed. It made him feel worse than he already did. Arch had said she wouldn't think less of him.

Then again Arch always said what you wanted to hear.

Another thought crossed his mind. What if Nic had told Evie about yesterday's surprise visit, a visit they'd agreed to keep quiet? In hindsight, he'd been a fool to trust someone he barely knew. She could've slipped over a glass of wine and *girl talk.* One thing he'd learned since walking into this apartment: Nic, Evie, and Jayne were like sisters. They didn't look anything alike and their personalities were distinctly different, but they shared a tight bond.

Maybe Nic had suffered a sudden case of guilt and spilled her guts. *You'll never guess who dropped by yesterday and confessed his sins. Lucky me. We got drunk, talked shit, ate Chinese, and he eventually passed out on my couch.*

Maybe Evie felt betrayed. Maybe she was jealous.

Wishful thinking, Beckett.

He jerked out of his musings when Nic jerked to her feet. "Anyone for more wine with dessert?" She didn't wait for an answer.

"I'll help." Milo cleared a few dishes and followed her into the small but tidy kitchen. Thankfully, Evie and Jayne were enthralled with Tabasco's accounts of celebrity look-alikes who delved too deeply into their roles and started passing themselves off as the genuine article.

"So, this Bobby De Niro impersonator started showing up at ritzy parties, seducing starstuck ladies, and…"

Milo came up behind Nicole just as she stabbed the corkscrew into their third bottle of merlot. "Did you tell Evie about my visit yesterday?" he asked in a hushed voice.

"No. Did you?"

"No." Watching her manipulate that corkscrew—full breasts jiggling as she twisted the implement deeper, her lush lower lip caught between her perfect white teeth—made him insane. He relieved her of the task. Christ. Even though he was annoyed with her, he was having erotic thoughts—specifically sliding off her pants, lifting her onto the counter, and burying his face between her legs. She looked that damned edible. The form-fitting pants and slinky blouse. The stiletto heels, spicy perfume, and bloodred lipstick. She was a walking sex toy and he wanted to play with her in the worst way. Considering their volatile relationship that pretty much made him a prick. He wanted to fuck Nicole, but he dreamed of Evie.

Definite prick.

"Arch should be here," she whispered gruffly.

"Instead of me, you mean." He extracted the cork with a soft pop.

She opened the fridge and nabbed the Italian pastries. "Don't take this personally, Slick, but he's her boyfriend, not you. Unless…" She narrowed her eyes while arranging cannoli, biscotti and almond macaroons on a large plate. "Is this your way of playing Evie's champion? Save her friend from the wicked psychic and maybe earn her adoration?" She grunted. "As Jayne would say, that's just sad."

"It's bullshit," he said then realized in a way she was right. When Arch had bailed, he'd gladly stepped up to the plate. Better than sitting home alone, wallowing in his sorry life. Also, last night he'd promised Nic he'd expose Madame Helene if he could, although she seemed to be skating over that part and focusing on his desire to impress Evie. Actually, it was more like trying to redeem himself in Twinkie's eyes, but he didn't aim on enlightening Nic, who had already accused him of being in love with her friend.

She whirled and folded her arms over her bountiful chest. "Did you send Arch away on some bogus mission?"

"No."

"Do you know where he is? What he's doing?"

"No."

"You could find out."

"Maybe."

"But you're not going to bother."

"Mind's on other things, like exposing that psychic and Crowe's hidden agenda."

She threw up her hands in…frustration? Disgust?

He wasn't sure, but he was intrigued. And distracted.

He nabbed a towel and gently brushed away the powered sugar on her satin blouse.

Sparks shot out of those killer green eyes as she yanked the towel out of his hand.

Okay. So he'd been a little out of line considering the dusting had been over her right breast, but it's not like he'd copped a feel. "What's with the pissy mood, Nicole?"

She ignored the question and picked up the dessert tray. "When are you going to broach the subject of—" she glanced toward the dining room "—you know who."

"Do you want Jayne to feel ganged up on, demoralized? Or do you want her to come out of this mess with her dignity?" He snatched up the wine bottle and rolled over her response. "Then let me handle it."

Back at the table, Jayne and Evie were entertaining Tabasco with a story about the time they'd impersonated the Andrews Sisters for a high-roller party. "I played LaVerne," Jayne said. "Evie was Patty and Nicole played Maxene. We didn't look exactly like them, but we copied their mannerisms and costumes, and we sang like them."

"Not *exactly* like them," Evie said.

"She's being modest," said Jayne. She looked at Nicole. "We were really good, weren't we?"

Nicole winked at her as she presented the dessert tray and took her seat. "We were great. Standing O after 'Boogie Woogie Bugle Boy,' remember?"

"Boy, do I. What a night! Remember when you tripped over that mic chord, Evie?"

Twinkie grimaced and took the opportunity to clear away more dishes. "Unfortunately."

"Only she covered by turning it into a comical gag," said Jayne. "Priceless."

Since he'd been a victim of a trip and hit by Evie, Milo

could easily imagine. He refrained from rubbing the faint scar on his forehead.

Reveling in nostalgia, Jayne held up her glass as he poured more wine. He didn't know if she'd already had too much to drink or if she was always this chipper. He should've made a pot of coffee while he'd been duking it out with Miss Attitude.

Knowing Evie was a lightweight, he only poured to the halfway mark. Nicole motioned him to fill her glass, but he wasn't worried about her. As for himself, he'd over-indulged last night. Tonight he was taking it slow.

"Evie arranged all of the vocals," Jayne went on. "She has a great ear for harmonies."

Milo nodded. "She also has a damn good voice."

Evie blushed, Nicole gulped wine, and Jayne smiled. "I forgot. You hired her to sing at the Chameleon Club. Is that for real or—"

"It's for real. She opens this weekend," Milo said with a quick glance at Evie. "If you're up for it."

She reclaimed her seat and cast him a shaky smile. "I'm up for it."

"Who's accompanying you?" Nic asked.

"Tabasco," Evie said. "He plays guitar."

Jayne smiled at the man and Milo conceded she, like most women, was smitten with the caring and talented re-formed grifter. If Arch was here, she'd probably be smitten with him, too. Both men possessed charisma and charm, two qualities Milo lacked.

"You trap scam artists, fly planes, cook gourmet meals *and* you play the guitar?" Jayne sighed. "Is there anything you can't do?"

Tabasco actually looked embarrassed.

"He can't stomach psychics," Milo said.

Nic kicked him under the table and Evie nailed him with a look of dismay. Granted, not the smoothest of segues, but suddenly he itched to get out of here. He'd thought anything was better than loitering around the club, obsessing on the Mad Dog fiasco. He'd thought wrong. Sharing dinner and wine with the woman he longed for and the woman he lusted after made him edgy as hell.

Nic recovered first. "We should probably tell you, Jayne believes in—"

"Never mind that." Jayne squeezed Nic's hand but looked to Tabasco. "What have you got against psychics?"

And they were off.

"To tell you the truth," Tabasco said as he passed around the pastries, "I didn't pay them much mind until two years ago."

"The Sylvia Evans case," Milo said.

"I remember her," Evie said, choosing a macaroon and easing into the game. "She had a cable show. Claimed she could talk to dead people. Her show was canceled after the second season, in spite of its popularity."

"I loved that show," Jayne said in an awestruck tone. "She was amazing."

"I'll give her that," Tabasco said with a sneer. "She had an amazing talent for snowing people."

Jayne helped herself to a chocolate-dipped biscotti. "Don't tell me you're one of those?"

"One of what?"

"A cynic."

"If you knew what I know, angel," Tabasco said, also opting for biscotti, "you'd be a cynic, too."

"No, I wouldn't." She followed his lead and dipped the hard cookie in wine. "So what do you know?"

Milo traded a look with Tabasco. This was their chance

to plant seeds of doubt and, if they were lucky, Jayne would conclude on her own that she'd been duped by Madame Helene. She didn't have to admit to them she'd been suckered, all she had to do was accept the ugly truth and to avoid any more *readings*.

"Sylvia Evans was a fraud," Milo said, keeping his tone casual. He and Nic both reached for a cannoli. At least they agreed on one thing.

"Let me guess," Nic said. "The people she called on in the audience were plants."

"Some, but not all."

"But she always connected to a deceased person in the audience member's life," said Jayne. "Always."

"You only saw what the show's producer wanted you to see," Tabasco said. "Botched readings ended up on the cutting-room floor. Or sometimes they were edited, questions and answers cut and pasted out of order so it appeared Ms. Evans's missteps were right-on."

"She did what's called a cold reading," Milo clarified. "Throwing out a name or initials. Seeing who responded. *Oh, so it's you who knew little David.* The bonus being the word *little*. Right away she knew she was dealing with a deceased infant or toddler. That's just one example of how she'd choose her mark. After that it was a matter of rapid-fire statements that also passed as questions. Right or wrong an expert medium has a way of twisting the answers to make it seem as though she or he has spiritual knowledge."

At this point they were talking about psychics in general. Cold readings were the norm. Some were better at it than others. Hopefully, Jayne would recognize various techniques, similar to those used by Madame Helene, as they explained them.

Tabasco leaned into the Bohemian free spirit who was

chewing thoughtfully on wine-soaked biscotti. "Evans studied her marks' expressions," he said. "Watched their body language and responded in ways that only someone with connections to the *other side* could. The statements were always generalized. The mark took the bait because they wanted to believe that the medium would connect with the person they'd lost. The person they were desperate to speak with. In their enthusiasm they invariably fed Evans clues. All she had to do was watch, listen and manipulate."

"This is fascinating," Nic said. "In a warped way."

"It's horrible," Evie said. "Preying on people's misery."

"I don't recall anyone ever looking miserable on that show," Jayne said. "Not after Sylvia connected with their loved one. On the contrary. She offered comfort and hope. Sometimes she even made them laugh."

Talk about a tough nut. Milo leaned back in his chair. "I think you're missing the point, Jayne."

"Let's get back to the so-called editing of the actual show," she said.

"Not so-called," Tabasco said. "It happened."

"If I'd been taped on a TV show," she continued as if he hadn't spoken, "you can bet I'd watch the broadcast and I'm certain I'd know if my segment had been altered."

Tough but not hopeless, Milo thought.

"The edits were subtle," Tabasco said. "But there were some who noticed. Most who lodged complaints were double-talked into believing no harm done. But a persistent few persevered until their concerns came to our attention."

"So Chameleon investigated Sylvia Evans's *Beyond the Grave* cable show," Nic surmised.

"We did," Milo confirmed. In a bid for nonchalance, he stood and started clearing away the remnants of dessert.

Evie helped. "And?"

"Audience members typically arrived more than an hour before showtime," said Tabasco. "Everyone was there for the same reason."

"To connect to a departed loved one," said Jayne.

"There were production assistants floating all over the place."

"Eavesdropping?" Nic asked.

"Why would they do that?" Jayne asked.

"Because everyone was talking to the person next to them about the dead person they hoped to hear from," Evie called over her shoulder as she and Milo ducked into the kitchen. She caught his gaze and whispered, "Right?"

"Right." They stacked dishes in the sink and Milo winked at her, a sign that things were going well. She smiled and, for a brief moment, he felt like her hero. Considering what he'd done on behalf of Crowe and Senator Clark, he desperately needed the ego boost.

They reentered the dining room where Jayne hung on Tabasco's every word. "There were cameras and microphones all over the studio," he said. "What the audience didn't realize is that Ms. Evans and her key people were backstage watching, listening, taking notes."

Jayne scrunched up her Cupie-doll face. "Are you saying she *cheated?*"

Tabasco nodded. "It's worse than that. She took advantage of and manipulated people who had lost someone dear. People in mourning. That cable show was only one venue for her treachery. She traveled and appeared in live concert settings. She wrote books. She and her 'production team' made millions off of everyday people's suffering."

Silence reigned and Milo hedged he wasn't the only one in the room holding his breath.

Jayne worried her bottom lip. Her eyes shone with disappointment. Her shoulders slumped, but then she straightened her spine and nodded. "Okay. So maybe Sylvia Evans was a trickster, but one bad apple doesn't spoil the whole bushel."

"Oh, for…" Nic dropped her head back and groaned. "This is hopeless."

Jayne folded her arms and turned to her tall, dark friend. After a long moment, she said, "You told them about Madame Helene."

Yup, Milo thought, *gullible but bright.*

"Actually," Evie said, as she scratched her neck, "I confided my worries to Arch and he asked Tabasco—"

"Don't you dare accept all the blame," said Nic. "I confided my worries to Beckett."

Evie stared at her, at him. "When?"

"Hellooo," said Jayne. "This is about *me,* remember? I can't believe my two best friends ganged up on me." She eyeballed Tabasco. "I can't believe you fed me all that hogwash."

"Hold up, angel. Everything we told you about Sylvia Evans was true."

"Maybe so, but still, that's an isolated incident."

Milo cleared his throat. "Not really. We could show you case files—"

"I don't need to see files. I know there are a lot of fakes and frauds in this world," Jayne said, "but some people are the real deal. Some people are gifted in extraordinary ways. Just because you don't understand, just because it's beyond the scope of your narrow minds…" She zeroed in on Nic. "I expected something like this from you. But *you!*"

Now she directed her fire at Evie. "You have an open mind. You put stock in dream interpretation. As for

Madame Helene's warnings about friends in trouble, every single one of her predictions came true and they all had to do with you. That's when I learned I was cursed because of something I did in a past life, something that's affecting those I love in this life. Luckily, Madame Helene knew how to lift that curse and now everything's fine. You've re-discovered love. You have a new job you're obviously excited about. You're surrounded by people who care about you enough to try to *snow* a friend you were worried about. After this morning's consultation, Madame Helene told me your future looks bright and I believe her."

Energized, she flipped back to Nic. "She also said she could give me some insight into your future and maybe some advice on how to break your unlucky-in-love streak. But I don't guess you'd believe me since you think I'm a pea-brained nut!"

"I don't think… I never said…"

Milo watched Nic grapple for words. A first.

Evie started to say something, but Tabasco cut her off. "How much did Madame Helene charge you to lift that curse?"

"None of your business, Mr. Hotshot Scam Buster."

Evie groaned. "Oh, Jayne."

"You were suckered, angel, and I can prove it."

Milo questioned this straight-ahead approach, but something in Tabasco's expression told him to let this roll.

The man pushed out of his chair and offered his hand to Jayne. "Let's go."

"Where?"

"We'll start with the gypsies on the boardwalk and work our way up to Madame Helene."

She fussed with one of her crystal rings. *Twirl. Twirl.*

"Worried I can prove they're frauds?"

Hell, yeah, she was worried, Milo thought. But then she grasped Tabasco's hand and pushed to her feet. "You are in for a rude awakening," she said as he guided her to the front door.

"No, angel. That would be you."

The door shut behind them and Nic glared at Milo. "*That* went well."

Evie sighed. "She didn't even say goodbye. I wonder if she'll ever talk to us again."

Milo reached over and squeezed her hand. "It'll be all right."

"How can you be sure?"

"Because Jayne's a bright and caring girl. She'll come around, with Tabasco's help, and she'll thank you."

"I hope you're right."

"Trust me."

She met his gaze and his heart bumped against his chest. She didn't say anything, but he knew, if nothing else, he did have her trust.

Nic stood so fast, her wineglass toppled. Fortunately, it was empty. "Do you need any help cleaning up, Evie?"

"No. I—"

"If you're sure, great. Because I've got a monster head-ache."

"I have some aspirin—"

"That's okay. I just…I need to go home."

Milo and Evie both rose, but Nic was already heading for the living room. She nabbed her purse and when she turned she faltered. "Dammit!"

Evie rushed to steady her. "Maybe Beckett should drive you home."

"I'm not drunk." Nic wrenched off her right stiletto. "My damned heel broke."

Milo moved in. "Let me see—"

"Don't bother." She waved him away and kicked off the other shoe.

"You can't drive barefoot," Evie said and ran into another room.

"I'm sorry things didn't go more smoothly with Jayne," Milo said, hoping to cool Nic's temper. "But you don't have to take it out on Evie."

She worked her perfect jaw. "I didn't—"

"You practically bit her head off when she suggested I drive you home."

"I'm *not* drunk."

"Maybe not, but you did consume a lot of wine. Enough to be over the legal limit—"

"Stow it, Secret Agent Man."

Evie hustled back in with a pair of fuzzy purple slippers. "My shoes are too small for you, but these should work."

Nic lifted a brow. "I can't drive wearing those."

"I know," said Evie. "That's why Beckett's going to give you a lift." She looked at him and he couldn't help but feel she was giving him the bum's rush. "You don't mind, do you?"

"Not at all."

Nic stuffed her black pumps into her oversized purse. "Jayne's not the only one who feels ganged up on."

"I'll drive your car over tomorrow and maybe we can go shopping," Evie said, following her friend to the door. "My car's on the blink and—"

"Shopping, sure," Nic grumbled. "Sounds good."

Milo opened the door and Evie held up the slippers. "You forgot these."

"No, I didn't."

"There are rocks in the parking lot," Evie said, undeterred. "What if you step on broken glass?"

"Or," Milo said, "I could carry you."

She grabbed the fuzzy slippers and slid them on.

"Night, Twinkie." He gave her a reassuring smile and finessed Nic out the door. Clearly, Evie was worried about her friend, but just as clearly she'd been eager for him to leave. She didn't want to be alone with him. He didn't know whether to be encouraged or insulted.

He and Nic didn't speak on the short drive to her condo. She was pissed about something and though she wasn't falling-down drunk, she was definitely inebriated. Now didn't seem the best time to pursue rational conversation. Instead he stewed on his own thoughts.

Where was Arch and what was he up to? Was Woody having any luck digging up dirt on Crowe? Who was Gina seducing for information? Not that it was his business, but he hated that she'd put herself out there like that for him. How was Tabasco faring with Jayne?

Did I really kill Mad Dog Turner?

Milo dug a travel pack of Tylenol out of his pocket as he swung his Honda into a parking space. Suddenly his head hurt like hell, but then so did Nic's. He offered her the pain reliever, but she waved him off.

"Why don't you just tell her?" she asked.

His brain glitched as he turned off the ignition. "Tell who what?"

"Don't play coy, Beckett. I saw you stealing looks at Evie all night. Saw the longing in your expression." She unbuckled her seat belt. "I'm out of here. Do yourself a favor, do Evie a favor, go back to her apartment and tell her how you feel."

He didn't say anything. Truth was, aside from aching

to win her affection, he wasn't sure how he felt about Evie Parish. Trying to put it into words would only make him sound like a boob.

Nic heaved a disgusted sigh. "Stealing a kiss didn't cut it, Slick. All you managed to do was confuse her."

He'd expected her to bring up this evening's brief embrace, something she'd witnessed. Not the late-night kiss, two weeks past. "You two talked about that?" Why was he surprised? They probably talked about everything.

"Don't get your shorts in a twist. And don't ask for specifics. I'm not going to betray her trust."

Great. So she'd torture him by making him wonder. Milo popped the pills dry and tried not to glare at the dark-haired siren.

"If you really want to be with Evie, make your play. If I were you, I'd play dirty."

Really. "Meaning?"

"Tell her everything you know about Arch's past. Reveal some of his tawdry secrets. I'm sure he has more than a few."

"Why?"

"Because he's going to break her heart. I feel it in my gut. And you wouldn't. I sense that, too." She wet her lips and looked away. "She feels something for you, and though I hate to say it, you're the wiser choice."

"Gee, thanks." He felt like a sacrificial lamb. "Your matchmaking skills need work, Nicole."

"I just…I don't want her to end up like me."

Alone? Wary? Bitter? He cupped the side of her face. Were those tears in her eyes? The urge to comfort and protect welled up, only Nic staved off the waterworks and closed him out. He leaned in, wanting to get closer physically and emotionally, even though his gut warned it was a dumbass thing to do. "Is this about that unlucky-in-love streak Jayne mentioned?"

Her eyes drifted shut. She didn't want to talk about it. Okay. They wouldn't talk. His gaze shifted to those sexy red lips. Possessed, he threaded his fingers in her hair and cradled the back of her head. Heat sizzled. Desire welled. He'd kissed her before, briefly. This wouldn't be brief. Or chaste. "Maybe you just haven't met the right man."

In a flash, she was out of his arms and out the door. Her curse echoed in his ears as she marched up the exterior stairs in her classy clothes and those fuzzy slippers. *"Go fuck yourself, Slick."*

The way things were going, he'd end up doing just that.

CHAPTER FOURTEEN

A DARK-HAIRED, GOOD-LOOKING man, wearing an expensive suit, rose from behind the cherrywood desk. "Simon Lamont," he said in a deep, pleasant voice.

Aka Simon the Fish.

He smiled and offered his hand in greeting. He didn't look like a criminal. He looked like a casino VP. "Pat them down," he ordered his hulking goon. "Security precautions," he said to us with a tight smile. "You understand."

I panicked. Arch's fake gut. The prosthetics. My heart pounded against my ribs. Did Arch carry a gun? Did the goons? "I don't feel so good." On instinct, I went limp, falling into a dead faint, directly in Hulking Guy's path.

I banged my head hard on the floor, suppressed a groan when he tripped and landed on top of me.

Still in character, Arch protested. "Get your hands off of me, old boy. Allow me to help my wife."

"He's wearin' a fat suit," Squirrelly Dude said. "And a fuckin' wire!"

Wire?

Cursing, shuffling.

Hulking Guy scrambled off of me, so I scrambled, too. Only I was disoriented from the head banging. Cross-eyed, I saw Arch clobber Squirrelly Dude with his cane, throw a *punch at Hulking Guy. Saw Lamont pull a gun. Aim it at Arch.*

"No!" *I lunged to knock away the gun. Only Squirrelly Dude pushed me. I whacked my head on the desk. Saw stars. Heard voices.*

Beckett?

I saw him choking Mad Dog. Foaming mouth. Bulging eyes.

No, no, no. Not a dog, a fish.

Not Beckett, Arch.

Me.

Head hurts.

Can't faint.

Hold on.

Grab something.

Hands.

Arch's hands? Fish's hands?

Bang! A loud sickening bang that reverberated in my ears.

Bang! Bang! Bang!

I BOLTED UPRIGHT WITH a scream. My heart pounded so hard, I pressed my hands to my chest to keep it from exploding through my skin. My T-shirt was soaked with sweat. My vision was blurred and my lungs burned.

Bang! Bang! Bang!

Body buzzing, I looked toward the sound.

Cops, goons, and guns. I'd fallen asleep on the couch with the TV on. I stared at the flickering screen—some black-and-white gangster film—trying to catch my breath, trying to reconnect to the living.

I'd been dreaming. The same nightmare I'd been having on and off since the Simon the Fish shooting. Only toward the end, the scene never played out the same. The sequence was always a little different.

"It's only natural," Arch had told me a dozen times. *"You hit your head. Twice. You suffered a concussion. Your memory's iffy. A good thing, yeah?"*

Not really. Arch wanted me to forget what I'm sure he thought I couldn't handle. The actual moment the gun smoked and Simon the Fish bit the dust. I'm thinking his face was mottled with rage and pain. There was probably lots of blood. I don't know. I can't remember. I blacked out, but that was after the gun went off.

I think.

I mean, I did hear the *bang*.

Still massaging my chest, I grabbed the remote and lowered the sound. Only then it was too quiet and I heard things bumping and creaking in the night. I flipped channels, settled on Nick at Nite and turned the volume back up. The ludicrous scene with Mr. Ziffel talking to Arnold the Pig lifted my morbid mood.

I thought about Beckett and his insomnia. How he'd confessed he spends late nights watching sitcom reruns— including *Green Acres*. I wondered if he was watching it now. I wondered if he was wrestling with Mad Dog's death the way I wrestled with the Fish's. Not knowing if he was truly responsible, the way I wondered if the gun really went off by accident. I only had Arch's word.

"Crap."

My cell phone rang. It took me a minute to find it. I still felt disoriented. What time was it anyway? "Hello?"

"Hey, Sunshine."

Arch. I wilted against the cushions. "I'm glad you called."

"You *dinnae* sound glad."

"I just…I fell asleep on the couch and I had a bad dream."

"Simon?"

"Yeah."

"Put it *oot* of your mind, yeah? Read a book. Watch a movie."

"I'm thinking it would be easier for me to forget if I could remember. If we could just talk about it—"

"I need you to let this go, Evie."

"So you've said. I know you don't feel bad about that man's death, but I do."

"*Dinnae.* The world's better off."

"I agree." The thug had bilked countless seniors out of their life's savings. That was just one of his many crimes. He was also guilty of at least two murders. Yes, he was scum. Yes, the world was better off without him. Still. "I know this is a touchy subject. I know it makes you think about what that rat bastard did to your grandpa, but—"

"The sting curdled. We struggled for possession of a gun. It went off. Simon took a bullet and died. End of story."

"But—"

"How was dinner?"

I pantomimed strangling him. Could he be any more infuriating? *Probably.* I blew out a breath and let it go because obviously the discussion I wanted to have wasn't going to happen. At least not with Arch.

I glanced at the vase of flowers, envisioned Zeke in all his Austin Powers glory. "The preshow was interesting."

"Overkill?"

"The orchids and the note would have been enough."

"I should have been there, lass. I'm sorry."

He sounded so sincere. If he told me the moon was

made of cheese, I'd believe him. Even with all of my research, I never knew when Arch was playing me. Jayne's voice whispered in my head, *"Who says he's playing you, Miss Cynic?"* Right. "Jayne was impressed by your creativity."

"And Nic?"

I scrambled for something nice to say. "She thinks you have good taste in champagne."

"Ah." I detected a smile in his voice, as if he knew exactly what Nic thought of his not being there. "How was the performance?"

I grinned. "Groovy, baby."

He chuckled. "Brilliant."

"Arch?"

"Aye?"

"Did you mean what he sang?"

"My head hasn't been on straight since I met you, Sunshine."

My heart bloomed. "I got you so you don't know what you're doing?"

"It's a bit disconcerting, yeah?"

I scratched my neck, anxious that he was saying all of this from miles away. "But not enough to make you run, right?"

"I'm not running, love."

I relaxed my jaw and switched off the TV. "Okay."

"Thought *aboot* you all night. How did the intervention go?"

I padded to my bedroom, focused now on Jayne.

"Things were going great until they went wrong. Tabasco practically dragged Jayne out of here, intent on proving Madame Helene's a fake. I guess I'll learn the outcome tomorrow."

"It'll work *oot,* lass."

"That's what Beckett said." I flopped down on my bed and braved an uncomfortable subject. "I have to say, I'm surprised you didn't object to him coming over here. To my apartment, I mean."

"I know what you mean."

"So, you're not worried about…"

"Beckett stealing you away from me?" He gave a humorless laugh. "*Cannae* say I've come that far, but I'm working on it."

The trust issue. "I'm working on it, too."

"I know." He paused and I imagined one of his sexy grins. "How hard was it not to ask where I was going?"

"Really hard."

"I'm on the West Coast."

I stared up into the darkness, breathing deep as Arch's words sunk in. The West Coast. Not specific, but it was something. And totally unexpected.

"I'll be home tomorrow."

More info. Wow. "You sound disappointed."

"A deal fell through."

I couldn't help myself. "A deal with Kate?"

"A deal with the devil."

Okay, that was unenlightening. That was…troubling. Was he falling back on old ways? Grifting for personal gain? Associating with bad sorts? Was *Kate* a bad sort? "Why would you want to do business with the devil?"

"Because the payoff is priceless."

He said it casually, but I sensed frustration and determination. I was dying of curiosity. I needed details. I needed—

"Heard anything more from Stone?"

I blinked at the change of subject. "No."

"I *dinnae* like the way he showed up unannounced, Sunshine. *Dinnae* like the way he touched you."

I thought about the way Arch had clocked him, and grinned. "Obviously."

"What if he comes calling again?"

"I'll send him away."

"Something else. Jazzman mentioned Crowe had him followed while we were on the Mad Dog case. What if he's still being tailed? What if Crowe is looking for other ways to get to Beckett?"

I envisioned bad men in black casing my apartment, waiting for the opportune moment to whisk me away to some secret room with no windows, a hostage until Beckett agreed to bend to Crowe's will. I cursed various espionage movies for filling my head with deceitful thoughts and grisly imagery. Starting tomorrow I was going on a strictly comedy diet.

Palms clammy, I scrambled to my bedroom window and peeked through the blinds. The moon was high and surrounding lights in the windows of other apartments were doused. I didn't see any suspicious activity but that didn't make me feel better. "Don't you think Beckett would've noticed if he was being tailed?"

"He *didnae* notice before."

"Yes, but, now that he knows it happened—"

"He'd be more sensitive to it, aye. Still…"

He trailed off and I got goose bumps. I stepped away from the window and flipped on the bathroom light. *Be gone, bogeyman.* "Still what?"

"If Chameleon goes head-to-head with the director of the AIA, things could get dangerous, you know?"

No. But I could imagine.

"I'd feel better if you were staying at my place."

Blindsided, I sank onto the edge of my mattress. I'd visited the London flat he'd inherited from his grandfather. I knew he owned a manor in Scotland—part of the barony he'd purchased. But I'd never been to his home here in the States. For most of the time we'd known each other, we'd been on the road. All I knew was that he had a condo in Margate. "You want me to move in with you?"

"Aye."

For good or for now, I wanted to ask, but didn't. Either way, the notion was daunting. If he meant for good, it didn't feel right. Not with my being confused about Beckett. Not without knowing the actual relationship between Arch and Kate. If he meant for now... What if he felt trapped? What if I felt smothered? What if I got used to being his live-in only to be booted out?

"Still there, lass?"

"Yes. I just...you took me by surprise."

"Think of it as protective custody." He paused. "Or a trial run."

Holy smokes. I fell back on my pillow, head reeling, heart racing. The man who'd never been in a committed relationship just committed. Sort of.

It scared the bejeebers out of me.

"Sleep on it," he said in a tender voice.

"Sleep?" He had to be kidding.

"Still on the sofa?"

"No." I massaged the center of my forehead. Brain full. Brain spinning. "I'm in bed."

"Brilliant." His voice dropped to a throaty growl. "Ever had phone sex?"

Zing. Zap.

Surely he didn't expect... But of course he did. And of course I would.

"What are you wearing, lass?"

"Aside from a smile?"

"You're cute when you're cheeky."

"So you've said. Luckily for me, cute turns you on."

"Got a *stonner* to prove it, yeah?"

"That anything like an erection?"

"Hard-on, stiffy, boner—"

"I get the picture."

"Do you now?"

Crystal clear. Arch's impressive appendage was branded on my corneas for life.

My inner thighs tingled. An erotic thrill made me bold. I slipped my hand beneath the elastic band of my Scooby-Doo pajama bottoms. "I'm wearing a short, pleated plaid skirt, knee-high socks and a white blouse with a Peter Pan collar."

"Schoolgirl uniform?"

"Yes, sir, Principle Duvall, sir." I sighed. "Oh, and I'm touching myself."

"Bollocks."

CHAPTER FIFTEEN

I DON'T REMEMBER falling asleep, but I remember what made me sleepy.

My cheeks burned when I thought about the sexually explicit things I'd said to Arch, the things he'd said to me. I'd touched myself exactly as he'd directed, and he'd followed my instruction as well. Or so he'd said. My imagination had worked double time. Orgasms had been plentiful. Exhilarating. Exhausting.

It wasn't like me to be so verbally uninhibited, but Arch had awakened my inner bad girl. Sex had never been so wild and fulfilling. Not with my ex-husband, or any of the few men before him. It made me wonder. Was the over-the-moon sex great because I'd evolved into a woman who grabbed the bull by the, um, horns? Or was it due to the connection I felt with Arch? A connection I couldn't define but one we both acknowledged?

I pondered the notion as I readied for the day, although I soon got sidetracked by an unusual sense of contentment as I primped and dressed for shopping with Nic.

Apparently I was in good favor with the style gods. I was having a great hair day even though my roots were in dire need of a touch-up. My skin glowed and my subtly applied makeup looked photo-shoot perfect. I didn't bemoan my curvy hips as I tugged on my jeans, and I happily settled on the first shirt and shoes I slipped on. A rarity. Typically, by the time I'm out the front door there are two to three discarded ensembles heaped on my bed. Not today. Today I felt comfortable in my skin.

Outside—clear and sunny. A beautiful spring morning. It was sunny on the inside, too. Call me Suzy Sunshine. I did a last-minute inspection in my full-length mirror trying to see the over-forty has-been I'd felt like since Michael had dumped me and my career had tanked. Because the entertainment business hypes youth and sexuality, I'd blamed my recent bum luck on my lack of both. But where my career was concerned, maybe I'd been blind to other factors. Maybe the rejections weren't solely about me being older, but about me being old news. I'd been working this town a long time. Maybe it wasn't so much about young blood as new blood. It was certainly an easier pill to swallow.

Needing to voice some new and interesting thoughts, I nabbed my diary and pen from my nightstand. Sitting on the edge of my unmade bed, I turned to a blank page.

Dear Diary,

Arch was right. I've been too focused on the physical. Talk about shallow and insecure. I wasted a good year comparing myself to twentysomething hard bodies instead of celebrating my good health and wealth of experience. Okay. So my upper arms and hips could use some work, but overall, I'm in damned good shape. I mean, jeesh. Arch is sizzling hot. He's younger. Six years younger. He could have anyone. Someone young and sex-a-licious like Gina. He did have Gina. Not that I'm jealous. Okay, that's a lie. But it's neither here nor there, because he doesn't want her. He wants me! Not only that, both Beckett and

Michael kissed me and expressed interest in…I don't know what. But it's weird. It's like I'm suddenly radiating sex-bunny vibes. Is it because I'm more confident? More aggressive? I don't get it.

I turned the page and doodled a heart. Then another heart. I connected the two with cupid's arrow. "What I do know," I said aloud, "is that I deserve my happily ever after. My very own too-good-to-be-true hero."

Unfortunately, if I went by the romance novels I loved, Beckett beat out Arch in the traditional hero department, hands down. If I needed a refresher, all I had to do was flip back a few pages to my pros-and-cons chart.

If only Arch would come clean about the shady aspects of his life. I desperately needed him to confide in me about that deal gone awry. About Kate. If we were going to pursue a serious relationship, we needed to go the extra mile. To share our hopes and dreams. Our fears and obsessions.

I stared down at my diary, the keeper of my innermost thoughts. A week prior, during a heated discussion about his own secrets, Arch had asked if I'd feel comfortable letting him read my diary—inferring some things are meant to be private. It would be a grand gesture, a supreme act of trust, if I allowed Arch to read my purple penned scribbles. Musings about myself, Arch…and Beckett. The notion simmered while I tucked the journal beneath my pillow and headed for the kitchen.

I needed to bounce my thoughts off of someone real. Since Nic knew more about my relationship with Arch, she won out over Jayne. I nabbed my cell off of the counter, but before I could dial Nic, she dialed me. "Good morning," I chirped while nuking a cup of hot water.

"What's good about it?"

Uh-oh. Was she hungover? Miffed because I'd insisted Beckett drive her home? Bent because Beckett had said something insensitive? "What's wrong?"

"Nothing. Ignore me. Blame it on PMS." She paused and I imagined her lighting up.

"Are you smoking?"

"No."

"Liar."

"Nag."

"I nag because I love you." Nic had a lot of vices, but smoking was the worst by far. "Those things will kill you."

"When it's your time, it's your time."

I rolled my eyes while searching the cabinets for tea bags and something edible. "Jayne's right. You're a cynic."

"Speaking of our Pollyanna friend, have you heard from her?"

"No. You?"

"No. I wonder if Zorro-dude showed her the light."

I laughed.

"What's so funny?"

"Nothing," I said, settling on a cereal bar. "It's just when I first met Tabasco I thought of him as Zorro, too."

"Jayne was also right about all of the Chameleon men being movie-star gorgeous."

"You think Beckett is gorgeous?"

"We were talking about Tabasco."

I blinked at her belligerent tone. "Yes, but you mentioned all of the Chameleon men and that includes Beckett. I just wondered—"

"Do you think he's gorgeous?"

"Arch is gorgeous," I said. "Beckett is…well, he's certainly handsome. And sexy…in an understated way."

"You're cracked, Evie."

"You don't think Beckett's handsome?" I sipped tea and nibbled on the stale oatmeal bar while she took a long drag on her cancer stick.

"I don't think there's anything understated about the man's sex appeal," she said at last. "He oozes sex. You know that cliché, it's always the quiet ones? Ten to one Slick's an animal in bed."

"You've thought about Beckett in bed?"

"You haven't?"

Honestly? "No." My musings and fantasies hadn't gone beyond a steamy kiss and some groping. I'd never actually thought about *doing it* with my boss. Hmm.

"But you are interested in him."

"Of course I'm interested. He's an interesting guy."

Puff. Blow. "Let me rephrase," Nic said. "You're infatuated with Beckett."

"I wouldn't say that."

"What would you say?"

Her insistence grated. I honestly didn't know. I wasn't sure if it was fascination, hero worship, or…something deeper. I chucked the remainder of my cereal bar in the garbage pail. "I'm *confused* about Beckett."

"What's there to be confused about? He's gorgeous. He's charming, in a stiff-ass sort of way. He's respectably employed. Intelligent. Trustworthy. Reliable."

"He's also trained to kill," I blurted. Not that I thought Beckett had intentionally killed Mad Dog, but what if Gina was right and he'd screwed up that choke hold. I didn't want to believe it, but the possibility niggled.

Nic grunted. "A former cop? A government agent? No. Gee. Ya *think?*"

My temper flared. "You don't have to be sarcastic."

"Why would you even say something like that, Evie?

Like it's a strike against Beckett? He's trained in self-defense and the use of weaponry. He's a law enforcer, not an assassin."

"I never said… I just meant…" *Dammit!* I couldn't say what I meant. Beckett's involvement in Mad Dog's death was hush-hush. "I just don't know how I feel about someone who's capable of killing another human being."

"First of all," Nic said, "I'd wager ninety-nine percent of us are capable of taking a life under the right, or maybe I should say, god-awful circumstances. Not to mention there is such a thing as accidental death."

I thought about Simon the Fish. Because of the god-awful circumstances, I'd fought to save Arch from the Fish's wrath, only I'd bobbled and Arch had fought to save me. The thought occurred that it could have just as easily been me grappling for that gun when it went off.

My tea soured in my stomach.

"Secondly, from what Beckett told me, I think Crowe set him up."

I blinked. "You know about Mad Dog Turner?"

"What can I say? Slick doesn't hold his liquor as well as I do."

But last night Nic had drunk twice as much wine as Beckett. At least I assumed she was referring to last night.

"The man's career is in a tailspin. Surely, you haven't already forgotten what that feels like?"

Was she calling me unsympathetic? Insensitive? My heart hammered as I grappled for calm and poured the rest of my tea down the drain. "Why are you trying to sell me on Beckett?"

"Because he's a straight-up guy."

"And?"

"Arch isn't."

I felt my TMJ flair. I knew she meant well, but her judgmental view chafed. "People are capable of change," I bit off. "Arch has changed. *I've* changed. Maybe we're perfect for one another."

"You're deluding yourself, Evie. Arch deals in deception. He has secrets. Christ, you don't even know where he is right now."

"The West Coast."

"Doing what?"

"Negotiating a deal."

"What kind of deal?"

"An important one. You know what?" I snapped before she could volley another question. "I think we should nix the shopping trip today."

"Good. I don't feel like shopping anyway."

I'd never known Nic to not *feel* like shopping, but I was too pissed to ponder the reason. "Fine. I'll just drive your car over and hop the bus home."

"Use my car to do whatever you need to do. I'm not going anywhere today. Drop it off whenever."

She signed off and I mimicked throwing my cell against the wall and tossed it into my purse instead. My hands shook, I was so dang peeved. I couldn't remember ever fighting with Nic. Then again I was the master of internalizing. Or at least I used to be. I thought about venting my anger in my diary but retrieved the cell and dialed Jayne instead. I needed to touch base with a *levelheaded* friend. Who would've ever guessed that would be Jayne?

She answered on the third ring. "Hello?"

"Jayne?"

"Evie?"

I worked my tight jaw. "Why are you whispering?"

"I'm not alone."

I glanced at my watch, 8:00 a.m. "Who's at your house at this hour?"

"Jimmy."

"Jimmy, who?" Then it dawned. "Tabasco?"

"The one and only."

So he'd failed to expose Madame Helene last night? He needed another day? "Why did he come over so early?"

"He didn't exactly leave."

I processed then spoke as though I was speaking to a child. "Are you saying Tabasco somehow ended up at your house last night and…never left?"

"I'm saying we had sex and he slept over. I'm sure you're shocked," she whispered, "but it was just one of those things and I'm not sorry it happened. Besides, I'm not talking to you."

I thunked my forehead, just to feel the *ouch,* just to know I wasn't dreaming. "Yes, you are."

"Not technically." She sniffed. "You went behind my back and spoke to people I didn't know about something that's near and dear to me."

My cheeks flushed. "I had your best interest at heart!"

"That's not the point. Instead of addressing what you considered my folly straight on, you constructed that sham of a dinner party. Getting to know the other faction of your life. Ha!" She snorted. "That dinner was an intervention. In the old days, you would have talked to me directly, in private. You wouldn't have been so…sneaky and manipulative. You've changed."

Tears stung my eyes. My stomach churned. "Jayne—"

"Whatever. If it makes you feel better, Jimmy showed me Madame Helene's true colors. Along with half a dozen psychics on the boardwalk. I may be optimistic and openminded, Evie, but I'm not stupid. I have to go."

She hung up before I could defend myself.

Well, hell!

Out of the three of us, I was historically the diplomat. The peacemaker. I was the nonconfrontational nice girl. Or at least I used to be. This morning I'd had heated rows with my two best friends, plus I wanted to give Tabasco hell. What was he thinking? Surely Jayne had been upset and vulnerable when he'd exposed Madame Helene. She'd no doubt felt like a fool. All marks do. I wasn't surprised that Tabasco would offer comfort. The man was a caretaker by nature. But comforting and boinking were two different things.

My aggravation mounted as I blew out of my apartment and hurried to Nic's sporty Honda. Part of me was hurt because she and Jayne had lashed out. One had called me insensitive, the other manipulative. I couldn't think of worse insults. Besides it wasn't true. *Was it?* "Of course not," I grumbled as I buckled up and keyed the ignition. "They spoke in anger."

Well, guess what? I was spitting mad, too. I peeled out of the parking lot, white noise roaring in my ears. Not only were my friends attacking my virtue, they were questioning my judgment. Nic's low opinion of Arch only fueled my determination to prove him the "prince of my dreams."

Instead of heading toward the mall, I veered toward the Chameleon Club.

Multiple agendas bombarded my mind as I drove to the inlet. A ten-minute drive tops, but plenty of time for my brain to stew. Because I was agitated, my thoughts kept bouncing all over and, okay, I admit it, my imagination got the best of me. At one point I thought I was being followed. That was Arch's fault for planting the notion.

Damn him and my scary good memory.

I'd been two seconds from jamming on my brakes and confronting the driver in the dark sedan—I was *that* pumped—but then the car had turned off and disappeared. Okay. So I wasn't being tailed.

Unless the guy was really, really good.

Damn my stellar imagination.

Regardless of the high drama, by the time I pulled into the Chameleon Club's parking lot, I had my agenda bulleted.

Address Tabasco's unprofessionalism. Seducing Jayne was just wrong.

Address the Simon the Fish shooting. Grill Beckett for specifics. Did he know something I didn't? Would he at least talk it out with me?

Address the friction between Beckett and Nic. Can't we all just get along?

Address my *confusion* about Beckett.

Yeah, boy. I'd be saving *that* one for last.

CHAPTER SIXTEEN

MILO HAD GIVEN UP ON SLEEP around three in the morning and flipped on the TV. He'd bypassed his standard nocturnal hangs—CNN and TV Land—opting for The History Channel. Instead of concentrating on an episode of *Decoding the Past,* he'd pondered Nicole Sparks's cynicism and belligerence. She was the mystery he wanted to solve. So much so he'd abandoned the TV for the computer. Normally, he utilized The Kid to find information on people, but Woody was holed up in The Cave trying to gain unauthorized access to government records in order to dig up dirt on Crowe. Milo's own efforts in that area had tanked early on. He didn't possess The Kid's patience or hacking skills. Not to mention, this was personal…too personal. He didn't want to explain why he wanted to know more about Evie's sultry friend. He didn't want to instigate gossip. Milo could navigate his way through a standard background investigation as easily as his cable channels. Besides, what better way to forget his own life and troubles than to dig into those of someone else?

Within a couple of hours, he had a basic rundown on Nic's family, education, financial and residential history. Her employment records were sketchy given she freelanced through various entertainment agencies. He'd found an interesting profile on an Internet site promoting trade-show models. Her publicity photos, though sexy as hell, were notably more discreet than several of the other models'. Knowing her, even as little as he did, he wasn't surprised that she opted to hawk luxury cars and medical supplies over beer and motorcycles. Hence, the missing bikini shot. What he didn't get was why she bothered working trade shows at all. It didn't jive with her no bullshit demeanor and God knows she didn't need the money.

Brain and body exhausted, Milo had dozed off just before dawn.

He'd dreamt of Nic. A first.

Even now, after a morning run and a cold shower, she was still on his mind. She'd been engaged once. He'd read the announcement in a newspaper's online archive. Her then fiancé was now married to another woman. Who'd broken the engagement? The prominent Philadelphia doctor? Or Nic?

He was rooting through his dresser drawer, looking for a matching pair of socks—why was that always so freaking hard?—when his cell rang. He glanced at the caller ID. "Morning, Twinkie."

"I need to speak with you."

He recognized that tone. Evie on the verge of a rant. This had to be about Arch…or Jayne. He hadn't heard from Tabasco. Maybe she knew something he didn't. Maybe things had gone bad.

Unless she wanted to talk about Mad Dog.

Explaining his strong-arm tactics to the tenderhearted cream puff he'd nicknamed Twinkie, wouldn't *that* be fun? "What's on your mind?"

"I'd rather discuss it in person."

Fuck. "I'll be over in—"

"I'm already here."

"At the club?" He gave up and tugged on mismatched socks, jammed his feet in his black Skechers.

"I'm at the front door. It's locked."

"That's because the bar doesn't open until eleven."

"Who drinks at eleven in the morning?"

"Dedicated barflies."

"Do you have many of those?"

"Two. Vince and Ollie. Friends of Pops."

"Ah, yes. Well, now I have names to go with the faces." She cleared her throat. "So, is there another way to get up to your apartment? An exterior stairway? A hidden elevator?"

Last night he'd been ticked when she'd intimated she didn't want to be alone with him. Now he dreaded the private time. Evie represented man's best qualities—compassion, tolerance, integrity. Everything he'd pissed away when he'd held that gun to Mad Dog's head. "Do you mind talking in the bar?" he asked as he loped down the stairs. "My place is a mess." A lame excuse, but the bar was a less intimate environment. Right now, he needed to detach.

"Maybe we could walk and talk," she said. "It's a nice day."

He'd once dreamt about them rolling around in the sand and surf. A walk along the beach didn't strike him as a good idea. Again, too intimate. Besides, what if Crowe had assigned a man to watch his ass? The last time Evie had needed an urgent word with him, she'd ended up crying in his arms. He didn't want the AIA to view her as someone special in his life. For once, he agreed with Arch. The more people know about you, the more vulnerable you are. "Pops took the day off and The Kid is in The Cave."

Temples pounding, he punched the code into the security pad. "No one will bother us, if that's what you're worried about."

He opened the door and saw Evie pacing the board-walk, alternating between chewing her thumbnail and scratching her neck. She was definitely worried about *something*. He pocketed his cell phone and gave a short whistle.

She dropped her own phone in her purse and hurried toward him. She looked damn cute in her faded jeans and formfitting T-shirt, her blond hair blowing in the ocean breeze. But his cock didn't twitch in response as it had in the past.

Huh.

"I apologize for intruding so early in the morning," she said as she brushed past him, "but this is really important."

"I got that." He locked the door and followed her into the dimly lit bar. "If you want coffee—"

"No, thanks."

"Juice?"

"Water would be great."

He nabbed two bottles from the fridge behind the bar. "Sit? Stand? Pace?"

She plunked her cute butt on a stool. He slid her a water bottle and took up the position of the all-ears bartender. "Shoot."

"Tabasco slept with Jayne."

"Huh."

"As in seduced her. As in had *sex* with her."

"Understood."

She waited a beat then spread her hands. "Is that all you've got to say?"

"Obviously, you're not happy."

"*Happy?* Jayne was in Tabasco's care. He was… working. Chameleon's supposed to protect the innocent and vulnerable, not take advantage of them!"

Milo uncapped his water. "I've known Jimmy Tabasco for six years. I've never known him to take advantage of a woman. I understand your concern, but I'm giving him the benefit of the doubt."

"Meaning?"

"Meaning, he must like Jayne."

Her blue eyes widened and her voice jumped an octave. "What's not to like? She's a fascinating, delightful person!"

"I agree. And attractive." He took a hit of spring water then set the bottle aside. "I take it you spoke to Jayne."

"Just a while ago."

"Was she upset?"

"Only at me. She's angry because she thinks I should have approached her about Madame Helene personally, instead of dragging Chameleon into it."

"She feels betrayed."

"Yes."

"Only natural."

"I know, but…" Agitated, she scratched a hand through her hair. "Jayne doesn't typically do one-night stands."

"Neither does Tabasco."

"You're kidding."

"For men everywhere, let me say, ouch."

She angled her head side to side. "Okay. That was petty and narrow-minded. I admit it. It's just—"

"Jayne's your friend and you're worried about her. To which I say, Tabasco's my friend and the man's a veritable mother hen. Don't tell him I said that."

She drummed her fingers on the bar. "You're right.

He's a nice guy. A great guy. I'm just surprised they hooked up like that."

"Then you need to work on your observation skills, Twinkie. You didn't notice the way they looked at each other last night?"

"I noticed." She frowned. "I also noticed the tension between you and Nic. What's up with that?"

He didn't know where to begin. "It's complicated."

She pursed her pink glossed lips. "Maybe I can help you sort it out."

"Maybe." Probably wouldn't be wise to tell her he'd snooped into her friend's background. She'd view it as an invasion of privacy even though the information was available to anyone who knew where to look. "Last night Jayne mentioned Nic's unlucky-in-love streak. Elaborate."

"I'm not sure if Nic would approve."

"She doesn't have to know."

"That makes it worse." She blew out a breath, shrugged. "Given your resources, I'm sure you could find out anyway."

Smart girl.

She sipped her water and gathered her thoughts. "Okay. Here's the deal. Nic's a tough cookie, but on the inside? A marshmallow. Don't tell her I said that."

He smiled.

"She's the kind of woman other women love to hate. Tall, beautiful, exotic. Killer figure. Flawless taste in clothes. The kind of woman men drool over. The problem with that is, most of these men, or at least the ones who managed to seduce her, are only interested in sex. They couldn't deal with the fact that Nic actually has a brain. She's smart and opinionated. Probably too independent for her own good, but we've all got our quirks."

"Are you saying there wasn't one man with the cajones to pitch in for the long run?"

"There was one."

The doctor.

"He even asked her to marry him. But the longer they were together, the more he tried to control her. In the end, Brad turned out to be much like the other bastards who'd stomped on her heart. Mostly, he wanted a trophy wife."

That had to hurt. "So she broke the engagement."

Evie shook her head. "He did. Nic really loved Brad and never lost hope that they could come to terms. He crushed her spirit when he walked away. Since then…well, let's just say, she no longer trusts her taste in men. If she's attracted to him, he's Mr. Wrong."

Maybe you just haven't met the right man.

Go fuck yourself.

"Huh."

"Why are you so interested in Nic's love life?"

Tread lightly, Beckett. "I'm trying to figure out what makes her tick."

"Why?"

Good question. Two days ago, he was just another one of those *bastards* fantasizing about getting Nicole into bed. Something had shifted last night in the car when she'd given him a glimpse of the marshmallow within the tough cookie. "Let's just say it's a welcome diversion from my own problems."

She pondered that then regarded him with compassion. "You feel guilty about Mad Dog."

"I do." No sense denying it. Not that he wanted to talk about it. He dipped in his pocket for a Tylenol and came up empty. No pain relievers, so he grabbed the next best thing: a beer. Screw the early hour.

"I know the feeling," she said.

"How so?" He took a long pull from the bottle and watched while she stared down at the bar and fought not to scratch her neck.

After a long moment, she reestablished eye contact. "I need to ask you something, Beckett, and I need you to be totally honest."

He rolled back his shoulders and braced for, hell, he didn't know what. "Go ahead."

"Simon the Fish."

"What about him?"

"Knowing the circumstances, do you believe Arch? Do you think the shooting was accidental?"

Tricky territory, but at least it had saved him from having to further explain the friction between him and Nic. In truth, he'd pondered that shooting from the get-go. He'd out and out asked Arch if he'd gone into that sting with an eye-for-an-eye intent. His answer? No. But when Milo asked specifics about the actual clusterfuck, the Scot danced around the subject. Typical Arch. In the end, he'd concluded that, although Arch was close to amoral, the man wasn't capable of premeditated murder. Even so, Arch was lying about something although he didn't know what or why. "What's your beef, Twinkie?"

"I keep having these nightmares about the Fish. I feel guilty. Logically, I can make sense of it. I got nervous and cracked out of turn. Because of me, Simon got suspicious and the sting curdled. So ultimately, the shooting was my fault."

"I don't see it that way, but you would."

"What's that supposed to mean?"

"Hate to break it to you, sweetheart, but you're a big softy."

"Meaning I feel too deeply." She frowned. "Arch sees that as a detriment in this line of work."

"Maybe he's right." He expected her to stiffen her spine, instead her shoulders sagged.

"This morning Nic called me insensitive and Jayne accused me of being sneaky and manipulative. She said I've changed. I *have* changed." She palmed her heart. "I feel it. I'm more confident. More assertive. I thought that was a good thing."

The hurt in her eyes touched his heart. "It is a good thing."

"Arch once said that he's afraid I'll grow cynical if I'm subjected to the grifter's world day in, day out. I scoffed. But maybe there's something to that. I want to be a Chameleon. I want to work for the greater good. But how do I do that without turning into a cynical bitch?"

He couldn't suppress a smile. "Twinkie, you could never be a bitch. But, I won't lie, cynicism comes with the territory." The very reason she intrigued him. Her optimism and innate goodness brought sunshine into his dark world. Like Arch, he mourned the potential loss. Even so, he wasn't about to strip her of her scales.

"Arch said he and Simon grappled for the gun. It accidentally went off. Simon took a bullet and died. Simple as that."

"I got the same story." Milo had been escorted out of the room along with Gina moments before, so he hadn't witnessed the fiasco. He did, however, listen after the fact, along with the local authorities. Arch had been wearing a wire. He'd gotten the entire episode on tape. Chaos. Chaos that supported Arch's story. "Are you saying you remember it differently?"

"Every night. Well, not *every* night, but certainly every

time I dream about it." She picked at the water bottle's label. "At first I couldn't remember much of the incident at all. But it's been trickling back to me, only always in a different sequence. I can't seem to remember it straight and Arch won't help."

"He won't talk it out with you?"

"He wants me to put it out of my head."

Interesting.

She leaned forward, lowered her voice. "Here's the thing. I was also involved in that scuffle. I was disoriented because of a knock in the head, but I grappled, too. I was falling and I grabbed someone's hand. I think." She swallowed. "What if *I* somehow made the gun go off?"

The possibility turned his stomach. He was having a hard time knowing he may have killed Mad Dog and *he* was a trained, hardened agent. But Evie… Being responsible for someone's death, even if it were an accident, would crush her.

Was it possible? Was that why Arch avoided the subject? Was he protecting Evie? "I listened to that tape numerous times. I didn't hear anything that suggested the shooting didn't go down just as Arch described it." Milo could dance, too.

"But what if—"

"You could *what-if* your way into believing you're responsible for the national debt, Evie. The price you pay for that valuable imagination of yours. The fact is dreams aren't valid memories. They're your subconscious at play. They're rarely literal."

"You sound like Jayne."

He smiled, hoping to lighten the mood. He itched to listen to that tape with a new ear. He wanted to prove her wrong. "Would you feel better if I pushed the issue with Arch?" He'd do so, no matter what.

"Would you tell me if you learned something bad?"

He wasn't sure. "Depends."

"Not the answer I hoped for."

"But an honest one." He set aside the beer, squeezed her hand. "One thing you can count on, Twinkie. I'll never lie to you."

She squeezed back, her expression relaxing then turning somewhat quizzical. "Did you feel that?"

"Feel what?"

"Exactly." She slipped his grip and rounded the bar.

He stood stock-still as she came toe-to-toe. He raised a brow. "Want another water?"

"No. I want another kiss."

Nothing could have surprised him more. "Pardon?" This was the first time she'd acknowledged that ill-fated kiss had ever happened. Now she wanted a replay?

"That night. Arch accused you of making a play for me. You didn't deny it. And before that, there were moments I thought I sensed interest from you. Romantic interest." Her cheeks burned. "Am I wrong?"

"You're not wrong." At least he'd thought he'd been interested in a romantic relationship. Just now he couldn't wrap his mind around making love to Evie Parish. Cherishing her? Yes. Protecting her? Absolutely. Fucking her? Didn't compute though he couldn't pinpoint why. Maybe he was just unbalanced by her direct approach.

"I allowed that kiss to happen, because I was curious." She rushed on. "But it only made matters worse, because I felt a little zing. I'm head over heels in love with Arch, so you can imagine my confusion. Except now…"

"What?"

She invaded his personal space. "Kiss me."

He'd dreamt about this moment. So, why wasn't he

taking advantage? *Maybe because she out and out said she's in love with your partner, bonehead.* Right. Only he honestly believed Arch was going to screw things up. This was his chance to do as Nic had suggested. To play dirty and steal Evie away. It's what he wanted, *wasn't it?*

They moved into each other's arms at the same time. He slanted his mouth over hers, feasted on her lips. It was…nice.

She backed away, looking annoyed. "For crying out loud, kiss me like you mean it, Beckett. Rock my world."

No pressure there. But in that instant, Milo thought he sensed what Evie was onto. The sexual tension that had subtly vibrated between them for the past several weeks hadn't been present during this conversation. When he'd squeezed her hand, he hadn't felt anything beyond affection for a friend. *This* was about knowing for sure.

So he kissed her like a lover. Passionately. He moved his hands over her compact curves. Intimately. She responded in kind. Aggressively. For all their fervor, he should've taken her then and there on the bar…only Mr. Happy wasn't keyed into the action north of the belt. What the…?

A few seconds later the kiss fizzled and they both eased back. Their breathing was even. Her gaze was clear. His heartbeat was steady.

Well, damn.

Evie spoke first. "You're a good kisser, Beckett."

"But I didn't rock your world."

"Please don't be insulted, but I'm happy to say I'm not the least bit dizzy."

"Don't be insulted, but you didn't exactly get a rise out of me."

She smiled. "The best news I've heard all day."

Stunned by this sudden development, Milo leaned back against the bar. "When did it fizzle for you? When you learned about Mad Dog?"

"I won't lie. It did make me see you a little differently. Knowing you're capable of violence. Although, Nic logically pointed out, it's what you've been trained to do. I just never thought of you as having a darker side."

"You and me both. I've always thought of myself as the good guy. Yet I allowed myself to be coerced into doing the senator's dirty work. It's a hell of a wake-up call."

"Nic thinks you were set up and so do I. The other team members are working hard to get to the truth. You're going to come out on the right side, Beckett."

He smiled. "That's what I like about you, Twinkie. Your unwavering belief that good conquers evil."

She angled her head. "Maybe that was the attraction."

"Definitely part of it. That and your determination. Not to mention you're cute as hell."

She batted her eyelashes and grinned. "Ya think?"

He chuckled and tugged at his earlobe. "Wow. When did we become *just* friends?"

"Haven't you ever been physically attracted to someone when you first laid eyes on them, but then as you got to know them, the attraction flatlined? I've had that happen with cast members in plays, fellow musicians. An initial *zing,* then nothing. Familiarity breeds—"

"Friendship?"

"Some friendships last longer than most marriages."

Milo toasted her with his beer bottle. "Here's to a long and loyal friendship."

Smiling, she touched her Evian to his Heineken.

He palmed his cell. "Do me a favor."

"Anything for a friend."

He keyed the newest number in his speed-dial and passed the phone to Evie. "Tell Nic what you just told me."

CHAPTER SEVENTEEN

FRIENDSHIP IS A MANY SPLENDID, and sometimes tricky, thing. I blinked at my new friend and considered an old friend. I stopped the call before it went through and passed the phone back to Beckett. "I don't mind sharing this development with Nic, but I'd rather tell her in person." At least if I told her face-to-face, she wouldn't be able to hang up on me. I'd have a chance to make her see reason. Maybe. She was PMSing after all. Or so she'd said.

Less than an hour ago she'd pushed me to drop Arch for Beckett. Instead, I'd cleared up the confusion. Beckett was no longer a contender for my affection. We'd kissed the hell out of one another but there'd been no heat. No *zing*, let alone *zing, zap*.

Beckett attributed my sudden disinterest to the fact that he'd fallen off his pedestal, but I think it had more to do with my deepening love for Arch. The man had promised to woo me and over the past two weeks, even though we'd been on the job three-quarters of the time, he'd done exactly that. I think the clincher had been last night when he admitted to being on the West Coast. There was a time he wouldn't have even told me that much. *Need to know basis, Sunshine.* Or maybe it was when he asked me to move in with him.

Things were far from perfect, but they were improving

and we were moving forward. All this time I'd questioned Arch's ability to commit. Like I wasn't hedging with my confusion about Beckett? Only now I wasn't confused. Evie loves Arch. Arch loves Evie. And if we didn't screw it up, we'd get our very own happily ever after.

As for Beckett…I couldn't help wondering if his interest in Nic's affairs went deeper than needing a distraction. The tension I'd felt between them, was it sexual? When they'd first met I'd sensed an attraction on Nic's part, but she'd denied it.

What if?

I studied the man while finishing off my water. "Why are you so eager for me to tell Nic we're officially just friends?"

He didn't hesitate. "So she'll get off my ass. If she had her way, I'd whisk you off to Vegas and put a ring on your finger. Pronto."

Even though Nic and I were currently on the outs, I felt compelled to defend her. "She just wants me to be happy. She thinks you're a straight-up guy. Arch? Not so much."

"Hate to tell you this, Twinkie, but her concern is grounded. Granted, Arch has changed, but he hasn't reformed. To reform, one has to admit he did something wrong. Ask Arch about any of his past cons and he'll put the blame on the mark."

I wanted to curse him for raining on my parade, but like Nic, I knew he meant well. "But he's not grifting anymore." At least to my knowledge.

"That wasn't my point, and you know it." His phone rang. After a glance at caller ID, he answered. "What's up, Kid?" His expression turned stony. "You already called the rest of the team? Uh-huh. No, don't worry about it. She's with me. We'll be right down." He disconnected and steered me toward the storage room. "Kid tried to call you. Did you turn off your cell?"

"No." Oh, crap. "But I did forget to charge it."

Beckett didn't say anything. He didn't have to. What if there'd been an emergency? A family crisis? An urgent Chameleon matter? "Woody dug up something on Crowe, didn't he?"

He whisked me down the stairs, toward the sliding snack shelves. "He did."

"COPRODEM." BECKETT SHOOK his head. "Never heard of it. What's it mean?"

"Don't know, sir." Woody got up from mission control and sat in a chair across from his boss. "But I can tell you *what* it is. A unit of unknown numbers, even more covert than Chameleon."

"What's their purpose?"

"According to the official mission statement—*to expose, discredit, or otherwise neutralize enemies of the State in order to maintain moral, social and political order.*"

Beckett frowned. "That sounds familiar. What do they do specifically?"

"I'm not sure."

"Maybe this meeting was premature."

"Covert Production Emissaries." I glanced up from the notepad I'd been scribbling on. "Sorry. Didn't mean to interrupt. But COPRODEM is likely an acronym. You know, like NASA or NATO." I loved this stuff. CIA, FBI, AIA. At first I'd thought Arch was a Bond-like super spy with an MI6. "Or maybe Covert Program…for Democrats? Wait. *Demarche.* Covert Program for Demarche."

"What's that mean?" Woody asked.

"In this instance," said Beckett, "*demarche* would be a political maneuver, a course of action. Impressed you know the term, Twinkie."

"Read it in a Regency romance novel. You'd be surprised what you can learn…never mind. Anyway, I'm thinking *covert* since Woody said…" I looked at them looking at me. "Never mind."

"No. It's good," Beckett said. "Keep at it."

My heart fluttered, not because of his smile, but because I'd contributed something to this meeting. I felt a little less like the untrained newbie, more confident in my Chameleon scales.

Just then Tabasco strode in. "I know why we're here. I just have to say this first." He sat beside me on the leather sofa, raked his fingers through his damp hair. He smelled of herbal shampoo and Tibetan incense. Jayne scents. "She got under my skin. I've never… It was… You're going to be seeing a lot of me."

"Okay." I didn't know what else to say. He seemed rattled. Like Jayne had knocked him for a loop. It was sort of sweet. "Heard you convinced her Madame Helene's a fake."

"It wasn't easy, but, yes. Doesn't mean I vanquished her belief in the supernatural though."

I smiled. Jayne wouldn't be Jayne if you stripped her of her spiritual beliefs. "I'm sort of glad. I mean it's not *all* hooey, right?" Fighting cynicism, I clung to the possibility that *some* spiritualist *somewhere* might be the real deal.

Tabasco and Beckett traded a look.

Cynics. "Never mind." I returned to my acronym.

"When The Kid's finished with his report," Beckett said to Tabasco, "I want a full update on Madame Helene."

"Will do, Jazzman." He leaned back against the sofa. "So what have we got?"

Woody filled him in.

"What am I supposed to do with that?"

"I know it's not much," said Woody, "but I've only been at it for twenty-four hours. The files on COPRODEM are classified. I'm still trying to crack a few passwords and codes. I can tell you this. COPRODEM is Crowe's pet project."

"Not Chameleon?" Tabasco pressed a hand to his heart. "I'm crushed."

"Did you get the names of any of the agents assigned to this special unit?" Beckett asked.

Woody scratched his scruffy beard. "I don't think he uses company men for this project."

"Independent contractors?"

"People who don't mind getting their hands dirty."

"Are you suggesting Crowe's abusing his power?"

"Of course he's abusing his power," I said, thinking about the men he'd instructed to cover up Mad Dog's death. "He tampered with a crime scene." My imagination revved as I got caught up in the sort of pulse-tripping intrigue indicative of spy thrillers. Only this was real life. My life. *Zowie.*

"You said Crowe mentioned hiring agents to keep tabs on us in Hammond," Tabasco said to Beckett. "Those same men tailed you to Mad Dog's and covered up your alleged crime. What if they weren't with the AIA? What if they're rogue operatives working for COPRODEM?"

"What if Vincent Crowe's a throwback to J. Edgar Hoover?" I asked. My heart pounded as a conspiracy theory rooted and spun out of control. I expected all three men to roll their eyes, but they angled their heads in interest. "A few months ago, I was watching this show with Nic," I explained. "I'm not into politics or the antics of political leaders, past or present, but she is. Anyway, this particular documentary was about the former director of the FBI. Given the business you're in, I'm sure you're all acquainted with Hoover's questionable practices—the gathering of derogatory information? Information he used to control people?"

Beckett nodded. "Keep going."

I got a heady rush, similar to when I used to brainstorm on a new stage show. The creative juices were flowing and my new fellow cast members were open to my ideas. Jazzed, I abandoned the notepad and copied Beckett's stance, forearms on knees. "Think about it. This whole thing about Chameleon utilizing their skills to win back the money Senator Clark's wife lost? It was kind of cheesy, right? Those two come from old money. Big money. They couldn't afford a ten-thousand dollar loss? I understand that Clark doesn't want it to get out that his wife has a gambling problem. He has a career to protect. So he goes to Crowe and asks for help. Why Crowe? Maybe Crowe buddied up to him at some event and said, *'If you ever need a favor…'* Blah, blah, blah. Or maybe Crowe is earning a reputation within political circles as some sort of *go-to, save-your-butt* kind of man."

Beckett considered. "Interesting."

That one-word response buzzed through my body like adrenaline. My imagination soared. "What if Crowe saw Clark's dilemma as a way of controlling a potential U.S. President? I know we touched on the fact that Crowe now has something on both you and Clark, but break it down then go beyond."

I paused for dramatic effect, plus, I needed to catch my

breath. This discussion equaled a roller-coaster rush. "Crowe not only knows about Mrs. Clark's gambling problem, he's privy to a sordid connection between the senator and a chiseler. In order to protect his political career, Senator Clark asked Crowe to make Mad Dog disappear. Or maybe Crowe was the one who suggested it, and Clark agreed only because he thought what you thought—that *disappear* meant leaving the country, not this earth. Bottom line—Mad Dog's dead, along with Clark's career should anyone learn about the connection."

Beckett arched a sardonic brow. "I wonder when and how Crowe broke the news of Mad Dog's demise to Clark. Naturally he'd remind the good senator of his dealings with me, the money that changed hands. Clark did, after all, compensate me for our hotel and travel expenses as well as staking us for those poker games. I can hear the spin now. Similar to the shit he fed me. *Don't worry, Senator. We've got you covered.* With the underlying implication, *I've got you by the short hairs.*"

"Moving beyond," I said, jazzed that he was taking me seriously, "what if Senator Clark runs for president and *wins?* Isn't it possible that Crowe could somehow use the Mad Dog fiasco to influence some of Clark's decisions? And move beyond *that.* What if this isn't the first time Crowe's done a *favor* for a politician? What if, like Hoover, he has a file of dirty secrets?"

Tabasco looked at Beckett. "The gathering of salacious material intended to be used as blackmail? Sort of like that DVD Crowe has of you offing Mad Dog?"

"A DVD that could have been doctored," Woody reminded them.

Beckett chewed the inside of his cheek. I heard his wheels turning, heard the *ah-hah* when something clicked.

"Now I know why COPRODEM's mission statement sounded familiar. It's a bastardized version of the FBI's motivation in the 1960s along with the goals of COINTEL-PRO."

Tabasco closed his eyes. "Holy shit."

I'd heard the term on that documentary, but Woody looked clueless.

"COINTELPRO was the brainchild of J. Edgar Hoover," Beckett clarified. "It stands for *Counter Intelligence Program.* A secret task force that investigated and neutralized dissident political organizations within the United States. Targets included everyone from the Black Panthers to Martin Luther King, Jr."

Woody slumped back against his chair. "Oh, man."

"What if Crowe actually *has* a Hoover fixation?" Beckett asked, jumping on my brainstorming bandwagon. "Though criticized by some for his methods, there are those who still view the infamous FBI director as an icon. If you asked Hoover himself, he'd probably say he played dirty for the greater good."

"Oh, yeah," Tabasco bit off, "he did a lot of good in the fifties when he ruined countless lives with his Communist witch hunt."

The Kid's pale complexion brought me down to earth. I realized the enormity and potential danger of my flight of fancy. "I could be wrong. I'm probably wrong."

Woody slid me a worried look. "But what if you're right? What if Director Crowe's a ruthless control freak?"

I felt a little ill. When I'd wiggled my way into Chameleon I'd anticipated participating in stings that brought down the bad guys, only I never imagined the bad guys being within our own government. This was huge. And scary. *"If Chameleon goes head-to-head with the director*

of the AIA, things could get dangerous, you know?" And
how. "I wish Arch was here." He would know what to say,
what to do. He always did.

I didn't realize I'd voiced my thought until Woody responded. "Ace is on his way. ETA, 4:00 p.m."

The wall slid open and my heart leapt. Had he taken an
earlier flight? My excitement was short-lived. Gina Valente slithered in. Okay. She didn't slither. She walked. But
it was hard for me to be kind knowing she'd slept with
Arch. I was jealous. I admit it. Not only was she young
and beautiful, she was smart and savvy. An ex-cop, she
was twenty times more qualified to work for Chameleon
than me. No wonder she resented my being a part of the
team.

"Sorry, I'm late," she said. "I took extra precautions
to make sure I wasn't being tailed. While trying to save
one friend," she said, eying Beckett, "I may have put another at risk."

Woody groaned. "Between you and Twinkie, I'm going
to have nightmares tonight."

Without looking at me she settled on the other side of
Tabasco. "What's he talking about?"

Beckett massaged his temples. "Evie has a theory."

"I'm sure it's fascinating." She may as well have rolled
her eyes. "But it can't be near as mindfucking as the truth."

Okay. That was rude. That was…challenging. But I
refused to rise to the bait. I'd just contributed a kick-butt
scenario. One that had fueled valid conversation and
concerns. Needing a moment to cool my jets, I sought out
The Cave's kitchenette. Thankfully, Woody had brewed a
pot of bean juice and it didn't smell too strong or stale.
Don't lower yourself to a catfight. Be cagey and confident.

Be a Chameleon. I stuck my head out of the tiny room. "Coffee anyone? Gina? How would you like yours?"

She glanced my way. She didn't smile, but she didn't glare, either. "One sugar, please. Thanks."

"Sure." Since everyone else asked for theirs black, it didn't take me long to pour and serve. I was surprised at the dead air. Were they waiting on me before resuming the discussion? Tabasco scooted over to make room for me. Woody looked at me with something akin to awe. Beckett winked. For the first time since I'd joined the team, I actually felt like I belonged. No one could spoil this moment. Not even Gina "Hot Legs" Valente.

Looking a little exhausted but still gotta-hate-her-gorgeous, the Chameleon I'd once dubbed Mata Hari leaned forward, expression intense. "Okay. Here's what I got. Don't ask how."

CHAPTER EIGHTEEN

"ACCORDING TO MY SOURCE, Crowe's collecting sordid material on various officials in the executive, legislative, *and* judicial branches. Typical scandal-sheet material. Alcohol and drug addictions. Extramarital affairs. Domestic employment of illegal aliens. Misappropriated funds. He's got conversations on tape. Documentations. Incriminating photos and videos." Gina eyeballed Beckett. "Made me think of you and that DVD. Anyway, Crowe enlisted one AIA operative and an assistant to oversee a special unit. They farm out the dirty work to a select group of independent contractors, one of whom is my source."

No one said anything. We just stared. I ping-ponged between horror that my Hoover scenario was grounded in reality and sheer joy that my Hoover scenario was grounded in reality. My signature happy dance seemed childish, not to mention inappropriate given this was a blow for our country. The director of the AIA was a bad sort. How bad, I didn't know.

"I didn't expect a round of applause, but some feedback would be nice," Gina said. "What the hell's wrong with you?"

The question wasn't directed at any one person, but Beckett stepped up to the plate. "That theory I mentioned of Evie's? I think we're all a little stunned that it's actually the mindfucking truth."

Gina gawked at me. "You *guessed* that Crowe's collecting incriminating evidence on key officials? Based on what?"

Okay. This was uncomfortable. Or rather Gina made me uncomfortable. She'd never liked me and now I'd stolen her thunder. This could get ugly. Or…maybe I could win her over. Life as a Chameleon would be easier if I earned her respect. *Cagey and confident.* "Woody learned about COPRODEM while trying to gain access to some top secret files, but he didn't learn specifics."

"Yet," he added, sounding insulted.

"He didn't mention COPRODEM when he called you?" I asked Gina.

"No. For the same reason I didn't share my news over the phone. You never know who's listening."

"Oh." I should've known. Not that I'd received official training or even a handbook on secret agent, antigrifting do's and don'ts. Still, I *have* watched a ton of spy flicks. "Anyway, I took what little Woody did know and what we'd determined about Crowe during our last meeting, in addition to a documentary I'd seen on J. Edgar Hoover and I…"

She arched a brow. "Yes?"

"Used my imagination."

I waited for her to make a snide comment. Instead, she borrowed from Beckett. "Huh." She glanced down and saw the scribbled acronyms on my notepad. "Is this your work?"

I stiffened my spine. "Yes."

"Close, but no cigar."

Amazingly, it didn't sound like an insult. "You know what COPRODEM stands for?" I asked.

"Covert Protection of Democracy."

I blinked. "Wow. I *was* close."

Her full lips curled into a semblance of a smile. "Guess Ace was right. You're not just a piece of fluff."

My heart swelled to the size of a cantaloupe: a) because Gina had just paid me a compliment. Sort of, b) because Arch had championed me. More than ever I wished he was here. Even though he wasn't keen on me being an active member of Chameleon, surely he'd be proud that I'd managed to impress everyone in the room, including my arch rival.

"Not to ruin this beautiful moment," Beckett said, tongue in cheek, "but if you've got more, Hot Legs, bring it on. The more we know, the better, obviously."

Curious, I nodded in agreement.

Gina sipped her coffee then picked up where she'd left off. "According to my source, Crowe claims he founded this unit to protect politicians and various VIPs from their own moral missteps."

"Their mission statement's a whole lot wordier," Woody said.

"The bullshit factor is off the chart," Gina said. "Bottom line, and my source only recently figured this out, Crowe covers for certain VIPs and confronts others. My guy, let's call him Syd, didn't use the word *blackmail,* but he did call Crowe a master of manipulation."

I'd always associated that phrase with Arch. Just now it sent a chill down my spine.

"So it's fact. Crowe's using his 'dirty files' to control powerful people," said Beckett. "People like Senator Clark."

"And you," she added. "He's kept a low profile thus far, but he's gearing up for something big," Gina said.

I leaned forward in anticipation and nearly fell off the couch. Luckily no one was paying me any mind. Everyone, including me, had glommed on to Gina.

"Lately, he's been concentrating on those who've declared interest in running in the next presidential election. Right now, Crowe's got dirt on three potential candidates, including Senator Clark, and he's digging, looking for ways to get his hooks into more."

Pensive, Beckett eased back in his chair. "No matter who's elected, Crowe wins. If he's allied with the president, he can use his contacts and propaganda to advance the president's policies. If he disagrees with our elected leader's agenda—"

"The exact opposite," said Tabasco. "This is bad."

"Bad?" The national anthem welled in my head, inspiring a patriotic rant. "It's unacceptable!" I couldn't believe my ears. "Doesn't Crowe answer to anyone? Isn't there some sort of check-and-balance system? You'd think after the Hoover debacle, something like COPRODEM would be frowned upon."

"Illegal or deceptive operations by various government officials and agencies fly under the radar every day," said Tabasco. "Once in awhile they get outed—Pentagon Papers, Watergate, Iran-Contra Affair—but not always."

"And sometimes they're outed but not prosecuted," said Beckett, "due to insufficient evidence."

"That's horrible!"

"That's life," Gina said. "Welcome to the real world, Twinkie."

"Believe me," Beckett said, "if the appropriate people were savvy to COPRODEM and privy to damning evidence, Crowe's ass would be in a sling."

"He gave the program a flag-waving name and mission

statement and buried the 'dirty files' deep," said Woody. "What a sneak."

Gina pulled an elastic band from her jeans' pocket and pulled her long hair into a let's-get-down-to-business ponytail. "The point is, we can use this information to get Beckett out of hot water."

"I'm not the priority here," he said. "Knowing what we know, we need to expose Crowe to protect the integrity of our political system."

"Noble," said Tabasco, "but out of our league."

"Don't be a weenie," I said, hopped up on righteousness. "Our country needs us."

Gina rolled her eyes, but she didn't disagree.

"Just think of Crowe as a mark," Beckett said. "All we need is a come-on."

"Why can't *Syd* just out him?" I asked. "Leak info about COPRODEM to the press or something?"

"Because *Syd* doesn't want to end up with a bullet in the back of his head," Gina said. "Remember, Crowe's got numerous people in his back pocket. Syd's one guy. But luckily, he's a well-connected, deviously talented guy. He's committed to helping us nail the bastard, but at best he's our inside-man, not our savior."

"Do I know him?" Beckett asked.

"No."

"Liar."

"You wouldn't believe me if I told you," said Gina. "Not that I have any intention of divulging my source."

Tabasco leaned into her. "I bet I know."

"I bet you don't."

"I'll find out."

"No, you won't."

Tabasco grinned. "Challenge accepted."

I'd been drifting, my mind spinning on Beckett's suggestion that we think of the AIA director as a mark. "I think I know how we can rope Crowe. Just a suggestion," I added when Gina slid me a look.

"Let me guess," she said. "We provide him with the means to get dirt on another one of the presidential hopefuls."

Well, darn.

"The obvious solution," said Beckett, "and a smart one."

Okay. That was sweet. That took the sting out of Gina's zinger, although she hadn't been cruel, just honest. It *was* the obvious solution. Manipulating the manipulator.

"We pitch the come-on, rope him, and set up a sting that will result in Crowe exposing his criminal intentions," Beckett said. "On tape."

"Hard evidence," said Tabasco.

"Syd's also working to see what he can learn about the Mad Dog cover-up."

"Sounds like Syd's got an in with Crowe," Beckett said, "or someone else within the Agency."

Gina shrugged. "Let's just say he's been around a long time."

Beckett narrowed his eyes. "Why would your source risk his neck for me?"

"He's not," she said. "He's doing this for me."

"Huh."

Tabasco got that mother-hen look. "Sure you know what you're doing?"

She smirked. "Call me the puppet master."

Meaning she was in control. Of the situation. Of Syd. Call me crazy, but I didn't believe her. Something— women's intuition?—told me she'd put herself out there big-time. Physically? Emotionally? I didn't know, but Gina vibrated with a subtle vulnerability I'd never sensed before.

Woody rose and headed for the console. "I'll start researching potential candidates, see if I can identify any weaknesses or quirks that will work to our advantage."

"Senator Wilson," I blurted.

Woody turned and looked at me.

"A democrat from Connecticut," I added.

"What about him?" asked Beckett.

"He has a quirk."

"What kind of quirk?" Gina asked.

"He consults an astrologer. That's quirky, don't you think? For a politician?"

"Franklin D. Roosevelt conferred with a psychic about post-WWII world relations," said Beckett. "Abraham Lincoln participated in séances and experienced visions. Woodrow Wilson…" He trailed off, after noting everyone's curious expression. "Recently watched a documentary on the subject."

With Nic? I wondered. *Hmm.*

"After the assassination attempt on President Reagan," Tabasco said, "the First Lady contacted a psychic asking if she could have foreseen the attempt on her husband's life."

"Joan Quigley," said Gina. "Knowing a good opportunity when she heard it, the noted psychic answered, yes. Mrs. Reagan ended up relying on Quigley for astrological advice throughout the rest of Reagan's terms."

"Definitely raised some eyebrows," said Tabasco. He drummed his fingers on his thigh. "A psychic angle. Interesting. Crowe could feasibly work that angle to smear or control Wilson."

"I don't know much about Senator Wilson. Certainly didn't know about his psychic interests." Beckett eyed me. "Thought you weren't interested in politics."

"I'm not."

"So you heard about Wilson's quirk from Nic."

"No. Jayne."

Tabasco scrunched his nose. "Jayne's interested in politics?"

"Only when it concerns electing the leader of our country. Somewhere or another she read about Wilson's interest in astrology. Guess who she'll be voting for?"

"Unbelievable." Gina sipped more coffee. "What else do we know about Senator Wilson?"

Silence.

Woody started clicking away at his keyboard. "On it."

Beckett asked Tabasco for an update on Madame Helene.

I only half listened, marveling over how so many parts of my life had intertwined. Jayne and Tabasco. Beckett and maybe Nic. Hoover and Crowe. Senator Wilson and Madame Helene. Talk about weird.

"Talk about destiny," I could hear Jayne say to which Nic would say *"bullshit."*

"What if we roped Crowe by introducing him to a so-called psychic?" I mused out loud. "Someone famous like Sylvia Evans. Or someone on the rise like Madame Helene? Someone the public perceives as all-knowing, but who we know, and hence Crowe knows, is crooked. Someone he could use to hook and manipulate Senator Wilson."

They didn't speak up, but they didn't say no, so I kept rolling. "What if Tabasco appropriates some place for us to use as the 'big store'? You know a location—"

"Tricked out to look like a real-life setting," said Tabasco. "We know."

I smiled. "Right. Anyway, maybe we could use some of those tricks Sylvia Evans used—hidden cameras and mics, stuff like that. Maybe you could teach me some of the gimmicks and tricks used by frauds like Madame Helene. What if—"

"Hold up." Beckett frowned. "What do you mean teach *you?*"

I didn't miss a beat. I was in my old element, plus, my *new* element. I was in Chameleon mode. *Cagey. Confident.* "You can't send in an actual psychic. It has to be someone you trust implicitly. One of us. A woman would be best, so that narrows it down to Gina and me. Crowe knows about her. He doesn't know me. Plus she's working the Syd angle. I'm a trained actress and a quick study. I vote for me."

"I second that vote," Gina said. "If anyone can pull off a star-gazing kook, it's Twinkie."

"Thanks. I think."

This time she gave up an honest smile. "Play to your strengths, right?"

"Right." There was a time I would've thought she was setting me up for a fall, but not this time. There was too much at stake. Also, something had shifted between us. Just like things had shifted between Beckett and me. Two life-altering "snaps" in the same day. My mind reeled. It wasn't even noon.

My heart pounded as I waited for Beckett to approve my plan. Before now I'd always been relegated to the sidekick, the shill. This was my chance to perform a starring role. To prove that I had the chops to be a full-fledged field agent. I had to do this for myself. For my country. And okay, to prove something to Arch.

Beckett rose from his chair, worked a kink from his neck. "Not saying yes, not saying no. Not saying anything until I speak with Arch. I want his input before we move forward."

Crap.

He moved away to have a word with Woody. Tabasco patted my knee, one of those *nice try* kinds of pats, before joining the men at the console.

I envisioned the psychic role going to an independent contractor. Someone with more grifting experience than me. Someone they'd used before. My stomach cramped with a premonition of rejection.

Gina leaned into me. "My advice? Beat Beckett to the punch. Only seduce Ace first, then spring your idea."

I narrowed my eyes. "The last time I took your advice, Arch had an allergic reaction to me."

"Just so you know, an apology is not forthcoming."

"Just so you know, I wasn't holding my breath."

We smiled at the same time.

"Take my advice," she said.

"I can't," I said. "Using sex to get my way, doesn't sit right with me."

"Doesn't bother me one bit."

"Liar."

She opened her mouth then closed it. She looked at me through wary eyes. "Anyone ever tell you, you're a pain in the ass?"

"Yeah. Arch."

"You mean you're making his life hell?" She chuckled and rose. "So there is some justice in this world."

CHAPTER NINETEEN

BY THE TIME I LEFT THE Chameleon Club, shopping for home decor was the last thing on my mind. Strike that. It didn't make the list at all. I had more important things to do. Like protect my country from a devious government official. Only I couldn't do that until Beckett gave my suggested sting—code name: Aquarius—the thumbs-up. *That* wouldn't happen until he got the thumbs-up from Arch. I told myself Beckett wasn't questioning my ability to pull off the role of the psychic as much as the viability of the plan itself. I told myself not to obsess. Or stress. The only way to avoid that was to occupy my time and thoughts with other matters.

Like dropping Nic's car at her condo and informing her that Beckett and I were officially "just friends." I called ahead and got her answering machine. "Nic, it's me. Hello? I know you're there. You said you weren't going anywhere today. Nic?"

She didn't pick up.

"So what? You're not talking to me now? Okay. Listen. I don't know why we're fighting but I don't like it. I'm coming over to discuss this in person."

I arrived five minutes later and knocked on her door.

She didn't answer.

What the heck? I knocked again. I called again. If she

was in there, she was ignoring me. I couldn't imagine. It wasn't her style. She must have gone out. Since I had her car, someone must have picked her up. Jayne? The thought of those two banding together to discuss my new supposed flaws chafed. It hurt, too. I didn't want to believe it. Instead, I told myself Nic was strolling the beach, getting some fresh air and exercise. She lived a stone's throw from the ocean and spent a lot of time there when the weather was nice. It was certainly nice today.

I redialed. "Okay. Last message. Since you're not here, I'm going to leave your car keys under the rear right floor mat. Thanks for the use of your wheels. Tabasco's giving me a lift home. The auto shop promised my car would be finished sometime today, so I'm set. Speaking of Tabasco, interesting development between him and Jayne. Call me for details, unless of course you already spoke to her and aren't speaking to me. Remind me again why we're fighting?"

I signed off with a heavy heart and schlepped back to the parking lot. After hiding Nic's keys, I slid into the passenger seat of Tabasco's car. "Thanks for waiting."

"You call thirty seconds waiting?"

"Nic wasn't home."

"So you'll catch up with her later."

"Right."

He hit the gas and zipped along the main drag at least ten miles over the twenty-five mile an hour speed limit. If I were at the wheel, sirens would be whirring.

I chewed my thumbnail contemplating my inability to bend or break rules without feeling the heat. That included meddling in a friend's life. "You discredit Madame Helene and yet Jayne's mad at me. How does that work exactly?"

"You're asking me to understand the mysterious workings of a lady's mind?"

"Good point. So, just how mad is she? Do you think she'll forgive me in this lifetime?"

His lip quirked.

"What?"

"This isn't about you."

Words failed as I flashed on a time when Arch had said something similar. It made me feel shallow and self-centered. I hate that.

"Transference," he said.

"What?"

"Jayne isn't mad at you, Twinkie. She's mad at herself."

I thought about that. It made sense. I'd felt the same way after I learned I'd been duped by a street hustler in the Caribbean. Seriously, who falls for the old "Rocks in the Box" scam? Lots of people, apparently. People like me. People enticed by a bargain. Arch calls it "Good Deal" syndrome. I call it stupid. Or rather I *felt* stupid. I'm betting Jayne felt the same when Tabasco exposed Madame Helene for a charlatan. She was kicking herself but taking it out on me. Which wasn't wholly unreasonable since I did set her up for the fall. Well, darn.

"Thanks for putting it in perspective," I said, and relaxed against the seat. I knew Jayne. She wasn't petty or vengeful. All would be right between us…soon.

"About tomorrow night," he said.

"What about it?"

"It's our first performance together. I know we've been shedding on our own and we've run most of the songs to establish the key and arrangement, but we should probably squeeze in at least one solid rehearsal."

"Probably." Although my heart wasn't in it. I wanted

to research crystal-ball gazing, astrology, and Senator
Martin Wilson. I wanted to prepare for Arch's arrival, not
opening night at the Chameleon Club. I could perform at
least fifty percent of our eclectic song list in my sleep. As
for the other half, I felt just confident enough with the
material to wing it. No way, no how could I wing a performance as a *"star-gazing kook."*

"We could rehearse now," Tabasco said as he veered
into my parking lot. "I have my guitar in the trunk."

"Shouldn't you be doing whatever it is you do in preparation of a sting?"

"Until I have specifics—"

"Beckett told you to keep an eye on me, didn't he?"

"Until Arch gets back, yes."

His honesty caught me off guard. Then again, Tabasco
was the least complicated, most forthright member of Chameleon. I was curious about his background, but, since I
wanted to be alone, now wasn't the time to ask. "Crowe
doesn't know about me," I said reasonably. "He doesn't
know Beckett took me on as a team player. If he had me
investigated at all, he thinks I'm an entertainer. A lounge
lizard hired to perform in a seedy bar, not that the Chameleon Club's seedy."

He slid me a look.

"Okay. It's seedy. My point is, if Crowe sent lackeys to
spy on anyone, they're spying on Beckett or an established team member. Like you. So you see, actually, I'd
be safer if you buzzed off. No offense."

He smiled. "You talk a good game, Twinkie."

"Not good enough. You're unfastening your seat belt."

"At least let me come in and give the place a once-over."

The thought of some thug hiding in my closet gave me
the chills. I almost relented, but it made me feel like a

wimp. Gina wouldn't need a bodyguard. I touched his arm. "You're being overly cautious, Tabasco. No one's lurking in my apartment, and if they are I'll…"

"Yes?"

Run? "Hit them with something."

"That would only make them mad." He reached over and nabbed something from his glove compartment. "This," he said as he pressed a palm-sized canister in my hand, "is Mace Pepper Spray. Someone attacks you, you press here. Spray him directly in the face then run."

That last part sounded good. "Mace makes your eyes tear, right?"

"That's putting it mildly. The OC pepper causes the eyes to automatically shut and spurs uncontrollable coughing, choking, and the sensation of suffocating. Most people freak out."

"Sounds awful."

"CN tear gas causes intense tearing, burning to the face and eyes, and disorientation. And the UV dye—"

"There's more?"

"—marks the attacker. Something that could prove useful later as a means of identification."

He may as well have handed me a loaded gun. The thought of causing another human being harm made me ill. Still, if I didn't take it, he wouldn't leave. And, being an intelligent person, I wasn't about to pass up a chance to protect myself from a dangerous lunatic. Not that I thought Crowe enlisted lunatics per se, but I could imagine.

I closed my fingers around the canister. "Aim, spray, run. Got it. Stop looking so glum," I said as I opened the door. "I'll be fine. Besides, Arch should be here in a few hours. Until then, I'll lock myself in my apartment. I have a lot of research to do if I'm going to pull off this psychic gig."

"That's assuming Ace and Jazzman give your 'Aquarius' plan the thumbs-up."

"It's a good plan," I said, trying not to look or sound churlish.

"I agree. That's why I'm going to spend the afternoon scouting a location for the big store."

"Your faith gives me hope." Smiling, I scooted out and waved goodbye.

"I'll wait until you're inside and wait another five," he called. "If I don't hear you screaming bloody murder, I'll take off."

"Mother hen," I mumbled under my breath, but honestly his protective streak was sweet. I thought about Jayne. I thought about Tabasco and Jayne. Oddly, they made a good match. Armed with Mace Pepper Spray and a boatload of determination, I slipped into my apartment and, after ensuring I was indeed alone, recharged my phone and fired up my computer.

IN THE TWO HOURS THAT PASSED, Beckett called to check up on me. Tabasco called to check up on me. Even my mom called to touch base, not that she knew I was mixed up in anything dangerous. She just wanted to know how I was doing and to ask if the *baron* and I had set a date yet. I tap-danced around that and asked if she and Dad were still planning a second honeymoon. She thrilled me by sharing details. Our discussion left me with the warm fuzzies and had me wishing Nic and Jayne would call so we could make amends.

Mostly, I'd been too immersed in my research to lament my friends' silent treatment. At least I think they were snubbing me. "Stop making this about you," I said, because Arch wasn't here to say it. Maybe they were busy. Running errands. Working out at the gym. Singing "Happy Birthday" dressed as Wonder Woman. "Yeah. That's it."

I glanced back at my computer screen. Jupiter, the planet of good fortune, stared back. Along with a lengthy description regarding its benefits, of which there were many. Each planet in our solar system had benefits. Each planet circled the zodiac for different lengths of time and stayed in each sign for varying periods. And this was only one aspect of astrology. There were the planets, the elements, the three qualities, and the twelve sectors.

Brain full, I broke into song. *"When the moon is in the Seventh House…"* I wondered if Tabasco would mind adding The Fifth Dimension's rendition of "Age of Aquarius" to our repertoire.

My phone rang. I glanced at the caller ID expecting to see the names of Mother Hen or Worry Wart and saw *Arch*. I squealed with glee, then pulled a poker face and tried not to sound too anxious. "Did you just land or are you already in your car?"

"Just merging onto I-95, yeah?"

Which meant he'd hit Atlantic City in an hour and fifteen. Yeah, baby, yeah.

"Where are you, lass?"

"Home."

"Alone?"

I resisted the urge to quote a line from that movie. He didn't sound angry but he didn't sound like his cocky self. That could only mean one thing. He was upset or pissed. "Don't worry. I'm protected."

"How?"

I glanced at the evil canister. I'd set it on the cocktail

table alongside Arch's exotic flowers. Beauty and the Beast. "Mace Pepper Spray. Tabasco gave it to me. Not that I'll need it."

"You *dinnae* know that. If Crowe—"

"When the moon is in the Seventh House and—"

"Why are you singing?"

"I just… You never know…" Who's listening. How could he not know that? Especially since he was savvy to electronic gadgets and surveillance gear.

"Noted," he said.

So he did know, but had slipped. He'd slipped the previous night, too, by talking about sensitive material over the phone. He wasn't in peak Chameleon form. A rarity. Which meant something was deeply wrong. My stomach knotted.

"Did you think about my proposition?" he asked.

"You mean moving in?"

"Aye."

"I thought about it."

"And?"

"I think we should talk about it over an early dinner."

"Right, then. See you in an hour, love."

"Wait. Have you talked to Beckett yet?"

"He's my next call."

I felt ridiculously pleased that I was his first. "There's something he wants to discuss with you, in person I'm sure, but I'd like to talk to you about it first."

"Like I said, see you in an hour."

He signed off and my hand shook a little as I laid the cell next to my laptop. Dinner. Right. Like I had an appetite. What would I bring up first? COPRODEM and my Aquarius sting? The kiss I initiated with Beckett that proved us "just friends"? Or my reluctance to move in with him until we tackled our trust issues which meant sharing our secrets?

Each topic was important and each one had the potential to blow up in my face. My thoughts raced and blurred. My mind jammed. Nic and Jayne weren't available to help me sort things out. "What's a neurotic girl to do?"

I shut down my computer and picked up my diary. I scribbled thoughts about the kiss that fell flat and stopped short of mentioning COPRODEM. It didn't seem wise to write down things of national importance. What if someone got hold of my diary? What if they leaked information to the press? What if they reported to Crowe and he sent someone to silence me…permanently?

My mouth went dry. My imagination leapt to the wrong side of the tracks. Fresh air and a brisk walk would clear my head and settle my nerves. Maybe I could pick up something for dinner at the corner market. Preferably something ready-made from the deli. Call me domestically challenged. Call me desperate to redirect my angst. I had to get it together before Arch arrived. I needed a plan. I needed to state my cases as calmly and succinctly as possible. Okay, so I'd be breaking my word to Tabasco by venturing out before Arch got here, but what he didn't know, didn't matter. To be on the safe side, I tossed the evil canister in my purse.

I was already halfway across the parking lot when I noted a dark sedan coming my way. The same sedan I thought I'd seen tailing me this morning. I'd swear it! A shiny black Mercedes with tinted windows. It screamed Fed. Or Mafioso. Warning bells clanged and my heart galloped.

Oh, my, God. Oh, my, God.

Even if I ran, I'd never make it back to my apartment in time to lock out whoever it was. Plus, your legs needed to work in order to run. I'd frozen as my imagination superseded sane thought. *What if they grab you and toss you into the backseat? What if they spirit you away and hold you hostage until Beckett bends to their will? What if they take you out on a boat, shoot you, and throw you overboard? Or tie a cement block to your ankles and toss you over while you're still alive?*

The car rolled to a stop right beside me and I had one last thought, a valiant thought. *They'll never take me alive.* Followed by, *if you incapacitate him, you can call the police.* Or Beckett. Only because he was closer than Arch.

I stabbed my hand in my purse, clasped the evil canister intent to blind, burn and stain.

The door opened and I fumbled with the flip-top safety cap. White noise. Tunnel vision. Operating on instinct, I hurled the canister just as the man unfolded from the car—and whacked him dead on the nose.

"Shit! *Fuck!*"

"Michael?"

"What the hell's wrong with you? Jesus!" Blood trickled through the fingers he'd pressed over his nose.

I swallowed a laugh. Not because it was funny, but because I was relieved he wasn't a dangerous lunatic. "I'm sorry. I thought you were…"

"Who?"

"Never mind." My body relaxed as the adrenaline rush ebbed.

Michael fell back against the car and pulled a handkerchief from his trouser pocket. Aside from his bloodied nose, I noticed his jaw was bruised. Compliments of Arch. I wonder how he'd explained that to his wife. Ten to one, he didn't tell her the truth. That would mean confessing he'd kissed me.

He winced as he pressed the monogrammed cloth over the bridge of his nose. Monogrammed. That was new. A purchase to impress Sasha?

Frowning, I moved forward. "Let me see—"

"Stay back."

I rolled my eyes. "I'm not going to hurt you."

"You just bashed me with…what the hell was that?"

I picked up the renegade canister. "Mace Pepper Spray."

"You're supposed to spray it, not throw it."

"I know. I panicked."

"Why?" He narrowed his watery eyes. "Who did you think I was?"

"Never mind." I stowed the can back in my purse. "Where did you get this car?"

"A dealership. Where do you think?"

"You bought it?"

"I treated myself."

Another move to impress Sasha? Or maybe the expensive wheels were her idea. I kind of liked the idea of Michael feeling pressured to impress his young trophy wife. Served him right for betraying the old wife who'd loved him for who he was. Or thought he was. "Why the tinted windows?"

"Why the third degree?"

I folded my arms and angled my head. "You were following me this morning. Why?"

"I wanted to talk to you. On the way to your place, I passed you on the bridge, so I made a U-turn. Figured I'd catch up to you, but Sasha called and I had to postpone my plans."

Can you say henpecked? Jeez. "You make your living with a phone glued to your ear. You could have called me."

"I wanted to do this in person. Can we go inside?"

I thought about the promise I'd made to Arch. "No."

"I'm injured." He folded the kerchief and reapplied it to his nose.

"You'll live. What do you want?" It wasn't like me to be so rude, but these days Michael brought out the worst in me.

"To offer you the opportunity of a lifetime."

I blinked. That line was a common come-on for a scam. I was instantly skeptical but curious. "Go on."

"Remember Charlie Lutz?"

A college bud of Michael's. A writer who enjoyed impressive success in show business, but who, even after winning an Emmy, kept in touch and never flaunted his good fortune. "What about him?"

"He's written and pitched a script to one of the cable networks and he's been given the green light. Think modern day *Scarecrow and Mrs. King* with a comical twist."

"An everyday woman who ends up working undercover for a government agency?" Talk about art imitating life.

"I know. The timing's eerie. Anyway, they're on a tight budget and have decided to go with an unknown for the female lead."

"What's this got to do with me?"

"Charlie thinks you'd be perfect for the lead and so do I. It requires the talents of a multifaceted performer, an aura of innocence, *and* the role was written for a forty-plus woman."

A year ago I would've been happy-dancing my butt off. A year ago, I'd been a lot less cynical. "You're joking."

He pinned me with an earnest gaze. "This is your big shot, Evie. You're washed up in this town—"

"Gee, thanks."

"But you're not washed up in the business. You're a

unique talent, hon, and you have a lot to give. I know you. Your hopes and aspirations. You were born to entertain. You're destined for the stage, whether live or in front of a camera. We probably should've relocated to Los Angeles long ago, but we didn't. But now…"

"My ship has come in? Fame and fortune await?" I arched a brow. "If I've learned anything from Arch it's if it sounds too good to be true, it is."

"You think I'm conning you."

"I don't know what to think."

"This is a legit opportunity."

"It's a pipe dream."

He reached into his inner suit jacket pocket and passed me an embossed business card. "Here's Charlie's contact information. Call him." He noted my skeptical expression and sighed. "Fine. Think it over then call him. But don't wait too long. You're not the only multitalented, over-forty performer in the mix. The longer you wait, the slimmer your chances." Still applying pressure to his nose, he climbed behind the wheel of his fancy new car.

"What do you get out of this?" I asked, assuming it was the real deal.

"Peace of mind. This town's not big enough for you, me and Sasha."

He drove off and I stood there dumbfounded. So, what? He still had feelings for me? More likely he was freaking out about being a dad. I felt a little sorry for Sasha. As for me… I glanced down at the card in my hand. If this was on the level, Michael was indeed offering me the chance of a lifetime. A shot at Hollywood fame. If I flew out there and nailed the gig, my childhood dreams would come true. My family would be relieved—*so all those years in entertainment weren't a waste!* My high school drama teacher would be so proud—*you, Evelyn Parish, are destined to become a big-time star!* Nic and Jayne would be over the moon—*you so deserve this!*

Except, I didn't burn to perform anymore.

Then what's with the fluttery stomach and giddiness?

I noted Charlie's phone number. I wondered…what if?

CHAPTER TWENTY

TODAY IN MY LIFE GONE WILD, I'd kissed my boss, given my ex a bloody nose, devised a sting to bring down a government bigwig, and been offered a shot at fame and fortune. Oh, and my lover, a sexy bad boy six years my junior, wanted me to move in with him. Not for the first time, I wondered if I'd inadvertently stepped into a reality program. Because, seriously, this was over-the-top drama at its best. Or worst. Depending on your view.

Speaking of TV, Michael hadn't been lying. Charlie Lutz was indeed casting for the pilot of a new series. A show that was perfectly suited to *moi*. He was shocked when I didn't jump at the chance to fly out to L.A. and audition and made it clear that this window of opportunity would soon close. I promised to get back to him in a few days. I should have turned him down on the spot. I had a new life with Chameleon. With Arch. Maybe. But my little girl dreams caused me to cling to that Hollywood star.

Bottom line, I had to figure out what I really wanted out of life. Where did I belong? The only thing I was sure of was that I wasn't certain. I hated that so much depended on Arch.

By the time he arrived, I'd paced a path in my carpet, but, by God, I had my agenda in order. My speech was burned in my brain. Too bad it went up in smoke when I opened the door.

Those mesmerizing eyes always knocked me for a loop. But this time Arch one-two punched my senses with frightening intensity.

Without a word, he pressed me against the living room wall and kissed me breathless. For once I was grateful for my lack of interior decorations. No framed paintings to knock crooked. No ceramic collectibles to crash from shelves to floor. Just plenty of stark, bare wall to flatten against as Arch melded his hunky body to mine and ravaged my mouth.

His hands moved over my body, caressing my curves and inciting lust. Call me dumb and dumber. I couldn't think. Agenda? What agenda? He'd reduced me to a mass of wanton flesh. I wanted him naked. I wanted him inside me. Was there a better way to say, *welcome home?*

I shoved him back to yank up his T-shirt, but I was anxious and clumsy and clipped him on the chin. He didn't flinch, but did take over, pulling his shirt over his head and treating me to a show of rippling muscles and that sexy Celtic tattoo.

My hoo-hah ached for his wa-hoo. Music welled in my head. A nitty, gritty R & B number composed for down and dirty sex. I smoothed my hands over his chest, nipped his biceps and traced the tribal markings with my tongue. Primal urges snaked through my body, making me bold. I kissed my way down his taut stomach. Lower, lower. I gently bit his hard-on through the stonewashed denim. JT was raring to go. *Bring it on, Big Boy.*

My heart hammered as I unzipped his jeans. I nearly climaxed when he threaded his fingers through my hair and cupped the back of my head. Only, just as I anticipated pleasing him with my mouth, he pulled me to my feet.

I barely registered the disappointment. His kiss was so…urgent. And…loving.

Okay. Call me royally undone.

Three seconds later, he had me naked and pinned against the wall. Sunlight streamed through the window blinds. I felt exposed and naughty. *Wanton.* I surrendered to his skilled touch, willing my knees steady as he savored my nipples then dropped to his knees and kissed a hot trail down my stomach. One hand kneaded my breast, one splayed my folds. Then suddenly his mouth was on me— there. Skilled and creative. Tongue. Teeth. *Ecstasy.*

Oh, God. Oh, please. Stop. No, don't…stop.

The music in my head intensified along with the erotic sensations. I shuddered and moaned. I climaxed with a throaty cry then a salty curse that caused him to smile against my damp skin.

Deliciously sated, I would've slid down the wall if Arch hadn't hauled me over his shoulder. He carried me to my bedroom, but instead of placing me on the bed, he set me to my feet in front of my mirrored dresser. I flashed back to the cruise ship and sure enough he maneuvered me around, my back to his front. A delicious thrill zinged down my spine when he stripped off his jeans and pressed his hot, hard body flush to mine. I couldn't believe how turned on I was by our racy reflection. My hair was tousled, my eyes glazed. I watched, electrified and mesmerized as his strong hands moved sensually over my soft curves. I trembled with anticipation as he brushed aside my hair and kissed the back of my neck. Whimpered when he reached between my legs and slid two fingers deep inside. *Oh, sweet misery. Just do it!*

Crazy for a hot shag, I cleared my dresser top with one clumsy sweep. Perfume bottles and a musical jewelry box thudded to the plush carpet. The theme from *Casablanca* tinkled from the open box. Given the movie's sad end, not a song I wanted to hear. I nudged it with my foot and "As Time Goes By" was gone.

Arch bent me over the dresser and smoothed his hands down my back, over the swells of my rear. My skin prickled and my heart raced. I was ready to beg when, at last, he gripped my hips and drove JT home.

I gasped.

He groaned.

I gloried in the raw sensation. He wasn't wearing a condom, was he? It felt different. No, *he* felt different. Something in his aura. His being. *What happened on the West Coast?* A deep thrust derailed that train of thought. I quivered and moaned as he rode me hard. I came and I came. Was that my life that just flashed before my eyes?

He turned me around and although I was knocking on heaven's door, the hungry look in his eyes zapped me back to life. I jumped up and wrapped my legs around his back, kissed him with sex-starved passion. We crashed into my closet and ended up shagging amongst my costumes. I'm not sure what rocked his world more. The things we did with my purple feather boa or the four-inch acrylic pumps—à la Cinderella—he'd slid on my feet in a very un-Disney-like moment.

At some point we ended up in the middle of my carpeted floor. That's when I took control—no mercy. I insisted on being on top. Call me nostalgic. I drove him to the edge once, twice. His endurance and control were exhilarating. Exhausted, I collapsed on top of him only to be swept up and placed on the bed where he revived me with a bout of tender lovemaking. Missionary-style. The ultimate intimacy.

He cradled my face, gazed into my eyes. *Zing. Zap. Meld.*

We climaxed in tandem. I wondered if planets exploded and stars shattered in his mind's eye.

Arch collapsed then shifted so as not to crush me. We were a sweaty, tangled mess of naked limbs. Breathless and blissfully satiated, we ended the heated coupling just as we'd begun—in silence.

One by one my brain cells sputtered back to life. A dozen concerns welled and bounced around my fuzzy brain. I'd had an agenda, though I couldn't remember it for the life of me. Crap.

When at last we eased apart, our eyes locked. My heart pounded with something new. Dread. What if that intense moment hadn't been a meld, but a snap? Had we just had breakup sex? Was he gearing up to tell me goodbye?

He traced a thumb over my swollen mouth. "Marry me."

I stared, blinked. *What?*

"Bugger. *Christ.*" He rolled to his back. "I *dinnae* know where that came from. No, wait. Yeah. I do." He looked into my eyes, grasped my hand and laid it over his heart. "It came from here."

My own heart tha-dumped as hard as his, only twice as fast. I peered around, certain my bedroom had been invaded by a film crew. *In the latest installment of* Evie's Life Gone Wild…

"I know this is sudden, yeah? But when you opened the door and I saw your sweet face, something inside me…"

"Snapped?"

"Burst to life." He brushed my bangs out of my eyes, stroked my cheek. "Being away from you, from your goodness…I need you, lass."

I'm sure his sentiment was heartfelt, but it didn't woo me as much as trouble me. "What happened to cohabitating?" I croaked. "You know. The trial run?"

"I *dinnae* need a trial run. I know what I want."

Must be nice. "I don't know what to say."

"Do you love me?"

"You know I do."

"Then say, aye."

My stomach and heart engaged in crazy gymnastics. He was offering me a happily ever after, but it felt doomed. "I can't."

"Are you still confused *aboot* Beckett?"

"No." Now would be the time to tell him about this morning's kiss, except it absolutely felt like the wrong time. Or maybe I was a coward. Knowing I'd initiated the kiss, then nudged Beckett to turn up the heat, would hurt Arch's feelings, not to mention piss him off. "I can honestly say I have no feelings for Beckett other than friendship." Did he really need to know the details?

"Are you certain?"

"Positive."

The corner of his mouth kicked up. "And you're over Stone, yeah?"

"Completely." Now would be the time to tell him about Michael's second visit and the once-in-a-lifetime opportunity. Except I didn't want to cloud this particular discussion with my rekindled career crisis. "Regardless, I can't marry you."

"Why not?"

"We're not ready."

"Speak for yourself."

Frustrated, I propped myself on one elbow and regarded him through wary eyes. "Less than two weeks ago you said you were cautious about our future. You said we'd take it slow."

"That was then, this is now."

"What about our trust issues?"

"Marrying me would definitely dissolve my insecurities about being your fantasy joyride, lass."

The charming smile did not amuse. "Well, that's peachy, but what about my insecurities? You once told me I could never trust you. Then you vowed to earn my trust. Let me tell you that part's not going so hot. Hard to trust someone with a bazillion secrets. Take that deal on the West Coast. You said the payoff was priceless. Was it illegal? Did it involve Kate? Are you grifting on the side? You live like a king. Strike that, a baron. I still can't believe you bought a title and lands. A flipping barony! And for what purpose? To impress someone? Con someone?"

"I bought it for my daughter."

I froze, inside and out. Poleaxed for the second time in five minutes. My voice turned thick and sluggish. "You have a daughter?"

A muscle under his left eye jumped. "With Kate."

My stomach twisted with jealousy and envy. "Were you married to her?"

"No."

"Did you love her?"

"Definitely not."

"Was she a one-night stand?"

He held my gaze. "She was the daughter of a mark."

Oh, God. I fell back on my pillow and palmed my chest. *Breathe, Evie, breathe.*

He shifted so that he was gazing down at me. Weariness dulled the normal sparkle of his eyes. "Remember when I told you there are some aspects of my life I'm not proud of?"

All I could manage was a nod.

"This tops the list, Sunshine. I seduced Kate in order to get to her father."

It just kept getting worse. "A big con?"

"A month and a half of my life."

"Big score?"

"Half a million American dollars."

He didn't look the least bit guilty about that part.

"He could afford it," he said, as if reading my mind. "The man was a millionaire ten times over, yeah?"

"Was?"

"Dead now. Boating accident."

"I suppose Kate inherited his fortune."

"Only a portion." He squeezed my shoulder. "So how much do you want to know, lass?"

This is what I'd yearned for. To know his secrets. I could either hear him out and deal or shut him up and avoid. Reality versus fantasy. *Welcome to the real world, Evie.* Nic was right. I'd somehow glamorized Arch's career as a con artist. "Basics only. Details are moot." A con is a con. And a seduction…unfortunately, I could imagine.

He nodded and smoothed my hair from my face, a tender gesture to temper the harsh truth. "I *dinnae* regret fleecing Harrison. He was a greedy, shifty bugger who took advantage of his employees. I *didnae* think twice about using Kate to get to him. She was and is a self-absorbed bird with a mean streak."

"Beautiful?"

"In a plastic way, you know?"

Several images came to mind. Most of them, blond, bronzed, and Botox injected. "Probably wasn't a hardship sleeping with her."

"Thought you *didnae* want details."

"Right. So how did she get pregnant? Weren't you using protection?"

"Johnnie broke."

"What?"

"Scottish for condom."

"Oh. You're kidding."

"Happens. I *didnae* sweat it, because she assured me we were covered. Said she was on the pill, yeah?"

"So…freak accident?"

He shrugged. "I'd disappeared by the time she knew she was pregnant. I *didnae* know *aboot* the baby until I read her father's obituary. I suspected the little girl was mine because the math added up, and Kate had named the baby after me or rather the alias I'd used—William Cassidy."

I scrunched my brow. "So your daughter's name is Willy? Billie?"

His lip quirked. "Cassidy."

So Arch had a daughter and her name was Cassidy. By the way his face lit up, I just knew he adored her. "Given her genes, I bet she's beautiful."

He rolled out of bed and plucked something from his pant's pocket. The cell phone he used for *private stuff*. He stretched back down beside me, pressed a couple of buttons, and handed me the phone.

Smiling back at me from the tiny screen was a gray-green-eyed, chestnut-haired little girl. She was just about the cutest kid I'd ever seen. My heart pounded with… something. Envy? Regret? *Why Kate and not me?* "She's adorable, Arch."

"She has the soul of an angel. Not sure how that happened, given her genes."

"How old is she?"

"Four."

My head reeled with a flashback. "I'm not my father's son."

"Your memory is bloody scary, Sunshine." He took back the phone and placed it on the nightstand.

"You went back to the scene of the crime, for your daughter."

"Once I knew for certain she was mine, aye. I contacted Kate. She was more furious with me for seducing and leaving her than fleecing her da. Not wanting the world to know he'd been scammed or that a con artist had knocked up his daughter, Harrison had talked her into marrying a company man."

"Why didn't she just, I mean I don't think I could but—"

"She saw the baby as a way of manipulating her da."

"But it sounds like *he* manipulated *her.*"

"*Dinnae* try to make sense of their twisted relationship. Just know Kate won in the end. She kicked that husband curbside as soon as Harrison kicked the bucket, yeah?"

"So what did she say when you contacted her?"

"She insisted that I return the money before she allowed me to see our daughter. I've been jumping through hoops ever since."

Something inside of me shifted. "You gave back five hundred thousand dollars?"

"I'd pay more if it would afford me more time with my daughter. But Kate doesn't need or want money. She wants to torture me, you know? She takes perverse pleasure in telling me I can have Cassie for a couple of days, only to change her mind after I arrive."

Noting the edge in his tone, I reached up and cupped his cheek. "That's what happened yesterday."

"It *doesnae* always go down that way, but the invites are usually last-minute and the timing often inconvenient. I've been struggling to get scheduled visitation with Cassie for years. I have no legal rights, and I *cannae* take Kate to court for obvious reasons."

"So you've been trying to work out a personal deal?"

"First Kate threw my sketchy profession in my face. I contacted Beckett, who'd been on my *arse* for almost two years, and struck a deal. I wanted my daughter to know her da, so I went straight. I wanted my daughter to have a respectable da, so I bought the barony. Over the years, Kate's allowed me just enough time with Cassie for us to bond. Fuck's sake, the kid lights up every time she sees me."

"Probably because you shower her with affection." I could easily imagine and that vision only strengthened my love for Arch.

"God knows Kate's a cold mother. She foists Cassie off on nannies, yeah?" He fell back on the pillow with a peeved sigh. "When Kate phoned day before yesterday, she swore she was ready to come to terms. When I got there… I *cannae* decide if she's evil or manic."

My heart ached for him. Jayne would probably view this as Karmic payback. I saw it as a sad twist of fate. Yes, he'd been wrong to use a woman in order to fleece a millionaire, but he'd tried to make amends. He'd returned the money. He'd walked away from a career he excelled at. *"Sometimes life throws you a curve, Sunshine. Sometimes you're forced to move on."*

Just as I'd been forced out of entertainment. At least here in Atlantic City. We'd had that conversation on the cruise ship, the first week we'd met. A shared misery that had helped to form our unique connection. A connection that held strong no matter how many times he stunned me with a dicey revelation.

Nic's voice rang in my ears. *"You must really love this guy."*

She had no idea.

"Does anyone else know about Cassidy?"

"Bernie."

His deceased grandfather. "What about Beckett?"

He shook his head. "Beckett has enough dirt on me, yeah? I've never volunteered the information. If he knows, he's keeping that card up his sleeve."

"The more people know aboot *me, the more vulnerable I am."*

I framed his face and urged him to meet my gaze. "Why are you telling me this now?"

"Because I want you to trust me, lass."

My heart swelled and threatened to jackhammer through my ribs. "Fair is fair." I nabbed my journal from beneath my pillow and passed it to him. I might as well have handed him my heart on a plate.

"But this is for private stuff, yeah?"

"Yeah." My mouth went dry as he grazed his thumb over the keeper of my innermost thoughts. "I want you to trust me, too. Just…don't read it in front of me."

"I *dinnae* have to read it at all."

"You shared your private stuff. I want to share mine. If we're going to make a go of this—"

"So you'll marry me?"

"I'll think about it." I blew out a nervous breath. "You may not feel the same about me after reading this."

He quirked a tender smile. "True. There's the risk I'll love you even more."

My heart skipped. "You have a dangerous way with words, Arch Duvall."

He winked. "A gift from the stars."

That comment triggered thoughts of astrology, COPRODEM and Aquarius. "Crap!"

"What's wrong?"

"This has to wait." I nabbed back the journal. While

we'd been engrossed in wild lovemaking and personal revelations, I'd left Beckett and Chameleon twisting in the wind. "I need to speak to you about a matter of national importance."

CHAPTER TWENTY-ONE

MILO BROKE AWAY FROM the document he'd been reading on Senator Martin Wilson and slipped into The Cave's kitchen for a bottle of water. He could hear The Kid tapping away at his computer, digging, searching. The boy was relentless.

Upstairs, happy hour was in full swing, which meant there were probably six to eight patrons drinking twofer beers, and that included the regulars, Vincent and Ollie. Pops had shown up on his night off, saying he needed to keep busy. What he really meant was that he wanted to watch Milo's back. The club was rigged with a surveillance system, but the old man didn't trust cameras as much as his own eyes and instincts.

Pops's concern was appreciated but unnecessary. If Crowe had men spying on him, Milo hadn't spotted or sensed them. And so far, he hadn't given Crowe cause to attack. He'd done exactly as the man had ordered. He'd kept a low profile, minded the club. No active fraud investigations. He didn't figure Madame Helene counted as Tabasco had handled that problem solo and off the books. Similar to how Milo had handled Mad Dog, only without the disastrous end.

He popped two Tylenol to reduce the headache he got every time he thought about the incident that had instigated this hell.

It had been three days since he'd tangled with Mad Dog. Media attention had dwindled day by day. No further clues as to the former athlete's assailant. It was only a matter of time before the case was labeled an unsolved mystery. There'd been no mention of Senator Clark or his wife. No reports of illegal gambling. Crowe and his cohorts were making the entire debacle disappear. At least publicly.

Meanwhile the AIA Director had his dirty files. He had the senator's and Milo's balls in a vice via phone taps, financial transactions, documentation, and that goddamned DVR. According to Gina, her source was working on confiscating that piece of equipment. If he did, then *Syd* was a top-notch thief. Crowe would no doubt blame Chameleon, although if the images on the hard drive coincided with those on the DVD, the director would still have Milo's balls.

They needed proof of Crowe's dirty dealings. So far, their mission wasn't time sensitive. The presidential election was two years away. Of course, that didn't insure Crowe wouldn't use his dirt to manipulate key people of power sooner. Although he'd be wise to wait until he was more entrenched. He'd only held his position for less than two months. Surely time was on Chameleon's side, yet Milo itched to expose the man as soon as possible. He wouldn't be free to live his life until he did. He wouldn't be free of the guilt-inducing question: Did he or did he not kill Mad Dog Turner?

He returned to his laptop, checked his watch. He'd expected Arch over an hour ago. He knew his plane had landed, but instead of answering his phone, he'd allowed his calls to roll over to voice mail. Unlike Evie, he wouldn't forget to charge his cell. An expert driver, odds were against his being involved in a crash and he sure as hell knew how to change a flat tire. Logic dictated he was with Evie. For the first time since Milo had known Twinkie, he didn't feel a pang of jealousy. It made working with her substantially easier. As for Arch... Milo was just about to call Evie's place when his pain-in-the ass partner strolled into The Cave. He looked wiped from the flight...or something.

"About time you showed up."

"Wanted to check in on Evie first, yeah?"

"You could've answered your phone."

"I said the same thing to you two days ago."

"You two sound like an old married couple," Woody mumbled without taking his eyes off of his computer.

Arch raised a brow at The Kid's uncharacteristic rudeness.

Milo minimized the document he'd been reading on Wilson. "The Kid's been trying to hack into sensitive files for almost two days straight."

"Almost there." Woody's fingers flew over the keys. "So close. Come on, come on. Damn!" He slammed a fist to the desktop and slumped back in his seat.

"Fuck's sake, Kid," Arch said, "take a break."

"Why can't I see it? It has to be... Wait." He resumed his frenzied typing.

"We're not racing the clock," Milo said, although he, too, was anxious. "Crowe's not planning to take over the world in the next week or even month."

"Not that we know of," The Kid snapped. "Who knows how his devious mind works?"

"You're starting to sound like Evie," Arch teased.

Oblivious, The Kid tapped away. "If I could hack into his dirty files, we'd have hard evidence."

"We'll get what we need. One way or another." Milo squeezed his shoulder. "Grab some dinner, Woody, or go up to my apartment and get some sleep."

"But—"

"That's an order."

"Yes, sir." Looking haggard even for his scruffy self, the gangly young man brushed past his boss then Arch. "Welcome back, Ace."

"Thanks, Kid."

The door slid open and shut.

Arch eased onto the sofa. "He's too hard on himself. I'm impressed he learned as much as he did, you know?"

Milo took an opposing chair. "I take it Evie told you about COPRODEM."

"Called Crowe a rat bastard rat and told me *aboot* her plans to trap him."

"And?"

"It's a good plan."

"But?"

"No 'but.'"

Milo frowned. "You do realize that Evie wants to play the role of the psychic?"

"Not crazy *aboot* that part. We'll just have to make sure nothing goes wrong."

"Did you try to talk her out of it?"

"No."

Milo pressed two fingers to his throbbing temples. "You've been giving me hell for bringing her on board in the first place. You said she's not cut out for our world and now you're willing to let her take center stage in a sting of this magnitude?"

"She's a natural," Arch said. "She's proven herself competent and intuitive on three separate cases."

"Precisely why I invited her to officially join the team. But we're a little out of our realm on this one. Which puts Evie—"

"On a more even keel?" Arch leaned forward. "Listen. Evie and I are at a crucial turning point, yeah? If I manipulate her professionally based solely on my personal fears, I'd risk losing the best thing I've ever had." He paused then added, "I asked her to be my wife."

Milo couldn't believe his ears. Arch, the man who'd enjoyed phenomenal success as a grifter by never allowing himself to become attached emotionally was going to commit? Permanently? Legally? "What's your angle?"

"Are you trying to piss me off?"

"I'm trying to get to the truth."

"The truth is—I love her."

Milo processed that. "Enough to take a homicide wrap for her?"

Arch didn't blink.

Milo crossed to the console then tossed a CD in the Scot's lap. "It's an enhanced copy of the recording of the Simon Lamont shooting."

Arch turned the CD over in his hands, placed it on the table in front of him. "Leave it be, Beckett."

"Gladly. But you have to come clean with Evie."

"Are you mental?"

"She already suspects the truth, Arch. Her memory is trickling back in nightmares."

"She talked to you *aboot* this?"

"Only out of desperation." Milo sat back down. "Listen, she's a big girl—"

"With a soft heart. Bloody hell, *dinnae* you know her at all?" He shot up and paced in a rare show of frustration. "Knowing she was responsible for another man's death would haunt her for the rest of her fucking life. The nightmares will fade. If we stick to my story…" He stopped and locked eyes with Milo. "You *didnae* know."

"Not for sure."

"The CD?"

"Enhanced like I said, but it didn't help. I still couldn't make out specifics in the chaos. All I had to go on was Twinkie's guilty subconscious."

Arch scraped his hand over his head then fell back on the sofa with a disbelieving chuckle. "You played me. *Me,* for chrissake."

"Yeah, well. I learned from the best."

"It was an accident, Jazzman."

"That much is clear."

"It went down exactly like I said, only it was Evie who caused the gun to go off. She was disoriented from a blow. I was struggling with Lamont. I'd managed to twist the barrel away from me and… Jesus, the timing. One of the thugs shoved her into the fray. She smashed her head, started to go down, and reached up to stabilize herself."

"So Lamont's finger was on the trigger?"

"Aye, but she grabbed his hand and…"

"Got it." Milo scratched his chin. "You know, if the local police had been less cooperative, you could've ended up in a foreign jail."

The Scot quirked a cocky grin. "You *wouldnae* have let that happen. I'm too valuable to you, yeah?"

"Maybe once upon a time."

He raised a brow. "The honeymoon's over?"

Milo had been in a funk for months about the state of Chameleon. He was tired of dealing with bureaucratic bullshit, wading through Arch's bullshit, and he was sick to death of spending his nights with his nineteen-inch television set.

As for taking on the scheming director of the AIA, he could end up a hero, in jail, six feet under, or ostracized. The need to instigate something positive in his life was overwhelming. God knows why he flashed on Nicole. She was anything *but* positive. "Let's just say, I'm contemplating major changes after the completion of Aquarius."

"So we're going to do this then. Rope Crowe and get him to hang himself."

"If we're lucky."

"And clear you of Mad Dog's death."

"If we're lucky and if I'm really innocent."

"Speaking of innocent," Arch said. "*Aboot* the Fish shooting…"

Milo didn't want Evie to know the truth any more than Arch. It's not like it would alter anything, other than her spirit, but he'd also made a promise. *Nice going, Beckett.* "I won't reveal anything to Evie…unless my back's against the wall. I won't lie to her, Arch."

"There are all kinds of lies, yeah?"

"Spoken like a true grifter."

"Former grifter."

"I'd have an easier time believing that if you explained all the impromptu trips over the years."

"Told you before. Personal business."

"None of my business. Maybe not. But if you marry Evie it'll sure as hell be hers."

"Already addressed, mate."

Coming clean about his secret life? Milo was shocked. Mostly he was relieved that he maybe wouldn't have to pick up the pieces of Twinkie's heart three months from now. "Looks like I underestimated the depth of your feelings for Evie."

"If you have any lingering hopes of stealing her away—"

"I don't."

"Good to know."

"But if you hurt her—"

"I won't."

For the first time in their six-year relationship, Milo saw Arch as a stand-up guy. Someone who cared enough about someone else to take the heat for something he didn't do. Someone willing to sacrifice his own agenda for a higher cause. Milo had sensed the potential four years ago when Arch had contacted him to strike a deal. At the time, Milo had collected key evidence that could put him behind bars, though probably not for long. Certainly not long enough to inspire Arch to make a life-altering decision. Yet the brilliant grifter had chucked a staggeringly lucrative career to play the good guy.

Though Arch had approached the transition with his cocky flair, it had been the one and only time, other than the Caribbean fiasco, that Milo had sensed vulnerability in Arch. For the most part, he had remained the shifty Scot, an infuriating pain in Milo's ass, but a valuable cohort. Chameleon was born and Milo had grudgingly looked the other way the times Arch went renegade. Now after working so hard to keep that part of his life under wraps, Arch had put his trust in a woman with the ethics of an angel.

Talk about a miracle.

Milo had never believed Arch capable of total reform. Until now. Maybe he wasn't there yet, but with Evie he stood a damn good shot.

One thing was certain, it altered the dynamics between the two men. Milo was used to having the moral edge.

"Have any ideas on how to launch Aquarius quickly and effectively?" Arch asked, swinging the discussion back to business.

"You're asking me?"

"If you're stuck for ideas—"

"I'm not."

"Then let's hear them, yeah?"

Milo leading the dance? Speaking of miracles… He downed more water and gathered his thoughts. The Fish shooting was history as far as he was concerned and faded to the recesses of his mind. He focused on the task at hand.

"Okay. Here's what I know. Evie was right. Senator Martin Wilson definitely has an interest in the supernatural. He wrote a college term paper on psychics, particularly those who channel readings through tarot cards, crystal-ball gazing, and astrology. The untapped resources of the human mind. I found current references that indicate his psychic interests are alive and well. Although the fact that he actually consults personal readers is veiled behind a cloak of *scientific versus spiritual* studies."

"A convenient spin that appeases both skeptics and believers, yeah?"

"He's smart and charismatic," Milo went on. "Popular with his colleagues as well as his contingency. He's got a clean record, personally and professionally, and there are rumblings that he's going to throw his hat into the presidential arena."

"A strong contender?"

Milo angled his head. "Possibly. Definitely someone Crowe would want to control or influence."

Arch scratched his unshaven jaw. "In this instance, having a psychic under his thumb would prove advantageous to Crowe."

"So we create a persona for Evie and feed her to the wolf. The wolf uses her to bait and hook Wilson."

Arch didn't flinch. "What's the come-on?"

"I approach Crowe, tell him I'm tired of sitting around with my thumb up my ass, waiting for the Mad Dog mess to blow over. If I'm supposedly innocent of wrongdoing, wouldn't it be better to conduct business as usual? So I suggest picking up with a case we abandoned right before the Caribbean fiasco."

Arch smiled. "A case involving an up-and-coming psychic, someone who's stirred a lot of interest, maybe attracted a celebrity client or two."

"I'm thinking she's charismatic and attractive, a modern-day psychic who takes full advantage of the Internet. A Web site that offers a bio, testimonials and services—readings in person, over the phone or via computer."

"A high-tech scammer," Arch said.

"With contrived credibility out the ass and an upcoming appearance in Atlantic City," Milo said.

"A special event held in a casino ballroom or an upscale catering hall." He shook his head. "Strike that. A private room in a restaurant. Easier to rig with cameras and microphones. Easier to book on short notice."

"Tabasco's already out there scouting. Hold up." Milo snagged his phone and made contact. "Nix the theater. Think intimate. Restaurant with a private room." He glanced at Arch. "A place that would hold say twenty to forty people. An event hosted by a paranormal society. Evie's going to be their guest speaker."

Arch nodded his approval.

Milo signed off with Tabasco. "He's on it."

"She *shouldnae* be a local," Arch said. "We'll fly her in. Base her close to Wilson but not too close."

Milo rose and moved to his laptop. "Massachusetts."

"Salem."

"Because it's associated with the supernatural? Too obvious."

"Trust me."

Milo laughed. "Not likely, but I do trust your grifter instincts." He pulled up a map on the Internet while Arch slipped into the kitchenette.

The man returned with two bottles of beer. He handed one to Milo then took the seat next to him at the console.

"We need an easy in and out." Milo pointed to a location on his monitor. "Here. Closer to the Boston airport."

"Brilliant. Now pull up a spreadsheet and let's create her profile, yeah? I'll prep her tonight while Woody gets her Web site up and running."

Milo set aside his beer while Arch drank deeply. "Considering she lives and operates in the next state, wouldn't Wilson be aware of this woman's existence?"

"If he's as intrigued with psychics as you say, by the time we finish planting her name all over the Internet, chances are he'll discover her pretty quickly. Not that it matters. Crowe's our mark, not Wilson."

True. "Our psychic needs a name. And we should alter Evie's image."

"Portia Livingston. Black hair. Straight. Chin length. Blunt bangs. You know, similar to Uma Thurman in *Pulp Fiction*."

"Never saw it," Milo said.

Arch grunted. "Your knowledge of the cinema is piss-poor at best, Jazzman."

"Maybe. But just ask me about any classic sitcom."

Arch swiped the laptop and Googled the movie.

"Ah," Milo said as he viewed the picture of the dark

and mysterious version of the naturally blond actress. He noted the hairstyle. "Barbara Feldon. *Get Smart.* Sixties' bob. Got it."

Rolling his eyes, Arch pulled up two photo manipulating programs then keyed into his personal files and located a head shot of Evie. Minutes later she was no longer a breezy blonde, but a sultry brunette.

"Alter her eye color," Milo said. He watched as Arch manipulated her vivid blue eyes to espresso-brown and deepened her pink lips to a sinful shade of red. "Christ, she looks hot. Just an observation," he added when Arch shot him a look.

"I'll have her fitted for brown contact lenses. She owns a wig like that. I spotted it on the shelf of her closet alongside several others, yeah?"

Milo was still staring at Arch's artwork. "Didn't realize you were such a wiz with this software."

"Do you know how many passports I've falsified over the years?"

"Maybe you shouldn't tell me."

"Probably not."

They worked like a well-oiled machine over the next two hours, inventing Portia Livingston and honing the sting. He noticed how they both opted to refer to Evie strictly by her alias. Obviously, they considered it easier to send Portia, a black-hearted con artist into the lion's den rather than softhearted Twinkie. Although they'd devised ways to ensure she'd never be without at least one of the team members at her side. If he didn't know better, he'd think Arch was oblivious to the potential danger to Evie should the sting curdle. What he was, was one hell of an actor. A man with amazing control over his emotions. A quality Milo prided himself on possessing as well. One of the things that allowed them to dance together—the G-man and the C-gee—without missing a beat.

They whipped up ideas and spun scenarios. Calculated and schemed. Milo's mind and body buzzed with adrenaline. Although he'd tired of Arch's bullshit, he never tired of his creative genius. In an odd way, severing their partnership would be like divorcing his wife. A relief, but not one without regrets.

Damn, he thought as they traded off typing fake testimonials, he really needed to get a life.

CHAPTER TWENTY-TWO

THE MOMENT ARCH HAD DRIVEN OFF to meet with Beckett, I'd hunkered down with my research books and the pages I'd printed off of the Internet. I'd been stunned when he hadn't balked at my idea to pose as a psychic to rope Crowe. He didn't give me the thumbs-up, either. He just said, *"I need to speak with Beckett."* But my gut told me Aquarius was a go.

I took it as a good sign that he was gone for more than two hours. I assumed they were working out the details of the sting. I thought positive and crammed on astrology and crystal-ball gazing. In a way it proved therapeutic. It kept my mind off of my friends who'd yet to call to make amends. Kept me from fixating on Arch's daughter and The Wicked Witch of the West, better known as Kate. It was useless to obsess on what I couldn't do much about, if anything. When Arch called I was neck-deep in casting my own astrological chart. I had to practice on someone. "How'd it go?" I asked in an anxious voice.

"You're moving in with me, Sunshine. No arguments, yeah? We're moving fast on this sting. I need to make sure you're properly prepped plus we'll be dabbling in a bit of smoke and mirrors. Pack for two. You and the psychic." Then he listed specific clothing in my closet in addition to the wig I wore whenever I portrayed a 1920's flapper.

"Jeez. What, did you take inventory while we shagged in my wardrobe?"

"Took stock the night you hauled out that French-maid costume, yeah? By the way, pack that, too."

"What for?"

"For fun."

Despite my jittery stomach, I smiled.

By the time Arch returned from the Chameleon Club, my bags were packed. I didn't know if I was moving in for a day, a week, or forever, so I overpacked. Then again I always overpack, according to Arch. He didn't raise an eyebrow when I presented him with two suitcases. He just loaded them and me into his James Bond-ish car and whisked us off to Margate.

"Tell me everything," I said as I adjusted my seat belt.

"Your name is Portia Livingston."

I crinkled my nose. "Sounds like a porn star."

"You watch a lot of porn?" he teased.

"Does ogling naked men in *Playgirl* count? Not that it's a habit or anything. Just skimmed the mag a couple of times with Nic and Jayne. You, know. For a kick. We were bored."

"Uh-huh."

Embarrassed, I turned the tables. "What about you?"

"I swear to you, I have never ogled naked men in *Playgirl*."

I rolled my eyes. "What about *Playboy?*"

"Haven't ogled naked men there, either."

"Ha, ha."

He grinned. "What can I say, lass? I'm a man. I like naked women." He reached over and squeezed my thigh. "I especially like you naked."

"Smooth."

"True."

I ignored the heat of his hand, the heat between my thighs. "Can we stop talking about naked people?"

"You're the one who brought it up."

"Well, just forget the porn reference, will you?"

"I'll try." But he was still smiling.

I focused on getting us back on track as he sped over the Brigantine Bridge, past Trump Marina, Harrah's and the newest, hippest casino, the Borgata. I tried not to think about all the times I'd performed in those places and the much younger entertainers who performed there now. That only made me think about Hollywood and the over-forty role of a lifetime that possibly awaited me there. I'd yet to mention the opportunity to Arch and now didn't seem like the time. We were moving fast on Aquarius.

Focus, Evie, focus. "Portia Livingston, huh? Doesn't scream psychic to me."

"*Doesnae* scream phony, either, yeah? Unlike Madame Helene or The Amazing Prescott."

"Point taken."

"Besides when I imagined you in that black wig, kohl-lined eyes and bloodred lipstick, I thought mysterious and sultry...Portia."

As in Portia Does Pittsburg.

"Here." He plucked an ultraslim, palm-sized device from his pocket, pressed a couple of buttons and passed it to me. Some sort of PDA. I didn't own one, but Nic did. Arch's was a whole lot fancier.

I stared at the touch screen and raised a brow at an altered picture of me. "Wow, you're right. I look...sultry." It made me wonder why I kept fighting nature. Maintaining golden locks was an expensive pain. Except I'd always felt like a blonde at heart. Plus I had a Doris Day/Meg

Ryan fixation. I related to their perky goody-two-shoes image. At least I used to. I was worldlier now. Sort of. That darker, edgier look appealed to my inner bad girl. Not to mention I wouldn't have to contend with dark roots. Hmm. "I recognize this head shot from my portfolio. I guess you manipulated it somehow on a computer?"

"Aye."

"Amazing. Makes you wonder what the models in fashion magazines *really* look like." I squinted closer. "Hey, my eyes are brown."

"We'll get you tinted contacts tomorrow. Tonight, let's concentrate on memorizing Portia's profile."

"Did you and Beckett write something up?"

He took back the PDA, touched the screen and pressed a button. Multitasking while driving—impressive. I'd be swerving all over the road. "Press here to scroll down, yeah? You'll also find background on Senator Wilson."

I palmed the device and skimmed the document as Arch tooled into Atlantic City then downbeach. Along with Wilson's rundown, they had provided me with a profile of scam artist, Portia Livingston, including a basic history of her supernatural shenanigans. I read through the documents twice. I absorbed. I memorized. Then just because I was anal, I skimmed the information again, keying in on specific details. Arch was quiet throughout. Or maybe he spoke but I didn't hear him. My concentration was that intense. All of a sudden, everything clicked and my shoulders relaxed. I passed him the PDA. "Cake."

His lip twitched. "You're cute when you're confident."

"Then don't ask me how I feel about casting an astrological chart."

"It *willnae* come to that. We'll focus on the lecture and readings via your crystal ball. You'll be appearing as a featured guest at a paranormal society event. We'll stock the audience with freelance players and a few nonsanctioned extras. You just need to talk a good game and most of it will be scripted. Considering your superior memory, that *shouldnae* pose a problem, lass."

It wouldn't pose a problem at all. Just like memorizing a monologue for a play. But… "I don't get it. How do I rope Crowe?"

"I'll explain in depth later tonight, yeah? One step at a time. The profile and the speech first." He glanced sideways, all levity gone. "You have to nail this, baby."

My stomach fluttered with butterflies. "I will." We fell into silence and I gave myself a pep talk. I could do this. I *had* to do this. For Beckett. For my country. Selfishly, I had something to prove to myself. To Arch. My gut knotted and I knew I had to chill or I'd break. I closed my eyes and willed nonchalance. I can do this. No big whoop. *Play it cool,* I told myself. *Be a Chameleon.* That mindset got me through the next ten minutes.

Arch pulled into the parking lot of his high-rise and I was further distracted by the subtle opulence of Ocean Heights Towers. The exclusive beach block residence was located in a super ritzy area. I felt underdressed in my jeans and T-shirt. If only I'd worn stiletto sandals instead of high-top sneakers. I noted a uniformed doorman with a groan. Funny, Arch was the one with a checkered past yet *I* felt like the riffraff. Note to self: *Make a good impression with your stellar manners.*

"What floor do you live on?" I asked as I stepped out of the car and gazed up at the stark-white skyscraper.

"Fifteen."

"Ocean view?"

He smiled.

Right. Dumb question. Arch always had the best. Clothes. Food. Accommodations. Jeez. He'd returned a half a million dollars to Kate and he could still afford to live in style. Just how many marks had he conned in his past? If they learned his identity would they be as vindictive as Kate? Would they seek prosecution? Or worse? His head on a platter?

I rolled my eyes heavenward, cursed my imagination. I noted the darkening sky and tried not to think ominous thoughts.

Oblivious to my musings, Arch handed his keys to the valet and instructed the doorman to cart up my luggage. We all exchanged pleasantries and Arch shook both men's hands before ushering me inside. "I hope you tipped Sam generously," I whispered. "Big Red weighs a ton."

"No more than usual, lass."

I ignored his teasing and openly ogled as we crossed the swanky lobby. When we stepped into the elevator, I couldn't help but pry. "Beckett's paying you a heck of a lot more than he's paying me."

He pressed 15 on the brass panel. The mirrored doors slid shut. "I *couldnae* afford this place on my salary from Chameleon."

I knew that, but I guess I'd hoped for a different answer. "So it's paid for with tainted money?"

"Yes and no. I invested my tainted money wisely."

"Oh." I told myself I'd be staying in a condo purchased from legitimate interest. Yeah, that was it. Exhausted, I moved into his arms and rested my head on his shoulder. He held me close, kissed the top of my head, and just like that, my concerns about his past shenanigans melted away. *How can this be wrong when it feels so right?* So what if he was several years younger than me? Financially and professionally, he was light-years ahead of me. He even had a kid. A child he'd gone to great lengths to claim. Did it get any more responsible and respectable than that?

A few seconds later the elevator doors opened and he ushered me down a carpeted hall and into his condo. *Spacious* was the first word that came to mind. Followed by tastefully furnished, albeit it with a manly flair. Lots of leather and dark wood. Fine art embellished the vivid blue walls. I recognized a Monet and a Renoir. "Your grandfather's work," I said in an awestruck whisper.

"Aye." His handsome face brimmed with pride.

No wonder. If I didn't know better, I'd think those beautifully framed paintings were the real deal. Wide-eyed, I moved deeper into the room and tripped over two huge cardboard boxes.

"*Shite.*" Arch steadied me then moved the boxes out of the way. "Sorry, love. Maria must've shifted these."

"Maria?"

"My cleaning lady."

"You have a cleaning lady?" I waved him off. "Never mind." Dumb question.

"They're for you. I had them sent over from London. I intended to bring them to your apartment, but—"

"What's in them?"

Smiling, he snatched a pair of scissors from a nearby drawer and slit the packing tape.

Heart racing, I dropped to my knees and opened the flaps. I dug through foam peanuts and attacked several bubble-wrapped items. "Oh, my God." His grandfather's knickknacks! A ceramic collection of animal figurines, first edition Sherlock Holmes books, an embroidered pillow—*Home is where the heart is*—and more!

After the Caribbean sting, I'd helped Arch clear out Bernard's flat. A flat filled with charming collectables, amazing art and beautiful antiques. There were a few special items that captured my heart. "These are the things I coveted."

"I'm not a sentimental man, Sunshine. But knowing they cheered you… Bernie would want you to have these."

I launched myself into his arms. "You are sentimental, Arch. And sweet. Thank you."

He held me close, kissed the top of my head. I reveled in his strength, his thoughtfulness, in the new thread that strengthened our already existing connection. "I'm thinking you're an old soul."

"That sounds like Jayne talking."

I sighed. "Speaking of Jayne, she slept with Tabasco."

He eased back and regarded me with surprise. "Come again?"

"I know. Crazy. The man exposed her precious psychic as a fraud and she falls into bed with him. I'm thinking she was more upset than grateful. I'm thinking he comforted her and it escalated into, well, sex. She said, it was just one of those things and she's not sorry. He said, she got under his skin and he intends to see her again."

"Sounds serious."

"What do you mean?"

He shrugged. "Just that I know Tabasco. He's not impetuous when it comes to women."

"So I shouldn't worry about him hurting her?"

"What *aboot* her hurting him?"

I narrowed my eyes. "Are you saying I'm sexist?"

"I'm saying there are some good men in this world."

"Like you."

His eyes sparkled with the cocky orneriness that weakened my knees. "What happened to my bad-boy image?"

"Nothing." Reformed or not he'd always be a rebel.

Rock on, James Dean. "It's just that I see beyond the badass attitude."

"You're good for my soul, Sunshine." He kissed me stupid then grasped my hand. "Let me show you around."

High on love, I practically floated through his condo. It wasn't excessively big—two bedrooms with a large living room, dining room, kitchen and two baths—but it was homey, in a guy way. Far and away more homey than my stark apartment. So much for women being superior homemakers. When he'd shown me the guest room, I couldn't help imagining converting it into a Disney room for Cassidy. Call me crazy, but knowing Arch had a little girl and knowing how much he loved her, suddenly I was imagining myself as a part-time mom.

Yeah. I know. Kate allowed him limited access as is. Like she was going to allow Cassidy to fly east?

Still…

Arch's phone rang. "Yeah?" His standard greeting. "Brilliant. On my way." He disconnected and stroked my cheek. "Tabasco located a big store. I'm going to check it *oot*. You settle in. When I get back I'll quiz you on your profile, yeah? Later we'll review your Web site. Woody should have it up and running in a few hours."

"I have a Web site?"

"Portia has a Web site and it's key to her success."

I'd been surfing psychic Web sites all day. I'd been stunned at the services they offered to conduct over the phone or the Internet. How could you spiritually connect without being in the same room? Surely most, if not all, of these people were scam artists. How could there be so many suckers in the world? Yet, I knew from all of my research on grifters that intelligence and savvy had little to do with falling prey to a scam. As long as you possessed some weakness, some vulnerability, you were a potential mark. Even U.S. senators had an Achilles' heel.

I squashed my anxiety and donned my poker face. I squeezed Arch's biceps. "I know you're worried. Don't be. I'm a good actress, a quick study and a wiz at improvisation."

His sexy mouth curved into a tender smile. "Not telling me anything I *dinnae* know, Sunshine."

I smirked. "You always say the right thing."

"Was I right telling you *aboot* Cassidy?"

My heart ached at his flash of vulnerability. "Absolutely." I squeezed his arms tighter. "I hope you know your secret is safe with me and that I'll do whatever I can to…to…" To what? To convince a manic, bitter heiress to have a heart?

"I know, lass."

He kissed me, soft and sweet, yet unbelievably potent. I swayed a little when he eased away.

He brushed my bangs out of my eyes. "So, what do you want for dinner, *Portia?* I'll grab something while I'm *oot.*"

I blinked away the sensual cobwebs. "Chinese?" I actually didn't mind that he hadn't invited me along to see the big store. It was nearly seven o'clock. I was wiped out and I trusted whatever he learned he'd share with me. Ah, trust. My skin heated from the warm fuzzies as much as from Arch's tender touch.

"Right then. Make yourself at home while I'm gone." He planted a quick kiss on my forehead then zipped out the door.

"Make myself at home. Right." This place was perfect. Nothing to clean or rearrange. I wasn't inclined to snooping in drawers and I didn't feel like watching TV. Arch had taken his PDA so I couldn't study Portia's profile. Not that

I needed to. The info was engrained in my brain. Still, I was feeling anxious about this gig. So much was at stake. My research books would have been nice, but they were in my suitcase, along with my clothes. I couldn't unpack because Sam hadn't delivered my luggage. He must have been waylaid. Or maybe he'd gotten a hernia trying to heave Big Red from the trunk of Arch's car. Speaking of cars, Al's Auto had yet to call about mine. Probably they were closed by now, but I could at least leave a message. Just as I reached into my purse, my phone rang. I looked at the screen. *Nic.* Not knowing her mood, my tone was wary. "Hi."

"I want to apologize for this morning," she said by way of a greeting.

I nearly sagged to the floor in relief. Argument over! Instead, I slipped out the sliding glass door and onto Arch's balcony. I breathed in the warm salt air, smelled rain. The view of the Atlantic Ocean and the Atlantic City skyline was flipping spectacular. "I'm sorry, too, Nic. I don't now why I got so huffy."

"Because I got huffy first?"

I smiled at that. "Are you okay? I left a couple of messages earlier. I even dropped by, but you weren't there."

"I went for a walk on the beach to clear my head. Then later Jayne called and I met up with her."

So they *had* been together. "Is she still mad at me?"

"We talked and got past that real quick. She knows we acted out of love. However, she is majorly pissed at herself. She feels like an idiot for being duped by Sheila Kurtz."

"Who's Sheila Kurtz?"

"Madame Helene. Apparently, Tabasco showed Jayne where the so-called psychic *really* lives and what kind of car she *really* drives. We're talking beach block in Longport and a brand-new Cadillac. When Jayne refused to believe him, he made her hide in the bushes while he knocked on the door and pretended to be an undercover cop."

"Isn't that illegal?"

"Probably a lot of what Chameleon does is illegal, Evie, but since they're working for the right side of the law—"

"Got it. Go on."

"At first Mrs. Kurtz played dumb, but Tabasco poured it on and the woman crumbled within five minutes. He got back the money Jayne paid the woman to lift that curse off of you, by the way. So do you feel any differently?" she teased. "Like a dark cloud is hovering over you?"

I glanced skyward. "Only literally. So…I guess you know that Tabasco and Jayne hooked up."

"Given the chemistry I witnessed during the intervention, I'm not surprised. She's nuts about him."

"He seems pretty nuts about her, too."

"Speaking of unlikely pairs," Nic said. "Did Arch get home yet?"

"He did. I'm at his place right now."

"Let me guess. Expensive digs."

I ignored the sarcasm in her tone. "It's amazing, Nic. A fifteenth-floor condo with an ocean view. I'm on the balcony right now."

"I'd scoot inside if I were you. A thunderstorm's lurking."

"I'm okay for now." I closed my eyes and focused on the calming sound of the waves lapping at the shore. I braced myself for Nic's disapproval. "I'm going to stay here for awhile, Nic. With Arch."

"You're moving in with the guy?"

"Think of it as a trial run." I opted not to mention his marriage proposal. He'd yet to read my journal. There was a possibility that once he did, the offer would be withdrawn. Until then, I decided to put wedded bliss with Arch Robert Duvall, the Baron of Broxley, out of my head. Besides, I needed to focus on work. On Aquarius.

"You have to nail this, baby."

I shivered. What if the sting curdled? What if guns were involved?

Bang!

"Evie? Are you still there?"

"What? Yes." I shook off an image of a gut-shot Fish. "I'm sorry. What did you say?"

"I asked you about Slick. Can't imagine he's pleased about you moving in with Arch?"

Here we go. I opened my eyes and saw a distant streak of lightning flash from sea to sky. "Beckett knows how much I love Arch. I'm sure he's fine with it. Listen, Nic, I have to tell you…" *Leave out the part about the kiss.* "I had an epiphany today and so did Beckett."

"What kind of epiphany?"

I heard her light up a cigarette. Was she going for aloof? Or did she need a smoke to calm her nerves? "That confusing bit of chemistry we had going? It flatlined," I said. "On both sides. We're just friends and, before you make a derisive comment, I mean that with every fiber of my being."

Puff. Puff. "So it's Arch all the way, huh?"

"All the way." I smoothed my windblown hair from my eyes. "I hope you can live with that."

"Are you happy?"

"Delirious."

"Then I can live with it. Unless, of course he breaks your heart, then I'll have to hurt him."

I laughed. "You're a good friend."

"Except when I'm feeling sorry for myself and suffering from a hangover."

I wondered if that had anything to do with Beckett. "Sure you don't want to talk about it?"

"I'm sure. So. You and Arch. Jayne and Tabasco. I need to get a hobby. I sure won't be spending as much time with you two."

I frowned. "That's not true."

"Yes, it is. But that's okay. Really." She sighed. "Christ, I sound pathetic. I'm fine, Evie. And I'm thrilled for you and Jayne. Honest. Listen, I have to go."

"Wait—"

"Are you still singing at the club tomorrow night?"

"As far as I know." Unless something changed because of Aquarius.

"Great. I'll see you there."

"But—" Why did most of our discussions end with her cutting me off?

Thunder boomed. The glass door rattled. I yelped and fumbled my phone. *"Noooooo!"*

I watched in horror as my cell plunged fifteen stories to its death. Then shrieked again when the clouds exploded and drenched me. "Crap!"

I flew to the door and yanked on the handle. It didn't budge. I tried again. Locked from the inside? "You have *got* to be kidding!"

Raindrops continued to pummel me. Lightning cracked. What had seemed beautiful a minute ago now seemed dangerous. What if I got zapped?

Okay. Don't panic.

What would Arch do?

He'd spring the lock.

I cursed myself for leaving my purse indoors. I could sure use a nail file. Or a credit card. I swiped my soaked hair out of my face, looked for something to jimmy the door with.

Nada.

When I spun back around, I saw a face in the fogged-over glass.

I screamed!

The door slid opened.

I scrambled back.

"Ms. Parish?"

I squinted through the downpour. "Sam?" The door-man. "*Sam!* Thank you!" I rushed into the air-conditioned condo and shut out the storm. "Your timing is incredible. I was afraid I was…" I trailed off when I realized he wasn't looking into my eyes.

Oh, no. Not again.

I glanced down. My pale yellow T-shirt was plastered to my shivering body. My sheer bra was soaked. Okay. This was embarrassing. This was par for the course. I folded my arms over my chest. "Thank you."

"Um. I put your luggage over there, Miss."

At least he hadn't called me ma'am. "I see that. Thank you."

"Can I do anything else—"

"No. I'm fine. Thanks. You can go. Wait!" Arms still crossed, I located my purse. The least I could do was tip him for saving me from electrocution.

"That's okay," he said with a grin as he rushed to the door. "You already made my day."

Color me mortified. What was it with me and my boobs? Did I have a secret desire to flash my miniblessings to the world one person at a time? I hurried toward the bathroom and a hot shower. I wondered if Sam was discreet or a gossip. So much for making a good impression.

Ten minutes later, steam clouded the generous-sized

shower. Or maybe it was my brain smoking. I mentally reviewed Portia's profile and Wilson's background over and over. Distracted, I washed my face with shampoo.

Snap out of it, Parish!

Right.

Relying on available toiletries, I differentiated between soap and shampoo and hurried about my business. I stepped out and toweled dry. Masculine scents wafted and mesmerized me. Suddenly, all I could think about was Arch and how he'd entrusted me with his most cherished secret. I wanted to make our first night together in his home a memorable one. I wanted to superseal that indefinable connection.

I dried my hair and considered my options. He'd be home soon. Greeting him naked would be clichéd. Frivolous, too, considering I should be gearing up for Portia's speech.

I looked in the mirror, rolled back my shoulders and channeled Beckett. "Franklin D. Roosevelt conferred with a psychic about post-WWII world relations. Abraham Lincoln participated in séances and experienced visions. And those are just *two* of our political leaders who sought advice through supernatural means." I flashed on a blurb I'd read on a professional astrologer's Web site. "Anyone seeking extra insight can benefit from a personal astrologer. Even government agencies have been known to hire an astrologer during times of crisis."

I talked a good game, but I could do better. I knew from past experience that my demeanor would change once I was fully in character. That required the appropriate costume, hair, and makeup. I instantly saw a way to combine business and pleasure and—bonus—a way to alleviate my stress.

I raided my suitcase and located my cosmetics and bobbed wig. Envisioning that doctored head shot, I transformed myself into a sultry brunette with kohl-lined eyes and bloodred lips. I couldn't do anything about my blue irises, but I could dress the part, starting with my, or rather Portia's, undergarments. Specifically the racy black lace undies Nic had talked me into buying when she was trying to urge me out of my postdivorce funk.

On our first job together, Arch had asked if I'd be comfortable reviewing my character's profile in my bra and panties. He'd been teasing and I'd been shy. Of course, I'd said, no.

That was the old me. The insecure me.

This was now. The new me. The confident me. The me prepared to take on the crooked director of a U.S. government agency.

I stepped into a pair of shiny black stiletto pumps.

I heard the front door open and shut.

"Baby, I'm home."

My body sizzled. Feeling naughty and anxious, I slinked out of the bedroom wearing my flirty lingerie. "Evie's not here, but Portia is and she's ready to show you the stars."

His eyes devoured me in a head-to-toe sweep. He fumbled the bags in his arms. "Bollocks."

My confidence level zoomed. Call me Super Chameleon. In that sexually charged moment I possessed the power to conquer the world.

Or at least one shifty government bigwig and the heart of one former con artist.

I glanced at the Chinese takeout, at Arch. I quirked a saucy smile. "Lo Mein? Tea? Or me?"

CHAPTER TWENTY-THREE

MILO ORDERED WOODY TO GO HOME around ten. "You're not any good to me dead and you've got one foot in the grave, Kid. Go home."

Woody didn't argue. He was exhausted. He hadn't managed to hack into the "dirty" files, but he had created a Web site for Portia Livingston. He'd included services, raving testimonials, a bio, and an altered image of Evie. Then he'd planted a dozen different stories about the charismatic psychic on targeted Internet gossip rags and paranormal blogs.

Portia Livingston was now an established force in cyber world. Tomorrow morning an article would appear in a local magazine touting Portia's rise to fame and an upcoming appearance in Atlantic City. Only twelve copies of that specific edition would be printed, via a media contact of Milo's, and all copies would be distributed per his instruction.

Tabasco had located the big store and tomorrow he and Woody would rig the place with surveillance cameras and audio.

Arch would prep Evie.

By the time Milo contacted Crowe for permission to pick up an investigation Chameleon had dropped, all of their ducks would be in a row.

He escaped The Cave around midnight, hung out long enough to make sure Pops went home instead of sleeping downstairs, then locked the doors and retired to his apartment.

He was too hyper to sleep.

He poured a Scotch, settled on his worn sofa, and flipped on the TV. He surfed until he came to the Discovery Channel and thought about Nic. Fifteen minutes into *MythBusters,* his cell rang. He ID'd the caller. Speak of the devil. "Are you okay?"

"That's a helluva way to answer the phone, Slick. Why would you ask such a thing?"

Noting her slurred words, he set aside his own drink. "Because it's—" he glanced at his watch "—one in the morning. What are you doing, Nicole?"

"Getting a hobby, *Milo.*"

He flicked off the TV. "That hobby involve drinking?"

"What are you, the police?" She snorted. "Oh, wait. You are. Sort of. Hey. Do you know how to play pool?"

He shoved his feet back into his shoes. "Sure. That your new hobby?"

"Well, Evie's with Arch and Jayne's with Tabasco. I have to do *something* to occupy my spare time." Milo heard the sharp crack of pool balls in the background. Damn. Was she at a skanky pool hall? "Except, I'm tired of fending off some amorous competitors, if you know what I'm saying. I'd go home, but I'm too drunk to drive. A couple of yahoos offered to take me home but—"

"Do not get in a car with anyone, do you hear me?"

"I'm drunk, not deaf. Hey," she groused off the phone. "Move it or lose it, dickhead."

Fuck. "Where are you?"

"The Beach Bar."

"On Brigantine?"

"You know it?"

He was already out the door and in his car. "I'll be there in ten minutes."

He tried to keep her on the phone but she complained about not being able to shoot pool one handed. Nine minutes later he walked into the dive and spotted her slouched in one of two booths. Just before Milo got to her, a man set a drink in front of her and slid in.

"Don't want it," she shouted over the canned music and shoved the drink away.

The bastard cozied up and said something in her ear.

She elbowed him. "Go away."

"You heard the lady," Milo said as he stepped up to the scene.

The man glared. "Who the fuck are you?"

"Her friend." He hitched back his jacket just enough to give the prick a peek at his Sig.

The man raised his hands in surrender and disappeared.

Nic cocked a brow at Milo. "Impressive."

Even dressed down in jeans and a black tank top, she looked classy…and totally out of place. "Come here often?" he asked.

"Almost never."

"Why tonight?"

She waved a limp hand at the pool table. "The hobby thing. Wanna play?"

"I'll take a rain check."

Those luscious lips curled into a taunting smile. "Worried I'll kick your ass? Nice ass, by the way."

"Thanks. Right back atcha."

"It's dragging a little now, actually. My ass."

He bit back a smile. "Need some help?"

Gratitude shone in her glassy eyes. "That would be great, Milo."

For once she didn't say his name with contempt. He helped her out of the booth, steadied her when she wobbled.

The bartender let out a sharp whistle.

"Oh, shit." She fumbled in her purse. "My tab."

"I'll get it." He maneuvered her to the bar and propped her on a stool. "How much?"

The bartender showed him the bill.

Milo shot her a look. "Surprised you're still conscious."

"Surprised I'm this lit."

He grinned and shook his head, slapped a large bill on the bar. "Keep the change." Then he wrapped an arm around Nic's waist, ushered her out and poured her into his car.

"Bad day?" he asked.

"Shitty day. And you?"

"Productive day."

"That's nice. Figure out how Crowe set you up?"

"Work in progress."

"Hush-hush," she said with a crooked smile. "Got it." She rested her head on the window. "Evie says you're just friends. That true?"

"Whatever was there fizzled."

"Sorry to hear that. You would've made a nice couple."

"Not really. No chemistry." He glanced over at Nicole's profile, felt a stir down below. "Gotta have chemistry."

She caught his gaze and sucker punched his senses. He nearly swerved off the road. "What do you call this?" she asked with a flick of her hand, indicating the sexual tension between them.

"Dangerous."

She sighed and slumped back against the window. "That's what I thought."

They didn't speak for the rest of the short drive. Nor when he half carried her up the steps to her apartment. She fished her keys out of her purse, but couldn't get the key in the lock. On her third try, Milo took over.

"Thanks," she said.

"Sure." He swung open the door and helped her over the threshold. "You going to be okay?"

"Sure." She turned to face him and balanced herself by grabbing two fistfuls of his jacket.

Her touch burned through his clothes. She radiated a sadness and sexuality that scrambled sane thought. *This is bad.*

"You should go," she said as she tugged him into her foyer and kicked shut her door.

Real bad.

A heartbeat later she launched herself at him. He slammed against the wall, groaned with misery and ecstasy as she grinded against him. Her mouth and moves were hot and wild. He knew he should end this. And he would. Soon.

One hand palmed her luscious ass. The other anchored at the nape of her neck, his fingers tangling in her thick, dark hair. She smelled of expensive perfume and smoke. Tasted like beer and tequila. Class and sin rolled into one beautiful enchilada.

She broke away long enough to tug him off the wall and down a hall. "Let's take this inside, Slick."

Cloaked in darkness, he assumed she was leading him to her bedroom. His cock throbbed in anticipation. *Down boy. Not going there. Not. Going.* "Nicole."

She responded with a passionate kiss. Christ, he

couldn't think straight with her tongue in his mouth. He kissed her back and lost himself in a sexual whirlwind. He wanted to touch that gorgeous face, but he was waylaid as she jerked his jacket over his shoulders and arms.

Then he felt her tugging at his shoulder holster. "How do you get this thing off?"

Kiss broken, his senses returned. He grasped her hands. "Stop."

She wrenched away and pulled her tank top over her head, revealing a black lace bra.

Moonlight streamed through her windows and shed light on those perfect breasts. Jesus.

"Don't play the gentleman, Slick. I know you want to fuck me." She moved in for another assault.

He shifted and hauled her off of her feet, flipped her onto the bed.

Startled, she stared up at him as he settled and hovered.

"Yes, I want to fuck you, Nic, as you so eloquently put it. But not like this. Not now."

He couldn't help thinking about the men who'd used her, the ex-fiancé who'd abandoned her. He wanted her to know that he appreciated her for more than her exotic beauty and kick-ass body. He wanted to be clear of his own baggage. Of Crowe.

Her eyes glittered with confusion and anger. A heartbeat later she slapped his face.

He ignored the sting, framed those stunning cheekbones, and thumbed away a renegade tear. "What if I'm the right man?"

"Then we're doomed."

"Not unless we both throw in the towel." He kissed her forehead. "Get some sleep, sweetheart."

She curled into a ball. "I hate it when you're nice."

His lip twitched. "I'll keep that in mind."

Milo wanted to crawl into bed with her. He wanted to hold her in his arms until they both fell to sleep. It sounded like heaven to him. Sounded like torture, too. He only had so much control.

He left while he still had the strength, only he didn't want to leave her alone. What if she staggered to the bathroom, tripped and hit her head on the tub? What if… He shook his head. Evie and her runaway imagination were toxic. Still, he bypassed the front door.

After draping his jacket and shoulder holster on a chair in the living room, he grabbed a bottle of water from Nic's fridge, snatched up her remote control and made himself comfortable on her couch.

Halfway through a rerun of *M*A*S*H,* he caught a whiff of flowery soap. He turned and saw Nicole leaning against the kitchen divider. She'd swapped her contacts for a pair of black-rimmed glasses. Changed into a pair of striped boxers and an oversize T-shirt, scrubbed her face clean and twisted her long hair into two braids. Shades of Lolita.

Mr. Happy danced with joy.

Forget it.

He shifted as she moved closer.

"What are you doing here?" she asked in a dry, hoarse voice.

He passed her his water. "I have this thing. Insomnia." He motioned to her plasma screen. "Your TV's nicer than mine." He watched her drink from his bottle, felt her unease. "Why are you up?"

"Couldn't sleep. The room kept spinning."

He quirked a sympathetic smile. "Come here." He dug a travel packet of Tylenol out of his pants pocket and passed it to her.

She sat next to him and chased the pills with water. "Thanks."

Noting her tense posture he opened his arms and pulled her into him. Either she was too tipsy or too tired to argue. His heart pounded when she rested her head on his shoulder.

"What's with the endless supply of pain relievers, Slick?"

"An endless supply of headaches."

"I guessed that much. Know the cause?"

"Stress."

"Your job?"

"My life."

She glanced up. "Sucks?"

"A little. Yours?"

"A little."

He tugged at one of her braids. "Looks like we have something in common other than getting blitzed when we're having a shitty day."

She smiled a bit, quirked a brow. "You're not going to hold anything I said or did tonight against me tomorrow, are you?"

"Think again."

"That's not nice."

"You don't like it when I'm nice, remember?"

She swallowed and licked her lips. "This isn't going to work, you know."

"Challenge accepted."

"I don't like bossy men."

"I don't like bitchy women."

She snorted. "Doomed." She looked away and focused on the TV. "What are we watching?"

"The best show ever written."

"Buffy the Vampire Slayer?"

"You're right," Milo teased. "This isn't going to work."

A few minutes passed. Hawkeye and B.J. sniped at one another. Klinger fell in love and Charles fell in love with the idea of love.

Milo held Nic in his arms.

He thought she'd fallen asleep until she cleared her throat. "So. We're just going to watch TV all night or until we doze off here on the couch?"

He kissed the top of her head. "Sounds like heaven, doesn't it?"

"A little."

His pulse kicked up when she slipped her hand into his. A small gesture of trust and affection. A moment of alcohol-induced weakness. He burned to know the marsh-mallow inside the tough cookie. Questioning Nic when her defenses were down seemed the fastest means to that end. Of course, instead of cooperating, she could easily shut down and kick his ass out the door. Knowing Nic, odds were on the latter. He didn't want to spoil this moment. At the same time... "You could do that."

"What?"

"Act on television. Or the movies. Why are you wasting your time and talent in Atlantic City? Why aren't you in Hollywood?"

She snuggled deeper into his arms and focused on the TV. Okay. Sucked that she didn't want to talk but at the same just holding her was thrill enough. Christ, she felt good, smelled good. But then it got better. She spoke. "Partly because my friends are here. Partly because I'm not that talented and refuse to trade on my looks. Mostly because I don't like playing games or kissing ass."

Although her words were slightly slurred, her senti-ments rang loud and clear. It only added to his confusion. "So you're not motivated by fame."

"Like I'd welcome paparazzi on my ass 24/7?"

"Or fortune."

"I have what I need and then some."

He knew that. From his research, he assumed she'd inherited the hefty chunk in her bank account. She came
from a wealthy family. Bottom line, she could live off her
savings and investments. "You mentioned needing a hobby
to fill your time. Why not apply yourself more to your profession? If you're not that talented, as you say—though I
don't believe it—take classes."

She snorted. "Because I'm not *that* driven to work in
entertainment."

"Then why are you in the field at all?"

She let out an aggravated sigh. "Partly because I'm a
Bohemian at heart. Mostly to piss off my family."

Huh. That said a lot, but not enough. He only burned
with a dozen more questions.

"Milo."

"Yeah?"

She glanced up at him through heavy-lidded eyes.
Damn, those eyeglasses were sexy. And those jade-green
eyes, beautiful even when they were bleary from booze.
"Either shut up or go home."

In other words, he'd hit a sore spot. Fair enough. He'd
back off. For now. He sure as hell wasn't going home. He
grinned down at her, brushed his lips over her furrowed
brow and settled in for the night.

They both focused on the antics of the 4077th. Too bad
surgeons couldn't mend emotionally mangled hearts.

"Just so you know, Slick," she said in a gruff voice. "I
come with a lot of baggage."

He smoothed a hand down her toned arm and clasped
her slender fingers. "Just so you know, Nicole, so do I."

CHAPTER TWENTY-FOUR

I BOLTED UPRIGHT, DRENCHED in sweat, a scream lodged in my throat. An image of Simon the Fish swam in my brain. A sea of blood. The smell of smoke. I blocked it out, blinked at my unfamiliar surroundings. Where was I?

Arch's condo.

Right.

I was safe.

"What is it, love?"

"Nothing." I fell back on the bed, into Arch's arms. What time was it? Still dark. *Go to sleep. Don't dream.*

"If this is *aboot* Crowe—"

"It's not. I'm good." *Go to sleep. Don't dream.*

"Sunshine—"

"I'm fine." I snuggled deeper into his arms, ignored my erratic heartbeat. No one would get hurt this time. No one would get shot. I would not crack. *I can do this.*

MILO'S ASS ITCHED. No. Vibrated. What the hell? He shook his head, but cobwebs clung. Where was he? He registered the woman in his arms, the posh surroundings. Hell. He reached for his phone, tried not to wake Nic. Maybe he could ignore the call. He glanced at the caller ID. Maybe not.

"What's up, Gina?"

He listened as his number-one shill spoke in coded sentences. Due to a glitch she wouldn't be joining the team tonight for the launch of Aquarius.

"I hope you don't think this is personal," she said in a hushed voice.

"I don't."

"No matter our differences, I wouldn't leave Twinkie twisting in the wind."

"I know."

"It's just that I'm tangled with…Syd, and he's…swimming with sharks. I have to go. Don't contact me. I'll be in touch."

"Wait. Shit. *Fuck.*"

"What's wrong?" Nic pushed off of him, her green eyes bright with alarm.

He swallowed hard at the early morning vision. Hungover and disheveled, she still roused primal urges. Even the imprint his bunched T-shirt had left on her cheek was sexy. "A teammate in trouble. Maybe. I'm not sure."

"Evie?"

"No. Gina."

She processed the name, nabbed her glasses from the cocktail table and shoved them on. "What kind of trouble?"

"I wish I knew."

"Do you think she's in some sort of danger?"

"I hope not." From what she'd said, *Syd* was the one in danger. But Gina wouldn't bail without trying to save the man's ass. *"He's doing this for me."* Bailing on a colleague was unthinkable.

Nic placed a hand on his arm. "Evie described Hot Legs as a realistic version of the character Angelina Jolie played in *Mr. & Mrs. Smith,*" she said, in a thick hoarse voice. "I'm betting she can not only kick a man's ass, but several asses at the same time."

Her attempt to offer comfort warmed him as much as Evie's description. "Leave it to Twinkie to cite a movie, but yeah, Gina's lethal."

"This trouble. Does it have anything to do with trying to clear your name in the Mad Dog murder?"

"Partly."

"I'm guessing this is a team effort."

"It is."

"So Evie's involved."

"She will be. We're launching a sting tonight. She's the central figure."

She narrowed her eyes. "How can you put her in that kind of danger?"

Guilt nipped at his conscience. "She's a Chameleon, Nic. She's doing her job."

"Without proper and extensive training. She's not Gina for chrissake."

"I know that." He grasped her hand. "Trust me. I know. That's why we're taking special precautions."

She looked away. "I hate this. I hate you."

He kissed her palm.

"I'm not fooled by your calm and casual demeanor, Slick. I know you're worried about Evie *and* Gina. I don't care if they were both Rambo incarnate. They're women." She waved him off before he could counter. "Don't bother denying it. It's the way you're built. You're a protector. Chivalrous, too. Pity for both of us, that last part."

"How so?"

"Because we missed out on great sex last night."

He recognized the dodge, a ploy to keep her mind off Evie. "I like my women sober."

"Too bad, because as long as I'm in my right mind, I won't be making that offer again."

Sober and defenses back in place. He'd expected no less. He cocked a brow. "We'll see about that."

"Bossy and arrogant."

"Bitchy and scared."

"I'm not—"

"I could use your help on Sunday. We're staging a paranormal event to sting Crowe. I need extras to perpetuate the ruse."

"Just tell me who I'm supposed to be and what I'm supposed to do."

"I will. Later."

"Why not now?" She glared up at him as he grabbed his coat and holstered Sig. "Where are you going? We're in the middle of an argument."

"No argument, sweetheart. Once I'm clear of this mess, I *will* seduce your pants off."

She followed him to the door. "Wait." She caught his arm, blew out a breath. "In spite of what happened last night, the things I said, did…I don't want this."

Another man might have cursed her a cock teaser. He knew better. He'd seen a glimpse of the marshmallow. "You want it."

"I—"

He smothered her protest with his mouth, kissed her hard and deep then with a tenderness that had her trembling in his arms. Confident he'd made his point, he eased away and out the door. "I'll be in touch."

I ROUSED AROUND 7:00 A.M. with a fiendish headache, feeling melancholy and sluggish. Damn that nightmare. I wondered if Beckett had spoken to Arch about the Fish shooting. I wanted to know, but I didn't. I needed to focus on Aquarius.

Last night after a hot and heavy shag, Arch and I had gorged on Chinese. Throughout, he'd quizzed me on Portia Livingston's profile and Senator Wilson's background. After, we'd studied my Web site, or rather Portia's Web site. Amazing what Woody had constructed in so little time. Then I filled Arch in on everything I'd read and learned about crystal-ball gazing and astrology. Together we wrote the speech intended to dazzle a faux paranormal society but mostly a crooked AIA director. He filled me in on details of the sting and, later, I fell asleep mentally rehearsing the gig play-by-play. I'd drifted off jazzed and confident.

Just now I felt disoriented and, okay, anxious. Not because Tabasco and I were debuting our barely rehearsed duo at the club tonight. But because afterward we'd be launching Aquarius. When Arch had said we'd be moving fast, he hadn't been kidding. The first leg of the venture would be the worst. It involved Tabasco flying me up to Massachusetts in his single engine Cessna in the middle of the night. It's not that I didn't trust his flying skills. I didn't trust my stomach. Surely that teeny plane would bump and bounce through the skies and I'd puke my guts out before we landed. Then I had to turn around and fly back into Philadelphia on a commercial airliner the next morning. I anticipated heavy turbulence because, hey, just my luck. When I stepped off that plane I'd be Portia Livingston. I needed to be sharp physically and mentally. Tough to pull off when you're woozy and green.

At least I'd have Gina by my side. If anyone could inspire me to suck it up, it was the woman who'd pegged me a piece of fluff.

"Morning, Sunshine."

Arch's sexy voice *zing-zapped* my senses. My heart pounded and my inner thighs tingled. Call me shallow, but his thick Scottish accent turned me on. Nothing new there. He'd had me at *"Where the bloody hell are you?"* The first words out of his mouth during our first phone call. Just minutes prior to our first meeting. It had been one thrill after another since then and I realized, as I looked into his mesmerizing eyes, I never wanted it to end. "Yes."

"Yes, what?"

"Yes, I'll marry you."

I'm not sure who was more surprised. Him or me? It's not like I'd thought it out. I'd been preoccupied with Aquarius. He smiled and I panicked.

"Wait! That just sort of popped out. I don't… God." I scratched my neck. "Can we just, you know, go back to sleep, wake up, and start the day over?"

"No." He rolled on top of me, weight braced on his forearms, fingers tangled in my hair. Mouth on mine— achingly tender. Then more insistent. Then—oh, my, God—this kiss freaking sizzled! Body—melted. Brain— melted. Senses—four alarm fire!

I burned for this man. So why was I frozen?

He eased off and regarded me with an arrogant twinkle in his eyes.

"No one's ever kissed me like that," I croaked.

"Good to know, Sunshine."

"I'm sorry I didn't respond properly. I was sort of…stunned."

"I know the feeling. *Wasnae* expecting an answer so soon, yeah?"

"About that." I could scarcely breathe.

"*Dinnae* mindfuck it, lass."

"But… You haven't read my diary, yet."

"I *dinnae* need to."

"Yes, you do!" My voice and strength returned full force. I pushed him off of me and sprang out of bed. Clothes flew in all directions as I rooted through Big Red in search of the spiraled keeper of my innermost thoughts. I pulled a baggy T-shirt over my head then bounded back on the mattress, journal clenched in my clammy hands.

Arch pushed himself upright. Relaxed against the headboard, he looked befuddled and amused. And sexy. Naked sexy. Bed-mussed sexy. I'd-like-to-do-him-in-twenty-four-different-ways sexy.

Focus, Evie, focus.

"We can't move forward without complete trust," I said. "You shared your private stuff. I want to do the same. I don't want you to think I'm keeping secrets."

He gestured toward my journal, the one he'd bought me in the Caribbean. "I *dinnae* have to read the words to know your mind, yeah?"

"What do you mean?"

"I know you, lass. I know how you think, how you tick. You telegraph your feelings with your expression, your body language. Except for the times you're intent on portraying a specific character, you're an open book. *Withoot* reading the content, I know what's inside that journal."

"No, you don't."

The left side of his mouth kicked up. "Yeah. I do."

I felt ridiculously insulted. Predictable. Michael considered me predictable. Boring. I narrowed my eyes. "Okay, smarty-pants. Let's hear it."

"Fine. Jesus." He dragged his hands down his stubbled jaw then crossed his muscular arms over his bare chest.

Sexy. "You ranted *aboot* the entertainment industry. In particular the Atlantic City casinos. You cursed them for hiring youth over experience. Sexuality over talent. You blasted Stone for leaving you for a younger bird. You blasted yourself for growing older. You wondered *aboot* your place in this world. You wondered what it would be like to be a super spy's sidekick. Only the super spy turned *oot* to be a con artist."

"Former con artist," I grumbled.

"You pondered your parents' troubles. Your troubled relationship with your parents. You obsessed on the Fish shooting, yeah?"

"Yeah." I swallowed and waited, hoping and fretting he was going to choose now to open that can of worms. He didn't.

"You poured *oot* your heart regarding me and Beckett."

I tensed.

"You penned your feelings *aboot* me. The things you love. The things you hate. The things you question. You did the same for Beckett." He angled his head. "You compared us, good and bad, in an effort to figure *oot* who was the better man."

"You read my journal. At some point in time—"

"I *didnae.*" He reached out and pulled me against him. "I *wouldnae* invade your privacy, lass."

I believed him. Which meant I was an idiot in most people's eyes. *Never trust a grifter.* It also meant I *was* predictable. Either that or Arch was a mind reader.

He skimmed his fingertips up and down my arm in a soothing gesture. "Even though I'm a confident man, I *dinnae* suppose I'd fancy reading the parts where you favored Beckett over me. If you jotted down any sexual fantasies *aboot* him, I definitely *wouldnae* enjoy reading that. You said that whatever you felt for him, other than friendship, is over."

"Completely."

"I believe you. This conversation is enough, you know?" He kissed the top of my head. "I *dinnae* need or want to read your journal, Sunshine."

Call me relieved. Deep down, I didn't want him to read everything I'd written about Beckett, either. On paper, the government agent definitely came off the better man. But that didn't make him the right man. Not for me. "Okay, but…I have to confess something that you don't know and didn't guess. Something that happened yesterday. I just…I don't want it to come out later and bite me in the butt."

"Okay."

I snuggled against him, my gaze fixed on his tattoo. Even though the incident was innocent at heart, I couldn't look him in the eyes. "It's just, I know it's going to hurt your feelings and…"

"Spit it out, love."

"I asked Beckett to kiss me. I needed to confirm what I suspected. That any romantic interest in the man was dead. Which it was. I didn't feel a thing. No zing. No zap. Nada. It was the same for him. Zilch. Even though we gave it our all. You can't imagine how relieved I was. I…" I realized suddenly that he was no longer stroking my arm. In fact, I wasn't sure he was breathing. Heart in throat, I risked his gaze. My stomach dropped. "I should have left out the *gave it our all* part."

"Could have done *withoot* that, aye."

I bit my lower lip. "I'm sorry."

"I'll live."

"But will you get over it?"

"Absolutely."

If only he would've backed that up with a smile. "Maybe I'm more trouble than I'm worth. I'll understand if you want to withdraw your proposal."

That prompted a grin. "Nice try." Still holding me, he nabbed his ringing phone from the bedside table. "Yeah? *Shite.* No. Let's hash it *oot* in person. Be right over." He disconnected and rolled out of bed.

My heart thudded and not wholly because he was gloriously naked. "What's wrong?"

"Gina *cannae* make it tonight," he said, while stabbing his legs into a pair of jeans.

Tha-dump. Tha-dump. "Why not?" I imagined the worst. "Did she and Syd get caught?"

"No, but they're in deep."

"That doesn't sound good."

"They know what they're doing." He pulled a striped oxford from his closet, tugged on socks and shoes.

I marveled at his calm. Then again Arch was always calm in a crisis. "Should we postpone the sting?"

"The sooner we rope and hang Crowe, the better." He nabbed his PDA from his dresser and settled next to me. "While I'm gone, I want you to study everything we went over last night. I know you have it memorized, but humor me, yeah?"

Throat tight, I nodded.

"Remember the password to get into my files?"

"Yes, but I'm not sure I remember how to work this thing."

"Watch and focus." He went through the process then made me do it. "Got it?"

"Got it."

"If you think of anything, have any questions, *dinnae* bother trying to input it and for fuck's sake, *dinnae* write it down anywhere. Use the digital voice recorder. Press the voice memo button—here—and dictate your notes into the PDA."

I blinked at the palm-sized gadget. "Jeez. Will it beam me up, too?"

He smiled and kissed my furrowed brow. "When I get back, we'll have you fitted for contact lenses then drop in on Tabasco and Woody. They're wiring the big store today. I want you to see the *layoot,* plus The Kid has some electronic devices we need to familiarize you with, yeah?"

Technical gadgets. Great. "No problem." I sensed an urgency that hadn't been there last night. My brain and heart raced. "If Gina's unavailable, who's going to act as Portia Livingston's personal assistant? Everyone else on the team has an assigned function."

"That's why I'm heading to the club. I'll pool my resources with Jazzman's. We frequently deal with freelance—"

"No. Not freelance. I'd feel better if it was someone I knew. Someone I trusted. What about Nic?"

He shook his head.

"Why not? You're using Jayne to pull off an illusion tonight."

"Jayne will be with Tabasco and then she'll be with me. You'll be with me and then Tabasco. You and Nic would be alone."

"Only on the flight from Boston to Philadelphia. Disguised as a member of the paranormal society, you'll be waiting at the airport to meet us then you'll drive us to our hotel in AC." I balled my fists in the sheets, dug in my heels. "Now who's mindfucking the situation? This first part, it's for show, right? Just in case Crowe puts a tail on Portia and her assistant? Just in case he wants to see them in the flesh before committing to the lecture? The only danger is in us not coming off as believable and that's possible if you stick me with someone I don't know and trust."

He chewed the inside of his cheek.

"You've seen Nic and me in action. You know we make a great team."

After a moment, he nodded. "I'll speak to Beckett."

"I'll speak to Nic." I scrambled off the bed and toward his landline phone before he changed his mind.

MILO WAS COMING out of The Cave's kitchenette when Arch strode in. He sensed the Scot's anger but he didn't anticipate the punch. He reeled back from the unexpected uppercut. "Fuck!"

"Bugger." Arch shook out his fist, massaged his knuckles.

"Christ." Milo shook off a daze. "For a nonviolent man, you pack a hell of a punch."

"*Didnae* realize I was that pissed. Part of that's a hold-over from the first kiss, yeah?"

"I take it Evie told you about yesterday. For what it's worth, it didn't mean anything."

"I know." Arch jammed a hand through his hair. "I just… Did you have to fucking go all *oot?*"

Milo wasn't about to say *she asked for it.* He rubbed his offended jaw. "We good now?"

"Good as we've ever been." Arch glanced toward the smell of freshly brewed coffee.

"Help yourself."

"Grab you a cup?"

"Grab me a beer."

"It's eight in the fucking morning."

"I'm not going to drink it, asshole. I want to use it as an icepack." Milo worked his jaw. "This fucker's swelling."

Arch moved into the kitchenette. "Sorry, mate."

"No, you're not."

"You're right, I'm not."

By the time Arch returned with their beverages, Milo had pulled up a file on local grifter, Sarah Fielding. "I'm thinking Sarah's a good fit for—"

"I've already replaced Gina."

"With who?"

Arch offered Milo an ice-cold Heineken. "Nic."

Damn. He pressed the chilled bottle to his throbbing jaw and suppressed his misgivings as the Scot relayed Evie's reasoning on the matter. Sound reasoning. She was right. They'd seen the women in action. Twice. An improvised ruse in an Indiana jailhouse and a calculated ruse devised by Arch and Milo. Both times he'd been stunned by their talent and cool control. "I don't like it." Bad enough he was concerned about Evie's safety. But to throw Nic into the mix?

"Neither do I, but I'm worried *aboot* Gina."

"Me, too."

"The least we could do is supply a distraction, you know?"

"Agreed."

Arch sipped his coffee. "So it's a go, aye?"

Damn. "Yeah."

"Everything else in order?"

Milo set aside the beer. "Good to go. Crowe returned my e-mail. I have a 3:00 p.m. appointment at HQ."

"Want to go over the come-on?"

"I know my part."

"You have to convince him that Portia Livingston is a fake. Someone he can manipulate into scamming Wilson."

"I know."

"Emphasize that she's appearing in Atlantic City—"

"We've been over this, Arch. I'll rope the bastard. Trust me when I say I'm motivated." Milo dragged a hand over his face. "Part of what made you the best damned grifter on the circuit was your ability to hide your emotions. Ever since you met Evie…" He shook his head. "Genuine emotions make a man vulnerable, compromise his judgment."

Arch quirked a brow. "You're reciting back my own words?"

"I thought you'd forgotten." Milo drummed his fingers on the console. "When Evie flies out with Tabasco tonight, she's no longer the woman you love, she's a Chameleon. That means thinking with your head."

"Not my heart, yeah? Now who's telling who how to do their job?"

"Fuck you."

"Bugger off."

Milo grunted. "Good as we've ever been." He opened a file on his laptop, the Aquarius checklist. "Let's dance."

CHAPTER TWENTY-FIVE

I ZOOMED THROUGH THE DAY like a zombie on crack. I know. Doesn't make sense. But it describes how I felt. My brain was full and bursting yet I kept taking in more information. I memorized what Arch told me. Went where he shuttled me. Brown contact lenses—check. New cell phone, Portia's phone—check. Inspection of the big store (a private room in a local Italian restaurant owned by an associate of Tabasco's)—check. Familiarization with the layout of the restaurant and the placement of hidden mics and cameras. Check, check.

I wasn't the only one who went through Aquarius boot camp. Nic and Jayne received grueling training as well. Nothing physical, unless you counted Tabasco teaching us the correct way to knee a man in the nuts. Yes, there's a right and wrong way. The right way incapacitates him. The wrong way just makes him mad. I couldn't see causing someone that much pain, but, like the Mace Pepper Spray, I wasn't about to turn down a mode of defense.

Jayne's role in the ruse was minimal but key, especially if Crowe's men were watching. We were the same height and approximately the same build. Together we'd create smoke and mirrors.

"Let's run it down one more time," Tabasco said to Jayne.

She fiddled with her crystal necklace as she sipped cappuccino. "For a tough guy, you're a bit of a worrywart."

"Better safe than sorry," Woody said, taking a break from his camera rigging to join us at a table in the otherwise deserted private room. "I don't know how you ladies can be so calm about this. You're not even professionals."

I raised a brow at the unintentional insult. *Ah, Woody.*

"You know what I mean," he hurried on.

Yeah, I knew. Even though we were trained actresses, we weren't trained in law enforcement or grifting or going up against government officials who used underhanded tactics to control people. Probably it was better that Nic and Jayne didn't know the specifics. If they were questioned by one of Crowe's flunkies, they wouldn't have to play dumb about COPRODEM. They were, in fact, clueless. They didn't know about the dirty files. They didn't know Gina was in deep, God knows where, doing God knows what, but almost assuredly risking her neck. They only knew that Crowe had set Beckett up and we were trying to clear his name. Arch had approached this meeting with his *need to know only* mentality. Only something told me Nic knew more than we thought. How that could be, I didn't know. Unless Beckett—

"Want to know our trick?" Jayne asked Woody, and I blinked back to the "calm" issue. "There's a saying."

"Never be more nervous than the person in charge," Nic and I recited along with her.

Jayne pointed to Arch. "Does he look nervous to you?"

"Ace doesn't do nervous," Woody said.

True. The man was a rock. On the outside anyway. Deep down I knew he wasn't thrilled about my main role in this sting. That he hadn't nixed my participation made me love him all the more. Even though he was worried about my safety, he trusted and respected my abilities. His faith in me bolstered my confidence and afforded me an inner tranquility. Or maybe I was just too focused to be scared.

"Running over a con multiple times," Arch said, "helps to cement details and assures everyone is on the same page, yeah?"

Tabasco nodded. "Redundant? Maybe. Effective? Definitely."

"Considering we won't get a dress rehearsal," I prompted.

"All right. All right." Jayne drummed her ringed fingers on the table. "Nic and I come down to the club tonight in support of Jimmy and Evie's debut. We listen to your music, have a few drinks and…"

I listened and absorbed. I embraced the zombie-on-crack feeling that would propel me through this gig…and said a silent prayer for my archrival, Gina, who, unlike me, was out there alone.

Fifteen minutes later, when Arch was convinced we all knew our parts, Woody rubbed his hands together. "Now for the fun part." He opened a briefcase and revealed an array of super-spy gadgets. I breathed a sigh of relief when he caught my eye and said, "Don't worry. Simple to use. Take this watch that doubles as a digital recorder…"

Focused and determined, I grinned as he fastened the device around my wrist. "Call me Bond. Jayne Bond."

"YOUR E-MAIL INTRIGUED ME, Agent Beckett. *'I'm ready to play ball.'*" Vincent Crowe lazed back in his chair, shuffled the papers on his desk with the eraser end of a pencil. He couldn't have seemed less interested in Milo's visit. "Meaning?"

Milo hitched back his suit jacket and sat in an opposing chair. Standing made him appear disrespectful, high-handed. He wanted Crowe to think he'd come crawling. "Permission to cut through the bullshit, sir."

The director of the AIA lifted a brow. "Go on."

"We clashed from day one. You had your agenda for Chameleon. I had mine. Only I fucked up and now you have me by the balls. Candidly speaking, sir."

Crowe said nothing, but Milo knew he had his ear.

"Per your order, I've spent the last five days lying low. Gave me a lot of time to think." He sniffed. "Why didn't you let me take the wrap for Mad Dog's death? Logical answer—even though I'm a pain in the ass, I'm a valuable asset to the AIA. Nobody does what I do, as well as I do, except for Arch Duvall. We both know if you ever tried to manipulate him, he'd be smoke. Instead you manipulated me. You cleaned up my mess and now I'm obliged to play by your rules or the ones enforced by a prison warden. Does that pretty much sum up my situation?"

Crowe picked up his phone. "Send in Agent McKeene." He replaced the receiver, looked at Milo. "Stand up."

Ten seconds later Agent Ass-Kisser searched Milo and his briefcase for a recording device. Did they think he was stupid? An encouraging thought, actually.

Convinced the head of Chameleon wasn't wired for sound, Crowe dismissed his yes-man. The moment the door shut, the director leaned forward. "Decisions were made to protect this agency and U.S. Senator Clark. You just happened to benefit, Agent Beckett. As for being a valuable asset, you've spent the last few years pissing away the talent of your team on cases that should be handled by local bunko squads. This is a national institu-tion. We handle cases of national importance."

Milo waited for an American flag to unfurl from the ceiling. Or maybe a poster touting COPRODEM's mission statement.

Protection of democracy, my ass.

"Even your own team members are fed up with your idealistic agenda for Chameleon. How long before the others jump ship in order to better serve their country?"

Milo didn't flinch. But... *What the fuck?*

"She didn't tell you yet." The corners of Crowe's fleshy lips curled. "When's the last time you spoke to Gina Valente?"

Milo's gut clenched, his mind raced. He didn't have a clue as to what was going on, so he played it safe, minimal details. "A couple of days ago. She was pretty steamed about the Mad Dog incident. Since then..." He shrugged. "She's not taking my calls."

"That's because she's no longer working for you. She's working for me. I'm utilizing her as we speak. Chameleon's not my only special task force."

COPRODEM. *Shit.* "My loss," he said simply. "As well as another sign that it's time to regroup."

"Meaning?"

"I'm tired of fighting a losing battle. Regardless of your opinion of me, I do want to make a goddamned difference and I'm not doing it by taking out your run-of-the-mill grifter. My pent-up frustrations compromised my judgment, caused me to fuck up that choke hold." Since he didn't really believe that anymore, he faked discomfort by loosening his tie. "Like I said, I've had five days to reevaluate my life. I'm ready to play ball. As a show of good faith, I have a case I think you'll find of interest."

Crowe shifted in his seat while Milo retrieved a set of files from his briefcase and placed them on the desk. "I ordered you to keep a low profile, Beckett. No active investigations."

Milo mentally rolled back his shoulders and settled in for the come-on. He tried not to think about Gina. *What the hell have you done?*

"Actually, this is an open investigation. One we were forced to set aside when you put us on suspension after that misstep in the Caribbean." Milo plucked a doctored 8 x 10 shot of Evie from the file and passed it to Crowe. "Portia Livingston."

"Sexy broad. What's her game?"

Milo hated the way Crowe leered at Twinkie, but at least he was intrigued.

"Purported psychic. Specializes in astrology and crystal-ball gazing. Ropes a substantial amount of clients through her Web site, which often leads to over-the-phone and in-person readings. She's built up quite a following along with a hefty bank account. Acting on two separate complaints, we looked into Ms. Livingston's business practices and we're convinced she's a fraud."

"Her and hundreds like her," Crowe scoffed. "I thought you said you were tired of taking down run-of-the-mill scammers."

"I don't think you'll consider her run-of-the-mill." Milo fished out a phony document. "A list of her clients. As you can see, several celebrities are listed. And here, a couple of government officials and scattered low-level politicians. Livingston is making a name for herself and she's aiming higher. We have it on good authority that she's going to go after U.S. Senator Wilson."

Crowe looked from the document to Milo.

"Hooked," Milo could hear Arch say. *"Now reel him in."*

"Wilson has a long-standing interest in psychics. Something his advisors try to downplay, but something they can't squelch. Livingston aspires to be the next Jeane Dixon, Astrologer to the Stars. Dixon," he clarified, "predicted Kennedy would die in office then went on to advise the Reagans."

"Before she lost the job to Joan Quigley," Crowe said. "I'm familiar with many of our leaders', shall we say, weaknesses, Agent Beckett."

As no doubt listed in your dirty file, you rotten son of a bitch. "There are rumors that Wilson might enter the presidential race," Milo continued. *Reel, reel.* "Imagine if Livingston had his ear. Or any other powerful politician for that matter."

Crowe didn't comment, but he did key Portia Livingston into his computer and pulled up her Web site. "So Chameleon wants to go after Ms. Livingston."

"We don't have to. She's coming to us." He retrieved a copy of the magazine printed specifically for his purposes and passed it to Crowe. He tapped the page featuring a story on the up-and-coming psychic. "She's flying into Philadelphia International tomorrow morning. A paranormal society booked her for a lecture and individual readings. Representatives of the local press are slated to attend. It's a prime opportunity for us to expose her as a fake. Considering her current and potential client list, I think this falls under the heading of national importance."

Crowe skimmed Portia's Web site. Glanced again at the client list. "Have any evidence to nail her pretty ass?"

Milo slid him the last file. "Statements from two fleeced marks. A report from Tabasco, who went undercover and experienced a personal reading. Her real background opposed to that concocted bio on her Web site. We'll get hard evidence this weekend. We have reason to believe her public appearances involve hidden mics and cameras."

Crowe read the statements and skimmed Tabasco's report.

Milo knew he'd roped the man. Felt it with every fiber of his being. He waited for Crowe to okay the sting. Either he'd want to be there for the bust or he'd ask Milo to bring Livingston into HQ. She was his ticket to Wilson.

The older man scrunched his nose, closed the files. "She's not worth the time and effort. Not now anyway. We'll keep an eye on her. In the meantime, I want you to take a look at this." He pulled a file from his desk and passed it to Milo. "Potential managed earnings scam. We could have another Enron on our hands. Look into this and get back to me on Monday with your thoughts."

Milo didn't blink, but his brain scrambled to process this unexpected twist. He took the MES file. Gathered Portia's papers. He studied Crowe all the while, searching for a *tell,* any expression, tick or gesture that suggested he was bluffing. He didn't believe for a second that Crowe was actually passing on an opportunity to manipulate a potential presidential candidate. He flashed Portia's picture one last time. "You're sure about this?"

"Quite sure, Agent Beckett. As to that show of faith, come up with a way to expose this managed earnings scam."

Beckett nodded, reached for the magazine.

"I'll hang on to this," said Crowe.

Huh.

Briefcase in hand, mind buzzing, Milo moved toward the door.

"Agent Beckett."

He turned and met the man's frosty gaze.

"You and Valente worked together for a long time. I know you considered her a friend as well as a valuable associate. Your casual acceptance of her defection doesn't ring true. Which gives me yet a tighter grip on your balls."

"Sir?"

"Fuck with me, I fuck with her."

CHAPTER TWENTY-SIX

"KEEP STARING AT THAT THING and you're going to start hallucinating, you know?"

"That's the idea. Sort of." I'd begged off dinner—who could eat when their stomach's stuffed with butterflies?—to cram in another session with the quartz crystal ball Tabasco had *appropriated* from Madame Helene.

Seated at Arch's desk in his condo, I cupped the square crystal base and gazed into the mesmerizing gemstone. "Diviners peer into the crystal in order to see things. Images pertaining to the past, present and future. Using the information derived, the psychic then guides her client in making important decisions." I glanced over my shoulder at Arch, who'd just finished wolfing down several slices of pizza. "Pretty sickening to think a greedy charlatan could influence a trusting soul's outlook on love and finances."

He came up behind me. "Or how to vote on a bill, yeah?"

"Yeah." I suppressed a blissful moan as he massaged my stiff shoulders. "You know, in reality, Portia Livingston will never have Senator Wilson's ear but, given his supernatural interests, some psychic will."

"*Cannae* worry *aboot* that, lass. Our focus is on Vincent Crowe."

I sighed. "So many crooks, so little time."

"*Cannae* save the world in a day."

"Right." I gazed even deeper into the clear stone and mentally recited a dozen visions. Visions I'd reveal to various planted "extras" during my lecture.

Arch leaned down and kissed the side of my neck. *Heaven.* "What do you see in our future, love?"

I smiled, enjoying his warmth, his strength. I peered deep into the gemstone and let my imagination soar. *I see the Scottish highlands and a man and woman kissing in front of a castle. I see a little girl with a big smile.* "I see a happy ending."

It was a corny thing to say, but it caused Arch to finesse me from my chair and into his arms. His possessive kiss rushed through me, seducing me, charming me. Call me dazed and loving it.

His cell rang.

Good thing, I told myself as he broke away to take the call. We didn't have time to fool around. My suitcase was packed for later tonight, but it was time to shower and dress for the club.

"Yeah?" He listened, took the seat I'd just vacated and fired up his laptop. "On it." He ditched the phone.

I watched as he entered a series of passwords. At last a mailbox appeared. A tiny chameleon blinked in the upper right corner, announcing incoming mail. Arch clicked on the post.

Not wanting to snoop, I eased away. Only he pulled me back and told me to read along with him.

Beckett had e-mailed the result of his meeting with Crowe. Apparently he didn't want to talk about it over the phone. I'm guessing Woody had secured the team's e-mail. The report was short and succinct. I felt sick and puzzled at the same time.

Arch whipped off a response. Business as usual.

Two seconds later, Beckett replied: Agreed.

Arch signed off the Internet and grabbed a pack of Marlboros from his desk.

"What do you mean, business as usual?"

"We're launching Aquarius as planned." Cigs in hand, he strode to the condo's balcony.

I trailed after, my heart thudding so loudly, surely Sam the doorman could hear it fifteen stories below. "But Crowe didn't take the bait."

"He took it. He's just cutting Beckett *oot* of the picture."

"Why?"

"He *doesnae* trust him." Arch lit up and blew smoke into the balmy night air. "Crowe's testing him. He'll assign a man to tail Portia Livingston. If anyone from Chameleon shows at any point, then Beckett disobeyed a direct order, yeah? Either way, Crowe will make a move on Portia this weekend. She's got something he wants."

"Power."

"Aye."

I swallowed hard. "He's also got Gina. He threatened to hurt her if Beckett messes with him."

"I know. I read."

I refrained from tugging my hair in frustration. I didn't want Arch to think I was freaking out. Which I was. I'd worked my butt off preparing for this sting and now half the script had been thrown out the window. I could improvise. I had good instincts. But what if I stumbled? I cursed myself for bringing Nic and Jayne into this. I fretted over Gina's safety. I wanted to scratch my neck, but didn't.

As if sensing my thoughts, Arch slid me a look. "As long as Beckett doesn't piss off Crowe, Gina's safe."

"You're just saying that to make me feel better. You're worried about her, Arch. And so is Beckett."

He blew out a stream of smoke, weighed his thoughts then came clean. "I think she's in over her head, aye. Signing on with Crowe's special task force *withoot* consulting us first? *Withoot* backup?"

"She has backup. Her friend, Syd. He's on the inside, right?"

"According to Beckett, *Syd* is the reason she acted rashly."

I thought about the mysterious independent contractor. A man who'd promised to work as a double agent of sorts as a favor to Gina. "She must think Syd's in danger and she feels responsible."

He eyed me hard. "She's letting her emotions muck up her judgment, yeah?"

Dread slithered down my spine. "We need to take down Crowe as soon as possible."

"Aye."

I ached to recite a movie quote, something to lighten the moment, only my brain wouldn't go there. "I'm going to shower and dress." Suddenly, a mambo clock ticked inside my head. Two hours until I hit the stage with Tabasco. Two sets of music and then…countdown to Aquarius.

I hurried toward the bathroom leaving Arch on the balcony with his Marlboros. Sure, he looked like his bad-boy self, but he didn't fool me. He was nervous. For Gina. For me. Where he found the wherewithal to command his emotions to such an insane extent, I had no idea. It used to infuriate me because I was never sure what he was feeling. Now I knew him well enough to see through the facade. Most of the time anyway.

I turned on the shower, toed off my shoes. I imagined awful things happening to Gina. Painful things. Bloody things. I shook off the graphic images and envisioned her cocooned in a protective pink bubble. So what if it was whimsical. It steadied my pulse. Gina and I had been enemies from the get-go—the pit bull and the poodle. Though I didn't think we'd ever be shopping buddies, I'm pretty sure we'd struck a truce. No matter what, she was a teammate. I couldn't, *wouldn't* let her down.

Damn Vincent Crowe's black heart!

Throat thick and dry with suppressed outrage, I left the shower running and zipped to the kitchen for a bottle of water.

"Bloody *hell,* Kate."

I froze in my barefooted tracks, steps away from the balcony. I hadn't closed the door all the way and though Arch wasn't yelling, he wasn't whispering, either.

He thinks you're in the shower.

I didn't want to eavesdrop. It was wrong. Invasion of policy. Only I couldn't move. They were arguing about Cassidy. I hung in the shadows, my heart aching for Arch. He told Kate this wasn't a good time, but then she said something that really pissed him off.

"I've turned my life fucking inside *oot* in order to prove I'm a proper da for Cassie. First you damned my career. Then my philandering. Jesus, I'm marrying a woman who's so fucking virtuous, she makes Snow White look dirty!"

My skin burned. My stomach soured. It didn't sound like a compliment. He sounded frustrated. *Resentful.*

I mentally lassoed my imagination. *Don't think the worst. Don't read into it.*

"What do you mean… We had a bargain, Kate. A good role model…" Arch blew out a breath, lowered his voice.

"Aye, it's worth the sacrifice. We're talking *aboot* my daughter for fuck's sake."

My world went black. I palmed the wall for balance. Marrying me was a sacrifice?

Can't. Breathe.

White noise roared in my ears. *Don't puke. Don't puke.*

I escaped to the bathroom on shaky legs. Snatches of past conversations assaulted my brain. Specifically Arch's comments about my goody-two-shoes nature. He liked that I'm a good girl, a nice girl. He didn't want me to change. Didn't want me mixing with bad sorts. He worried that I'd grow cynical.

He didn't want me to *change,* because marrying a *nice* girl would advance his campaign to gain greater access to his *daughter.* He'd made a bargain with Kate. If he found a good role model… Oh, God. *Sucker.*

He'd given up a lucrative career for Cassidy. Spent a fortune on a title and lands. Marrying a modern-day Doris Day, creating a stable home, proved he'd stop at nothing to *be a proper da.*

Oh, my, God. Oh, my God. He *conned* me.

I sank to my knees and hurled into the toilet bowl.

Nic warned me. Beckett warned me.

Arch warned me.

"How can I trust you?"

"You cannae."

Had that admission two months prior been the sole honest moment in our relationship?

Idiot! I pushed to my feet and rinsed out my mouth. My blood boiled. I was so hurt, so *angry* I could…I could… I wrenched off my undies. *Dammit!* I couldn't do anything. Not now. Not yet. Too much was at stake. Beckett's career. Political leaders' reputations. Gina's *safety.*

I had to suck it up. Stay strong. I had to do what I'd done for most of my life—*internalize.*

I stepped into the shower. *Don't cry. Don't cry.* I squashed down my emotions. Deeper and deeper until I felt…nothing.

I envisioned my own protective bubble and channeled Yoda. *Do, or do not…there is no "try."*

CHAPTER TWENTY-SEVEN

EMOTIONAL LOCKDOWN is a beautiful thing. Between that and being a damned good actress, I managed not to implode when Arch strode into the bedroom.

"You look stunning, lass."

"Thanks." Snow White in basic black. A color suitable to my mood. Slim-fitting pants and a long-sleeved satin tunic. A costume appropriate to the Chameleon Club. "My metallic hot pants and sequined bra seemed a bit much given the venue."

He grinned at that. "I meant the whole package, yeah? Hair, makeup, clothes. Subtle, but classy."

Nice and respectable. I concentrated on zipping my chunk-heeled boots. Steady hand. Steady heart.

He moved into the bathroom. "I'll be ready in ten minutes."

No mention of Kate. If I'd misunderstood, if he had nothing to hide, wouldn't he have vented his frustration? Asked my opinion on how to handle the woman he'd dubbed devil? Yesterday, we'd confessed our secrets and established trust.

Ha!

There's a sucker born every minute.

In my case, I'd been reborn for the umpteenth time. But by God, it would be the *last* time. I would not be played again. I sure as hell wouldn't fall prey to Arch's hypnotic charm.

I heard the faucet running, imagined him splashing water on that gorgeous face. Normally, I'd join him in the bathroom. We'd had dozens of conversations with me standing on the threshold watching him shave or raking gel though his hair or applying some disguise. Usually, he was half-naked and I openly gawked at his buff torso. Drooled over that Celtic tattoo. Not now.

Not ever again.

Ten minutes later we were on our way to the Chameleon Club. A ten minute drive. *Tick, tock.*

Arch veered into the club's pothole-riddled lot. "You're awfully quiet, Sunshine."

"So are you."

"Just going over things in my mind, yeah?"

"Same here."

He rounded the car and opened my door. I didn't want him to hand me out. *No touching!* But he was always a damned gentleman and sure enough I felt a *zap* when his fingers curled around mine. I was furious with myself, with him.

"You're trembling."

"I'm cold."

"You're nervous."

Yeah. Okay. Let's go with that. "There's a lot at stake. I don't want to screw up."

"You *willnae.*"

I arched a brow. "I have before."

"You've come a long way." He leaned in and my senses glitched.

I palmed his shoulders to fend him off. "I can't think straight when you kiss me, Arch." Yeah, boy, *that* was the truth. "I need to focus. My brain is bursting with the details of…" I lowered my voice even though no one was in sight. "Aquarius. If I seem on edge, detached, it's because I'm in the zone."

He eased back and regarded me warily.

I hated that the moon was out. Hated that it illuminated his handsome features. Hated the stars glittering in the sky, the sound of the ocean, the feel of the warm breeze, and the spicy scent of Arch's cologne. I hated every romance novel I'd ever read for brainwashing me into thinking I'd get a happy ending with my fantasy man.

"When this is over, Sunshine—"

"I need to focus on now."

He brushed my windblown hair out of my eyes. "Right, then." Unsmiling, he grasped my hand and escorted me toward the Chameleon Club. "Let's do this bloody thing."

EVEN THOUGH WE'D HAD minimal rehearsal, Tabasco and I sailed through two sets of music with minimal clams. I'm pretty sure the only people who heard our flubs were Jayne and Nic, because they were the only ones paying close attention. Devoted friends (and as Aquarius dictated), they'd shown up moments before we'd hit the first note of our first song, claiming a table just a few feet away from the entertainment. Otherwise, seven men sat at the bar, including the two regulars and, except for the time he escaped outside for a smoke and the few moments he'd disappeared with Beckett, Arch.

Mostly the barflies gave Tabasco and me their backs. They were here to drink and talk about sports or whatever men talk about in dive bars, not to listen to a live duo performing jazzy versions of pop music. I wasn't offended. Over my twenty-some years in entertainment, I've been ignored plenty. Don't get me wrong, I've enjoyed my share of delighted audiences and standing ovations, but mostly if you're not a star, people tend not to go ga-ga over you-you. Especially if you're misbooked or the sound system is bad or the setting is inferior. We weren't even on a stage. We were crammed into a corner alongside an antique jukebox. The sound system Tabasco had *appropriated* was decent, but, since we were strictly *atmosphere,* he'd kept the volume low so as not to disturb the chatty patrons or the game playing on the TV hanging above the bar. To cinch our non-existent status, there was no special lighting. We were confined to the shadows which, given my somber mood, was fine and dandy with me. Call me Morticia.

Let's just say I wasn't surprised or hurt that Jayne and Nic were the only two who faithfully applauded after every song. Then again I was also detached. The zombie-on-crack feeling was not only welcome but also vital. If I allowed genuine emotions to seep through I'd shatter.

Throughout the two sets, I conjured images of Gina kicking butt. I avoided looking at Arch. I blocked his betrayal from my mind and focused on the music. Okay. So maybe I glanced his way while singing Norah Jones's version of "Cold Cold Heart." But other than that, I closed my eyes and lost myself in song or focused on the rest of the audience, sparse though it was.

A man and a woman floated in during our first set, but they only had eyes and ears for one another and after a couple of drinks, they were history. At one point I wondered if they were working undercover for Crowe. I wondered the same thing about one or two of the ratty-looking dudes at the bar. Then again it could have been the vagrant who'd stumbled in during our second set looking to bum a drink off Pops.

Possible I was imagining things, but Arch *had* warned that given Beckett's meeting with Crowe, chances were stronger than ever we, or at least Beckett, was being watched. That's why Tabasco hadn't flown Nic and me to Boston earlier today. The plan was to make it look like business as usual, every one accounted for. Then under the cover of night, a little cloak and dagger. As Tabasco and I wound up our last song, I mentally prepared for that moment.

Tick, tock.

I shifted into character. Not Portia, but a fake me. A woman pleased with a gig well done. A woman looking forward to celebrating with friends. A woman who couldn't wait to get the man of her dreams alone so she could kiss him senseless.

The real me wanted to blast Arch a rat bastard rat. The real me wanted to blow this town for Tinseltown. Trading a broken dream for a pipe dream would be a step up. But that would have to wait.

Tick, tock.

"Thank you and good night." I acknowledged the scattered applause then turned to Tabasco, who was already unplugging his acoustic and shutting down the amps. "I just wanted to say...I really enjoy your playing. It was a pleasure working with you, Tabasco."

"The feeling's mutual," he said. "You have a pretty voice. Unique. I look forward to our next performance."

There wouldn't *be* a next performance. I couldn't end things with Arch and continue with Chameleon. Not that I'd thought that far ahead. Okay. That's a lie.

Don't think. Don't feel.

Luckily, Jayne rushed up. "I know I said it on your break, but *wow.* You two are great together. The song se-

lection was *awesome*. Too bad the other bozos in the room
tuned out."

"Arch and Beckett were listening," Tabasco said.

"When they weren't jabbering about something," she
said.

"Pops listened," I said. The leathery bartender had applauded almost as often as my friends. I'd really miss that
sweet, caring man.

Stop it! Focus! Stay in the moment.

"Sure. When he wasn't serving drinks." Jayne frowned.
"There's a difference between listening and being atten-
tive."

Tabasco looked bewildered but I got her meaning. It
was the difference between being polite and truly interested. Clearly, Arch and Beckett's minds were on things
other than music.

"Doesn't matter. We're used to it," Jayne said, kissing
Tabasco's furrowed brow. "Come over and join us. Nic
ordered a round of drinks. Arch said he'd be right over."

"I'll be there as soon as I put away my guitar, angel. You
girls go ahead." But before Jayne got away, Tabasco caught
her up in a four-alarm lip-lock.

My cue to leave.

"How can she be so over the moon about a guy she just
met?" Nic asked as I sat down next to her. A heartbeat later
she rolled her eyes. "Why am I asking you? You were in
love with Arch after what, thirty seconds?"

I swallowed a lump. Thankfully, Jayne saved the day
once again.

"Isn't he amazing?" She wilted into a chair and released a dreamy sigh. "Talented, sexy, kind. Exciting *and*
interesting."

"I'm sure he has some faults," Nic drawled.

"He does leave the toilet seat up," Jayne said, "but that wouldn't stop me from marrying him if he asked."

Nic grimaced. "Don't joke."

"Who's joking?"

"You've only known him a couple days."

"It only takes a moment." Jayne glanced at me. "Isn't that a song from some movie?"

"Hello, Dolly!" I said.

"Barbra Streisand and Walter Matthau," Arch said as he slid over an additional chair.

"See." Jayne motioned to Arch and I. "Meant for one another."

My stomach turned. I ignored Arch's sexy smile and sipped Chardonnay.

He smoothed a hand over my back, tender yet possessive.

Zap! I bobbled my wineglass. A few drops splashed on his lap. "Sorry."

Shaking his head, he dabbed at his jeans with a cocktail napkin. "'Dolly Levi, you are a damned exasperating woman.'"

A quote from the movie. I knew that quote. He would know that I knew that quote. He expected me to followup. It was our thing. Well, that and boinking in various places and positions. For the first time ever, I blanked.

"'Why, Horace Vandergelder,'" he prompted in a girly voice. "'That is the nicest thing you have ever said to me.'"

Jayne laughed.

Nic smiled.

I tried not to look forlorn. Was this a sign that our special connection was truly severed? "I knew that," I said with a little laugh. "Of course I knew that." I thunked my forehead. "Brain's full of lyrics."

Before Arch could comment, Tabasco joined us and Jayne directed the conversation toward his musicianship. Thank God.

Small talk ensued. As planned.

We had a couple of rounds. As planned. Pops had watered down our drinks. Also planned. *Must stay in control.*

Tick, tock.

Beckett finally joined us.

Nic smiled up at him. I gave her two points for genuineness. I knew she was irritated with him. Again. Though I didn't know why. "About time, Slick."

"Sorry. I got caught up talking to Pops about a liquor shipment." *Planned.*

"Why *dinnae* we take this party to my place?" Arch said, grimacing as he drank his Scotch. "No offense, mate, but this is swill compared to my stock, yeah?"

"Anything would be swill compared to your stock," said Beckett.

"Only the best for Arch," Nic said dryly.

Jayne finished off her seltzer. "That's why he's with Evie."

I smiled even though my heart was breaking. *What I am,* I thought bitterly, *is the best stepmom he could find for Cassidy.* I squashed down the sentiment as quickly as it occurred. I felt like a jack-in-the-box. If anyone opened the lid they'd be in for a rude shock.

"As much as I'd like to continue the fun," Nic said, "I'll beg off. I've been drinking all night. I'm spent."

She was as sober as a teetotaler. We all were. But she slurred her words just enough for effect.

"Well, I'm not tipsy or tired," said Jayne.

"I'll drive Nic home," said Beckett. "Appreciate the invitation but it's been a long day."

And it wasn't over yet.

Tick, tock.

We stood to take our leave. Said goodbye to Beckett and Nic while the rest of us agreed to meet at Arch's condo. Not that we'd be there for long.

Tick, tock.

Two minutes later, Arch handed me into his car. My heart pounded as he rounded and settled into the driver's seat. *Play it cool.* "So do you think one of tonight's patrons was a spy for Crowe?" I asked as he peeled out of the parking lot.

"*Dinnae* know if there were men on the inside or simply stationed *ootside* the club in cars, but, aye. I think we're being watched. You were brilliant, lass."

"No better than anyone else." I resisted the urge to look over my shoulder. Were said watchers tailing us? Or were they stuck like glue on Beckett? Was there one thug? Two? Five? My skin prickled with apprehension. Crazy, but I preferred imagining scary scenarios as opposed to being alone with Arch.

The air vibrated with tension. His. Mine. I closed my eyes and zoned. *Don't think. Don't feel. Just act.*

Ten minutes later, he broke the brittle silence. "Detached is one thing, Sunshine. Disconnected is another. What the fuck's going on?"

CHAPTER TWENTY-EIGHT

"ON SECOND THOUGHT," Nic said as soon as the others were out the door. "I don't feel like going home."

Milo smoothed a thumb over the woman's spectacular cheekbone. "Want another drink?"

"Sure." She slid her hand suggestively up his thigh. "But not here."

"I know just the place." He cursed the hard-on that had been plaguing him all night. Ever since she'd strolled through the club's door in her tight jeans and low-cut blouse. Nothing risqué, just sexy as hell. Then again the mocha-skinned beauty would look hot wearing a burlap sack.

Christ.

He palmed the small of her back and guided her to the door marked Private, the door leading up to his apartment. He traded words with Pops for the sake of the remaining patrons. Scripted words. This whole evening was scripted, more or less, including this *tryst* with Nic.

He hadn't been familiar with every person in the bar tonight. It was possible that Crowe had sent a man in to check up on him. Possible that person was still hanging out at the bar. Also possible that Crowe had men watching the club from parked cars or the abandoned building across the way. If they were spying on his apartment with high-tech surveillance cams or binoculars—this show was for them.

Nic climbed the narrow stairs ahead of him, giving Milo a prime view of her beautiful ass. The unconscious sway of her hips sent a jolt of lust from the top of his head to the tip of his cock. She had to be wearing a thong. Satin? Lace? Red? Black? His fingers itched to peel off her jeans. To smooth his hands down those mile-long legs. To explore that thong with his teeth and tongue. He'd take his time. He'd drive her crazy. He'd make her beg for release.

Mr. Happy twitched.

Not gonna happen, boy.

Although she played the part of tipsy lover with conviction, he knew Nic was pissed at him. She hadn't said so. Hadn't suggested so. She was too skilled of an actress for that. He just knew, and he had a good guess why. He didn't have time to talk her down from her offended rage. He sure as hell didn't have time for a genuine seduction. Milo had to sneak Nic out via a secret passage, drive her to the airport, and haul his ass back to the club before closing time.

They reached the top of the stairs. He unlocked the door and ushered her into his apartment. He'd purposely left on a living room light. The window blinds were half-mast. Anyone with the means could witness the forthcoming action.

Nic swept her green gaze over his secondhand furniture. "Evie was right. Looks like Sam Spade decorated this place. Got a thing for the 1940s, Slick?"

"Just know what I like when I see it." *Mocha skin. Lush red lips. Jade-green eyes.* He pinned her against the wall, seared her neck with hot kisses.

She threw back her head to allow him greater access. She whispered, "Bastard."

He nibbled her earlobe. "You're pissed because I could've asked you to fill in for Gina this morning, and didn't. But I *did* offer you a role in the sting."

She pushed and twisted and suddenly he was the one pinned. Her back to the windows, she worked the buttons of his shirt. "As an extra. One of the members of the paranormal society. An insignificant role. Big freaking deal."

He buried his hands and face in her luxurious hair. *Christ she smelled good.* "I didn't consider substituting you for Gina because—"

"Because I'm not a former cop." She raked her nails over his bare chest, nipped his collar bone. "Because I haven't been trained to kill a man with my pinkie. I get it, Secret Agent Man."

She didn't get it at all. "Because I care about you. Because I don't want to put you in harm's way." Frustrated and turned on as hell, he flipped her around. Once again the aggressor, he stripped her silky blouse over her head. "What's done is done. You're in and you've got a major role. Happy? I'm not. Now kiss me like I'm your fucking knight in shining armor."

He registered something interesting yet unfathomable in that lethal green gaze before she launched a full body attack, knocking him to the opposite wall.

Milo grappled for a sane thought as he endured her atomic kiss. He punched the light switch and plunged them into darkness.

"I DON'T WANT TO TALK ABOUT this now," I said, wishing Arch hadn't broken the silence to pry into my "disconnection."

He drove a little too fast and crazy for my taste, fighting nightlife casino traffic in a bid to get to his condo in Margate. I'm not sure if he was upset, angry or confused. Frankly, I didn't give a damn. If it weren't for the impending sting I would have told him straight-out what the flip was going on. I would have called him a few names, told him what I thought of his manipulative Scottish hide, and where he could shove his marriage proposal.

But too much was on the line for me to lose my composure.

Later. I could lose it later. I *would* lose it later. I tried not to think about how long it would take me to get it back.

Swallow. Lump.

I also felt bad for Cassidy. If anything of what Arch had told me was true, she'd benefit from more time with a loving father and less time with the shallow, bitter mother who foisted her baby on nannies. I couldn't imagine. If I had a child I'd want to spend as much time with him or her as possible. I loved kids, and if Michael would have been willing, I'd have a couple of my own by now. I cursed him. I cursed my over-forty ovaries. But mostly I cursed Arch. Being a part-time stepmom would be better than being no mom at all. For that reason, it was almost worth marrying the lying bastard.

The fact that he had gotten my hopes up for such a thing made me shove my anger down even deeper.

"I *dinnae* want to send you into the fire, knowing you're upset. Emotions compromise judgment."

"I'm not upset."

"Liar."

Look who's calling the kettle black! I realized then, I was scratching my neck. Damn! "I'm not compromised. I'm confused."

"*Aboot* what?"

"I had an offer." I had to give him something, and sure

as hell didn't want to admit why I was truly upset. Not now. His betrayal was too huge and the clock was ticking on Aquarius.

"What kind of offer?"

"A chance of a lifetime."

He shot me a look.

"Yeah, yeah. It sounds like a scam but it's not." I told him about Michael's last visit and my phone discussion with the Emmy award-winning screenwriter, Charlie Lutz.

"He's trying to break us up."

"Charlie?"

"Stone. He wants you back."

"If he wanted me back, he wouldn't be offering me a new life on the West Coast." I glanced sideways, noted Arch's expression and posture. He'd gone very still, his focus on the late-night traffic. But I knew he was seething on the inside. I'd just thrown a monkey wrench into his grand plan, after all. His control was astounding. I wanted to blow past this but at the same time I wanted him to feel the same disappointment and hurt he'd inflicted on me. How mean was that? I swallowed and focused on the tail-lights in front of us.

"I *dinnae* trust it," he said.

"You mean you don't trust Michael. Me, neither. But like I said, I spoke to Charlie. This is the real deal. My shot at the big time."

"And you want to take it."

"Maybe."

"Why *didnae* you tell me *aboot* this earlier?"

"Because I didn't think I was interested." *True.* "But then tonight, with Tabasco, I realized how much I miss being on stage, performing." *Lie.* "Only I don't want to go back to what I did before." *True.* "But…this is a chance to realize my childhood dream. I'd never forgive myself if I didn't try. I owe it to myself. My family." *Kind of, sort of, true.*

"Your family would love you if you were hawking papers at a newsstand, Sunshine."

"Yes, well…" My throat clogged with grief and lies. I could hear his wheels turning. *But what* aboot *us? What* aboot *Chameleon?* I nearly sighed with relief as we pulled into his condo's parking lot. "I'm sorry. I told you I didn't want to talk about it now. Although I do feel better now that I got it off my chest." I made a show of shaking off my angst. "I'm good. I'm focused. Let's get this show on the road and save Gina's and Beckett's butts." I unfastened my seat belt and scrambled out before he could do or say anything to shatter my composure. I feigned a levity I didn't feel. "Chop-chop, Ace. Time's ticking."

THE NEXT HALF HOUR SPED BY, a blur of focused energy. Arch calmly drilled me one last time on the events to come. "Everything is in order. If there's a surprise, improvise, and know that someone will have you in sight at all times, yeah?"

I nodded. "I'm not worried." Oddly enough, that was true. Even though I was angry with Arch, I knew he wouldn't let anything bad happen to me. In addition, Beckett, Tabasco and Woody had my back. I was battling a lot of emotions but "fear of personal danger" wasn't one of them.

Next came the switch. Hopped up on her own nervous excitement, Jayne helped to transform me into, well, Jayne. We switched clothes and I donned a red wig. I looked in the bedroom mirror and smiled. I didn't look exactly like her, but close enough to fool anyone watching from a distance. What pleased me the most was that I *felt* like her—optimistic and carefree. Dressed in her ankle-length tie-dyed sundress and flirty sandals, her tasseled shawl draped over my shoulders, it was hard *not* to feel like a Bohemian free spirit. The shoulder-length wig with the bouncy curls topped off the whimsical persona. Now all I had to do was pretend I had the hots for Tabasco.

"You look good as a redhead," Jayne said. "Then again you'd look good bald. You can pull off any look. Any character. You truly are a chameleon, Evie."

For the next few days anyway. I swallowed past the lump in my throat. "Thanks, Jayne." I gave her a quick hug, strove to make light of the upcoming ruse. "I promise not to tongue-kiss your man."

She chuckled. "Ditto."

She'd be sleeping here tonight as me. I'd be leaving with Tabasco as her. Portia's luggage was already on board the Cessna thanks to Woody.

Jayne glanced at her/my watch. Right on time. "Let's go."

Tick, tock.

Tabasco and Arch were on the balcony. Tabasco took one look at me as Jayne and smiled. "Excellent." Then he moved into the living room to kiss the real Bohemian whack-a-doodle goodbye.

"Brilliant," Arch said of my getup, but he didn't smile. He took a drag off of his Marlboro and blew out a stream of smoke. The sexy, infuriating bad boy who'd stolen my heart.

Emotions welled, but I squashed down the tender ones, leaving anger. I marched up to him. "Give them to me."

He blinked.

"Your cigarettes. If you want to be a *proper da*, you

should give up smoking. Bad for your health. Bad example for Cassidy. If you can't manage cold turkey, buy nicotine gum or the patch or suck on lollipops like Kojak." I wiggled my fingers. "Hand them over."

Expressionless, he crushed out his butt and placed a pack of Marlboros in my hand.

I chucked them into Jayne's/my purse.

He nabbed me by the wrists and hauled me against his body. One arm anchored around my waist, one hand cupping the back of my neck, Arch kissed me with a tenderness that left my knees quaking and my heart crying.

Don't say you love me. Please, God, don't say you love me.

"See you tomorrow, Sunshine."

"No," I said, backing away on shaky legs. "You'll see Portia."

THE DRIVE FROM ARCH'S CONDO to the airport went off without a hitch. When I boarded the Cessna, Nic was already dressed in her Delia Jones disguise. As the personal assistant to an up-and-coming psychic, she'd gone with a semi-geeky beatnik look. Slim-fitting capris, a long-sleeved T-shirt and ballet flats—all black. She'd pulled her thick, long hair into a high *I Dream of Jeannie* ponytail. Instead of her normal contact lenses, she was wearing a pair of oval, black-rimmed glasses with blue-tinted lenses. They weren't the most flattering frame for her face and gave her a distinct quirky look. Quirky was good given her character.

Once in the air, I did my own quick change morphing from Jayne into Portia. Even though it was a small plane, it seated six so I had some wiggle room. My look was similar to *Delia's,* at least for tonight, only I covered my own hair with the blunt bob wig. For now I nixed the brown contact lenses. When we deplaned in Boston, like Nic, I'd don tinted glasses. Dressing our parts now seemed over-the-top considering we were arriving in the dead of night. But Beckett and Arch had left nothing to chance. Just in case someone was watching Portia's apartment, they'd see Portia and Delia going in and out.

For the most part, Nic and I spent the trip in companionable silence. We both knew our parts although I knew she was going over details in her head just like me. I wanted to ask her if everything was okay between her and Beckett, but then she might ask me about Arch. I couldn't go there.

Suck it up. Squash it down.

So I pulled Arch's PDA from my purse and went over Portia's profile. I studied the crystal gazing and astrology documents he'd uploaded for me. I went over the lecture and the phony readings. At one point I showed Nic the picture Arch had inputted of Vincent Crowe.

She squeezed my hand. "Don't worry, Evie. We'll nail the prick."

Assuming she was battling her own private war with nerves, I squeezed back. "Ever thought about moving to L.A.?"

"What?"

"Never mind."

Four hours after leaving the ground in Atlantic City, Nic and I were ensconced in a furnished one bedroom apartment in a suburb of Boston, Massachusetts. Portia's apartment. Tabasco was bunking in the apartment next door— *Call me if you need me, ladies.* Chameleon had gone all out in a very short period of time to create a grand illusion. It only served as a reminder of the high stakes and their superior skills.

Exhausted, Nic toed off her shoes and I pulled off my wig. With a united sigh, we sank down on the double bed.

"Okay," she said, massaging the balls of her feet. "Now that we're alone, tell me what's wrong."

"I can't. If I do, I'll fall apart."

"If you don't, you'll explode. What if you blow at an inopportune time? Like tomorrow during the ruse." She nudged me in the side. "Want me to find a notebook so you can write your feelings down?"

Her thoughtfulness caused tears to well. "No."

"Are you scared we're going to mess up?"

"No."

"Worried about Gina?"

"Yes, but…that's not it."

Nic blew out a breath. "It's four o'clock in the morning, Evie. If you tell me now, we can squeeze in a few hours' sleep. If you make me play 'one hundred questions'—"

"Arch asked me to marry him," I blurted, then burst into tears.

She blinked. "I…uh…shit. Okay. I'm pretty sure those aren't happy tears."

"He doesn't love me."

"He asked you to be his wife. A loner. A guy who never attaches himself—"

"I'm just a means to an end," I blubbered into my hands.

"I don't understand."

"He…he doesn't love me," I sobbed. "He loves… the…idea of me!"

"I *really* don't understand."

And I couldn't explain. I'd promised Arch I wouldn't tell anyone about Cassidy and I wouldn't break that promise even though he'd broken my heart. "B-b-bastard."

"Most men are," Nic said, then at long last, took me into her arms. "I'm not good at this comforting thing, Evie."

I hugged her tight and wept against her shoulder. "You're—" *sob, sniffle* "—doing okay."

She gave my back an awkward pat. "I know I've never been Arch's champion," she said, "but I've seen the way he looks at you, touches you. I can't believe I'm saying this, but I think his feelings are genuine."

"That's because he's a master manip-manip…"

"Manipulator. Got it." She groaned. "So he manipulated you into falling in love and tried to manipulate you into marriage because…"

"Because I'm Snow White."

"Huh."

I'd been damning up tumultuous feelings for hours. Sobbing released the crushing pressure. Losing control helped me to gain control. Even though I hadn't shared the total truth, I felt lighter. I could feel my strength and focus returning. A few hiccups and sniffles later, I pushed off of Nic and swiped my arm across my swollen, watery eyes. I blew out a breath. Then another.

"Feel better?" Nic asked.

I did. "I do." I massaged my throat. "You were right. Better to let it out. Thanks, Nic."

"Sure, but…"

She trailed off as I stood and rooted through my/Portia's suitcase. I was exhausted, but oddly focused on the day to come. I wouldn't screw up. I'd take every precaution. One thread in the plan had felt too loose so I'd packed in preparation. I handed Nic a box of black dye and a pair of scissors.

She looked from the beauty supplies to me. "That's what the wig is for."

"I don't trust it. Remember that gig where I dressed up like Marie Antoinette?"

"Some patron pulled you onto the dance and spun you around so many times, your wig whirled off your head."

"Exactly." I located a box of tissues and blew my nose.

"You won't be dancing with Crowe, Evie. And the Antoinette wig was a two-foot bouffant. This is a sleek bob and we'll make sure—"

"I'm a magnet for bad luck, Nic. I can't…I *won't* risk it." She'd eyed the box, the scissors, me.

"If you don't want to help, I'll do it myself," I said.

"With your luck?" She snorted and headed for the bathroom. "Let's do this so we can get some sleep."

I released my long bleached blond hair from a tight bun. So long, Doris Day. Toodles, Snow White. Okay. So, Snow White had black hair. That wasn't the point. I sat on the toilet and draped a towel across my shoulders. I shook off the remnants of my crying jag and focused on duping Crowe.

Nic emptied the contents of the box. "About Arch…"

"I'd rather not talk about him."

She concentrated on the printed directions. "I just meant, if not him, there's always Beckett."

I noted a slight flush in her cheeks. "I told you, Nic, no chemistry."

"Maybe…"

"He's a good man, but not the man for me. You, on the other hand…"

She fumbled the nozzle of the plastic bottle. "What's that supposed to mean?"

Ignoring the pang in my heart, I just smiled. At least one of us would be getting our Prince Charming.

CHAPTER TWENTY-NINE

PHILADELPHIA INTERNATIONAL was bustling as usual. Milo had no trouble blending in with the vast assortment of humanity flying in and out of the airport. Dressed in ratty bell-bottom jeans, a Grateful Dead T-shirt and a denim jacket, he slouched in a seat reading the latest issue of *Rolling Stone.* A jazz connoisseur, Velvet Revolver was foreign to him, but he pretended interest. His current ego, Kirk Tatum, was a rocker. If nothing else, the sixties throwback would be interested in the article on Bob Dylan.

Instead of a long wig, he'd topped off the disguise with a black baseball cap, Ray-Bans, and a full beard—à la Jerry Garcia. Instead of a joint, an unlit cigarette dangled from the corner of his mouth. A cup of Starbucks sat alongside his backpack on the empty seat to his right. Anyone looking would peg him as a Dead Head or a burned-out musician.

He hadn't given Nic or Evie a heads-up about his disguise. Any sign of recognition could tip off Crowe's men. Though he hadn't spotted anyone suspicious, his gut said he wasn't the only one watching for Portia Livingston's arrival.

He and Arch had discussed multiple scenarios. They both agreed one or two of Crowe's lackeys would be waiting to confirm the psychic's arrival. They'd watch as Portia and her assistant were greeted by Preston Spock, a colorful representative of the Paranormal Society of New Jersey. Spock, aka Arch, would drive the women to the hotel the PSNJ had booked as part of their appearance fee. At the special guest's beck and call, he'd be staying in the room next to theirs.

The lackeys would report back to Crowe—*looks like the real deal.*

Best-case scenario: Crowe himself would show up the following day for the paranormal lecture. After seeing the psychic in action, he'd corner Portia, flash his credentials, denounce her as a fraud, and blackmail her into manipulating Senator Wilson.

Worst-case: Too cautious to attend the event himself, Crowe would appoint his right-hand man in COPRODEM to carry out the manipulation, in which case Portia would demand to speak to the man in charge.

Either way, the objective was to get Crowe to incriminate himself on tape. Both Evie and Nic were armed with digital recording devices. In order to bring in major guns, Milo needed more juice to back up what little information Woody had already amassed on COPRODEM.

Milo looked up from his magazine as their plane taxied to the gate. "Let's rock and roll."

"Brilliant," Arch responded via the team's covert audio transmitter.

"Standing by," said Woody.

"I'm live," said Tabasco.

Like Milo, each man sported a custom earpiece. A small lapel-mic was clipped into their clothing enabling low-profile radio communication. Each man was in disguise and stationed at various points of the Philadelphia International Airport. Milo was loitering at the gate, seemingly awaiting the departure of his own flight. Arch, as the paranormal society contact, waited just outside the security checkpoint. Tabasco, also in disguise, was onboard the commercial airliner with Evie and Nic—or rather Portia and Delia—although he was seated alone. He'd return later for the Cessna. Since the women weren't trained in self-defense, the objective was to keep them in sight at all times.

Woody was parked nearby in a surveillance SUV, keeping tabs with various technical gear while using his laptop in a continued effort to crack codes that would allow him deeper access to COPRODEM.

Pops was keeping up pretenses at the club and acting as liaison with the sanctioned extras who'd act as members of the paranormal society. Fortunately they'd used all of these players in the past. As always they'd been given minimal information. As always Milo knew they'd turn in performances worthy of an Oscar.

Gina…God knew where she was or what she was doing. Milo just hoped she was safe. Although the team's focus had turned to exposing COPRODEM, part of him obsessed on the death of Mad Dog Turner. Selfishly, he hoped Syd and Gina got their hands on that DVD or the DVR so that Woody could analyze whether or not the recording had been tampered with. Resolving the situation would bring either relief or resignation, but at least closure.

He thought about Evie and the Fish. As much as he didn't want to tell her, she deserved to know the truth.

Speaking of Evie, Milo flipped to the next page of the magazine and watched as she and Nic flowed into the terminal along with the other passengers. No. Not Evie and Nic. Portia and Delia. He barely recognized them. They were deep in character. They *were* the characters.

Impressive.

His gaze flicked down the hall where Arch waited. "Coming your way, *Spock.*"

"Noted, *Kirk.*"

"No disrespect intended," said Woody, "but you two are showing your age. You should be Riker and Picard. You know the *Next Generation* not the old—"

"Can it, Scotty," Milo said.

"Aye, aye, sir."

"McCoy on deck." Tabasco emerged in a suit and tie, dark hair slicked into a low ponytail, briefcase in hand. He looked like a record producer or a drug lord with the arrogance to match.

The fact that they'd borrowed character names from the original *Star Trek* cast had been Arch's idea. Something about "The needs of the many outweigh the needs of the few." Milo didn't recognize the quote, but Twinkie would. *"The Wrath of Evie,"* he'd said to Milo, whatever the hell that meant. Evie and Arch had a thing about movies. He figured the quote was a tribute to her. Or maybe it was Arch's way of assuring himself she'd sail through the sting and kick Crowe's butt. Even though the Scot was keeping his emotions in check, Milo knew he was worried about Evie and Nic.

He wasn't alone.

That's why they'd gone overboard with today's surveillance.

The real action would take place at tomorrow's paranormal event. No reason to assume Nic and Evie were in danger now. Still…

Milo stood and slung his backpack over his shoulder as the women passed by. He ignored the urge to sweep them in the opposite direction, to put them on a plane to somewhere safe while he figured out another way to crush Vincent Crowe. He told himself they were big girls, talented girls. *Be a professional, for chrissake, Beckett.* God knew Evie and Nic were prime examples.

He chucked his empty coffee cup and followed at a discreet distance. He noted and admired the way they walked and talked in character. Wearing ballet-type slippers Nic as Delia appeared shorter than usual. Between her thrift-shop attire, high ponytail and chosen eyewear, she looked more nerdy than glamorous.

Evie, on the other hand, had transformed into a dark beauty. The brown contact lenses and shiny black bob were a startling change. Combined with the heavy eyeliner and deep red lipstick, the slim black skirt, belted jacket and pointy-toed high heels, she looked more Devil's Food than Twinkie.

Portia Livingston, a psychic with attitude.

Not surprisingly, heads turned.

Schlepping a few feet behind the psychic scammers, Milo as *Kirk* checked out the taverns and eateries—just a dude passing time until he boarded. He wondered where Crowe's men were lurking. In one of these shops? A nearby gate? Baggage claim? Would he recognize them? Would they be undercover?

Didn't matter. What mattered is that they called Crowe with a Portia sighting.

He wondered if Nic and Evie were experiencing adrenaline rushes like him. He slowed his pace as the women prepared to leave the terminal. Tabasco strode past him. Milo would loiter another few minutes then slip down to join Woody in the SUV.

Just ahead, he could see Arch, or rather Preston Spock, nursing his own cup of Starbucks and holding a sign that said PSNJ.

Paranormal Society of New Jersey.

Just beyond…

"Shit."

"Elaborate," said Arch.

"This could be bad."

"I see them," said Tabasco.

"Who?" Arch asked.

"Two suits in dark shades," said Tabasco.

"Where?" the Scot asked. He tossed his coffee cup in the trash and made a show of recognizing Portia Livingston. He raised the sign higher, squealed like a groupie and waved.

Christ. "Coming up behind you, Spock," Milo said. This had clusterfuck written all over it. "Agents McKeene and Burns."

"Shite," Arch said.

"Oh, man," said Woody.

"Anticipate an interception," Milo said.

"Got your back," Tabasco said, stepping aside to take a feigned business call.

Milo ducked into a newsstand and searched the magazine rack while keeping an eye on the action. "Whatever you do," he said to Arch. "Don't let them separate you from Livingston and Jones."

THE MOMENT NIC AND I STEPPED off of the plane we were on stage. We lived and breathed Portia Livingston and Delia Jones. We'd done our homework, so improvising was easy. We knew we were within Tabasco's and Beckett's sight and that we'd soon be with Arch, so we weren't nervous. We were too focused, too motivated.

The fact that it all seemed surreal was an added blessing. Two friends, two entertainers, on a covert mission to bring down a crooked government official. Too bizarre to be real. I pictured myself waking up, only to realize that the past two months had been a dream. That would suck. Even though I'd been manipulated by my fantasy man, I didn't regret my time with Arch and Chameleon. I'd rediscovered passion and purpose. I was comfortable and confident in my over-forty skin. Last night I'd been too hurt to think straight. The crying jag and a few hours' sleep had worked wonders. The new hairstyle and color also contributed to my new attitude. This weekend I'd kick butt. First Crowe's, then Arch's, then I'd decide my future. One way or another I would have my happy ending.

My spike heels clicked on the floor. My sleek hair swung just below my chin. Adrenaline and power buzzed through my veins as *Delia* and I wheeled our carry-on suitcases behind us and navigated the crowded terminal. She spouted the virtues of traveling lighter, reminding me of the two times the airlines had lost our baggage. Made-up story. Funny story. Nic actually made me laugh. I listened and nodded as we pushed toward our contact. In the back of my head floated the notion that I'd first met Arch in this very airport. He'd been in disguise as Charles Dupont, a man in his sixties with gray hair, jowls, and a doughy stomach. His transformation into woo-woo dweeb Preston Spock was just as convincing.

"Good grief," Nic said in Delia's nasally tone. "Our contact's not only a geek, but a flaming geek."

I could scarcely believe my new brown eyes. Instead of covering up his buff physique, he'd accentuated it. He wore a green silk shirt that clung and showed off the hard sculptured torso beneath. His overall look was trendy, in a hairstylist to the stars kind of way. He'd bleached his dark hair platinum and wore steel-framed glasses that had a European flair. Bad boy looked like a pretty boy. Color me stunned. I nearly lost it when he let out an excited yelp and waved like a girlfriend to get our attention.

Delia groaned. "What a waste."

"As long as we can manipulate his mind," I said with a slight British accent, "who cares about his body."

Delia pushed her glasses up her nose. "Speak for yourself, Portia."

"Portia Livingston!" *Spock* practically floated toward us. "You look exactly like the picture on your Web site, only better! And those *shoes!*" He laid a hand over his heart. "To die for. Oh, dear. Where *are* my manners?" He stuck out his big palm and gave me a limp-fish handshake. "Preston Spock. I'm with the Paranormal Society of New Jersey."

Delia pointed to the sign he was holding. "We got that." She hiked her satchel higher on her shoulder, stuck out a hand in greeting. "Delia Jones, Ms. Livingston's personal assistant. We appreciate the lift, Mr. Spock."

He clasped her hand and ditched the sign. "Please, call me Preston, and it's my pleasure, Ms. Jones." He turned to me. "I can't tell you how excited we are about your lecture and readings, Ms. Livingston. We would have flown you into Atlantic City directly, but what with the four hour layover in Philly…I'll have you down at the shore and in your hotel room in ninety minutes flat. Barring any unforeseen traffic, of course."

"I'm sure we'll enjoy the drive and the company," I said.

Preston flashed a dazzling smile. "Gifted *and* lovely."

My heart fluttered and ached at the same time. *Dammit!*

"Allow me to take your bags," he said, moving in between Nic and me. "I parked in short-term. Walk this way."

Uh, right.

I noted the swish of his hips and suppressed a giggle.

My amusement was short-lived. Two stern-faced men in black suits blocked our way. I registered the entire package. White shirts. Black ties. Black shades. FBI? AIA? Rogue agents? Independent contractors?

Definitely trouble.

"Ms. Portia Livingston?" the taller one inquired.

"Yes?"

"I'm Agent McKeene."

"Agent Burns," the darker, shorter one said.

The men who'd escorted Beckett to Crowe. Holy crap. They flashed their badges.

"I'm sorry," I said, tamping down a flurry of dread. "I'm not familiar with the AIA."

"Is that anything like the CIA?" asked Spock, eyes wide.

"Similar," said McKeene.

"Let me guess," Delia said, "you read that Ms. Livingston was flying into town and decided to take advantage of her psychic gifts. What's the case? Missing child? Serial killer?"

"Something like that," said Burns.

Spock gasped. "Oh, dear."

Delia reached into her satchel and pulled out a pad and pen. The spy gadget pen that offered up to eight hours of digital recording time and stored the audio in a flash memory. *Go, Nic!* She flicked her Bic and triggered the recorder. "If you give me the basics—"

"Not here," said McKeene.

I noted the crowded terminal. "You don't want people to overhear specifics of the case," I said in a soft voice. "I understand. Just as well. If I'm to help, I need a less chaotic atmosphere. If you give us your number, perhaps we can set an appointment for Monday."

"This matter is urgent, Ms. Livingston."

"Heavens," said Spock. He looked at me with Arch's calm and confidence. "I don't mind driving you and Ms. Jones over to the police station or wherever these agents need you to be."

"This case is for Ms. Livingston's ears only," said Burns. "You go ahead with Ms. Jones. We'll escort Ms. Livingston to Atlantic City after our meeting."

"And that meeting would be where?" Delia asked, pen poised.

"In Philadelphia," McKeene said.

Could he be any more vague?

"I must protest," said Spock. "Ms. Livingston is a guest of the PSNJ and under my direct care. If—"

"This is a matter of national importance," Burns said, looking directly at me.

Okay. This wasn't going according to plan at all. I wondered where Beckett and Tabasco were. I assumed they were listening in. They were all connected via secret agent hidden mics and earpieces. Normally, I would have broken out in a nervous rash by now. I marveled at my calm. All I could think was, *this is it. My chance to save Beckett, Gina, and my nation from a dangerous power monger.* "When you put it like that, Agent Burns." I squeezed Nic's hand. "You and Preston go ahead. I'll be fine. I'll meet you at the hotel later and we can all go to dinner." I turned to Arch. "If my psychic abilities can help these men capture some fiend, I'm obligated to go. I'm sure you understand." I relieved him of my carry-on suitcase.

"You won't be needing that," said McKeene.

"Yes, I will. In order to conduct readings, I need my crystal ball."

The agents traded a look. Burns took my bag.

Arch touched my arm. "Ms. Livingston—"

"We'll want to turn in early so I'm properly rested for tomorrow's event." I glanced at my watch, the one fitted with a recorder similar to the one in Nic's pen. "Would you mind making our dinner reservations for five-ish, Preston? Thanks. You're a doll."

I turned away and focused on my marks. "You have an interesting aura, Agent McKeene. What sign are you?"

CHAPTER THIRTY

MILO STEPPED OUT OF the newsstand. He saw McKeene and Burns flanking Evie and steering her toward an escalator. Spock was guiding Delia across a skywalk to short-term parking. "What the fuck, Arch?"

The Scot addressed Woody instead. "Have you got her, Kid?"

"Signal's strong, Ace. Real-time updates. We're good."

Pretending he was still talking on his cell phone, Tabasco pushed off the wall and headed out. "That GPS tracking device we wedged into Twinkie's mirrored compact is top-notch. All she has to do is keep her purse with her and we'll know where she is at all times."

"I'm aware," Milo ground out as he headed for an exit.

"She can do this, Jazzman," Arch said. "I saw it in her eyes. Whatever's said in that meeting, she'll get it on her digital recorder."

"Look at it this way," said Tabasco. "We're a day ahead of schedule. Sooner this is done, sooner Gina's out of the danger zone."

"How's Nic holding up?" Milo asked as he stepped in a deserted elevator and hit the button for ground level.

"If anyone's in danger," Arch said, "it's me, yeah? The woman's got bloody murder in her eyes."

"You did just let the bad guys walk off with her best friend," said Woody.

"Evie knows we're tracking her," Arch said. "If things get rough, she knows to trigger the SOS button on the GPS."

"Stand by," said Milo. He tapped off his mic, speed-dialed Nic on his cell.

"Don't worry," she answered. "I won't murder him. Not just now anyway. He's behind the wheel."

"You're in his car already?"

"Pulling out of the parking space."

"Crowe needs Portia to work with him long-term to manipulate Wilson. He'll threaten her but he won't hurt her. I'm not happy about it, babe, but Arch was right to let her go."

"Agreed."

"Then what's the problem?"

"Don't worry about it. We'll work it out."

The elevator doors slid open. "There's a time and place, Nicole."

"Noted, Slick."

"You were amazing back there."

"You expected less?"

His lip twitched.

"Milo?"

"Yeah."

"Be careful."

That was downright sappy for the woman. "Always." Smiling, he signed off and worked his way through the mob waiting to claim their baggage.

"I've got a visual," Tabasco said in a quiet voice. "Black four-door sedan."

"Figures," said Woody.

Tabasco chuckled. "Oh, man. This is priceless."

Milo neared a set of glass doors, spotted their blue SUV. "What's so funny?"

"Burns is putting her suitcase in the trunk."

"Fucking hilarious."

"No, it's the exasperated look on McKeene's face."

"What's Evie doing?" Arch asked.

"Reading his palm."

"Brilliant."

Milo crossed the street and slid into the driver's seat. He tossed the backpack over his shoulder. Woody was stationed at a miniconsole in the back. "Still got her?"

"In 3-D glory, sir. This unit is amazing." He narrowed his eyes. "They're on the move."

"Target in action," said Tabasco.

"What's your location?" Milo asked as he pulled into traffic. "I'll pick you up."

"They're pulling onto 95 North," said Woody.

"I'm there," said Arch.

Milo swung by and Tabasco hopped in.

The team fell quiet as they sped along the multilane highway.

"I've got them in sight," said Arch.

Milo had Arch in sight. "Don't follow too close."

"I know the dance, yeah?"

Shortly, Woody told them to take the Broad Street exit. He continued to relay directions using the GPS tracking unit as his guide.

"I don't know if this is good or bad," Milo said when the agents' intent was clear. "Looks like they're taking her to HQ."

I LEARNED TWO THINGS WITHIN the first ten minutes I spent alone with Agents McKeene and Burns.

1. They were humorless.

2. They were not suckers.

Neither one of them showed any interest in my psychic gifts. I was tempted to tell them their auras were black and to offer a horoscope prediction that would strike the fear of God into their hearts. Only I wasn't sure they *had* hearts. They were go-to men for a man who used his position and dirty files to control people. Surely McKeene and Burns had been decent men at some point. They were government agents. The "white hats." Although, now that I thought about it, they *were* the good guys in this instance. *I* was the bad sort. The scammer who tricked gullible marks out of their money with my fake readings.

Right.

The story about needing to utilize my *gift* had been a ploy to get me away from my friends and alone with Crowe. So far we were still playing that game, although we'd fallen into silence.

Purse clutched in my lap, I sat in the backseat alongside McKeene while Burns chauffeured us toward Center City. I feigned interest in the passing sights and mentally reviewed the technical aspects of my spy gear. Thankfully, the recorder on my watch was simple to activate. The GPS unit was hidden in my purse and already in action. If I was in serious danger there was a panic button that would alert Chameleon to storm in and save me. I didn't intend to use it because that would mean I'd screwed up. I refused to crack out of turn. Too much was riding on this moment.

I recognized Independence Square and felt a burst of patriotism. "The Star-Spangled Banner" welled in my ears. How dare Vincent Crowe discredit a government agency!

Burns parked the car in an official-looking parking lot. McKeene released our seat belts. I ignored the way his hand brushed my thigh. *Pig.* "Is this case somehow tied into Independence Hall?" I asked. "Or the Liberty Bell? Is that what you meant by national importance?"

He pointed to a historical-looking brownstone. "That's AIA Headquarters."

Mentally, I pumped a fist. *Yes!* Better than rendezvousing with Crowe in a seedy hotel or secluded area where they could whack me with nobody noticing. Not that a dead psychic would further his cause. Still, it only boosted my confidence knowing I was being escorted into a law enforcement facility. Surely, I'd be safe in there. "I would have thought your headquarters would be in D.C."

"Local," Burns said as he opened my door and helped me out.

"I see." He tugged me toward the building, only I dug in my heels. "I need my crystal ball."

He started to say something, but McKeene stepped in. "I'll get your suitcase."

I noted the area. Lots of traffic and pedestrians. Obviously, he meant to play this game until we were inside and out of sightseers' view. Fine by me.

My pulse kicked up as we headed toward the brownstone. I trusted Chameleon was nearby, watching. I hoped they trusted me. Once I disappeared inside that building, they'd have to be patient until I came out. I wasn't wired into their audio system thingee. No way to communicate to let them know I was okay. Only the SOS button if things curdled. I could see a couple of hours going by and Arch or Beckett or *both* getting twitchy. It would royally suck if they jumped the gun and ruined things just because they didn't trust that I could take care of myself.

Too bad I couldn't at least give them a visual. But Woody had rigged the wireless button camera into the black designer jacket I was supposed to wear for tomorrow's lecture. That suit jacket was packed in my suitcase and I had no sane reason to change clothes.

Unless…

I saw a teenaged couple and an opportunity coming my way. I braced myself. This was gonna hurt. Due to my impeccable timing and pratfall skills, I caught my heel on a crack in the sidewalk and plowed forward into a teenager eating a triple-scoop ice-cream cone. He fell back on his butt. I landed on my knees and elbows. The yelp of pain was for real. Mine, not the kid's. The kid just cursed.

Chaos ensued. Apologies and concerns flew from both sides as Burns helped me to my feet and McKeene pressed a bill into the kid's hand to cover the cost of the cone. Two minutes later we were all on our way. A minute later the agents escorted me into HQ and to the nearest bathroom where I changed out of the red jacket smeared with chocolate ice cream and into the video-rigged black jacket. Amazing how all six buttons looked exactly the same. The third one down was a camera. I activated the device and hoped the team had recognized my fall as purposeful and guessed my intent. The team's SUV, like the van we'd used in Indiana, was tricked out with high-tech surveillance gear. I knew the console included a wireless receiver and video monitor. It was just a matter of if they were turned on.

Someone knocked on the door. "You okay in there?" asked Burns.

"Just washing off my knees. Be right out." I'd skinned them pretty good, but I was more concerned with my tricked out watch. *Crap.* The second hand was no longer moving. Had ice cream seeped in and shorted something? Had I damaged the watch in the fall? If the time mechanism was broken did that mean the digital recorder was busted, too? I pressed the appropriate button. No. The dial didn't look right. Something was definitely wrong. So, what? Now I had visual, but no audio? And I wasn't even certain I had visual. *Dammit!*

"Ms. Livingston." McKeene poked his head in. "We're expected."

I smiled and grabbed my suitcase and purse. "I'm ready."

I kept the watch in activation mode just in case it worked. My heart hammered as they escorted me through a deserted lobby and past a security checkpoint. "Where is everyone?"

"Traditional office days are Monday through Friday," said Burns.

Today was Saturday. I'd hoped to be surrounded by a combination of agents and office workers. I spied a janitor and one desk jockey. Okay. This was disappointing. This was…scary. I squared my shoulders. "Guess you're working overtime," I said as they whisked me down a hall. "This case *must* be urgent. I'll certainly do my best to help."

"We appreciate that," said McKeene. He opened a door and nudged me inside.

A fiftysomething man with white hair and bad posture was seated behind a large antique desk. I knew him from his picture. Crowe. My stomach fluttered with dread and excitement. Was the camera working? Could the guys see him? Maybe read his lips?

He smiled. "Ms. Livingston. Thank you for joining us. Please sit down."

I sat. I smiled. "And you are?"

"Vincent Crowe. Director of the AIA."

"What exactly is the AIA?"

"A government agency devoted to fighting corruption."

"Aren't they all?" Purse at my side, I relaxed against the chair and crossed my legs. "So, you're the top man in this outfit, I assume. When your agents said this case was of national importance, I guess they weren't kidding."

"We never kid, Ms. Livingston."

"Did you search her purse?" A woman's voice. A familiar voice. *Gina!*

McKeene and Burns mumbled a sheepish, "No."

I turned and saw her move out of the shadows. She looked like one of them, dressed in a black suit and a white shirt. Whatever. She was safe! She was here! But why? Since Portia wouldn't know her, I frowned when she snatched my purse and started looking through the contents. "What are you doing?"

"Security precautions," said Crowe.

"Wallet, keys, makeup bag." She opened it. "Lipstick, powder, eyeliner." She closed my compact and I thanked God she hadn't exposed the GPS device. She rooted some more. "Paperback book by Sylvia Browne, cigarettes." *Arch's.* "An inhaler."

"I have asthma."

"Then you shouldn't be smoking," said Crowe.

I raised an offended brow. "I realize that, thank you."

He glanced at Gina. "Is that it?"

"That's it." She handed me back my purse and perched on the corner of Crowe's desk, arms crossed.

But that wasn't it, I realized with a start. Arch's PDA. They couldn't get into the sensitive content without his passwords. Still…

Then I remembered. The PDA contained a digital voice recorder. Did she know that? Had she switched it on? "I came here of my own free will to help you with a case, Director Crowe," I said in Portia's faint British accent, "and yet you're treating me like a criminal."

"You are a criminal."

"Excuse me?"

He shoved a file across his desk. "Agent Valente formerly worked with a special branch of the AIA that investigates scam artists."

"We know your real name is Becca Price and that you were raised in Georgia not the U.K.," said Gina. "We know you've been swindling marks with bogus astrological charts and crystal-ball readings. We know you plant cameras and mics at your public readings and listen in on conversations prior to the lecture to gain insight on your audience members. We know…"

She went on to detail all the dirt Chameleon had dug up on Becca Price aka Portia Livingston. I licked dry lips and scanned the files, which included Portia's financial statements—wow, I was rich—and IRS forms—I'm pretty certain I cheated the government—and complaints against me by several people I'd bilked.

Being a—*cough*—con artist, I danced around the truth.

Being law officials, they weren't having it.

Crowe leaned forward. "You have a golden tongue, Becca, on top of being quite attractive." He dragged his wretched gaze over my body. "I suspect you could talk most any man into believing anything."

I pretended boredom, traded the British accent for a southern drawl. "Is there a point to this, sugar?"

He smiled. A wicked smile that made my skin crawl. Then he asked his men to leave. "You, too, Agent Valente."

She looked surprised, but she nodded and took her leave along with McKeene and Burns. I hoped she didn't go far. The door clicked shut and I faced my fate alone.

Portia/Becca would be nervous, but she wouldn't scratch her neck. "Mind if I smoke?"

Crowe took an ashtray from his desk drawer and placed it in front of me. "I have enough evidence to send you to prison for several years, Becca."

I reached in my purse for the pack of Marlboros, spotted the PDA. I couldn't tell if the button for the recorder was on. "Do you have a light? Because of the flight restrictions…"

"Luckily for you, my dear," he said, while reaching back in his drawer, "I am a fellow smoker."

I touched the button. ON. *Thank you, Gina.* But could the teeny mic pick up what Crowe was saying? I better positioned the PDA, leaving my purse cracked open.

He came around the desk to light the cigarette. *Yes! Sit in the chair next to me! All the better to hear you!* I uncrossed and recrossed my legs as enticement. He'd been staring at them since I'd walked in, skinned knees and all. The use of my first name suggested a sleazy intimacy that I intended to take advantage of. I could do sexy. Arch said so.

The thought of the man who'd stolen my heart, filled me with renewed confidence. Crazy, even though I was mad at him, he inspired me and pumped up my courage.

I inhaled as though I'd been smoking for years. Lord knows, I'd watched Nic and Arch smoke enough to know the ritual. Not gagging was the hard part. I blew out smoke and quirked an easy smile. "I wouldn't look good in prison garb. Can we work a deal here, Vince?"

"Play by my rules, Becca, and you'll prosper. Cross me—"

"I'll play." I shifted so that I was facing him, thrust out my breasts, just enough to tease him, and just enough to give the button cam a prime view of his crooked, smarmy face—just in case the video thingee was actually working. "What's the game, sugar?"

CHAPTER THIRTY-ONE

NOT THAT I TRULY PUT STOCK in the stars, but the planets were aligned or the moon was in the Seventh House or some such lucky such. Over the course of ten surrealistic minutes, Crowe pitched his deal, just as we'd imagined. He sugarcoated it with a whole lot of hooey about the protection of democracy. Bottom line, he wanted Portia Livingston to cultivate a relationship with Senator Martin Wilson. "Become his personal reader, win his confidence and we'll take it from there," he said.

I pushed, trying to get him to incriminate himself further. "I assume you want me to influence his decisions in some way?"

"We'll take it as it comes."

I pushed a little more, backing off at the first sign of irritation. I hoped I had enough. I hoped the digital recorder in the watch worked or the PDA worked or the button cam worked. *Something.* If nothing else, I suppose I could always testify in court. Except it would be his word against mine. Lounge lizard versus Agency snake.

Great.

Before he dismissed me, he made another point of threatening me with prison, or worse, should I cross him.

That's when I *knew* I had enough to nail him.

I did an internal happy dance and made one request. I

was surprised when he agreed, but then I am a damned good actress and my dislike of McKeene was genuine.

Five minutes later, I left HQ flanked by Burns and Gina.

"This is bogus," Burns said, as he wheeled my suitcase back to the car. "McKeene did not touch her inappropriately."

"Whether he did or did not," Gina said, shoving on a pair of dark shades, "Director Crowe instructed me to partner with you for this ride."

"Bogus," he repeated, tossing my bag in the trunk.

"Hey," I complained with a southern drawl. "Be careful. There's a crystal ball in there."

"You," he said, jabbing a finger in my face, "shut up."

Hopped up on adrenaline, I narrowed my eyes. "I'd be nice to me if I were you. I have something your boss wants."

Burns opened the back door. "Don't push me."

Catching a warning glance from Gina, I bit my tongue and slid into the car.

She started to join me, only Burns dropped the keys in her hands. "I've been driving all day. You take the wheel."

"The idea," she said, "was to have a female agent sitting alongside Ms. Livingston."

"Tough shit." He slid in beside me and slammed the door.

Jeez. Nothing like a partner scorned. Well, too bad. No way was I leaving a team member behind.

Gina took the driver's seat and steered the car into Center City traffic.

I trusted Chameleon was following us. It was all I could do not to rubberneck and look for a blue SUV and a black Jaguar.

Trust.

I rested my head against the seat and closed my eyes,

trying to wrangle runaway thoughts. They all revolved around Arch. Confusing thoughts. Conflicting thoughts. I wanted to hate him, but I didn't. The best of me wanted to believe the best in him. What if I'd heard wrong? What if I'd misinterpreted his words? What if Nic was right and his feelings for me were genuine? So what if he considered me an asset where his daughter was concerned? I *was* an asset. I'd make a great mom!

I shoved aside the notion. This was nuts. This was…dangerous. I needed to stay in character until they dropped me at my hotel in Atlantic City. That was the plan. They'd drop me off. I'd lecture to the PSNJ tomorrow then I'd fly back to Boston where I'd initiate contact with Senator Wilson.

Supposedly.

In reality, I'd hand over my recording devices and Beckett would sic the FBI on Crowe.

Then I'd figure out what was what with Arch…and my life.

The car jerked and swerved. I gasped and jerked.

"Idiot drivers," said Gina.

I realized with a start that my purse had flown off my lap. The contents littered the floor. *Oh, no.*

Burns and I bent over at the same time.

He scooped up the PDA. "What the hell is this? You didn't mention a PDA when you searched her purse," he said to Gina.

She glanced over her shoulder. "What?"

My stomach clenched when he hit a button and I heard Crowe's voice. The world jerked into slow motion. Burns pulled a cell phone from his pocket. "We've been had, McKeene."

He reached for his gun and I freaked. I snatched up my inhaler, sprayed him in the face. He *screamed.* His gun slipped from his hand as he palmed his swollen, watering eyes. "You fucking blinded me!"

"Grab his gun!" Gina shouted just as a car rammed us from behind.

What the hell? I whipped around, glared at a black four-door on our tail. "McKeene?"

"Bitch!" Burns swung out at me, but I ducked. He lurched forward and puked.

Gina punched the gas. "What was in that inhaler?"

"Mace Pepper Spray!" A brainchild of Tabasco's and Woody's.

"Beautiful. Now get his *fucking gun!*"

Another ram from behind. Where was Arch? Beckett? I thought about the GPS. The SOS button, but it was in my compact which was…where?

Coughing and wheezing, Burns reared up.

"Don't touch me. Don't move." Since he couldn't see me, I tapped the barrel of the gun to his forehead then eased back and aimed at his chest.

Oh, God.

Gina drove like a freaking NASCAR racer, zipping in and out of city traffic at lightning speed.

Another ram. I heard it, but I didn't feel it. I glanced out the back window. A blue SUV was muscling McKeene's car off the road. Metal clashed. Rubber burned. *Sparks. Smoke.* This was like a scene out of any one of a dozen action movies.

In this episode of my life gone wild…

A black Jaguar zipped alongside us. I saw Nic, Arch.

Burns wheezed and growled. His face was swollen and red. His eyes watered profusely. "Kill—" *cough* "—you." Disoriented, he struck out but clipped Gina in the back of the head.

"Goddammit! Grow some balls, Twinkie!"

Desperate to protect us both, I leaned in and pressed the barrel of the gun to Burns's chest. "I've killed before. I'll kill again. Don't. Move."

My words boomeranged and knocked me ill. *Killed before?* Where had that come…

A memory flared.

Me. Fading. Falling. Grabbing hold. A hand. *Fish's* hand. *Bang!*

I'd wondered. Now, deep down, I knew.

Gina swerved to the side of the road and hit the brakes. The world stilled.

I heard tires screech. Doors open and slam. A loud roar buzzed in my head.

I felt someone move in behind me. "Leave off, lass."

I blinked to clear my vision.

Gina yanked a snot-nosed, wheezing Burns from the car. "Bastard."

Drenched in sweat, my arms sagged with the weight of the gun. I dropped it. "I'm going to puke."

Arch hauled me from the car. He settled in the grass, held me and stroked my back. "Breathe, Evie."

I trembled in his arms, massaged my tight chest, and fought nausea. I couldn't voice my sin. If I did, I'd fall apart. Now wasn't the time. I was still on the job. Crowe was still on the loose.

I heard sirens. Nic. "Jesus, Evie. Are you all right?"

"Peachy."

Arch smiled. "You were brilliant, Sunshine."

"How do you know?" I was embarrassed by my mini-anxiety attack, unhinged by my realization.

He tapped the third button on my jacket. "Got it on video." He kissed the back of my head. "Brilliant."

"But it didn't have audio."

"Aye, it did. Via a wireless transmitter."

"Oh." I didn't have the energy to ponder how I'd missed that. I sleeved sweat from my clammy face, looked up at Nic. "Do you have a ginger ale?"

She blew out a breath of relief, smiled. "No. But for you, Miss Kick-Ass Chameleon, I'll find one."

She hurried off and I wilted against Arch. I focused on the sting. "I think I broke the watch, but I'm not sure. I used your PDA as backup. Crowe hanged himself, Arch. Where's Beckett?"

"Dealing with Burns and McKeene."

"How did the police get here so fast?"

"While you were inside HQ, The Kid finally hacked into COPRODEM. *Aboot* the same time you cracked Crowe, yeah? Talk *aboot* teamwork. Beckett alerted the FBI. Crowe's going down, Sunshine."

Relief blew the lid off of my tightly contained emotions.

I burst into tears.

He rocked me in his arms. "Shush, lass."

"I killed Fish. It was me, not you."

"Christ."

"I grabbed a hand. Not yours. Simon's. I grabbed and the gun went off. Why did you lie, Arch?"

"Because I *didnae* want… Because…I love you. Christ. Why do you think? I'd do anything to protect you, Evie. I *didnae* want you to have to live with this."

I gazed into those tender gray-green eyes. I thought about the way he made love to me. The way he'd carved our names in a tree.

I sobbed.

"Shite."

I didn't doubt Arch's love, but I did doubt the man. There'd been too much deception.

There are all kinds of lies, Sunshine.

Maybe. But my inner bad girl would never conquer my innate good girl.

I blinked through my tears at the chaotic scene. The banged-up cars. Gina in a huddle with Tabasco. Beckett with his hand on the small of Nic's back as he talked to the police. There was something right and easy about those two. I knew they were meant to be. I knew that, no matter their differences, love would conquer all.

Why didn't I have the same faith in my relationship with Arch? Why couldn't things be right and easy between us?

My brain exploded with a dozen what-ifs. What if the last couple of months had been a test? A transition? Some sort of midlife growing pains? What if Arch's fears were grounded? What if he'd been no more than a joyride, a sexy fantasy to distract me from my previously crappy life? If I truly, deeply loved him, wouldn't I be willing to accept him as is? Flaws and all?

I felt a snap. A sickening disconnection. How could I commit to Arch when I didn't know my own heart?

As for Chameleon, knowing I'd been responsible for Simon the Fish's death tainted everything.

Logically, now wasn't the time to make rash decisions. But sometimes a person has to go with their gut. I looked into Arch's eyes and felt numb to the charisma that usually melted sane thought. The surrounding chaos faded to white noise. The fantasy shattered. I wasn't Emma Peel or any one of Charlie's Angels. I was Evie Parish and I owed it to myself to get my head and heart straight before I considered a future with Arch or any other man.

In a nanosecond of clarity, I knew what I had to do.

CHAPTER THIRTY-TWO

Nine days later...

MILO WALKED THE LENGTH of the Reflecting Pool, reflecting on his meeting with the President of the United States. He wondered how the team was going to take the news. Unwilling to cool their heels in Atlantic City, Chameleon, with the exception of Twinkie, awaited him on the steps leading up to the Lincoln Memorial.

They sat side by side—Arch, Gina, Tabasco, Woody, Pops. Milo experienced a rush of pride for all they'd accomplished together. Their work wasn't finished. It would never be finished. Grifters had been scamming unsuspecting souls for centuries and would continue to do so, feeding off of mankind's strengths and weaknesses. His vision hadn't changed, but his priorities had.

He loosened his tie as he jogged up the steps.

Woody spoke first. "Sir?"

Milo took off his suit jacket and sat in between Gina and Tabasco. He gazed out at the long column of water, conscious of the tourists drifting up and down the National Mall. Potential marks, every one. Christ.

"First things first," he said. "Thanks to Syd's sticky fingers, I've been officially cleared in Mad Dog's death."

Arch nodded. "Brilliant."

"Right is right," said Pops.

"No denying the audio/visual evidence," said Woody.

Gina just smiled.

Her mystery friend had infiltrated HQ and managed to steal the damning DVR before the busted director had had a chance to destroy it. The Kid had been right. The DVD they'd shown Milo had been tampered with. Mad Dog had been alive when Milo left him. McKeene had finished him off, per Crowe's directive. McKeene hadn't been aware his antics had been caught on tape until he and Burns had tossed the room and discovered the DVR. The only reason Crowe had kept the damning evidence was because who knew when he'd need dirt on McKeene? The depth of Crowe's dirty deeds seemed bottomless, as proven by the FBI's ongoing investigation.

Milo cleared his throat. "Naturally, the president's shocked and outraged by Crowe's corruption. He's intent on replacing the crooked official with a proven straight arrow."

Arch raised a brow. "You?"

"He offered me the job, yes."

Tabasco whistled. "The Director of the AIA."

"Man, oh, man," said Woody.

"About time," said Pops.

"I didn't take it."

"You said no to the President of the United States?" Gina snorted. "Only you, Jazzman."

It hadn't been easy. The president had been insistent. But Milo had his own agenda and it included a life with Nic. She didn't know it yet, but she was going to marry him. Eventually. "I'm still committed to busting scams, but I'm through with answering to the AIA." He glanced at Arch. "A wise man once told me that if I really wanted to make a difference, to go freelance." He looked at the others. "I don't expect you to give up the security of working for the government—"

Pops grunted.

"Don't insult us," said Tabasco.

"Your mission is our mission," said Woody.

Gina nudged Milo and smiled. "Chameleon. Free to pick and choose our own cases. Free to play by our own rules. Sounds like fun."

Arch didn't comment.

The rest of the team stirred with discomfort. They all knew he was grieving Evie's absence, but they didn't expect him to abandon Chameleon.

Milo, on the other hand, had been anticipating this moment since the day Evie flew out to Hollywood.

Pops stood. "Have me a mind to take in the Smithsonian before we fly back to AC. Kid?"

"Sure." Woody scrambled off the step. "So long as we're back home before eight o'clock. I've got a date."

They all slid him a look.

"Does this mean you're finally over being lovesick?" asked Gina.

Woody had been trying to win back his old girlfriend for weeks. He nodded and rubbed a hand over his new short haircut. "I was talking to Twinkie the other night. She convinced me it was time to move on and... What?" It dawned on him then that he'd brought up the woman who'd broken Arch's heart. "Oh. Yikes. Sorry, Ace."

The Scot waved off his apology. "Enjoy the museum, Kid. Have fun with your new lady, yeah?"

"Uh, sure. Thanks." Blushing, The Kid hurried down the steps. Pops followed and smacked the younger man in the back of the head.

Tabasco stood. "I'm going to hit the National Air and Space Museum." He whipped out his cell. "Just need to call Jayne with an update. Don't want her to worry."

"The Bohemian fruit loop and the Latin Chameleon," Gina teased. "It'll never last."

Tabasco just grinned. "Coming with?"

"Nope." She stood and brushed off the seat of her form-fitting jeans. "I'm meeting up with Syd. The least I can do is buy him dinner."

Tabasco narrowed his eyes. "It's Roger Lions, right? Dan McNaught?"

"Nice try." Smiling, she descended the stairs.

Tabasco followed. "Nimble Fingers Newton?"

Milo watched them go. "You have any idea of Syd's real identity?" he asked Arch.

"No. You?"

"None. Huh." Milo fell silent. He was used to Arch taking the lead, but the Scot seemed tongue-tied. A first. "Guess this is it," Milo prodded. "The end of our partnership."

"You *dinnae* need me anymore."

Milo buzzed a hand over his cropped hair. "I know I've said some shitty stuff over the past few weeks—"

"Nothing I *didnae* deserve." Arch rolled back his shoulders. "So, The Kid got a call from Evie, yeah?"

"Sounds like."

"What about you?"

Damn. "Day before yesterday. She got the starring role in that cable series."

Arch didn't flinch. "I'm not surprised. She's a damned good actress. When you talk to her again, tell her I said congratulations, yeah?"

"Tell her yourself."

"I *cannae*. She asked me to give her space. Said she needs time to sort *oot* her feelings and… *Fuck*." He looked away. "I'm bloody miserable."

There was a time Milo thought Arch would slice and dice Evie's heart. He'd never expected it to go the other way. "For what it's worth, Nic said Evie confided she's not all that thrilled with the Hollywood scene."

"*Doesnae* help, considering she's even less thrilled with me." He bit the inside of his cheek, considered. Finally he said, "I could use a friend, Milo. A real friend, yeah?"

Well, hell. Aside from being courted by the U.S. president, nothing could've surprised him more. "Okay."

"I fucked up and I *dinnae* know how to fix it."

Milo listened while Arch confessed to a past con that resulted in a daughter. The shockers just kept coming. His opinion of the man dipped and rose as he went on to explain how he'd handled the situation with *Kate* as well as Evie.

"I keep replaying the night we launched Aquarius," he said. "Evie turned cold and the next day Nic gave me hell for using her as a means to an end. I *didnae* know what she was talking *aboot*. Then it clicked. I think…I'm afraid she overheard an argument I had with Kate and misunderstood. It's the only thing that makes sense only…I *cannae* clear the air because I promised I *wouldnae* call her for at least a month."

Not that Milo was an expert on relationships, but he had a pretty good handle on Evie. "Want my advice?"

"I'm all ears."

A few minutes later, Arch took his leave and Milo dialed Nic. She answered on the first ring which made him think she'd been anxiously awaiting his call. Not that he expected her to admit it.

"How'd it go, Slick?"

"Good. Better than good. I'm clear." He gazed out at the patriotic landscape feeling lighter than he'd felt in years. "Of everything."

"Think you could spare some details?"

"I'll tell all over dinner."

"Is that your way of asking me out on a date?"

He grinned at her sarcasm. "Will you have dinner with me tonight, Nicole?"

"Yes. But only because I want to know what the president had to say."

"Uh-huh."

"I'm not going to sleep with you, Slick."

"Who mentioned sleep? I'll pick you up at eight, babe." Smiling, he signed off then dialed a florist. "I'd like to order two dozen roses."

CHAPTER THIRTY-THREE

HOLLYWOOD IS WHERE DREAMS come true and stars are born.

I had fantasized about it all of my life.

Three weeks into what should be bliss and I felt like an alien. The only place where I felt comfortable was Disneyland. I'd rather hang with cartoon characters trying to create smiles than with too beautiful people concerned only with their careers.

Running away to Tinseltown hadn't been a complete bust. I'd still nailed the dream. Unfortunately, I'd found no joy in the accomplishment. Okay. That's a lie. Directly after acing the audition, I'd reveled in a burst of renewed confidence. Over forty and still in demand. Call me vindicated. Except, soon after, the thrill was gone.

After a few days, all being here did was remind me that I hadn't come with all of my energy in front of me, pushing toward something. Hollywood in my heart. All of my energy swirled behind me, leaving a huge wake. With Arch in my heart. I was running from my true passion instead of toward it. Being here felt empty and hollow and left me with little conviction to carry out my childhood dream.

I also thought about the other actresses who'd lost out. Talented actresses, trained actresses. Actresses who wouldn't need a crash course in performing on camera. I felt like one of the fledgling lounge singers I had complained about in AC. The ones who hadn't paid their dues but who got the gig because of an edge. Like youth or big boobs or a high-roller daddy. Had Michael's longtime friendship with the show's writer/director been my edge? I knew that was how Hollywood worked, and, at some other time in my life, this might not have bothered me so much. Plus, to give myself some credit, I would've worked my butt off to rock Charlie Lutz's Armani socks.

But the truth wouldn't be denied. Again and again it made itself evident.

My heart wasn't in it.

Charlie (who'd personally coached me prior to the audition) had been stunned when I'd graciously declined the studio's offer to star in their show. In fact, he thought I was nuts. But luckily he liked me, so when I asked him if he could line me up with a job more suited to my areas of expertise, he'd complied. Okay. So this gig as Snow White (what were the chances?) was only temporary, but at least I had my foot in the park. There were dozens of costumed characters. Hey, if I survived the gorilla suit, I could handle Tigger or Goofy. If not a character then there were several shows and attractions that involved singing, dancing, and/or acting. Perfect for a veteran variety performer.

Working for a company that created fairy tales? Bringing joy to countless children and adults? Yeah, baby, yeah. My ex's friend had landed me a primo gig. Too bad it wasn't my happy place.

I looked up at the starry sky, breathed in the wafting scents of grilled burgers and cotton candy, and counted my blessings.

There's something to be said for distancing yourself from every place and everyone you know. In addition to testing your survival skills, it's a supreme way to gain perspective. Space and time had allowed me to sort fantasy from reality. My love for Arch "Ace" Duvall was achingly real. The good memories outweighed the bad and if the journal I'd received in the mail two days ago was any indication…

"Can we have a picture with you?"

I blinked away thoughts of the rebel Scot who'd penned and shared his innermost thoughts. I smiled down at a little boy and girl. So cute! Since they were holding hands, and since a man and woman reminded them to say *please,* I assumed they were brother and sister. "Why, of course." I stooped down and opened my arms. They hugged me and I got the warm fuzzies—a feeling I'd enjoyed countless times over the past ten days.

"Where's Grumpy?" asked the boy.

I made a pained face. "Off grumbling somewhere, I imagine. Know what I do to get rid of his sour puss?"

"What?"

"I tickle him!"

The freckle-faced kid shrieked with laughter when I ruffled his tummy.

"Does Prince Charming really ride a white horse?" asked the girl.

No, he drives a black Jaguar. I cursed myself for asking Arch to stay away for an entire month. Every day felt like a year. What if he'd decided I was more trouble than I was worth? But then, why send the journal? A journal filled with details of past scams, stories about his mom and grandpa, his history with Beckett, his dreams for Cassidy and his deeply intimate thoughts about me.

Talk about a token of faith and trust.

I felt the girl tug on my puffy sleeve. *"Did he say he loved ya?"*

"Did he steal a kiss?" asked the boy.

I realized they were quoting a song from the 1937 classic *Snow White and the Seven Dwarfs.* In spirit, I sang my reply. *"He was so romantic, I could not resist."*

"So where is he?" asked the girl.

I swallowed past a lump in my throat, but before I could answer, someone else did.

"He's right here. I hope."

Arch.

Tall, dark, and handsome. Sexy. Vulnerable. Heart pounding, I rose and met his tender gaze.

Zing. Zap.

If not for my acting skills, I would have burst into tears. *The connection.* Only, thanks to the handwritten journal he'd entitled *Private Stuff,* a bazillion times stronger.

The little girl frowned up at his denim jeans and leather jacket. "You don't *look* like Prince Charming."

"Close enough," said the mother with a be-still-my-heart expression I'd witnessed so many times before.

"Come on, kids," said the dad and the family disappeared.

Everything disappeared. Everything but Arch. I could scarcely breathe.

"You're a hard woman to find, yeah?"

So, he'd come looking a whole week early. To mend things? To end things?

My neck itched. Great. A nervous rash. My only consolation was the absence of Arch's cocky aura.

The more people know aboot *me, the more vulnerable I am.*

Considering the extent and depth of what he'd shared in his journal, he had to be feeling pretty raw just now.

"Beckett told me you landed the lead in that television series."

"I did, but…I didn't want it." I hoped I didn't sound ungrateful. I tried not to think about how sexy he looked when he cocked his head in wonder. Yeah, right.

"You passed up a chance at fortune and fame?"

Anxious, I tightened the red bow in my hair. "I don't want fortune and fame. I want…"

"Aye?"

You. "To be happy."

He indicated the bustling theme park. "Are you happy here?"

"Yes…and no." I licked dry lips and quelled the urge to break into "Some Day My Prince Will Come." After all, Arch was a baron and he was, well, here.

He moved closer and my knees went all noodly under my voluminous yellow skirt. He held my gaze and, yeah, boy, the numbness I'd felt three weeks ago was nonexistent. My entire body sparked like a live wire. Plus, I tingled in, what had to be, inappropriate places for a virginal Disney icon. The thump-thumping of my heart, however, was extremely in character. "Why are you staring at me?"

"'I don't know,'" he said in an American accent. "'It's just that…it's like you escaped from a Hallmark card or something.'"

I recognized the movie quote. I couldn't help but reply in kind. "'Is that a bad thing?'" I asked, affecting the childlike innocence of Giselle. Then I smiled. "*Enchanted* starring Amy Adams." Not a typical guy movie. Then again, Arch wasn't your typical guy. "You saw it?"

"On the cross-country flight."

"Oh." I scratched my neck. "So…I guess you came out to visit Cassidy." It had been a little weird knowing Arch's daughter lived close by. Sometimes I wondered if we would ever cross paths in the park. I'd seen her picture. I'd recognize her sparkling gray-green eyes—so like her daddy's.

"Yes…and no."

He leaned in and I had visions of being arrested by the Keystone Cops for indecent behavior. This was all kinds of wrong. "I can't do this. I mean not dressed like this. Wait here." I hesitated, then took off like a flash, nearly tripping over my own two feet as I looked back to make sure he wasn't a figment of my powerful imagination.

Please be there when I get back.

The dressing rooms were a good distance from where Arch waited. I prayed he didn't lose patience. Or get a phone call that would take him away. Or… Decorum be hanged, I changed my clothes with the speed of a minute-man and sprinted the whole way back. Well, except for the last few yards. I didn't want to appear anxious, even though I was. *Play it cool, Parish. For all you know he's here to blow you off in person.*

Right.

I let out a breath of relief when I spied him sitting on a bench.

"You're blond again," he said as I neared.

Free of my character's dark wig, I self-consciously fluffed my hair. "Yes, well, it just feels more me."

He tugged at the hem of my Tinkerbell T-shirt. "Sit with me?"

I didn't see the harm, even though I was certain I wouldn't be able to keep my hands off of him. Dressed in civilian clothes, I blended with the mob. Although the crowd had thinned. Only the most hearty made it until midnight. At any rate, I was off duty, so whatever happened from here on out was off the record. In my mind anyway. "About the journal."

"Beckett's idea."

The notion warmed my heart. Beckett had not only made Nic deliriously happy, he'd turned out to be one of my most steadfast friends. "Yeah, well. That's why he's raking in the big bucks. The man's full of unique ideas."

"So it wasn't a mistake?"

"Are you kidding?" I'd cherished every handwritten page. Every story. Every sentiment. No matter how shocking. Or bitter. Or sad. The harsh truth made the funny and passionate entries all the sweeter. "Arch, you gave me something you've never given anyone else. An intimate look inside your life."

"When I *didnae* hear from you—"

"I was absorbing. I was…overwhelmed. I *should* feel manipulated."

"But?"

I thought about what it had cost him to bare his soul. I interlaced my fingers with his. "Now I know you better."

He skimmed a thumb over my palm. "Better than anyone, lass. Even Bernie."

It made me sad to know he'd only ever been his true self around his grandfather. At the same time, my heart bloomed knowing he trusted *me* with his secrets and dreams. "That part in your journal where you wondered why I'd turned cold. You were right. I did overhear your phone discussion with Kate. When you said…" I looked away. "I thought you only wanted to marry me because I'd be a good role model for Cassidy—my Snow White image and all that. When you said you had a bargain, I thought…"

"I can guess what you thought, yeah?" He caressed my chin, beckoned my gaze. "The bargain was for me to transform my*self* into a good role model, and in return Kate would consider joint custody."

I swallowed a lump. "So marrying me wouldn't be a sacrifice?"

"What?" He scrunched his brow as if in deep thought, as if conjuring that night, that conversation. "Oh." He shook his head. "*Shite.* The sacrifice Kate referred to was giving up my previous lifestyle and profession, my freedom, in order to care for a little girl. You, Sunshine, *you* are a bonus. The biggest score of my life. I *dinnae* deserve someone so good and kind, yet fate steered you my way." He glanced skyward. "Maybe Bernie put in a good word for me, yeah?"

My heart pounded. My eyes burned. "You always say the right thing."

"Except when I say the wrong thing."

I smiled through my tears. "I should have confronted you that night instead of internalizing, or after the sting instead of running away, but between that and the gunplay with Burns and the memory of Simon the Fish…"

Arch leaned in and rested his forehead against mine. "I'm sorry I *didnae* handle that better, Sunshine."

"Your heart was in the right place, but…I don't want to live a lie. I don't want to second-guess your every word. I deserve the truth, Arch. Always. I can handle the truth. Admittedly, I talked to a therapist about the Fish shooting—no names, place, or time—but I *am* handling it."

His eyes twinkled with tenderness and respect. "I suspect you can handle anything life throws your way, Evie. The truth is you're one of the strongest, most talented women I've ever known, yeah? The way you suppressed your emotions, the way you handled Crowe and his men. You impressed and scared the hell *oot* of me at the same time. If you want to go back to work for Chameleon—"

"I don't." His compliments warmed me head to toe, but the thought of violence, blood and death chilled me to the bone. Maybe later, under different circumstances, part-time…just not now. "What about you? Beckett told me you quit."

"Sometimes life throws you a curve."

My mouth went dry. "Another opportunity?"

"You." He brushed his lips over mine and I nearly swooned. "I've been miserable *withoot* you, Sunshine."

"Ditto, Ace." A tornado of emotions ravaged my spirit. Excitement. Fear. Skepticism. Awe. This was the single most important moment of my life. A turning point. A *starting* point. The springboard to my happily ever after. Call me a drama queen. No. Call me the Baroness of Broxley. A girl can dream. And serendipity had landed us in a place famous for making dreams come true.

Arch smoothed his thumb over my knuckles and I marveled at the racy desires that innocent gesture roused.

"I need to say this straight out, yeah? I want to marry you because I love you. Because you light up my life, lass. Not because you'd advance my chances with my daughter, you know?"

I choked back an emotional sob. "I know. I mean, I do now. I mean, I'm sorry I doubted you. I just… I guess I always thought you were too good to be true."

"No, baby. That would be you."

This is it, I thought. The Hollywood ending of my life gone wild. *My happy ending.* I felt it with every fiber of my body.

I noted Sleeping Beauty's castle in the background, remembered the vision I'd had compliments of my imagination and Madame Helene's crystal ball. *I see the Scottish highlands and a man and woman kissing in front of a castle. I see a little girl with a big smile.* Okay, so we weren't in Scotland and, though there were plenty of beaming little girls around, they weren't Cassidy. But the castle and the kiss had been dead-on. Maybe there was something to Jayne's mystical hooey after all.

Arch pulled me into his arms.

Passionate music welled in my ears. Fireworks exploded in my brain. No, wait. Fireworks exploded for *real.* We both glanced up at the colorful sky. I'd witnessed the midnight spectacular several nights running, but it had never been as magical as this precious moment.

"Arch?"

"Aye, lass?"

I framed his gorgeous face and poured my heart into a kiss. "I want to go to my happy place."

He grinned, that sexy grin that made the back of my knees sweat.

"And that would be?"

"Anywhere with you."

EPILOGUE

Three months later...

DEAR DIARY,

Today in my life gone real, Cassidy and I made traditional Scottish shortbreads. It wasn't a total disaster. At least we had fun. So what if the result tasted... How did Cassidy put it? Yucky. We'll be walking down to the village bakery later today to purchase the real deal.

Broxley is everything Arch described and more. Can you say magical? And, okay, his barony doesn't include a castle, but he does own a lovely stone manor. As for his daughter, let's just say, he wasn't exaggerating when he called her an angel. Cassidy is adorable—sweet and shy. Although the longer she's with us here in Scotland, the more she's coming out of her shell.

Arch is still in shock that Kate gave him partial custody. Not me. In fact, I'm pretty certain by this time next year, Cassidy will be with us permanently. Kate's new fiancé doesn't like kids and Kate...well, from what I've witnessed, there isn't a maternal bone in that witch's body.

But I digress...

Did I mention Arch is working freelance as a scam-and-

fraud expert for a global private agency? I hope to join him on a few missions, but mostly I'll have my hands full with Cassidy—yay!—and the community theater I'm organizing for the village.

The wedding is next week. I know I've mentioned that a bazillion times, but I'm so excited!! Mom and Dad and my brother are flying in. So are Nic and Jayne, Beckett and the entire Chameleon team. This place is going to be a madhouse. I can't wait!

"Evie! Evie!"

I looked up from my journal, smiling as Cassidy barreled into the room. "What is it, honey?"

"Da said fairies live in the woods. He's gonna show me! Will you come?"

I cupped her dimpled cheek and plucked a twig out of her wild curls. "Of course, I'll come. Fairies, huh? Wow."

She pumped her little fist in the air and did my signature victory dance. Hey, can I help it if I'm rubbing off on the kid?

I heard Arch laugh. Blushing, I glanced up and delighted in his amused gaze.

Zing. Zap.

"Go and grab your sweater, baby," he said to Cassidy. "We'll meet you in the garden, yeah?"

She zipped off and I doodled a parting thought in my journal. Stick figures of Arch and me in front of the manor, kissing. A stick figure of Cassidy playing with the Scottish terrier puppy Arch intended to give her as a present on our wedding day.

My Scottish rebel looked over my shoulder, kissed my neck, then commandeered my purple pen. His penmanship was truly awful, but the sentiment reminded me of why I loved this man so much.

And they all lived happily ever after.
* * * * *

*Turn the page for an exciting preview of Beth Ciotta's
hot new contemporary romance,
OUT OF EDEN
Coming in early 2010*

FAYE AND HER slightly blurry twin snapped their fingers two inches from Kylie's face. "Earth to McGraw. Are you zoning or comatose?"

Kylie adjusted her red cat's-eye glasses and blinked away the double image, conceding cosmopolitans packed a mighty punch. Either that or Boone had screwed up the ingredients. Possible, since he'd referred to a mix recipe and his reading glasses were forever perched *on top* of his balding head. "Okay. Maybe I am a teensy bit tipsy, but I am not, absolutely *not* drunk. And even if I was…" She grappled for a righteous excuse. "It *is* my birthday."

"I'm not saying you aren't entitled to cut loose," Faye said, nursing a frosty mug of Budweiser. "It's just that you always drink beer."

"Exactly!" Kylie jabbed her shoe in the air to emphasize her point. "I always drink beer."

Faye sighed. "I have no idea what that means."

"It means I can't take it anymore."

"Take what?"

"The predictability. The routine. The mundane. The run-of-the-mill, unremarkable, habitual sameness—"

Faye shrugged, smiled. "Not following."

"Every year we celebrate my birthday the same way.

Pizza King. Movie. And since we turned twenty-one, Boone's Bar and Grill."

"Except we skipped the movie this time and came straight to Boone's," she said with a frown. "It's 7:00 p.m. We're the only ones here aside from a few guys throwing back happy-hour brewskies and you're already half-tanked."

Kylie scrunched her nose. "Did you really want to see that slasher flick?"

"Not really. But since the Bixley runs one feature at a time, it's not like we had a choice. We could have closed our eyes during the gory parts."

"We would've missed three-quarters of the movie!"

"That's not the point! We always celebrate your birthday the same way. Pizza. Movie. Boone's. It's *tradition*."

Kylie wrangled her natural blah-boring brown, overly thick, overly long hair into a loosely knotted ponytail. "It's hot in here."

"Blame it on the cosmos or your heated rant," Faye said calmly. "It's the same as always—comfortable. Boone keeps the thermostat set at sixty-eight year round. You know that."

Kylie wanted to scream at yet another example of predictability. Instead she propped her elbow on the table, footwear in hand. "My life is like this shoe. Sensible. This town is like this shoe. Practical."

"Isn't that your family's motto? Practical shoes for practical people? It's written on the plaque hanging behind the cashier counter."

Kylie narrowed her eyes. "That plaque is so gone. In fact, I am going to redecorate the entire store. Bright colors. Maybe even pink. Pepto-Bismol pink with banana-yellow trim. Acrylic racks. Art posters splashed with funky period high heels. I saw this Andy Warhol print on the Internet. *Diamond Dust Shoes.* Weird, but fun."

"Ashe sent this over." Wanda, Boone's wife, who usually manned the kitchen, whipping up her locally famous, kick-butt chicken wings, seasoned mozzarella sticks and other assorted yummies, was currently working the floor due to a server shortage. She set another cosmo on the table. "Be warned, the silver-tongued dog paid Boone for a double shot of vodka."

"Happy birthday, Kylie," Ashe called from his bar stool.

He probably thought that winking thing was sexy. Smarmy was more like it. "Thanks." She saluted the cocky car dealer with a dismissive smile. Ashe Davis had been trying to score with her since her fiancé, make that *ex*-fiancé, had fled paradise two years ago. At no point in time had she suggested he had a snowball's chance in hell, but the man was persistent. Not that there was anything outwardly wrong with Ashe. Handsome and successful, thirty-six and never married, he was considered the perfect catch. Only, thus far he'd proven too slippery for any of the eligible women in Eden and even a few of the not-so-eligible. With Ashe it was all about the hunt. Once he bagged his prey, he lost interest. If Kylie wanted a brief, hot fling, he'd be the perfect choice.

"He's thinking tonight's his lucky night," Faye said with a roll of her blue-shadowed eyes.

"I'd have to be blitzed out of my gourd to sleep with Ashe."

"Drink that third cosmo and consider yourself boinked," said Faye.

Kylie pushed her glasses up her nose and focused, sort of, on Wanda. "Do I appear inebriated to you?"

"Well…I did see you talking to your shoe, dear."

"That's because this shoe represents the crux of my discontent."

"Don't ask," Faye said, then sipped her beer.

Ashe approached Kylie with another cosmo and a smarmy grin. "I'll show you mine if you show me yours."

Kylie dropped her head in her hands with a groan.

"Go away," Faye said. "And take that evil drink with you."

"Hey, I'm just trying to please the birthday girl. She said she wants a sensation."

Kylie banged her fists on the table and frowned up at the man. "I'm talking about something *extraordinary,* you thick-skulled bozo. People expect you to seduce me and they expect me to fall under your spell. Boone knows the gang will show up every Wednesday and Friday at 6:00 p.m. to play pinochle and *they* know they'll get twofer beers, kick-butt chicken wings and a comfortable room temperature of sixty-eight degrees. Faye expects me to drink beer because I always drink beer. The Bixley will never expand to a multiplex theater, and storefronts on Adams Street will always look as they did in 1955 because progress moves at a snail's pace in Eden! Nothing out of the ordinary *ever* happens!" Kylie vented, voice slurred and shrill. "You can set your watch by this town. *We* are boring, people!"

"Ooo-kay." Ashe backed away with the drink, his free hand raised in surrender.

"That does it," Boone called from behind the bar. "You're cut off, Kylie."

She jabbed a finger in his direction. "I *knew* you'd say that."

"Predictable," Faye said.

"Exactly."

"But wise." Looking puzzled and worried, the normally

unflappable woman rooted in her oversize purse and pulled out her Orchard Inn souvenir keychain, *available at the front desk for the bargain price of $3.99.* "I'm taking you home and you're going to tell me what set you off, Kylie McGraw. This is very un-Zen-like of you. You're making a spectacle of yourself."

Fueled by years of frustration and three cosmopolitans, Kylie pushed out of the booth, her compact body trembling with Godzilla-like rage. "Well, get used to it. All of you! Because starting tomorrow, there's a new Kylie McGraw in town. I'm going to shake up paradise. Just you wait and see!" She made it halfway across the hardwood floor before her feet slid out from under her and Kylie went ass over heels.

One of the bar patrons whistled low. "Wasn't much of a wait."

Dazed, she squinted at the sea of faces spinning above her. "Stand still, you guys."

"We're not moving." Faye stooped and inspected Kylie's noggin. "How hard did you hit your head, sweetie? Are you seeing double?"

"Of course she's seeing double," Boone said. "She's shit-faced."

Swearing, Faye tried to pull her friend to her feet, but Kylie's arms and legs went all noodly. "I could use some help getting her in my van," she said to the men.

"I'll do it," Ashe said with a smile.

"I'll do it."

Kylie knew that voice—deep, sexy. Hard to forget the voice of your first major crush. Best high-school bud of her infuriating brother, this man had made tofu of her early teen hormones. She adjusted her crooked glasses and blinked up at the obsession of her youth. Dark cropped hair. Steely blue eyes. A buff body and a boyish smile. Hands on denim-clad hips, Jack Reynolds—the most handsome man in the universe *ever*—towered above her. Then again, she was flat out on the floor. She hadn't seen him in several years and usually her heart fluttered when she did. Either she was completely over him, or the mass quantities of vodka had paralyzed her vital organs along with her limbs. "Heard you were back in town."

"No secrets in Eden."

"Is it true you're taking over for Police Chief Birch?"

"It is."

"You been in here long?"

"Long enough."

She quirked a hopeful grin. "Going to arrest me for drunk-and-disorderly behavior?"

"Nope."

"Shoot," she complained when he hauled her up and into his arms.

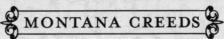
  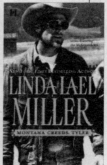

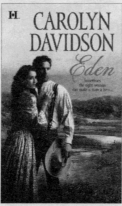

REQUEST YOUR FREE BOOKS!

2 FREE NOVELS FROM THE ROMANCE/SUSPENSE COLLECTION PLUS 2 FREE GIFTS!

YES! Please send me 2 FREE novels from the Romance/Suspense Collection and my 2 FREE gifts (gifts are worth about $10). After receiving them, if I don't wish to receive any more books, I can return the shipping statement marked "cancel." If I don't cancel, I will receive 4 brand-new novels every month and be billed just $5.49 per book in the U.S. or $5.99 per book in Canada, plus 25¢ shipping and handling per book plus applicable taxes, if any*. That's a savings of at least 20% off the cover price! I understand that accepting the 2 free books and gifts places me under no obligation to buy anything. I can always return a shipment and cancel at any time. Even if I never buy another book from the Reader Service, the two free books and gifts are mine to keep forever.

185 MDN EF5Y 385 MDN EF6C

Name	(PLEASE PRINT)	
Address		Apt. #
City	State/Prov.	Zip/Postal Code

Signature (if under 18, a parent or guardian must sign)

Mail to **The Reader Service:**
IN U.S.A.: P.O. Box 1867, Buffalo, NY 14240-1867
IN CANADA: P.O. Box 609, Fort Erie, Ontario L2A 5X3

Not valid to current subscribers to the Romance Collection,
the Suspense Collection or the Romance/Suspense Collection.

Want to try two free books from another line?
Call 1-800-873-8635 or visit www.morefreebooks.com.

* Terms and prices subject to change without notice. N.Y. residents add applicable sales tax. Canadian residents will be charged applicable provincial taxes and GST. Offer not valid in Quebec. This offer is limited to one order per household. All orders subject to approval. Credit or debit balances in a customer's account(s) may be offset by any other outstanding balance owed by or to the customer. Please allow 4 to 6 weeks for delivery. Offer available while quantities last.

Your Privacy: Harlequin is committed to protecting your privacy. Our Privacy Policy is available online at www.eHarlequin.com or upon request from the Reader Service. From time to time we make our lists of customers available to reputable third parties who may have a product or service of interest to you. If you would prefer we not share your name and address, please check here. ☐

BOB08R

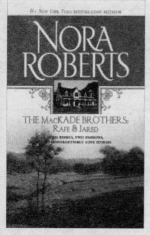
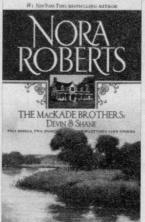

Beth Ciotta

| 77298 | EVERYBODY LOVES EVIE | ___ $6.99 U.S. | ___ $8.50 CAN. |
| 77207 | ALL ABOUT EVIE | ___ $6.99 U.S. | ___ $8.50 CAN. |

(limited quantities available)

TOTAL AMOUNT	$ _____
POSTAGE & HANDLING	$ _____
($1.00 FOR 1 BOOK, 50¢ for each additional)	
APPLICABLE TAXES*	$ _____
TOTAL PAYABLE	$ _____

(check or money order—please do not send cash)

To order, complete this form and send it, along with a check or money order for the total above, payable to HQN Books, to: **In the U.S.:** 3010 Walden Avenue, P.O. Box 9077, Buffalo, NY 14269-9077; **In Canada:** P.O. Box 636, Fort Erie, Ontario, L2A 5X3.

HQN™

We *are* romance™

www.HQNBooks.com

PHBC0309BL